Art in America

Also by Ron McLarty

The Memory of Running
Traveler

Art in America

Ron McLarty

VIKING

VIKING
Published by the Penguin Group
Penguin Group (USA) Inc., 375 Hudson Street, New York, New York 10014, U.S.A. • Penguin
Group (Canada), 90 Eglinton Avenue East, Suite 700, Toronto, Ontario, Canada M4P 2Y3 (a
division of Pearson Penguin Canada Inc.) • Penguin Books Ltd, 80 Strand, London WC2R 0RL,
England • Penguin Ireland, 25 St. Stephen's Green, Dublin 2, Ireland (a division of Penguin
Books Ltd) • Penguin Books Australia Ltd, 250 Camberwell Road, Camberwell, Victoria 3124,
Australia (a division of Pearson Australia Group Pty Ltd) • Penguin Books India Pvt Ltd, 11
Community Centre, Panchsheel Park, New Delhi–110 017, India • Penguin Group (NZ), 67
Apollo Drive, Rosedale, North Shore 0632, New Zealand (a division of Pearson New Zealand
Ltd) • Penguin Books (South Africa) (Pty) Ltd, 24 Sturdee Avenue, Rosebank, Johannesburg
2196, South Africa

Penguin Books Ltd, Registered Offices:
80 Strand, London WC2R 0RL, England

First published in 2008 by Viking Penguin,
a member of Penguin Group (USA) Inc.

1   3   5   7   9   10   8   6   4   2

Copyright © Zaluma, LLC, 2008
All rights reserved

Publisher's Note
This is a work of fiction. Names, characters, places, and incidents either are the product of the
author's imagination or are used fictitiously, and any resemblance to actual persons, living or
dead, business establishments, events, or locales is entirely coincidental.

Library of Congress Cataloging-in-Publication Data
McLarty, Ron.
Art in America / Ron McLarty.
p.   cm.
ISBN 978-0-670-01895-6
1. Authors—Fiction.   2. Colorado—Fiction.   3. Water rights—Fiction.
4. Land tenure—Fiction.   I. Title.
PS3613.C573A89 2008
813'.6—dc22   2007040454

Printed in the United States of America
Set in Berkeley with Trixie
Designed by Daniel Lagin

Because she knows the stage so well,
and because she understands,
this book is for my beloved wife,
Kate Skinner McLarty

Acknowledgments

I am beholden to my editors, Ray Roberts and Paul Slovak, for their support and guidance; grateful to Maureen Sugden for her funny and forceful copy editing; and happy to have had Shasti O'Leary and Jethro Soudant design the jacket for *Art in America*. I am indebted to Rhode Island College, the Rhode Island Public Library, and its Reading Across Rhode Island Program. Thank you, Joyce May of the East Providence Library and Louise Moulton of Adult Education at the Rhode Island Center for the Book at the Providence Public Library. I am joyous for our granddaughter, Ava, and for my children, Zachary, Lucas, and Matthew, with love and appreciation.

Art in America

Prologue

The Selected Works of Steven Kearney

THE BUDDHA OF WOMEN

A novel
1,962 pages

The story of a man who knew everything you could possibly know about women. A man nearly religious in the pursuit of knowledge regarding the feminine human being. Along the way, in his world travels, Cagey Larson meets a woman traveling a coextensive route. She knows everything about men. The fun begins when they meet an old man and an old woman who show them they don't have to know everything and who help them forget, so that they can be a couple.

© 1978
Currently without a publisher

THE LENSMAN OF HOLLAND

A novel
1,821 pages

The adventures, successes, and tragedies of the fabulous Antoni van Leeuwenhoek, father of protozoology.

© 1978
Unpublished

MISSION TO DOGS

A novel
1,102 pages

In 1929, Betty Durand, a wealthy Rhode Island widow, begins rescuing dogs and having them neutered and spayed. Although she loses everything in the crash of '29, she has the indomitable spirit to continue her crusade to give nice homes to dogs and eventually other small animals except cats.

© 1981
Unpublished

PURDAH

A novel
1,807 pages

A man searches for information about his grandmother, who disappeared before he was born. He follows her in retro investigation and finds an amazing path of affairs and betrayals. It is also an immediate mystery, because someone is trying to block his informal inquest.

© 1982
Submitted to agents and publishers
Unpublished

Note: New revision of last 223 pages to make the work more accessible.

Resubmitted August 1991
Unpublished

CHRONHIMER TRILOGY

Three interrelated plays
822 pages, 11 acts, 55 scenes (prose, free verse, rhyming couplets, music)

A Catholic choir director/composer struggles with faith, love, family, and cancer of the tongue over a fifty-year span.

Note: Many of the 126 characters can be doubled up.

© 1984
Hand-carried to every theater in the *Guide to New York Playwriting* handbook. Hand-carried back to the apartment.

TURN-DOWN MAN

A novel
15 poem-chants
1,211 pages

A man is kidnapped in Botswana, Africa, and remains a prisoner for ten years. He becomes spiritually entwined with the ancient soul of a shipwrecked Carthaginian sailor. After he is freed, he goes to live with his brother, then becomes a movie star and loses his ability to conduct souls.

An allegory

Completed January 1984 while recuperating from concussion received falling three stories with wheelbarrow on a construction site in Queens.

© 1989
Unpublished

Note: New revisions and additional poem-chants brought current version to 1,722 pages.

THE CONCENTRIC SQUEEZER

Book by Steven Kearney
Music by Lynn Lamas

A musical (28 songs, 14 dances)
231 pages

The fabulous life of Henry Burden (1812–92), inventor of the Burden Rotary Concentric Squeezer, which was described as "The Niagara of Water Wheels." It was capable of doing the work of twelve hundred horses. In a blend of comedy, drama, song, and dance, the story is told of how Henry not only saved Pittsburgh manufacturers over half a million dollars with a machine that heated, cut, bent, and forged iron into completed shapes with one movement, but also did more than any ten men who ever lived to make his adopted hometown of Troy, New York, a great manufacturing center.

Completed June 1991
Currently unproduced

ARROWHEAD

A novel
1,522 pages

An orphan, raised by the Rhode Island Children's Society, gathers followers among fellow institutionalized children through wondrous acts as a child and teenager. This core group ascend to successful careers and aid the orphan in reaching great political heights.

© 1995
Unpublished

THE BARRELLI RETROSPECTIVE WORKS:
1958–98

A novel
1,930 pages

A failed Rhode Island artist looks back over his long career as oil
painter/short-order cook at Manny's Big Eats in Cranston.

© 1998
Submitted: NEA Grant
Jackson LaRue Literary Award
PEN National Fiction Award
Unaccepted
After twenty-two letters, scripts (except NEA) returned.
Reworked to fully shape and clarify the characters in chapters forty
through forty-seven, where the early paintings are mysteriously eaten
by a young admirer.
Submitted: Rhode Island State Council on the Arts
    Not eligible due to not being currently a Rhode Islander.
Submitted: Henry Holt & Co.
    Not returned or accepted, although four previous novels were re-
turned.

THE INFRANGIBLENESS OF HENRY HUGHES

A semiautobiographical novel with 2 interrelated novellas, 14 short
stories, and 61 poems
3,852 pages

Henry Hughes has an unhappy childhood and, when his parents divorce, spends much of his time with his imaginary friend, the author
Judith Tobit, who teaches him how to become a great and meaningful
writer. He becomes so proficient in language he is asked to translate
Ibsen's *Wild Duck* for the Trinity Square Theater in Providence.
Drafted, he wins a Purple Heart, returning to his home a hero. But his
imaginary friend, the author Judith Tobit, committed suicide when
she heard of his being wounded. And so he must recapture his mas-
tery of the language arts without her spiritual guidance.

Work in progress
1982–98

In 1991 three long one-act plays added to text regarding Henry's meeting with Molière in a Providence coin shop.
(Currently 4,172 pages)

1

The taxi grazed him, turned him, and left him facedown in a pool of dirty water. The driver stepped out, realized that no one had witnessed the accident, and drove off. It was after ten in the evening but seemed later. Steven Kearney rolled slowly onto his back and pushed himself into a sitting position. A fine mist came.

April had been a cold month. Earlier that day it had snowed. Steven couldn't remember the last time he'd seen an April snow. He also could not remember what day it was. A young couple walked wide of him. He tried to say something to them, but his words were slurred and a smile spread across his fat, red face.

For ten minutes he sat in the puddle. He remembered his two black garbage bags and spotted them on the edge of the sidewalk. He could feel a throbbing in his head that ran to his tailbone. He wiggled his toes and then his fingers. The mist gave over to a freezing rain, then a downpour. The ancient black cashmere overcoat, worn smooth and shiny, absorbed the water like a sponge. He pulled himself onto the sidewalk and sat with his feet in the street, between the garbage bags.

His stomach rolled. He pulled his knees up to his chest like a gargoyle, and the nausea passed. He shivered.

"Jesus," he uttered.

The heavy rain came again and left again. He reached for the bags and checked for rips.

Two young men noticed him and crossed to the other side of the street. The rain now came in pellets of half-frozen water pinging onto his huge forehead, laying a tiny gray-brown ponytail flat against his collar. He stood, took a bag in each hand, and moved as if in slow motion, downtown. Thoughts returned and arranged themselves. Had Beverly left?

"Yes," he said out loud.

He'd written a long poem all night and didn't get to bed until dawn.

She was by the door when he woke that afternoon. Small and angry.

"Good-bye, Steven."

"Huh?"

"I'm leaving."

"Leaving?"

"Good-bye."

"Is the coffee on? I mean, what about your stuff?"

"I already moved my things. I've been moving them all month. The apartment is empty. Haven't you noticed?"

He glanced around the room.

She hung her head and shook it side to side. Long black hair brushed her back and made a swishing sound.

"Did . . . did my agent call?"

"Your agent hasn't called in a long, long time. Nobody has called you, unless you count Roarke, who by the way I don't."

He stared at her face, then his feet, then back to her face. Her lips twitched. He saw loathing. He saw disgust. There was toast on her teeth.

"What . . . what time is it?"

She laughed without smiling. Steven realized he was standing naked. His forty-eight-year-old body, the personification of failed art, part-time employment, and contemporary farrago, flinched.

"I thought I'd feel bad about this. I had constructed a deeper meaning to our relationship. Now I can see there wasn't enough there to feel bad about," she said.

"I'm moving in with Toby Hunter."

She said it evenly and low, like a slap on the ass. He really needed coffee, and he needed his pants. Now he could see that she had been moving. The furniture was gone, and most of the pans and plates and the bathroom rug. He stared at the bathroom. It could use a door so close to the kitchen. *In* the kitchen, actually.

"I love him," she said flatly.

"Oh," he said. He sat back on the bed and covered himself with the sheet.

"You don't care, do you? You don't fucking care. Four years!"

He felt wobbly. He needed coffee.

"You love that pile of shit more than you ever loved me!" she shouted, pointing to a plywood table next to the stove.

"What pile of shit?"

She walked over to where a yellow writing tablet was neatly laid out and half filled with words. "Number 91" was circled at the top right-hand corner. Thirty stacks of manuscripts in varying sizes lined the back of the table.

She picked one up and tossed it on the floor. "*This* pile of shit."

"Hey," he said pathetically.

She threw another one.

"*Heart Redoux*, shit!"

Another.

"*The Ship and the Spider*, shit!"

Another.

"*Arnie*—Jesus, what kind of title is this? *Arnie and Alice*, shit."

"It's a verse play. It didn't work, but—"

"Shit, shit, shit."

He watched her empty the desk.

"Do you know why the plays have never been produced? And the novels published and the . . . the . . ."

She reached down and brought up a piece of paper.

" 'The pigeons are sidling
The birds
Agora in the tub a
Sweet . . .'

"Jesus . . . and the . . . poems. Shit!"

"They . . . they did *Moon Play*," he said with a dry mouth.

"It's still shit—and it was only a reading."

"I mean . . . well . . . Toby Hunter? The designer?"

"You know who he is. I think I love him."

"Toby's gay, isn't he?"

"Fuck you."

"I mean . . ."

"Fuck, fuck, fuck, fuck, fuck, fuck you!"

Beverly threw the door open and stormed past Rose Marmar, who stepped into the room followed by a burly cop.

"Uh . . . hello, Mrs. Marmar."

"This officer is here to escort you out."

"Huh?"

"Let's go, pal."

"No rent in eight months," Mrs. Marmar said.

Steven stood, and the sheet dropped away. He quickly covered his pecker.

"Hey, c'mon, pal," the cop said.

"Sorry. . . . But Beverly always brought you cash, Mrs. Marmar. I gave cash to her," he said. The sheet fell again. Rose was not impressed.

"Not for the last eight months she didn't. Officer?"

"You got stuff?"

"My plays and things. Some clothes . . ."

"These the plays?" he said, pointing to the pile.

"Yeah . . . uh . . . the top one is *Moon Play*. That was done in a workshop reading at the—"

"Got something to put this shit in?"

"I think Beverly borrowed my suitcase."

"Garbage bags or something?"

He had descended the narrow stairwell behind them. Garbage bags stretching under the weight of the word. In front of the building, Steven stood facing Rose and her enforcer.

"Now, don't you try coming back," the policeman said. "I mean, c'mon. Law's the law. No hard feelings."

Steven used the ATM at the corner of Fourteenth and Broadway. A kid of indeterminate sex and an elderly couple viewed him and his bags skeptically. He inserted his card and punched up his code. He pressed "Savings Withdrawal" and then "$40." "Insufficient Funds" flashed in green and below it "Card Being Retained."

He turned to them and pointed at the machine.

"I had eleven hundred dollars in here."

At University he turned down toward Washington Square, not noticing the fine snow until it warmed into a steady drizzle. Beverly had completed a clean sweep. The money he'd saved from the day-labor gig was gone. He called Roarke from a pay phone.

"Roarke? Roarke? It's Steven. . . . Uh, listen, I'm . . . Are you there? Pick up if you're there."

He listened for another few seconds, then hung up. He walked through Washington Square and crossed down to West Broadway.

He stopped to light a cigarette. He heard laughter and cheers. The glass-fronted Jan-Wac Galleries diagonally across the street seemed warm and inviting. A delicate light illuminated the large crowd. A limo pulled to the front, and two young men stepped out. He recognized them both as New York Yankees.

"Hey, man, good luck next season!" Steven called.

They glanced at soggy Steven Kearney and his black plastic bags, and the tall one with the blond hair and the $90 million contract and the $1,400 per diem gave him the finger. Then they joined the party.

Then the taxi got him.

2

Steven stood on the corner of Franklin looking across to the One Bird Theatre, the corner basement apartment that served as Roarke's home and performance space. There were no lights on. He crossed the street and rang the bell anyway, because with Roarke you never knew. That's it. You simply didn't know. After a few moments, he pushed the two garbage bags against the building's stairs. His stomach pressed tightly against the overcoat. He poked at it.

"My belly is soft," he said to the dark street, "But . . . my art . . . is . . ."

"What?"

Across the street a black woman, layered in blankets, pushing a shopping cart filled with bags and newspapers, stared at him.

"What you say?"

"I . . . I said my belly was . . . you know . . . kind of soft."

"Something about art."

"My art . . . is . . . firm."

"I hear that, big boy. I hear that."

She walked to the corner and moved slowly uptown. Steven wondered if a round and layered woman, complete with wonderful things in her cart, could hold sway over an audience. A narrator? A commentator? What if he took one of his unpublished novels—*The Central Society*, maybe—and turned it into a play? She could sit on the corner of the stage. . . . Hell, she could sit right there with the audience. She could be the one who illuminates, who puts his very thoughts out there. Could it work? Would it be produced? And then there's the problem of distilling an almost-seven-thousand-page unpublished novel into a stage play. What about the First World War and gassing the trenches and the hippie girl simulating oral sex with the Washington Monument, not to mention the Los Angeles earthquake? His head hurt. He had to pee.

Steven walked to the corner of the building, just out of the throw of light.

"I wish I could do that."

"I can teach you how."

"Fuck you, Steven."

"Fuck you, Roarke."

When she saw him in the light, she gasped. "Steven! Jesus!"

She put her powerful arms around him and held him while she unlocked the door. She pulled off his coat.

"Take your clothes off. You're cut. Steven!"

"My bags."

Roarke brought them inside, pulled his shirt off, then his T-shirt. She unbuckled his belt and yanked his corduroy slacks down to his ankles.

"Raise your foot. Help me. I have to take your shoes off."

She pulled at the shoes, then the pants, and reached up to his shorts.

"Will this be embarrassing?"

"Humiliating."

Roarke pointed to her bed between the stove and the refrigerator.

"Get under the covers and take them off."

He passed his shorts to her. She picked up the rest of his soaked clothes.

"I'm going to wash these. You got any more?"

Steven pointed to his garbage bags. She squatted and opened them. She looked inside and became still. After a moment she removed the clothing. She fluffed his pillow, brought the bedspread up to his neck, and kissed him.

He was snoring when she returned from the laundry room. A large bruise was coming up under his right eye and spreading crazily down his neck onto his shoulder and chest. Roarke stood over him wondering if she should wake him. His mouth was set in a kind of smile, and inside himself Steven was experiencing book signings and opening nights. She decided to leave him pressed into a corner of his dream.

One half of Roarke's living area was taken by a kind of stage, raised a few inches off the floor by nubbed two-by-fours. Fifteen folding chairs were leaned neatly against the back wall, and the windows were curtained in heavy black. Four lekos and one work light hung from a water pipe. To Roarke— Director, Master Teacher—this was a space of dreams.

She switched off the living-area lights and switched on the work light above the stage so that Steven fell into an orangey dim. She carried his heavy garbage bags to the stage. Roarke was six feet tall, with long, sloping shoulders. Bones that would seem brutish on the frame of any other woman were luxurious on her, almost elegant, and her large hands had a symmetry approaching perfection.

She took the manuscripts out and set them in neat piles. Plays, novels, poetry. Every now and then, a title would pass her that she remembered, and she would brush her short black hair to the side and read a line or two. Pink skin shone under the light. The phone rang.

"Roarke here."

"Roarke?"

She closed her eyes and brought her knees up to her chin and made herself small.

"Roarke? Are you there, Roarke?"

"Uh-huh."

"I feel so terrible. I mean . . . I mean, Roarke, we have to help each other. That's what friends do."

Roarke sniffed. "We're friends, huh?"

Roarke closed her eyes tight.

"We're cronies, then? We're amigos? We're chums?"

"I don't want to fight."

"Me either."

"Then, I mean . . . let's not fight."

A small, nervous breath.

"I hope we can be friends, Roarke."

They hung there a few seconds in silence.

"So we're pals?" Roarke whispered. "So we're sidekicks?"

"Stop."

"Buddies?"

"I'm hanging up now, Roarke."

"No."

"I've got to go out."

"Where?"

"I can't love you, Roarke. Okay? We should be able to be friends."

"I don't want to be friends!" she yelled. Her angry eyes. Her tears. Her beautiful, strong hands encasing the silence. She curled into herself and wept. She tilted and rolled onto the floor. Steven woke but did not move. He listened to her choppy breath. She reached out from a fetal curl to replace the receiver.

"Judy?" he asked in a whisper.

She cried softly and then stopped.

"I'm sorry, Roarke," he whispered.

"Fuck you," she whispered.

"Fuck you, too, Roarke."

3

Steven put on his damp clothes and limped to the bathroom. He splashed cold water over his face. One eye was black and almost closed. A bruise the color of ripe eggplant spread across his right cheek, jaw, and neck. He hobbled as quietly as he could into the kitchen, taking four dollars in change out of a bowl on top of the refrigerator. It was not yet six o'clock. Roarke was sleeping on a couch pushed against the wall of her studio stage. He wrote her a note and slipped out into the icy morning.

He took the subway up to Thirty-fourth Street and walked to the Campanella & Girardi construction site on Twenty-ninth. No one had arrived yet. Steven stood in the chilly spring sun and closed his swollen eyes.

Tubby Vinitti arrived ten minutes later.

"Tubby."

Tubby kept moving to a makeshift row of lockers behind a high chain-link fence.

"What the fuck happened to your face? Somebody kick holy shit out of it?"

"I got hit by a car."

"Get the fuck out."

"Honest to God."

"Honest to God? When?"

"Last night."

"Well, what the fuck? Jesus. A truck? A car?"

"Taxi I think. I'm not sure. Listen, Tubby, I need some work."

"I thought you put enough away for a while. You told me you had to finish something."

"Yeah, I'm trying to finish a new collection of poetry."

Tubby nodded thoughtfully. Steven was embarrassed. More sun came, and it was actual morning. Tubby took a leviathan set of overalls out of a locker and pulled them over his gargantuan belly.

"The money . . . didn't go as far as I wanted it to."

"You up to it? 'Cause you look like shit."

"I look like shit, but I'm up to it."

"Same deal, then. I'll pay cash at the end of the day. A hundred fifty bucks. Anybody asks you, don't say 'pay.' Remember? Say 'foreman's prerogative.' "

"Thanks, Tubby."

"Had breakfast?"

"Uh-uh."

Tubby gave him five dollars.

"Go to the Greek place. Come back in fifteen, grab one of my sweatshirts out of the locker."

Most of the morning, he unloaded bags of concrete, rode them to the tenth floor, and piled them out. Then it was the sand, delivered by wheelbarrow. Tubby was pointing something out to an electrician on a pinned-up blueprint when Steven rolled by. He nodded.

"Barrows. Some things never change. Never will. Try moving sand with a fucking computer. Thatta boy!"

In the afternoon he assisted in steel-rod cutting. Stacking, really. "Still look like shit," Tubby said, passing him cash. "I took out the five I gave you for breakfast."

"Thanks, Tubby."

"Sure you're all right?"

"Feel great, man."

Steven felt himself already stiffening. He flexed his fingers. Blisters were coming up. Forgot to wear gloves. Forgot good shoes.

Tubby grinned. "Tomorrow?"

"Cool."

"That mean yes?"

"Uh . . . yes."

He picked up a six-pack of Pabst Blue Ribbon, two cans of Manhandler Bean with Bacon Soup, and a pack of Marlboros. Roarke wasn't in. He sat on the stoop, smoked a little, and drank some beer.

"Your art still firm?"

The shopping-cart woman. He was tired. He was so tired.

"Your art still firm?" she called again.

He could have fallen asleep, but he stood up.

"My art . . . my art is adamantine."

"I hear that," she said.

He popped another beer. He lit another cigarette.

4

hile Steven dozed on her steps, Roarke had a beer in Hell's Kitchen with playwright Awky Rand. She handed his play script to him.

"I'm really flattered, Awky. I read it and everything. But . . . well . . . I'm looking for a directing project that will pay a bit. I need to make some money."

"I thought you do phone calling or some shit?"

Awky Rand had a beard like a Chinese elder. Wispy little hairs hung off his plaster skin like snots. Head hair curled into a ball. At only twenty-five, he had somehow blended his major themes of nudity, obscenity, and the elimination of waste material into a reputation as a dramatist on the rise.

"Telemarketing."

"Yeah."

"It's one of those things that keep you going."

"Yeah. See, I saw *Hand Motion* at INTAR Arts."

Roarke smiled. "That was a great experience. The actors were a director's dream."

"I thought—what's her name? the old one—I thought she sucked dick as the mother, but you directed it fucking great. Shit. I'm watching it, I'm thinking, you know, fucking shit, I mean . . . I'm thinking, shit, there is my director for *Measuring Remnants*. C'mon. Fuck."

Roarke didn't have to think about it. *Measuring Remnants*. He should have been killed at birth. She feigned being thoughtful for a moment.

"I'm awfully sorry, Awky."

Awky didn't say anything. They both sipped their beers. Roarke felt sorry for the pasty tatterdemalion.

"But it's a terrific . . . terrific piece," she lied.

"It *is* great." He nodded at his beer and said, "It's perfect. You think?"

Roarke took a drink now.

"I mean, I don't, I honest-to-God don't think it can be improved."

Roarke took three huge swallows, and it was gone. She signaled the waitress for another.

"I mean, shit . . . fuck . . . it's motherfucking great shit. . . . I mean, it cannot be improved it's so fucking perfect."

The beer arrived, and she quickly drank half of it.

"I'm right about that. Shit. You abso-fuckin'-lutely know. Right?"

"Well, hey. I wish you the best."

"But, hey . . . right?"

"I'm not an expert on plays, Awky."

"No shit," he laughed. "That *Hand Motion* you directed. Fucking gag me. All those fucking women. I mean shit. Fuck."

Hand Motion was the autobiography of an ancient matriarch who remembered her three daughters at various moments of their lives. It quite moved the audience when they could find one and was a revelation for Roarke and the four women involved.

"That old one. She sucked dick. Who gives a shit about those fucking crybabies?"

Roarke took a small swallow and put the glass down.

"You know, Awky, the scene in *Measuring Remnants* where you have the three orphaned male prostitutes urinating out toward the audience may be difficult to stage."

"They just face the fucking audience and piss. What's so fucking hard?"

"The audience might not like to get urine on them."

"Fuck them. When we did it in workshop, the motherfuckers ate that shit up. No compromise. That's why I got the fucking National Endowment grant. I do not fucking compromise."

"So the bowel movement that the Baby Eater takes onstage in act two is not simulated?"

"The Baby Eater shits right there. What we did was take this, like, fucking cellophane or some shit, and the Baby Eater just shits. It's fucking magical. Baby Eater needs to eat a lot of roughage, though."

Roarke took another swig. Then another.

"You got a fucking problem with that?"

"Nope. If that's what you want."

"Yeah, you got a problem. Up-fucking-tight. I thought you dykes weren't supposed to be up-fucking-tight."

Awky's whiny voice started to rise. He liked it when people knew he was passionate about his art. He liked the world to see his passion.

"Up-fucking-tight!"

"Don't yell at me, Awky," Roarke said evenly.

17

"I'll yell at you! I'll fucking yell at you! You fucking impostor!"

Roarke looked across the table into Awky's fiery nostrils. Her cheeks high under opaque eyes. Beautiful skin coming crimson. For a moment, synaptosomes at the base of Awky's brain stem tried sending a warning. But it was halfhearted, and it was garbled in transmission.

"Cunt!" he said.

Later, all Awky remembered was her fist coming across the table. He saw a beautiful vision of Mary Magdalene, which he hadn't seen since catechism. He was running in a field, and the trees and grass all smelled like Mennen Skin Bracer, and there were old women chasing him, and they were naked and swatting him with long wooden spoons.

5

Ten days later, hands hardened and back throbbing, Steven sat at the table finishing a beer. Roarke was in her rocker next to the stage, a reading light clipped to the back.

She turned the page of her paperback and brought her knees up so that the rocker held her separated from the floor. She looked up and caught Steven staring.

"What?"

"What, what?"

"Why are you looking at me?"

"It looks like you're floating, with your feet up and everything."

"Oh."

She turned back to the book.

"Hey, Roarke."

She kept reading. "What?"

"I've been thinking that if it wasn't for you, I'm a homeless person."

She closed the book, put her feet on the floor, and folded her hands. "Will this be a short whining session or a few hours of self-flagellation?"

"Well, I don't know. I'm pretty disgusted with myself."

"I think you're great. Have another beer."

"I drank all the beers."

"Write something."

"I'm too tired."

"It's eight o'clock."

"It feels like midnight."

Roarke opened a folding chair and sat next to him. "Look you asshole, you are not a homeless man. You're just a guy who's been victimized. I figured Beverly would do something like this. She didn't get it."

"Get what?"

"Get that an artist has to be an artist. That's your job. Being an asshole is second."

Steven looked at his hands. "I don't know."

"Besides, how great could she be if she took all your money and moved in with Toby Hunter, who by the way is indeed gay?"

"What do you think was going through Toby's mind?"

"I haven't the foggiest."

They sat quietly.

"I'm sorry. Go back to reading."

"You ruined reading."

"I'm sorry."

"You're tired. When a person gets tired, he can't see the forest for the trees."

"I'm forty-eight, Roarke."

"I'm forty, for Chrissake."

Roarke looked at the stage. She felt tired, too.

"The hard part of this artist thing . . . is going on. Getting . . . getting the energy . . . back."

"I don't feel like an artist." He sighed.

Roarke moved back to the rocker. "You're an artist, asshole. Trust me."

6

The stage setting was naturalistic. Couches, chairs, tables. A few paintings, contemporary and bright, were pinned to the side walls. It was the enormous papier-mâché buttocks serving as the backdrop that added a visually unique metaphor to the year's most challenging theatrical production, *Bottom Dwellers*, a hip-hop musical about the seasoned Catholic priests who, through a seemingly endless parade of sexually aberrant acts, bore testimony to the vileness of religious life. As Richard Poore, syndicated theater critic, gushed, ". . . at last off-Broadway has a production *about* something. It's hot! It's now! It's America!"

Two and a half hours of Catholic hegemony later, the cast members emerged from the anal canal for curtain call. Steven and Roarke walked quietly into Tribeca. Steven lit a cigarette.

"Look." Roarke pointed up. "A star."

Steven looked up. "It's a plane."

"It's a star."

"You can't see stars in New York, Roarke."

"That is a goddamn star."

"Okay, it's a goddamn star."

"Maybe not."

"Whatever."

"It's moving. It's a plane."

Five minutes later Roarke looked up again. "Why?"

"Why what?"

"Why can't you see stars in New York?" she asked.

"The lights of the city muddle up the sky."

She thought about that and then said, "That play . . . took place in a gigantic asshole."

"The *Times* said it displayed 'high moral sense.' "

They laughed.

"What are you doing day after tomorrow?" Steven asked.

"Teaching acting."

"What time?"

"Two classes. Eleven to one and three-thirty to five."

"Want to go to dinner at Tubby's?"

"Who's Tubby?"

"Guy runs the construction job I'm on. He says I can bring somebody. I thought I'd bring a lesbian."

They laughed again and held hands. At Hudson Street, Roarke threw her head back and shouted, "I LOVE theater!"

Her oath lingered above them and followed them, and later, after she had called Judy again, and wept again, it still hung there like gossamer.

7

She picked up on the second ring.

"Roarke here. Oh, hi . . . uh-huh . . . well, he's here. Why don't you just write on the envelope to forward it?"

Steven watched from the sink.

"Uh-huh. Uh-huh. Well, Beverly, I'll see if he can come to the phone. You know how he is when he's writing. . . . I'll see if I can get him."

Roarke looked over to Steven and held the phone. He hesitated for an instant, then took the receiver. "Hello?"

"Steven?"

"Hello, Beverly."

"How are you, Steven? I've been so worried. Have you been there all this time?"

"At Roarke's. Yes, I have."

"I've been so worried."

Steven watched Roarke and waited.

"Are you there, Steven?"

"I'm here."

"Mrs. Marmar forwarded some of your mail to me. I put it in a manila envelope."

"Oh . . . could you send it over? I'll give you Roarke's address."

"Maybe I could just bring it over."

Steven kept his eyes on Roarke, who held her stomach and pretended to vomit.

"It'd be easier just to mail it, Beverly. You really don't have to bring it."

Roarke pointed a finger at her temple and cocked her thumb.

"I miss you, Steven. I need . . . I need to see you. . . . Toby . . . it's . . . he's . . ." Beverly choked, and her breath quavered.

Roarke held the end of an imaginary rope and hanged herself.

Beverly came back on. "Toby . . . Toby is a homosexual."

"Well . . . yes he is, Beverly."

"What?" Roarke whispered.

Steven cupped his hand over the mouthpiece. "Beverly just found out Toby's gay."

Roarke collapsed on the floor.

"C'mon, Roarke. . . . Beverly . . . what kind of mail?"

"What?" she sniffled.

"I mean . . . the mail Mrs. Marmar sent."

"Well . . . I don't know. . . . I can bring them over now."

"Uhh . . . sure. . . . You know where Roarke lives."

Roarke threw her hands up in the air.

"Yes. Is it . . . you know, uncomfortable?"

"Is what uncomfortable?"

"Roarke. The whole lesbian thing."

"I'll meet you outside, Beverly. I'll be on the steps."

He sat on the apartment steps for half an hour. It was a damp night, but not uncomfortably cold. A Yellow Cab pulled up, and Beverly got out. She saw him and pushed her teeth down onto her lower lip. She looked nice in a tight short skirt. A ribbon held her hair up.

"Hi, Beverly," he said, standing up.

"You got a haircut."

"Roarke cut it."

"It's very neat."

"It's short. I'm working for Tubby again, so, you know . . . construction guys."

Roarke's building rumbled a little from the subway. Steven wondered if all his mail could fit into her little teddy-bear knapsack.

"I've been exercising," she said.

"What?"

"I've been . . . you know, working out. Pumping iron. That's why I look different."

Steven did not think she looked different.

"You look great. Pumping iron?"

"Lifting weights. Nautilus. Jogging."

Steven reached for his cigarettes.

"Can I have one?"

"You don't smoke, Beverly."

"I've been smoking a little. I've been really nervous."

He handed her one.

"Thanks."

Beverly watched him through dramatic tiny puffs.

"I guess there wasn't a lot of mail, huh? I mean, I thought you'd have it in a big envelope or something."

She reached into her coat pocket and brought out three letters and some bills.

"Here. I don't know what they are. Mrs. Marmar says we still owe some utilities. I can help when I get it all together."

Steven nodded. "Well, thanks for bringing the mail over. You look great, working out and everything."

"Toby is homosexual," she croaked, throwing down her cigarette. "He has a boyfriend. He may have more than one."

Beverly shivered and hunched into herself. He patted her shoulder.

"I have to go inside now, Beverly."

She looked up at him. She made her eyes big. "I want . . . I want to go inside with you."

She let her hands drop helplessly. Another train made the street tremble, but she did not feel it.

"The trains really make the street rumble, don't they?" he said.

"I didn't feel it," she said.

She took his hands now. She stood back and held Steven Kearney at arm's length. She nodded knowingly. He nodded reflexively.

"I really have to go to work," he said.

"Steven, I'm nervous and things."

"I'm sorry, Beverly. I don't know what I can do about it."

"We live together, Steven!"

"We used to live together. You moved out."

She dropped his hands. "And now you're throwing that in my face?"

"I'm not throwing that in your face."

"Then why'd you even mention it?"

"I just meant . . . you know, we don't live together anymore."

"And whose fault is that?"

"You moved out."

"So it's all my fault?"

"You moved in with Toby."

"I didn't know he was homosexual."

"He is."

"I know he is . . . now."

She moved in and took up his hands again. "I mean . . ."

"How's that art, big boy? How's that art?"

He looked across the street to the shopping-cart lady.

"Adamantine," he answered.

"That's my big boy. That's my big art boy."

Beverly ignored her.

"I love your writing. I know I said things. I didn't mean to say them. I didn't feel them."

"It's okay not to like my stuff. Nobody likes my stuff."

"That play . . . that play about the old woman . . . the old woman and the hurricane."

"*The Hurricane Tontine.*"

"*The Hurricane Tontine*, that was great."

"That was a short story."

"That's what I said."

"You said 'play,' but it doesn't matter."

"It matters. It matters because when you live with someone—"

"Beverly, we don't—"

She pushed away. "Stop it! Stop it! Stop it! We live together. If people live together for years and years and don't for just a little while, it doesn't mean they don't."

The bag lady yelled, "Let the big boy do his art!"

"Who is that?"

"I don't know."

"Please take me inside, Steven."

"Roarke's inside."

"I am so sick of Roarke. You are living with a lesbian, Steven. Do you know what lesbians do? What do you do when she has other lesbians over? It's so gross."

"I really have to get back to work."

"You can write that shit anytime."

The bag lady yelled, "That's right! Write that shit, big boy! Write that shit!"

"Jesus, Steven!"

"I have to go now."

"What about me? I brought you mail. I . . . I . . . we live together. I'm nervous and things."

Steven took a deep breath and looked at his feet. "Look, Beverly . . ."

She moved in again and put her head against his chest.

"See . . . after . . . after you walked out . . ."

"Stop."

"I got hit by a taxi."

Beverly looked up at him.

"After I got hit—or since I got hit—I've been having a terrible time writing again. Then I had to go back to working for Tubby, and I'm all out of shape, and it took a couple of weeks to get over my aches and pains. And—"

"I would run a hot bath for you. I would make sure you soak your muscles."

"But now I'm working good. I'm working on a book of poetry as a companion to my novel about the poet from Maine."

"I loved that."

"I never showed it to you."

"Yes you did."

"I never showed it to anybody but Roarke."

"She's a lesbian! You showed it to me!"

"So I'm working good, and it's probably all for the best that you took the money I saved working for Tubby so I could have time to write the poems. I mean, working construction has lent this immediacy to the poetry, and the language itself has—"

"Throw it in my face, why don't you?"

"No, I just—"

"Four years. Four years I labored at our relationship. You never made any money. All that paper piling up. Nobody wants it because, Steven, hello, it's no good. It's irrelevant. You have wasted your life on crap nobody wants. Your only friend is a fucking lesbian. You're a couple of losers! Why do you have to hurt me so much?"

Steven shrugged. "Well . . . I hope it all works out for you and . . . you know . . . Toby."

"He's a fag! Roarke's a dyke."

"Good night, Beverly."

"Fuck, fuck, fuck, fuck, fuck, fuck you!"

* * *

He tossed the bills onto the table and opened the letter addressed to Mr. Steven Kearney, Playwright, from Miss Wilma Kirk of Creedemore, Colorado.

MISS WILMA R. KIRK
26 Bachelor Drive
Creedemore, Colorado 17701

Dear Mr. Kearney,

Several years ago I was on a play-reading committee assigned to select a play reflective of, but not limited to, the silver boom of western Colorado. I was chosen for this honor because I was a teacher of English in the Creedemore Regional School and a member of the Del Norte Players (our most recent production being *Les Misérables* at the Regional High School).

27

I was quite taken with your entry, *Poker Alice Tubbs in Love*. While it was not ultimately chosen for presentation (the revue *Wagons, Wine, and Silver* received that honor), I felt *Tubbs* displayed not only a savvy understanding of the time but a poetic tone that makes English what it is. This was especially evident in Alice's monologues given over the bodies of the various cheaters, liars, and frauds she shot throughout the work.

I am retired from my profession and am now president of the Creedemore Historical Society (CHS). Last year I applied for funding to present a broad-based, language-intensive, historically accurate spectacular at the Creedemore Outdoor Lumberjack Amphitheater in Creedemore, on or about August 30.

Now that funding has been approved, I would like to offer to you the position of town Playwright in Residence. The appointment would be for three months beginning June 1 and would involve researching and writing an historically accurate piece on Creedemore and its environs (no allegories, please).

Accommodations and board would be at the Ute Guest Ranch, and included in the employment package of $300.00 per week is a three-month enrollment in the Puerite County HMO health plan.

I do so hope you can accept this position. The actors in the county are equal to none, and the jagged cliffs that form the amphitheater's natural backdrop offer a rare opportunity to spread your artistic wings and encompass an entire landscape.

Sincerely,
Miss Wilma R. Kirk

P.S. Puerite County has experienced some mild disagreements over water and property usage. I firmly believe that ART, and her sister BEAUTY, can bring our community back to the fold.

W.K.

8

The whole awful thing happened because of old Ticky Lettgo's refusal to negotiate the use of his stretch of the Upper Rio Grande River. At least that's the take Miss Wilma Kirk had on it. Although the big-shot "Mountain Man" Red Fields out of Boulder didn't help matters any with his condescending attitude and stupid little grin. Even Sheriff Petey Myers, who had retired from the Boston police and was new to all this Puerite County jazz, had told him to go slow.

The Mountain Man had come into the county last spring and rented the Quonset hut next to the Western Market. He brought fifty-five mountain bikes with him from Boulder, where he'd just gotten his master's in mathematics, and set up shop as Mountain Man's Guided Tours and Bike Rentals. It wasn't that the folks in Creedemore were cynical or anything, but they just didn't know. About Boulder or touring bikes. This little bit of Colorado was about fishing and hunting and some people who just wanted to watch the leaves turn gold on the aspen. When the summer folks went home in November, what was left was something under three hundred valleyers. Nothing happened in the spring, and Mountain Man Red Fields should have put two and two together and gotten four-get-it.

Old Ticky Lettgo spent winters in Wichita Falls, Texas, where him and old Minnie Lettgo ran seven, count them, Feed 'n' Seed stores. It was an operation as ripe for an antitrust suit as Standard Oil used to be. Old Ticky had them all by the short hairs and let them know it.

"I got you by the short hairs," he'd cackle, "and you know it."

The fact that both Mountain Man and Ticky came up to Creedemore on the same April day last year is pretty unremarkable, because Ticky usually arrived on May 1. As Miss Kirk had it, Red Fields's mountain bikes and guide service was not yet headed on the collision course of the following year, and most likely the only contact the burly, red-haired, twenty-seven-year-old bicycle entrepreneur might have had with the bald, bony, ninety-six-year-old, six-gun-wearing Ticky Lettgo was when Minnie rented a two-wheeler to see what it was all about and had a heart attack not half a mile from the store that put her in bed for six days except to cook for Ticky.

Their place, between Creedemore and the Rio Grande Reservoir, was where the big river hooked almost completely back onto itself in three wild zigzags. It was magnificent water, and Ticky loved to stop at the high gate just off Creedemore Road, in his pristine GMC Lettgo Feed 'n' Seed red, white, and blue pickup and say to Minnie, who sat on three San Antonio phone books so she could see out the passenger window, "That is my water, Mrs. Ticky Lettgo."

"I know," she'd say, looking at it as if for the first time.

"I know you know," he'd say proudly.

It's about endurance and thoughtfulness and mostly patience, is how Miss Wilma Kirk had it. Mountain Man Red Fields had everything but patience, while patience was Ticky's middle name. And this is how bad things happen almost to formula. Take an idea, even a good idea, and blend to a smooth consistency with endurance, thoughtfulness, and patience. It's a recipe, see, and Miss Wilma Kirk knew about cakes rising or whatever.

So it wasn't lost on Mountain Man with the master's degree that the spring start on bike rentals was a mistake in judgment. Business picked up in June, and by August it was actually brisk. When he tallied up his summer receipts, he saw that while his guide service was a bust, the bike thing, the lure of the athletic, made a profit. There had to be another angle. Mountain Man pondered the mathematical probability that there was money in these hills, then ran his pondering through the small computer on his desk. There was indeed the probability of further cash flow and a one-in-seven chance of actual wealth. But what, where, and how?

Mountain Man walked up Main Street to Rowdy's Chili Bar, ordered a beer, and took it onto the back porch that hung over Bachelor Creek. The narrow stream was running hard to the Rio Grande a few hundred yards below. The shining black stones caught the three-quarter moon and showed its shimmering reflection. A small tree floated by, dislodged somewhere above by a rockslide or snowmelt. Mountain Man watched it on its way to the big river, and he smiled to himself and drank deeply. The next morning he designed flyers and drove into Monte Vista to have them printed up. For the flyer's cover, he chose a picture of the Grand Canyon he tore from a *National Geographic*. Beneath the picture he had printed in bold half-inch lettering:

MOUNTAIN MAN
SPRING RIVER RAFTING

Then he wrote his phone number in Creedemore and his girlfriend's number in Boulder. He would decide on the price later. He could put in at Box Canyon where the river came out of the cliff range, public land, and get out by the old train trestle outside of South Fork. Then, when the spring thaw settled down, he'd segue into the trail bikes.

The flyer proved inexpensive, and he had five thousand made up. Roughly, his plan was to paper the valley, leaving the flyers at groceries and drugstores and gas stations, and take the remainder to Boulder with some drop-offs in Alamosa, Pueblo, and Denver. He experienced a verve and confidence he hadn't felt in quite a while. That dreams-coming-true connection to a place and time. It was in this feeling he first spoke to old Ticky Lettgo. He had just set down a pile of thirty or forty flyers at Ryan's Barbershop.

Ticky, who was having his small, hard head buffed by Ryan, said, "What's that?"

Mountain Man turned to Ticky, lost in the high barber chair, and said, "It's a flyer for a new operation I'm starting out of my bike shop, old-timer."

"What?"

"River rafting."

"No. What did you say after 'bike shop'?"

"What?"

"Old-timer?"

Ryan gave Ticky a look. "Stop moving around. You want the shine on the top to match the shine over the ears, don't you?"

"Hell yes."

"So sit still."

"I'm going to offer action rafting on the Rio Grande," Mountain Man said, hands on his hips, holding in his belly, feeling like a frontiersman.

Ticky chuckled. "Jesus."

"Only in the spring when the water's high. Start at the Box and end at the trestle."

Ryan seized the wild little noggin and held it. "It's important to keep still while I'm buffing."

"It's an offer of high excitement," Mountain Man stated.

"Well, now, let me ask you this. What are all the dudes gonna think when they have to get out of the damn floats and carry them around private land?"

Ryan checked both sides of the gleaming head. Satisfied, he pulled off the barber cloth. "You're a new man, Ticky."

Ticky wasn't listening. "They pay their money and they carry the floats?"

"I thought that out," Mountain Man said with a mathematician's certainty. "Nobody owns the water."

"What?"

"I said, 'Nobody owns the water.' It stands to reason that if everybody stays in the rafts and they don't touch the river bottom, which I suppose technically belongs to the landowner, although personally I find it an archaic law at best, it should be smooth sailing."

Ticky sat still for a moment, then climbed down from the chair. "That's very interesting."

"Thanks. Take a flyer home."

"How about I take a flyer and shove it up your keister," Ticky said, drawing the huge Colt .45 from his holster.

Ryan continued folding his buffing cloth. The Mountain Man stood stone-frozen. Some of the flyers slipped out of his hands and drifted to the barbershop floor.

Ryan said, screwing on the top of the head polish, "Now, goddamn it, Ticky. This isn't 1932."

Ticky kept his small eyes hard on the Mountain Man. His lips curled in an ancient smile. "You remember '32?"

"Course I don't remember '32, you old fart. My dad told me."

"Last gunfight in Colorado."

"Shot his nuts off."

"What?"

"His nuts. You shot his nuts off."

"I shot him here," Ticky said, slapping his skeletal thigh.

"Well, I heard it was his nuts."

"Well, you heard wrong."

"I heard it was his nuts and then you stood over him and kicked him."

"I shot him here, and then I helped him over to Doc Wheeler."

"Well, that's not the way I got it."

"Well, you got it wrong."

"Maybe."

Ticky narrowed his black eyes onto the Mountain Man as if he were a can of frozen orange juice with the word "concentrate" on the label.

"Now, you listen to me, you big son of a bitch. I see you on my river or in my river, you're gonna be under my river. Now, git."

Mountain Man staggered from the shop. Fear turned to anger. He took his pounding heart up the street to the county sheriff's office. Petey Myers's wife was on dispatch. She looked up from her station to see the Mountain Man standing there. Fists clenched. Neck clenched. Clenched.

"Yes, sir?"

Mountain Man Red Fields took a snatch of air. "Old man pulled a gun. Old man. Gun on me."

"Someone pulled a gun on you?"

"Old man. Barbershop."

The switchboard buzzed and lit.

"Will you excuse me a moment? Sheriff's office. . . . Yes. . . . Oh, dear. . . . Yes. . . . Oh, gee. . . . Well, it's good no one was hurt. . . . That's right. I'll get the sheriff out there as soon as possible. . . . All righty."

She turned back to the Mountain Man. "I'm sorry."

"Some old man took out his gun and pointed it at me in Ryan's Barbershop."

"Oh, dear."

"I need to talk to the sheriff."

"Well, Sheriff Myers isn't in right now, but I expect he'll be checking in."

"Will you tell him an old man pulled a gun?"

"Tell me again."

The sun had dropped in the foothills by the time Petey Myers knocked on Mountain Man's door.

"Somebody pull a gun or something?"

Petey was fifty-eight years old. Some rural towns hired retired, experienced policemen from big cities. Petey was from Boston. Thirty-two years on the force. Seen it all. Done it all. Had it all done to him. Creedemore hired Vi, too. Soon as he got the hang of it and stopped calling everybody "cockhound," which was his pet name for offenders or possible offenders or anybody else, then small-town sheriffing was a piece of cake.

Mountain Man Red Fields stood in the doorway and explained the incident in meticulous detail. A gun was pulled. An old man pulled it. His entire enterprise had been threatened. He had a witness.

Petey Myers drove the county Jeep out to Ticky's place between Creedemore and the reservoir. He opened the gate, drove in, and closed the gate after him. Before he got back into the vehicle, he checked the river and its zigzag. There were trout here, and they were big ones, not the little brookies he'd taken in the Berkshires. These were browns the size of his arm. He knew it. Under the low moon, Petey heard them rising for cow flies and mosquitoes. He imagined them on the end of his eight-and-a-half-foot boron western fly rod, their yellow bellies, their great snouts, their runs into the deepest pools.

Petey drove on slowly, crossing two narrow wooden bridges. A quarter of a mile farther, the Lettgos' huge TV glistened through the porch window like an aurora. He rang the bell and talked business.

"... anyway Ticky, a man can't draw anymore. Period. You might have had a reason, you might not have. I'm not here to judge you, just to let you know that the charge was leveled."

Ticky listened to Petey and kept an eye peeled on the TV, where the Undertaker was wrestling two men, both black. When he spoke, he looked at Petey, but his eyes shifted back to the set as if in some midconsciousness. This gave him a kind of conditional authority. Minnie sat close to him, completely lost in the action.

"Well, okay," he said slowly, between body slams. "Okay and yes maybe, but . . . see now, Sheriff, you're a fisherman, right? I seen you. That'd be the catch-and-release business. The State Fisherman's Area. Yes? Fruitcakes in Denver won't let you keep 'em. Now, Jesus, that Undertaker . . . Minnie, look—lifted up the black bastard and dropped him onto his old mau-mau. Jesus K. Christopher . . . well, well. . . . Now, what if I see you throwing flies at the ones in the state area, the release area, and I honk my horn, and you walk over, and I say, 'Petey, why don't you come over to the Lettgo Ranch, where my Rio Grande zigzags three big times and I got stretches that meander and get deep and I know, I know personally, where there's a goddamn German brown with a mouth like a steam shovel that Minnie and me named Dave after Dave Santi from Lake City, who tried to get him for years and who died sorry about one thing, and that was not catching that German brown? And what if you come over and catch fifty fish and take home dinner, and what if that happened?"

Petey caught the ramble about the steam shovel German brown. He caught the ramble about the invitation.

"That'd be great."

"Damn right. And I'd get old Minnie Lettgo to cook up a meat loaf, and later we'd have some— Minnie! Jesus, the black bastards have got the Undertaker tied up in the ropes!"

The Undertaker kicked one in the chest, then disentangled himself before knocking both men out. He arranged them, for viewing, amid boos, and sprinkled flowers on them. He had R.I.P. tattooed on his chest.

"Undertaker beats the snot out of the black bastards and gets booed. See? You never know. Okay, yes, well . . . So it's all great. Meat loaf, fish, whiskey. But now what if I come home one day and there you are throwing into the river, or maybe you got Dave on the end of your goddamn line and I haven't invited you? You just saw the river turn on itself three specific times and said, 'Well, hell, I can just fish here.' What do I do? Well, I'll tell you what I'd do. I'd drop you like yesterday's pancakes. Jesus, look!"

Ticky gave full attention to the entrance of Nicotine Nick Nomad. A long-haired biker driving his hog to ringside. A man who thumbed his nose at authority by smoking king-size unfiltered English Ovals while he wrestled. Ticky pointed to the screen.

"Minnie! Jesus!"

Petey watched the quick little brawl, too. By the time Nicotine Nick smashed the No Smoking sign over the ref's head, Ticky's eyes were closed.

9

The tortellini floated in her big yellow bowl. They bobbed and rolled in the clear broth.

"Put lotsa cheese on it. Sarah, slide the Parmesan over to Roarke."

Roarke looked up at Sarah and smiled.

Tubby turned to Steven. "What was I saying?"

"You were telling us how you met Sarah."

Tubby ripped a piece of Italian bread from the loaf and dipped it into his broth. He spoke between chews. "You eat, I'll talk. See, I never knew a lot of Jews, being from Newark and everything. I knew a lot of Portagees, I knew a lot of Puerto Ricans, I knew a lot of blacks, but Jews? No, I can honestly say I just didn't know a lot of Jews."

"Say it again, we didn't hear you the first forty times," Sarah said sweetly. She was as delicate, pretty, and demure as Tubby was enormous, tough, and loud. He ignored her.

"So. I'm on this construction gang on the Lower East Side. I remember it was my first union gig. Now, your Lower East Side has got what you might call your whole lot of Jews. Every shape and story."

"He thought I was a dago."

"I did not think you were a dago. See, Sarah worked in the coffee shop I'd stop in to get my breakfast in the morning and—"

"Second breakfast."

"All right."

"His mother cooked him a big breakfast, too."

"—and here's this beautiful little girl waiting on me. One look at me and she flipped her kosher cookies."

"There was less of him then."

"Twenty-three years of marriage."

Roarke applauded.

"Thank you, thank you. Four kids. One still at home. Three in college. Same time."

"I'll bet it's expensive," Steven said.

"Fucking A."

"Tubby, watch your mouth. We have company."

Roarke said, "I say 'fuck' all the time."

"That's my girl, but yeah, it's expensive."

Sarah sipped her broth, then said, "It's a good thing Tubby's in the mob."

"The mob, listen to her."

Steven said, "I can't believe how great this is."

Roarke said, "What's in the stuffing?"

"She uses the hamburg, pork, and veal, but the key is the broth. I make the broth. Chicken and beef. I marry the flavors."

"I don't mind Tubby being in the mob. He's in the good part of the mob. He's a construction mobster."

"Then how come I got a lot of micks on my crew? How come I probably got more blacks than Carter has little liver pills? Right, Steven? I got micks, blacks, I got it all."

"What did I say? I didn't say Mafia. I said mob. It helps with college. Now you tell us. Where did you meet? Tubby, fill up Roarke's glass."

Tubby filled it up and scooped some more tortellini into the bowls.

"When did we meet, Roarke?" Steven asked.

" 'Eighty-six, was it? I directed a reading of one of Steven's plays. It was at the Public."

"The literary department gave my play to Roarke."

"You mean, you read it?" asked Tubby.

"A reading," Roarke explained, "is when a director gets a group of actors together to see how a play sounds. To get it off the printed page. Sometimes, if there's rehearsal time, you can have some movement, some deeper interpretation, but I think we just sat around and read Steven's."

"Raul Julia read one of the roles," Steven said.

"I loved him." Sarah sighed. "So sad."

"So what happened?"

"They didn't like it. Joe Papp didn't even come to it."

"Well, fuck Joe Papp."

"You heard of Joe Papp?" Steven asked.

"I don't have to hear of him. Fuck him."

"I love the theater," Sarah said. "If you do something, we'll come. Tubby likes theater, too."

Tubby shrugged and sopped up the last of the broth.

"We saw *Cats*, *Les Misérables*, *Miss Saigon*, *Phantom of the Opera*, which I loved, but you had to see it with the original cast," she said.

Tubby wiped his mouth, crumpled up the napkin, and plopped it into the bowl.

"We saw Dustin Hoffman in *Death of a Salesman*. We loved that, didn't we, Tubby?"

"I didn't love it but I like Hoffman. But I don't know, I couldn't hear that other asshole."

"Malkovich?" Steven asked.

"The creepy-looking guy?"

"Yeah."

"Tubby said 'Louder' twice. Twice! I could have died."

"I paid seventy-five dollars a ticket, and this prick is up there talking to himself. He's supposed to tell *me* about it, right?"

"I hate it when actors mumble," Roarke said.

"Yeah, but Hoffman was great. He can do anything. What'd you guys think of that homo thing? What was that, Sarah?"

"Don't be crude."

"Oh, sorry. What did you guys think of the homosexual thing?"

Sarah said, "*Angels in America*. I didn't see it. Tubby went with Niki."

"My baby sister."

"She's always broadening his horizons."

"Well, she wanted to see it for some reason."

"Niki is a daughter of Sappho."

"If my old man had stuck around, she'd be . . . I don't know, the regular daughter or something."

"Niki teaches at Hunter. Art history. Very bright."

"That's no lie."

"Niki teaches at Hunter, and Tubby is a construction mobster," Sarah said sweetly.

"Anyway. Seventy-five bucks to sit there and have these guys wave their bananas at you."

"A little nudity. God, you're such a prude."

"I just don't get it."

Roarke smiled. "When I walk into the theater, I'm looking for something I can recognize. It can be a feeling or a sense or a shared emotion, but it's got to be there."

"Here, here," said Tubby.

"Speaking as a daughter of Sappho myself, I want a theater of inclusion. Don't lecture me. Don't judge me. Let me connect."

Everybody chewed for a second. Tubby topped off everyone's wine. He chuckled.

"Roarke, when Sarah said my sister was a daughter of Sappho . . . well, you're *not* one."

"Yes I am."

"No, no, you're probably, like, a feminist or something. I mean, Niki's a . . . you know . . . lesbo."

"A lesbian," Sarah corrected.

"When she stops calling me a fat-ass, I'll stop calling her a lesbo."

"She doesn't call you a fat-ass."

"Sometimes she does."

"Sometimes you are. She is a wonderful woman."

"Okay, stop. Hold it. Steven. Roarke. Did I ever say she wasn't wonderful?"

"Nope," Roarke answered. She glanced over to Steven, her eyes twinkling.

"She's an amazing girl . . . woman . . . whatever. She graduated college at nineteen. She's amazing. But I want her to be happy. She'd make a great mother. Her kids would be geniuses or something."

"Maybe she can adopt," Roarke said.

Tubby shrugged. They drank the table wine. They finished the tortellini.

10

An inch of fine, dry snow had drifted onto the valley floor during the night. The Rio Grande at its beginning, cold and luminous, blue and green rolled high, occasionally spilling out at the turns and charging at the riffles. Later, pivoting at South Fork toward Alamosa, much of the big water dove underground, becoming a river of potatoes and barley and hops. But Mountain Man Red Fields's High Adventure plan included only the most majestic of the Rio Grande, the twists and curves of rocky grandeur. A glorious procession through Creedemore's timeless valley.

At 5:35 A.M. on May 14, Mountain Man secured the third rubber wilderness raft to the trailer. He briefly inspected each adventurer's gear. In all, twenty-four participants, including his girlfriend, Felicia "Cia" Brun, a graduate student at the University of Colorado, and Ronald DeFreeze, editor-publisher of Colorado Wild Folk magazine, had reserved space on Mountain Man's inaugural High Adventure Raft Trip. The evening before, Mountain Man had driven Felicia's minivan to the old train trestle at South Fork and parked it. When the happy party ended their rafting at around 4:30 P.M. (according to his loose calculations), Mountain Man could pass out his Certificate of Rafting Excellence to everyone, then ferry them all back to their vehicles. He was feeling his authority and wore his new rank as "Raft Professional" in a powerful and steady step, a robust hand on hip, a deeper, satisfied voice.

It was a cold morning, but the coffee was hot and the small talk invigorating. By 6:15 the caravan pulled away from Mountain Man's High Adventure Mountain Bike Rental and River Rafting storefront in Creedemore proper. The seven vehicles—three Explorers, two Jeep Cherokees, two Land Cruisers—snaked by the played-out bottom mines outside of town, past the Landings Guest Ranch, by the National Campground at Ute Bend. At Phil's Gravel Depot, they turned onto the icy dirt road that sloped dangerously close to the spring mud of Boynton's horse farm. Mountain Man pulled his Land Cruiser to a halt and slowly stepped out, surveying the situation in a purposeful 360-degree swirl. He signaled four-wheel drive to the others. They moved on. Four cow gates later, the convoy crossed the bridge at the Box and turned in to the public parking area.

Rafts were laid side by side on the snowy spring grass and loaded with supplies. Oars were the last essentials, secured by a riveted leather strap. The rafts had cost Mountain Man thirty-two hundred dollars apiece. Their very newness spoke of vision and commerce. He placed his hands under his concho belt as his eyes swept the lay of the Box. He did not know much about the big river except that it poured madly out of the mouth of Box Canyon. He had never been above the Ten Mile Camp to the reservoir, the twelve-mile water valley created jointly by Colorado, New Mexico, and Texas to satisfy their ribbon of farmers. He knew nothing of the creeks that filled it. Nothing of where the clarity came from. Nothing of where the big fish began their colors. A light snow began again.

The Ferrinis, John and Lorraine, and their three boys joined DeFreeze and Felicia in the first raft, named *Wil* after Mountain Man's mother. The large contingent of young men from the Colorado Springs Zion Bible Institute filled the second raft, *Bozo,* and spilled over into the third one, *El Capitan.* Mountain Man himself and the two retired couples, the Philos and Handlemans from the Navajo Estates outside of Denver, completed the hearty circle. Mountain Man said, "Let's rock."

"Cool," said Liz Handleman, and they pushed out onto the river.

The Ferrinis were first off, followed by the Zion Bible Institute and finally Mountain Man at the oars of *El Capitan*, commanding the rear guard. In seconds the three orange and green rafts reached a disconcerting speed. Despite having been required to view a fifteen-minute video entitled *ProFloat and Oarsmanship*, each oarsman immediately lost control of his raft. The trees on either side of the river passed in a whistling blur. At the first bend, where a large boulder protruded into the water, the river miraculously slowed, spun all the rafts in a gentle whirlpool, then guided them away from the rock.

Hiding his astonishment at the goodness of the river, Mountain Man said strongly, "The main thing to remember is, the river runs us, we don't run the river."

Tommy Philo, who had pissed himself a tenth of a mile back, nodded his understanding.

As the flotilla approached Wright's Lower Ranch, the Rio Grande split into two equally frightening runs of white water, divided by an island of silt and sand. Mountain Man signaled right; the river took them left. Not at all sure what to do, Mountain Man pulled his long oars, one, then the other. In a moment of natural symmetry, the rushing spring water turned the rafts and formed them into a perfect line so that the party progressed backward. Mountain Man thought this might be a good time to stop for lunch, even if 7:00 A.M.

41

seemed a little early. But it was a moot point. You didn't get off the river. The river gets off you. By the time the river rejoined itself, Mountain Man estimated they were traveling about two hundred miles an hour.

The river again spun them around, and Mountain Man glimpsed that the young men from the Colorado Springs Zion Bible Institute had lost their oars. They seemed to be praying. Landscape passed as if they were on a train.

His heart racing, Mountain Man said, "Beautiful country, isn't it?"

He considered the mountain bikes and he thought, It's true there's a seasonal thing to contend with, but the variants aren't as unpredictable as rafting. Then he thought, Fuck, we're all gonna die.

11

Steven sat at the little table, and Roarke read by the dresser. The night was cool, and a big moon came through the steel-barred window.

"I'm gonna take this job."

Roarke looked at him, then looked back at her book.

"I like the idea, you know, the idea of writing a kind of history thing."

Roarke kept looking at her page. Steven doodled on the writing tablet.

"Maybe not, though. I don't know."

He lit a cigarette and smoked it. When it was done, he tapped it out on the empty beer can and dropped it into the hole. He stared at the white writing tablet in front of him. Fragments of thoughts. Partial ideas. Half sentiments. Where had his language disappeared to? In two hours at the table, he had written:

Vision   Water or

       Beverly

                       Something about water

       Roarke Reading

Grandmother leaves Family—Mother?

                 ?

He picked up a clipping from his hometown newspaper that he kept in his workbook. It was thirty years old and yellowing. It showed a photo of Miss Alda Bradford, Teacher of the Year, sitting in the center of six high-school English students, reading aloud from her battered volume of the complete works of William Shakespeare. From left to right, they were identified as Sally Soares, David Wolfe, James Spigott, Allison Aguire, and Robert Fonse. The boy on the far right side looked intense and sweaty. He did not wear a jacket like the other young men, and his hair was hopelessly wild. He held a pen, and his mouth was half open, as if he were caught in the act of reading over Miss Bradford's shoulder. He was referred to as Unknown Boy on Right. He had kept the picture because he thought it was funny. Now Steven Kearney wasn't so sure.

"Roarke?"

She looked up. "What?"

"I have this feeling that I'm not feeling. Does that make sense? I'm drifting. If I took this Creedemore thing, I'd have a structure to work in. I'd have boundaries. And it would get me going. I know it would get me going. How hard could it be? A little local history. It ought to be fun."

12

For a long moment, not one of the adventurers moved. They sat astonished, the rafts gently beached onto a grassy island by the mighty river. Mountain Man checked his Swiss Army G-Shock watch. In twenty-two minutes, they had completed approximately two-thirds of the trip. He was six hours ahead of schedule, but he was alive.

He stepped confidently from the raft. "Let's get a fire going for coffee."

"Cool," said Mrs. Handleman, leaping from the craft.

The young men from the Colorado Springs Zion Bible Institute, equating labor with faith, joined the search for driftwood. Theirs had been a particularly trying few minutes. Abounding in firm belief at Box Canyon, they had quickly lost all certitude as they careened backward downstream, concluding that man was on an empty, godless journey to final oarless despair. Life was a cruel hoax, and perhaps drinking and sex were the answer. Now, preserved by the Lord's mighty hand, they found their faith renewed.

Cia walked over to Mountain Man and looked where he was looking.

"That was great," she whispered.

"You liked it?"

"It got me hot. It got me so hot."

Mountain Man thought about that. He kept scanning the high ridges for answers. One thing, though. It had not gotten him hot. Jesus.

"I bet it got you good and hot, too," she whispered.

"It did," he said. "It got me hot."

The coffee break stretched for two hours. The young men from the Colorado Springs Zion Bible Institute did not drink coffee. They sat in a tight circle and discussed Revelation. Ronald DeFreeze was particularly quiet, walking to the edge of the sandbar jotting notes in a small leather notebook. Mountain Man wondered if the editor-publisher of *Colorado Wild Folk* magazine was reviewing his rafting adventure right there.

"We're only twenty-two minutes into it," he mumbled.

"What?" Mrs. Handleman yelled over the river.

"I said I'll have to secure raft number two to raft number three. They've lost their oars."

"They're a bunch of pussies."

"Mrs. Handleman, please."

Mountain Man tied the Bible Institute raft behind his own and gathered the adventurers.

"As we move on to what I like to refer to as Phase Two of our adventure, pay special attention to the particular arrangement of cliffs and ridges on this next section of river. The valley was formed by glacial cuts, and the rocks reflect that."

"The valley is volcanic. There wasn't any glacial movement."

Mountain Man looked over to Mrs. Ferrini, standing by raft number one with her husband and children.

"Actually," she continued, "the glacial incidents were to the north."

Mountain Man looked over to Ronald DeFreeze, smiled knowingly, and looked back at Mrs. Ferrini. "Well, then, I guess you must be the foremost expert on the Rocky Mountains in the world."

"I wouldn't go that far. But I have published several textbooks on the subject."

"Okay, let's hop in the rafts."

The four miles between the sandbar and where Texas Creek joined the river were exceedingly gentle and bore the flotilla calmly through meadows and aspen ridges. Tiny spring flowers pushed up through the snow. Deer stared wide-eyed at the delighted humans.

Mountain Man could hear the Ferrinis laughing ahead. Behind him, in the secured raft, sat the Zion Bible Institute, oarless but seemingly at peace. Mountain Man checked the time: 9:40. Maybe it was going to be okay. If he could stop for lunch at the Fork Campground, this side of Lettgo's property, kill a few hours there, the float through the Lettgos' place and Beaumont's Ranch should take approximately two more hours to the old railroad bridge in South Fork.

Now he could hear DeFreeze and Cia laughing also, and he wondered if the Ferrini bitch was holding class on volcanic formations. He knew she was wrong. He had always understood the glacial movement as pivotal to the great mountain ranges. She could take her theory and shove it up her bony ass.

"They're signaling you," Mrs. Handleman said, pointing to the young men in the last raft.

Mountain Man looked back to see them holding up one of their lost oars, which had floated up to them. Several of them flung victorious fists into the air.

"They got an oar back," said Mountain Man.

"Pussies," said Mrs. Handleman.

13

Tubby gave him a ride home from the construction site in his Cadillac. "Last day on the job. You get the royal treatment." They crossed Twenty-third Street to Broadway and took it downtown. It was past seven. Tubby had arranged two more hours of overtime. He handed Steven the cash.

"Thanks, Tubby."

"You earned it."

"You know . . . thanks for everything."

"A lot of times I get these cocksuckers working for me. They show up late. They work like grandmothers. You work your ass off."

"Thanks."

"See this car? It's a 1983. How come? It's cherry, that's how come. Every now and then, they make one cherry. That's gonna happen with your fucking writing. Swear to God."

Steven smiled. "From your mouth to God's ears."

"You gotta get in line for that. I get a hold of God's ear, I'm gonna have him set Niki straight."

"Your sister."

"My sister the lesbian."

"But you like her."

"I like her and I love her, but I got a big responsibility. I don't know. Am I going right?"

"We go all the way until we cross Canal. I'll show you. Or you can turn on Canal, and I can walk from there."

"Hey. Door-to-door service," Tubby said. "See that number 241? There. I worked on the renovation. I crewed it up. That used to be a library, then a slaughterhouse for pigs, then a Chinese import joint. Swear to God. Fucking city changes. Jesus. So you happy or what? You ready? When do you leave?"

"I'm taking a Greyhound bus to Denver on Tuesday and then another bus to Alamosa."

"Alamosa?"

"Then this woman picks me up and takes me to Creedemore."

"Dempsey was from Colorado."

They glided across Varick.

Tubby pulled in front of a fire hydrant across from Roarke's apartment. He shut off the engine.

"Let me give you some good advice. You are at what I call a discouraging age. You're what? You're forty-five, forty-seven?"

"I'm forty-eight."

"Yeah. Now, that is a piss-poor age."

"Tubby. You're younger than me."

"I'm not talking about me. I'm talking about guys that think things up and write things down and turn around and get all crapped out about being forty-eight. You gotta keep doing what you're doing. I gotta use your pisser."

Steven tapped on the door a couple of times. "I guess she's not in."

He opened the door with the key Roarke had given him and switched on the kitchen light. There were forty people in the room. They just watched him quietly for a moment. He watched them. Tubby knew that Roarke had planned this, but he was astonished at how quiet they were. How some were dressed outlandishly and some were dressed in rags. Old and young and wary. They smiled and embraced Steven. For some it was easy, some difficult. He thought about Niki's faculty get-togethers and, like this, how strange everyone had seemed.

Roarke kissed Tubby and hugged him. "Thanks, Tubby."

"I think he was surprised."

"I got beer and wine and food over on the stage."

"Stage?"

"I live on a stage. Pretty nutty, huh?"

"You ain't nutty, Roarke."

Junior Kay grabbed Steven from behind. The author of *Don't Look at Me Like That*, a celebrated collection of poetry about black soldiers in Vietnam, said, "Don't take no shit, my man. They eat black people out there."

"Out where?" said Steven.

"West, motherfucker, west."

Toby Hunter handed a can of beer to Steven. "Oh, honestly, Junior, you are so full of shit."

"They ain't eating us? You saying that?"

"You're thinking of Milwaukee."

"No I ain't."

"Dahmer."

"Okay. That's west."

"That's midwest."

"Fuck you." Junior moved toward the food.

Toby rolled his eyes. "Poets. I mean . . . Gawd. Steven, now, listen. This Beverly of yours is off it. Jee . . . sus. I can't get rid of her. She got it into her head that I was a breeder."

"How did she get that?"

"I have not the foggiest. I only talked to her once. That was at Roarke's Christmas bash. I mean, no offense, but I thought she was wacko. Then she shows up at my place once a week and wants to leave stuff there—clothes, coffee table, towels, I don't know, tchotchkes. Then she wants to leave *herself* there. Jesus. Andrew is crazed, *crazed*."

Steven saw Roarke staring at him and smiled. "Look, Toby, you're a good guy. Hide your bankbooks."

By eleven, Tubby was sitting cross-legged on the floor in a circle of young men and women passing a joint around. He did what they did. He drew in the wet smoke and held it. There was darting intensity in their eyes, and they spoke earnestly.

"The big things. Abortion. Race. Women," a heavy, black-haired girl intoned.

"No shit," they agreed.

"The big things, the big topics."

"Issues."

"No shit."

"The theater . . ."

"No shit."

"Where's it going now that it won't discuss?"

"It don't discuss shit," said a beautiful black girl with pearls woven into her cornrows.

"*Angels in America*," Tubby said, looking at the floor, shaking his olive head.

"No shit," they agreed.

"Hoffman," he said sadly.

General agreement and quiet. There was something to this. He was colliding with minds now. Tubby suddenly threw back his head and yelled, "John fucking Wayne!"

They nodded. They passed the joint. They lit the pipe.

Steven sat next to Roarke on the apron of the tiny stage. He held his beer with both hands.

"You drunk?" she asked.

"Yuh."

"Me, too."

"You get tipsy, Roarke, you don't get drunk."

"I'm very tipsy, then."

They watched Tubby, enormous on the floor, now leaning back against the fridge. A balmy breeze flitted through the open window. Roarke hated the sentimental in drama, but Steven would be gone in three days.

"Now, after this thing, you're coming back here."

"Yeah?"

"Sure. You're my best friend."

"You're my best friend, too, Roarke. I don't want to get in your way."

"You don't get in my way."

Steven put his head on her shoulder like a big boy getting ready for summer camp and sniffled.

"You crying?"

"I'm such an asshole."

Roarke patted his big face. Tubby threw back his head again and yelled, "Tony fucking Bennett!" His new circle of friends nodded, and the whole room nodded.

14

Low clouds huddled over Fork Campground, where Mountain Man's contingent of High Adventurers had stopped for lunch. Cia passed out bologna-and-cheese sandwiches.

"We've got Gatorade to replace the body fluids," Mountain Man announced importantly, holding a large jug in each hand.

"Do we have mustard or mayo?" Mrs. Ferrini asked.

"Cia? Where's the mustard?"

"I thought you packed it."

He turned to Mrs. Ferrini. "We're out of mustard."

"You're out or you forgot it?"

"We don't have any mustard."

He moved away from the volcano bitch. Who puts mustard on an adventure lunch? What an unbelievable bitch. He sauntered over to a fallen tree where Ronald DeFreeze sat chewing and writing in his notebook and squatted next to him.

"You believe that?"

The editor stopped writing and looked up.

"Mustard. Mayonnaise."

"Sandwich is pretty dry, all right."

"Sure it's dry. We're on an adventure, for cryin' out loud. That Ferrini . . . I mean, some people." Mountain Man shook his head and stared off. "You see, Ron, it's my dream to offer a primal outing. To give my customers that sense of self-reliance our forbears had. I think I've got a mission."

Ronald DeFreeze chewed thoughtfully.

"Ron, do you have any questions I can maybe answer for your article?"

"What article?"

"About the rafting adventure."

"I hadn't really thought about writing an article."

"Oh . . . well . . . I just . . . I saw you writing."

"I've been writing some poetry. I'm in a poetry workshop in Denver."

Mountain Man stood. "Okay, people. Let's saddle up for what I like to call Phase Three of our High Adventure."

15

R oarke had lent him her huge black duffel bag and insisted on carrying it from the cab to the Port Authority bus station.

"It's got your name on it. Inside and out, and my address."

Steven took the bag and put it next to him in the bus line. "Thanks, Roarke."

She gave him a paper bag.

"You don't have to give me anything, Roarke."

"It's a Walkman and some Ry Cooder. Batteries are in it."

Steven held the present as if testing its weight.

Roarke took a step away from him and put her hands in the back pockets of her chinos. "Promise me you'll work hard and write well."

"I promise," Steven said seriously. "And you promise me you'll work hard and be happy."

"I'll work hard. Happiness is for pigs."

The bus was clean and smelled of disinfectant. Steven had planned to spend the time writing "an epic prose poem" about the space between cities, but two minutes out he discovered a certain motion nausea whenever he read or wrote. He decided to do a "memory piece" in the Kerouac vein by recording his thoughts at each stop. It was a good plan, because they stopped a lot. Newark, Trenton, Philadelphia, Baltimore, Wheeling, Columbus (to change drivers), Dayton, Indianapolis, St. Louis, Kansas City (another driver), Junction City, Salina, Oakley, Limon, and of course Denver, where Steven slept in the bus station. At 9:35 Friday morning, May 30, Steven boarded Lon's Express to Alamosa and his rendezvous with Miss Wilma Kirk, president of the Creedemore Historical Society.

This time the bus made stops at Englewood, Littleton, Castle Rock, Larkspur, Palmer Lake, Monument, the Air Force Academy, Cascade, Colorado Springs, Security, Fort Carson, Pinon, Pueblo, Colorado City, Walsenburg, La Veta, Fort Garland, Blanca, Alamosa East, and finally Alamosa.

The driver pulled his duffel from the luggage compartment and drove off, leaving Steven standing on a narrow sidewalk. He moved his bag onto the grass and lit a cigarette. A dry sun played on his head. He took a Boston Red Sox cap from his bag and put it on. He squatted and lined up the distant mountains and felt New Mexico somewhere across the high desert plateau and barley fields. He rose and became light-headed.

"Mr. Steven Kearney? Playwright?"

Miss Wilma Kirk stood at the edge of the grass. She was about seventy, short and round. She was wearing khaki safari shorts, a white blouse, brown kneesocks, and hiking boots. Her white hair was in pigtails tied with red ribbons. She held out a tiny hand.

"The playwright Steven Kearney?"

Steven shook her hand. "Yes."

"I'll bring my vehicle around."

She walked off, swinging both arms in a kind of military march, and a moment later pulled a blue Volkswagen Beetle in front of him.

"Put your bag in the backseat."

When he had squeezed into the passenger side, she extended her hand once again.

"I am Miss Wilma Kirk from the Creedemore Historical Society and your producer of sorts. How was your trip?"

"It seemed kind of long, but it was okay. This sure is beautiful."

"This?"

"The mountains and everything."

"Well, we consider Alamosa and most of Alamosa County pretty barren. Now, Creedemore is beautiful. The valley was Ute Indian until the 1870s, when Kit Carson came in from Fort Garland and cleared them out so that the gold and silver hunters could come in. Men like Jacko Creedemore and the Jacko Mine. They made millions, but the boom lasted only a few years. There's a lot of history to tell."

"I'm excited to tell it . . . and . . . hear it."

Miss Kirk drove the speed limit on the two-lane Highway 160. Cars and trucks followed close behind. She slowed at Monte Vista.

"We travel through Monte Vista, another twenty miles or so to Del Norte, then at South Fork we turn off 160 into our valley. Creedemore is seventeen miles into the mountains, Mr. Kearney."

"I used to go to the White Mountains in New Hampshire with my mother and father."

"Those are hills, really. I mean comparatively."

"I guess."

The road seemed to rise steadily into Del Norte, where Miss Kirk slowed again.

"Railroad came through seven times a day at the height of things. Made the towns along the way as surely as the barley and potatoes. All these towns have suffered so, but Creedemore is tourism-driven. Trout fishing, hiking, riding, hunting, rock climbing, et cetera."

South Fork unfolded like the end of something, as if there had been no plan of a town, just a vague idea.

"I don't enjoy South Fork, Mr. Kearney. I was raised here. None of these junk shops and trailers were here when I was a girl."

She slowed at the junction of 160 and 6.

"Or if they were here, people knew enough to keep them at the back of their property. There's the meeting house, though, the log building. The winter festival is held there. Extraordinary. Cowboy Bob Panousus read his poetry last festival. Do you know his work? *I Am Seeing Cleveland, but My Bad Eye Says It's Rome*? Do you know it?"

The Volkswagen turned onto Route 6, and immediately the hills became clean and the mountains, mountains.

"No, I don't know him. My God, look at the cliffs."

" 'I am seeing Cleveland, but my bad eye says it's Rome,' " she began in a pointy voice.

" *'I am seeing Cleveland, but my bad eye says it's home.*
I may be lost forever in this sixteen-wheeling rig.
And I'm eating southern-fried tonight, but my bad eye says it's pig.' "

"I don't know that, no."
"Gutting the Elk and Taking It Down?"
"Uh . . . no . . . I don't think I've—"

" *'Gutting the elk and taking it down,*
I stumbled on the road.
A tiny pebble in my shoe
So I dropped my heavy load.'

"Cowboy Bob Panousus has several pamphlets of his work for sale around Creedemore. You can pick one up at the Western Market. Now, here we cross the great Rio Grande."

The big river was wide and crystalline, and Steven could see the bottom shimmering. Shadows darted long and dangerous from rock to rock.

"What are those shadows?"

"You see them?"

"Yes ma'am."

"That's odd you see them. Most people don't. Those are the big ones. Rainbows and brown mostly, but there are some enormous eastern brookies there and, of course, cutthroat trout. They congregate here because in a mile or so, just outside of South Fork, the river becomes the farmers' property. Then it goes underground."

The pass narrowed to sheer cliffs. On the other side of the pass was an aspen grove.

"Kit Carson camped here, going and coming. This is called Ear Grove. He divided up the ears of the Utes here. A jeweler in Del Norte bronzed them to sell in the East."

"Ears?"

"Carson was a hard man. He took many scalps."

"I thought the Indians—"

"Carson was a hard man. Now, here our valley opens."

And it did. A long, flat field of brown grass stretched out to connect gentle hills and high peaks. Some of the surrounding mountains had been capped with fresh snow. A herd of black cows colored the pastures.

"These are the Watchem herds. There is no other herd of cattle like them. Nicholas Watchem bred them from the wild steers the conquistadors left behind. This is Watchem land all the way into Creedemore. On the other side and up the far valley are the brown Norgans."

"They're beautiful."

The Volkswagen maneuvered the valley at the speed limit. They pulled around a giant mound of gray and black crushed stone.

"Slag heap. We've got several slag heaps. There is Bachelor Creek and Creedemore, under that Cathedral Rock."

Creedemore's Main Street, postcard perfect, reached up from an antique railroad bridge to the base of an enormous brown-gold rock that indeed resembled a sharp steeple. Hardware, bank, and post office nestled comfortably in historic storefront settings alongside art galleries, coffeehouses, and bed-and-breakfasts.

"Creedemore," Miss Wilma Kirk said, with an understated spread of her hand.

"Beautiful," Steven said.

The Volkswagen passed the county police station, and the paved road became gravel.

"Fire department," she said, pointing to a hole in the side of a mountain, the opening of which was sealed with a bright red garage door.

They continued up a steep rise. The Volkswagen slowed to a crawl.

"High," she said.

She pointed out the Common Man Mine and the elaborate Kill Robin Mine and the small holes bored in impossibly high and awkward places.

"How could they work up there?"

"One-man operations. Desperate one-man operations."

Miss Kirk turned the Volkswagen around in the parking area of the Kill Robin.

"Tourist mines now. Lots of people, though, believe that the boom of 1884 barely touched the ore."

They rumbled slowly down, back toward Creedemore, and the tiny town lay out sensibly under them.

"It's difficult to imagine, but from 1884 to '94 this town grew to over fifteen thousand people. Miners. Con men. Prostitutes. It was a vital time. An historic time. A dramatic time. I hope it piques your interest."

"It does," he said.

"Look here."

Miss Wilma Kirk pulled the Volkswagen over Bachelor Creek, which ran parallel to the road. Several eccentric homes of stone and logs were pressed against a boulder that jutted from the base of a hill. The cottages seemed actually a part of the rock. Wildflowers bloomed all around, even on the sod roofs.

"In 1885 the boys from the mines brought in Flapjack Janey O'Reilly from Denver and built this as her 'house.' She always maintained twelve women, whom she called her 'disciples.' They managed most of the urges of the town in the early years. The cottages were abandoned for a long time. Then, in the sixties and seventies, hippies took them over. Bad times, those. Tensions over the war, et cetera, but in time a community blends. And, of course, the hippies got older. Artists' community now."

She turned again, back toward the road. A thin, bald-headed woman, wearing jeans and a black T-shirt, smiled at the general vicinity of the car. Steven smiled back.

"Artist," Miss Wilma Kirk said evenly.

They drove into the center of town and through the parking lot of the Western Market. Behind the low buildings were two portable viewing stands, a large carved totem, and a banner proclaiming THE CREEDEMORE LUMBERJACK AMPHITHEATER. She stopped the car and got out. Steven followed. He was tired, and the images of the West ran into one. She walked into the space between the two stands.

"Now, each stand seats one hundred and twenty-five. They're movable. After the annual Lumberjack Contest in July and our play in August, the stands return to the football field. We play eight-man football. Our players are wiry but western hard. Cal Majenovic went from the Creedemore fields to the Chicago Bears in 1932."

She pointed over the supermarket roof.

"From the center you can frame your performers on Cathedral Rock, which is lighted in the evening. Exits and entrances from the alley or the back of the Western Market. Light grid stretched pole to pole."

She watched him now, and he nodded and smiled tiredly. They got back into the Volkswagen and drove deeper into the valley. She pointed to the distinctive brown cows with the white noses.

"Norgans."

"Beautiful."

The Volkswagen moved past a tiny airport and then a cluster of nondescript summer homes.

"Ugly Acres," she said. "Went up in the sixties. Now the town knows that planning is everything. You'll see that the rest of the valley's homes built after Ugly Acres retain a certain western integrity inherent to the valley itself."

The valley turned sharply right, and the mountains bordering either side turned, too. Cows. Horses. Fences. The character of the big river down below them seemed to change at each curve. The Volkswagen slowed. Fifty or so people milled by a gate just off the pavement. Outside the gate half the crowd were carrying signs and banners. They seemed to be chanting. Inside the gate were five pickup trucks. Each one had several rifles displayed in the back window. The other half of the crowd leaned tensely against their trucks. Some of each group waved to Miss Wilma Kirk, who nodded. As soon as she had passed the gate, she powered the Bug up to speed.

"What was that?" Steven asked, looking back.

Miss Wilma Kirk took a deep breath. "Do you see that wiggle over there? That wiggle of water?"

"Kind of a zigzag?"

"That . . . is Ticky Lettgo's property."

"All of it?"

"All of it."

She pulled to a stop on the shoulder of the road and looked over river and meadows pushing up against the Weminuche Mountains. Miss Wilma Kirk squinted as she scanned the land. Steven tried to see what she saw. A deer came out of the far trees, took a few steps toward the river but changed its mind and retreated.

"In many ways our project this summer has as its foundation this very stretch of river and soil."

Steven felt heavy. His body still rolling over the West.

"Water, Mr. Kearney, is everything. Water brought the valley into being,

59

and as surely as we sit parked here, water can drive it apart. This is why your historical play should endeavor to find common ground. You see, our community has been deeply divided. On the one side is a group of citizens who believe powerfully in the concept of 'nongrowth,' status quo, et cetera. And on the other, equally passionate in their position, are the 'growth' people. Those who rely on tourism, et cetera."

She took a deep breath, eyes still distant, searching.

"A . . . cataclysmic event took place. There. On that beautiful portion of our valley. Tension reigns. Anarchy could be close behind. You see, Mr. Kearney . . ."

Miss Wilma Kirk swiveled emphatically toward the passenger side. Steven's head tilted back, eyes closed, and a tiny stream of drool edged cautiously down his chin. He snorted, and his fat mug rolled so that it faced Miss Kirk. She started up the Volkswagen. The turn of the little engine didn't wake him. Ute Ranch, whose owners had agreed to supply room and board for Creedemore's playwright-chronicler, lay twelve miles deeper into the mountains. As she turned off the two-way road onto the rugged little jeep path toward the ranch, she thought of a line by Cowboy Bob Panousus.

I'm high on the mountains
But low in the heart.

Art, she thought, was not easy.

16

For nearly three miles, from Fork Campground to the puerite slide that marked the beginning of the Lettgo property, the big river raged relentlessly. The speed of the rafts discouraged any effort even to put an oar to the water. The young men from the Bible Institute flowed into a separate jet stream and moved easily from third to first.

"Those pussies are passing us! Come on!" urged Mrs. Handleman.

But there was nothing Mountain Man could do as he watched them, holding each other and sobbing, pass his raft as if shot from a cannon.

"Come on!" Mrs. Handleman screamed.

"I can't, Mrs. Handleman," he said over the thunderous rush.

"What?"

"I can't control the raft."

"What?"

"Take the shit out of your ears!"

"Can't you catch them?"

"Mrs. Handleman, I can barely stay in the—"

Suddenly Mountain Man's raft shifted into the rocket path of water. It passed the Ferrini raft as if it were standing still and went roaring after the weeping Christians.

"That's kicking ass, Mountain Man!" Mrs. Handleman said, pumping her fist and holding a "number one" finger up to the Ferrini raft. Mountain Man looked across sadly to Cia and thought again about the mountain bikes. The Ferrini bitch looked calm, and her family looked calm. Mountain Man wanted to hit her in the head with an oar.

In the amazing roil of snowmelt, the raft of the Zion Bible Institute seemed to disappear beneath white foam so that the hysterical young men appeared to be floating on the foam itself.

The sound was the first indication. The river's roar seemed to dissipate a minute or so before it calmed into a wide, low, sandy stretch of water that more resembled a millpond than the mighty Rio Grande. Sensing that something good had happened, Mountain Man began to row over to where the Bible Institute's raft bobbed against a high, grassy bank. The young men clung to the grass roots and held the raft immobile. Several of them prayed. Several of them seemed to be talking to themselves.

"How are you boys doing?" Mountain Man said, flashing what he felt was a reassuring grin.

"Not good. Not good at all," one of them gasped. "Maybe we'll carry the raft back."

"That's another eight miles."

"Maybe you could come and pick it up after you finish."

"See, this is private property."

"Maybe we can carry it up the road."

"Look, this is the last of the white water."

"It is?"

The Ferrini raft pulled next to Mountain Man's. Her kids were actually laughing about something. Cia also. He looked at them evenly and turned back to the shaken congregants.

"Now we sort of meander down through the Lettgo land, which is said to be the most beautiful ranch in the whole county, and from there we ease on over to the old railroad bridge, where I've got transportation waiting."

"Transportation is waiting?" one of the young men asked cautiously.

"It's a smooth ride all the way," Mountain Man said, again flashing a grin he hoped would one day be celebrated.

"No it's not."

All of the adventurers turned together to Mrs. Ferrini.

"What?" Mountain Man asked.

"It's not a smooth ride."

"Yes it is."

"No it's not."

"Yes it is."

"No it's not."

"Oh, yeah?"

"Yeah."

"It goes all smooth in little loops through the whole Lettgo Ranch," Mountain Man said.

"And then it comes out the Lettgo Ranch into Hell's Basin and Slackjaw Chute."

"Hell's Basin?" one of the young men choked.

"The river sways here," Mrs. Ferrini said, demonstrating with both her hands. "Then it drops, and I mean *drops,* about sixty feet over a half a mile into Hell's Basin—which, by the way, is a perfect name for it. There's so much mist from colliding water it looks like smoke."

"But it's not smoke," Mountain Man proclaimed triumphantly.

"Of course not," Mrs. Ferrini said, rolling her eyes.

"What about Slackjaw Chute?" Mrs. Handleman asked.

"It's two miles of white water."

"Cool. Let's do it."

The young Biblists looked at each other for answers.

"Can we meditate on the question for a moment?" one of them asked.

"Jesus," Mrs. Handleman muttered.

"Okay," Mountain Man said, pulling a short distance away from them. Ferrini's raft also gave the young men space to bow their collective heads in a grope for spiritual guidance. Mountain Man closed his eyes and took a deep breath of thin air. He felt as if he had been on the river for weeks. He heard them laughing again but kept his eyes closed.

"They're signaling!" Cia shouted.

Mountain Man opened his eyes and looked over to Cia, then to the young men of the Bible Institute.

"We're putting our trust in the Lord!" one shouted.

"We have a friend in the Lord!" another shouted.

"Well, move your asses, then!" Mrs. Handleman shouted.

The young men began to sing "What a Friend We Have in Jesus" in an up-tempo, not-unpleasant harmony. The Ferrini bitch automatically took the lead position heading for the first soft curve of the Lettgo property. Mountain Man reattached the pull line onto the Zion Institute's raft, and the seasoned adventurers glided around the gentle bend of the river.

"You can easily see how eons of silt rushing down from the spring thaws treated this section of the valley particularly generously."

No one in his raft seemed to be listening, but Mountain Man found the timbre of his voice personally soothing.

"While nature tends to be indiscriminate with its bounty and some benefit more than others, we are indeed fortunate to live in a land that says, 'This land is your land. This land is my land.' "

He looked around and felt good.

"The land isn't private?" Mrs. Handleman asked.

"I meant that even though it's technically private, it's really everybody's." Mountain Man Red Fields turned and waved at his attached hymn singers, and they waved back. The rafts followed the Ferrini raft around a second easy turn and then a third. The Lettgo lodge came into view. A two-story log house with freshly whitewashed chinking between each piece of rich brown wood. The roof gleamed a metallic dark blue. Flowers were everywhere, and horses seemed to roam free all around the property. He noticed a tiny figure walk onto the corner of the open porch that faced the river and watch the rafters. Then the distant figure reached up for something, and a bell rang out three times.

17

Ticky Lettgo had risen at 4:00 A.M., made coffee, and eaten two of the boiled eggs Minnie Lettgo had prepared the night before. Minnie hadn't been feeling too well, and Ticky had noticed she moved slowly about the kitchen.

"How's your ticker, Mrs. Lettgo?"

"Well, it's sore a little."

"Sore or achy?"

"Yes."

"You know what I'm going to do? I'm going to put you in bed right now and bring you a toddy."

"Well, I've still got these dishes to do."

"I'll do the damn things."

Minnie snorted.

"What was that?"

"That was me."

"Why'd you make that noise?"

"Because whenever you do the dishes, I have to do them over again."

"What?"

"Truth hurts, but you don't rub hard enough."

Ticky turned back to the Houston Astros baseball game his satellite dish had picked up and shook his head. After Minnie had put the dishes away and dry-mopped her kitchen, she poured two small glasses of Christian Brothers brandy and sat up against Ticky in the middle of the big plaid couch. She gave him his brandy and watched with him.

"These guys pitch a couple of innings and just quit," she said disgustedly. "You don't get the real guys."

"You don't," Ticky agreed.

"What's-his-name gets millions."

"They all get millions."

"Pitch a couple and quit."

They watched Atlanta score seven times, and there were still no outs.

"Jesus."

"Jesus."

Ticky switched off the huge TV, and they walked to their bedroom on the second floor. Ticky tucked Minnie under a green down comforter.

"You sleep in. I'll just eat those eggs you did."

"And the prune juice."

"Okay. I'll get you up around six-thirty."

"Okay."

So next morning Ticky took his coffee onto the porch. One of his horses clopped over, and Ticky rubbed its nose hard.

"Hello, Two-Dollar. Hello, old boy. What are you doing?"

The horse moved off, and some light flipped and danced over Phinney Mountain down the valley behind Cathedral Rock, starting there to make its way deeper into the hills.

At five, as he did every morning of Creedemore time, Ticky began to call each of his seven Lettgo Feed 'n' Seed stores in Wichita Falls, Texas. He asked about the daily receipts. He asked about deliveries. He asked about the weather.

"Good morning, Lettgo Feed 'n' Seed."

"Henry, this is Ticky Lettgo."

"Why, hello, Mr. Lettgo. How are you?"

"I'm fine. How'd we do yesterday?"

"Three thousand eight hundred eight and four pennies."

"That's the way to sell."

"Thank you, Mr. Lettgo."

"We get that dog food yet?"

"Yessir, they delivered yesterday afternoon."

"How's it been?"

"Hot."

"Well . . . 'bye, Henry."

"Good-bye, Mr. Lettgo."

It took Ticky thirty minutes each morning to touch base with his seven stores. By then the coffee and prune juice kicked in. It was past six-thirty by the time he walked into the bedroom. Minnie was lying in bed awake.

"Good morning, Mrs. Lettgo."

There was a moment before she spoke, and when she did, Ticky could barely hear her.

"Want to stay in bed?" he cackled quietly.

Minnie scooted up slowly so that her small head rode higher on her pillow.

"I said I am ninety-six years old."

"Not till August, old girl."

"Well, almost ninety-six."

"I *am* ninety-six."

Minnie thought about this. So did Ticky. "I'll be ninety-seven in . . . February, is it?"

"February sixteenth. I was lying here, and I heard the river, and I didn't know if I was awake or asleep, and then I thought that Jefferson would have been seventy-seven."

"I don't know."

"We had him in '27."

She lay still, and Ticky sat on the edge of the bed.

"I still wear the pin the Marine Corps sent. I wear it on my blouses. All my blouses."

They listened to the water, the room almost yellow with sun.

"Want to stay in bed?"

"No."

"Okay."

"Okay."

"I'm going to go over to that fern ledge above where the river straightens just before public land. Remember?"

Minnie sat up and dangled her ancient legs over her bed.

"I'll get your thermos. I'll get you some sandwiches."

"I'll get my Winchester."

∗   ∗   ∗

The first crack of gunfire split Mrs. Ferrini's right oar, and she fell back onto the raft's floor. The second shot blew the tubing apart. The next three discharges hit Mountain Man Red Fields's tubings in one straight line, and the raft flipped. The young men from the Colorado Springs Zion Bible Institute required no bullets as they abandoned their vessel at the first salvo. The river was icy, but at the point before it left the Lettgo property it became extremely wide and shallow, with a fine pebble bottom. The stunned adventurers slogged through knee-deep water to a sandy, sloping bank.

"Take the rafts with you," a voice tinned from the cliffs above them.

"What the hell's going on?" Mountain Man yelled back.

"I don't want to say this twice, so listen up, you fence-cutting, dirt-hugging interloper. Take those damn silly things and follow the path to the horse road and get the hell off my land. And close the gate, you tinhorn son of a bitch, or I'll put an ounce of iron in your butt. Now, git!"

"All of us?" Mrs. Ferrini shouted reasonably. "Or just him?"

"Sorry, lady, but them's the rules."

Mountain Man and several of the others waded to the rafts and brought them ashore. Some water had gotten into the canvas covering the tubes, and they felt soggy and heavy.

"They're very heavy!" Mountain Man yelled up to the ledge.

A bullet smashed into the only raft with air remaining, and it sizzled.

"Okay, everybody grab a side of the raft you were in!"

The adventurers struggled dripping wet up the tiny path and out of the river basin to a meadow above. They followed a horse path to the main road. Mountain Man thought about not closing the gate behind him but did. They struggled along in the direction of Creedemore.

"I thought you said the land belonged to everybody," Mrs. Handleman reminded him.

"Who said that?" Mrs. Ferrini asked.

"Him."

"You said the land belonged to everybody?"

"I was talking metaphorically. I mean, sure there's private property, but who shoots at people?"

"Nuts shoot," said Cia.

Mountain Man forced a smile and nodded.

"We had permission, right?" asked the Ferrini woman.

Mountain Man set his jaw tight so that the insides of his cheeks went raw against his teeth. In an instant the sun disappeared and a drizzle began to fall.

"Right? We had permission?"

Bitch woman.

"Eminent domain," he snarled.

"What?" Mrs. Handleman asked.

Mountain Man stopped, and the others stopped. He put his portion of the raft down, and they all put theirs down.

"Nobody—N-O-B-O-D-Y—nobody owns the water. If you stay on the water. If you don't leave the water— Let me say this again for the writer of bogus volcano textbooks. If you stay on the water, no one can invoke the rule of property. Eminent domain."

The young men from Zion walked as a group to the side where Mountain Man faced off with Mrs. Ferrini.

"Isn't it joyous?" a short one said. "No one was hurt. Jesus has taken us again out of darkness. Shall we give Him thanks?"

Mrs. Handleman shivered. "Blow it out your ass."

But the young men were now on their knees in a low murmur of orison.

Mrs. Ferrini pushed it. "So you're saying you constitute a government?"

"Jesus," muttered Mountain Man.

"Hallelujah," added the young men.

"Eminent domain gives a *government* power to take private property for the greater good."

"You know what I meant."

"I only asked you if you had permission to float through private property, and you mentioned eminent domain."

"So you think that old fart had the right to shoot us?"

"He didn't shoot us, he shot *at* us. And how do you know he's an old fart?"

"Because he threatened me."

"He threatened you?"

"Why do you repeat every fucking thing I say?"

"Don't swear in front of my children."

Cia stepped up to him. "Let's just go. It's a long walk."

And she was right. And the rain wouldn't make it any shorter. Or the marching hymn sung with gusto by the young men from the Colorado Springs Zion Bible Institute.

In the deepest heart of the Rockies,
In the land of Ute and deer,
Lies a town whose feet are silver
And a soul that's filled with beer.

And they say that old Kit Carson,
With the boys they called galoots,
Cleared the Redman from the valley
With their knives and guns and boots.

So if you're searching for heaven,
Or whatever you're looking for,
There's a town that's bound for glory,
And we call it dear Creedemore.

18

Steven could barely breathe and slept with his upper body propped up on two pillows. He kept his hand over the thump of his heart so it wouldn't pop out of his T-shirt.

"I guess this is me dying," Steven muttered to himself.

He had arrived at dusk and had the formal introductions by Miss Wilma Kirk. Al and Janice Overstreet, owners of the Ute Ranch, their son, Buck Overstreet, outfitter, and daughter, Skyo Overstreet. Janice took him through the stone-floored kitchen into a large room of pine and aspen, filled with overstuffed sofas and recliners, all facing a huge television set. The walls were covered with arrangements of arrowheads. They climbed stairs to the second floor, which consisted of a long, narrow hallway with old cowboy photographs on the wall and five bedrooms on each side. The door at the end of the hallway was the lone bathroom.

Janice Overstreet opened the door marked three. "This will be your room. And as you can see, it's Room Three."

"Thank you."

She opened the lace curtains. The view out the window was like a picture on a calendar. The aspen across the stream shook against the wind, and the mountain sloping to them seemed to sway. Steven touched his heart again and thought of himself dropping dead right there before he began.

"Now, Miss Kirk said you'll be here until the end of August?"

"I hope. Yes."

"That's a long time."

"I'll be . . . I'll have to write and . . . stuff."

"It must be exciting."

"I hope so."

"Now, Miss Kirk's group is sponsoring the room and contracted me to do linens and towels. Is once a week all right for the linens?"

"That's great."

"I line-dry, so they'll get lots of sun. Buck and his wranglers take breakfast early. You're welcome to scrounge something up then or wait for Skyo. Sometimes Al gets up early, sometimes not. I'll be at the ranch store from seven on. Close at six. We're packed with guests until middle of September, and Buck and them will be guiding or leading day or hour rides or whatever."

She looked around the room again, and Steven looked where she did. The small brass bed was spread with a heavy quilt of faded blue and green. The reading lamp with Victorian shade. The side table of rough pine.

"I'll just let you get settled. Dinner's around six-thirty. Miss Kirk's staying for it."

Janice and Skyo cooked fried chicken and mashed potatoes and corn and catfish cakes the Texans in Cabin 4 brought up, and rolls and pie. Albert and Buck and Jimmy the Kid, his wrangler, and Skyo's boyfriend, Ralph, a counselor at the Outward Bound camp down below the reservoir, and Janice and her sister Deb, who was visiting from Oklahoma, all pulled up to the long oak table and passed the food.

"Pull yourself up here, boy," said Al.

"Get on that feed bag," said Buck.

Steven let Janice scoop his potatoes and choose his chicken.

"Brain food," she said.

Jimmy the Kid chewed thoughtfully.

"Where's that joker pal of yours?" Buck asked.

"He's not back from Ruby Lake yet," Jimmy the Kid said.

"His dad called, didn't he, Mother?"

"Why, yes, he did. You tell Jude to call him back."

"Yes, ma'am."

"His dad's from New Jersey," Skyo explained to Ralph.

"New Joisey," Al said.

The kitchen fell into a wonderful percussion of knife and fork and plate. Buck stood and scooped another round of potatoes onto his plate and Jimmy's plate.

"How do you stay so skinny, Kid?" Al asked.

"I do all of my work and all of Buck's work, too."

"Thatta boy."

"Mr. Kearney is writing a play about Creedemore," explained Skyo.

"Get out," said Ralph.

"He is. It's gonna be put on at the Lumberjack Amphitheater."

"Amphitheater?" said Al. "Amphitheater? It's the parking lot behind the Western Market."

"When the football stands are in, it's an amphitheater."

"Well . . . maybe. I believe I'll take another piece of fried chicken."

"I believe you will."

Janice pushed the platter across the table to him.

"How does a person go about that, Mr. Kearney? Writing seems like such a difficulty in itself, let alone a play."

Steven finished chewing his chicken and laid his fork and knife across the plate. Skyo watched him carefully. She was short and pretty, with an oval face. Pixie blond hair framed her green eyes.

"That is not a fair question, Mother."

"Not fair?"

"You can't expect an artist to have to defend his methods."

"I'm not asking anybody to defend anything. Al?"

"Mother's right. But who knows? Coffee?"

Steven spoke softly.

"Actually, I'm not sure. Every play I've written is . . . different. More often than not, they just float around in your thoughts for months or even years, and one day there's a little voice saying, 'Write it down.' "

"That's the ticket." Jimmy smiled, satisfied with the answer.

Miss Wilma Kirk dabbed at her lips. "Of course, this is history. The challenge for Mr. Kearney will be the blending together of the factual chronology of significant events with the literary and creative process."

Everyone thought about that as the forks and knives glided over pale blue porcelain.

"There's a lot of history in the valley okay," said Jimmy.

"History is fact. Fact is truth. Truth is history," Miss Wilma Kirk stated, followed by an emphatic swallow of milk.

"One person's facts, though, may not be another person's truth," Skyo said.

Her mother sat back against the chair. "I don't think I understand that one."

"Something can happen, and we all know it happened, but when we look closely at it, we may all interpret it differently. Like the Lettgo trial."

"I'm taking my coffee outside," said Al.

Buck filled his cup and followed his father.

"Now you've upset Daddy," Janice said.

"All I'm saying is nothing is black and white. Anybody want pie?"

Ralph waved his fork. "That Lettgo shot up three rafts full of people. There's nothing black and white about that?"

"He only shot the rafts," Skyo said.

Jimmy the Kid stood and plopped a big beaten-up brown Stetson over his blond hair. "Al would have shot more than the rafts. Me, too."

"Why, Mr. Jimmy the Kid!" scolded Janice.

"Well, it's true, ma'am."

"It is true, Mommy," Skyo said. "But in Creedemore proper, where they don't want the tourists to get the wrong idea, they're all ready to put him in jail."

"He belongs in jail," said Ralph.

Jimmy the Kid put a Marlboro between his teeth and headed outside to light it.

Miss Wilma Kirk stood up. "Janice, I believe I've eaten too much."

"Oh, you've got room for pie, I'll bet."

"I really better be leaving for town."

Steven excused himself also and walked with her to the Volkswagen. He rubbed his heart unconsciously.

"Can't breathe, can you?"

"Well . . . actually . . . no."

"It's the altitude. Three or four days, it'll go away as your body adjusts. We're eleven thousand feet at Ute Ranch."

"Three or four days?"

"Then you'll be breathing like a baby. I'm sorry I don't have a car for you, Mr. Kearney. However, I shall call for you early tomorrow morning for the grand tour. How is six?"

He watched the little car until it cut behind an aspen grove and disappeared. Steven started to light a cigarette but remembered his shallow breath and fitted it back into the pack. Some children ran by, chasing an ancient horse wearing a dusty blanket. A woman called to them from one of the guest cabins.

Ute Ranch lay above the reservoir, and its egg-shaped meadows were cut by ribbons of feeder streams. He could not see them in the early darkness, but he heard Ute Creek, Savoy Creek, Snow Creek, Sheep Creek, and the odd beaver streams tumble purposefully somewhere close, out of the short willows and brush.

19

The same morning Mountain Man Red Fields led his convoy to the inaugural float of his Rafting Adventure, Sheriff Petey Myers was taking coffee at the office with his dispatcher wife, Vi, when the call came out of Lake City that Sheriff Shari Tobias had been shot to death at a roadblock just below Slumgullion Slide and that the perpetrators, a man and a woman in a light blue Dodge pickup, were last seen moving in the direction of Creedemore.

"My God," Petey said.

"Shari?" said Vi.

"Killed her, they said. Where's Bobby?"

"Some man hit an elk with his motor home near Masonic Park. Bobby's at the scene."

"Damn. Well, hon, listen. When Bobby gets back, tell him I'm gonna put myself at North Clear Creek Road."

"Not the main road?"

Petey kissed her on the top of the head and reached for the pump shotgun. "If they stay on the main road, the staties will get them."

"You think they'll come over by Brown's Lake?"

"Well, I fished up there, and I know there's a jeep path from outside Lake City."

"I hope they stay on the main road."

"You ain't kidding."

Petey put the shotgun in its rack on the floor of the Jeep, then went back into the office and took an M16 out of the closet.

"Where are the cartridges, hon?"

"File cabinet."

He took three clips, made sure they were filled, and kissed her head again.

"Tell Bobby, okay?"

"North Clear Creek."

"Right. And put in a call to Dan Cryer. I know he's retired, but maybe he could mind the store till I get back."

Petey drove with one hand, balancing his coffee. He drove deliberately, staying at the speed limit. Several miles out of Creedemore, before the main road rose into the mountains, he noticed the rafters' caravan turning down toward the river. The road crested at a scenic overlook, and he pulled in to the parking area. For fifteen minutes he watched the distant dirt road that ran along Brown's Lake and the beaver stream that would become part of North Clear Creek. Wet spring snow fell heavy and made his binoculars useless. Back inside the Jeep, he called the office.

"This is Sheriff Myers. Over."

"Hon?"

"Any luck with Bobby?"

"I called him."

"Dan?"

"He's here now."

"Put him on."

There was some shuffling. He could hear old Dan moaning himself up and out of the chair.

"Sheriff Cryer here."

"Thanks, Dan."

"No problem, buddy, but listen. As long as I'm filling in, I'm going to call myself Sheriff Cryer. Is that all right?"

"Sure. Sure. Listen, now. I'm at the scenic overlook up above Brown's Lake. I'm going to go into the North Clear Creek Road."

"Well, hell now, Petey, I don't want to tell you how to do your job, but they ain't gonna come out of the jeep trail."

"Why not?"

"Too rough."

"Maybe. Hey, thanks, kemosabe."

Sheriff Petey Myers turned off the main road at the campground and rolled slowly a half mile into the valley. At the lake he turned up onto the jeep trail and went another mile before pulling behind a boarded-up sheepherder's cabin. He got out and stretched his tall, narrow body. The snow had stopped now, but the feeling of gray was still all around him.

Petey enjoyed the cool, dark mornings of Colorado. They reminded him of Boston. The early shifts, parked in the patrol car with Reedy, drinking coffee, telling jokes you could only tell to another cop. Then Reedy getting killed over that stupid, stupid argument those kids were having on the basketball court. He walked over and told the kids to watch the language and two of them shot him. And Reedy black, and Reedy thinking he understood. Understood what? Even now Petey didn't get it. Probably never would. How the hell could those little fuckers ever play basketball with goddamn guns in their pockets? Jesus Christ. "Hey, young men, please watch your language in a public place. Okay, gentlemen?" Gentlemen. Jesus Christ. And that was it. No more him and Reedy up to the bass lakes in Maine. No more Reedy. And then the kids saying they were provoked? Watch your language? Petey gets there, and they got the kids in custody, and the kids are laughing. Laughing!

He was angry now, and he knew that would not do. He took the shotgun and the M16 and instinctively shifted them butt-first on his car seat and left the door ajar. He checked his own nine-millimeter and flipped the safety off. He remembered Shari Tobias as one of his instructors during the Colorado Law Enforcement certification class. A heavy woman around thirty-five who was a little uncomfortable in front of the class but not one-on-one at the range or in a confrontation. He'd seen her in action, bracing a biker in a Lake City bar. The girl can handle herself. *Could* handle herself. Jesus Christ. First Reedy. Now Shari. Of course he had loved old Reedy. Maybe the only real friend of his warrior life. Then he heard the engine.

He could hear the low gear grinding it forward, losing the sound for a moment, then catching it again, louder, as the engine climbed out from behind the rocks and aspen. Petey stepped to a corner of the cabin and watched the farthest portion of road before it dipped and rose again. The blue truck jiggled forward slowly, gears stripping out in the high, cool morning. Petey took the shotgun and leaned it next to the cabin. He balanced the M16 on the window frame next to his shoulder. He checked the safeties, making sure they were off, rechecked the safety on his nine-millimeter, then stepped out into the jeep path.

He heard the engine again, and felt its irrevocable roll to him, but it did not appear immediately. There were corners to negotiate and dangerous muddy stretches clinging precariously to the rocky side of the gorge. Finally, with a grating squeal, it pulled up and onto the plain, thirty yards in front of him. The truck stopped. Inched forward and stopped again. Petey's heart was thumping, but he kept his Boston face on. Hard and resigned. Through the tinted front window of the truck, he could see the woman turn to the driver and back to Petey. The man never took his eyes from Petey. He shut the engine off.

"Please step out of your vehicle."

Petey kept his hand on the nine-millimeter. Canvas holster unsnapped.

He watched them. He watched the man's hands on the wheel. His thumping heart settled.

"Step out of your vehicle."

A cool breeze flew from behind. Petey shivered. The passenger side of the cab opened, and the girl stepped cautiously out. The driver slid over and also stepped out. She was quaking and appeared to be sobbing. She wobbled. She was dressed in a waitress uniform. The man behind her had a Colorado Rockies baseball hat on backward over his short hair. Beefy in jeans and jean jacket. He held her arms behind her and had a gun to her head.

"She shot at me first. That fat sheriff woman. I wasn't doing nothing."

"Help me," the girl wept.

"Shut up. Just shut up. I'll do this, bitch. I swear I will."

Petey took his hand away from his gun. Play it like a pro. Like the amateur shrinks cops become in Boston.

"Now look, son, if what you say is true, everything ought to turn out in your favor. I can tell just by looking at you you're telling the truth."

The man sounded soothed. "You can?"

"I can honestly say there's a light at the end of your tunnel."

"A light?"

"Now you know what you have to do. Put the gun down."

"But . . ."

"No buts now. C'mon, son."

The man wavered for a moment, then tossed the revolver on the meadow grass a few feet away. Petey felt air rushing into his lungs. A tiny bit of relief played over his mouth. That's when the girl brought the handgun from behind her back and shot him.

It felt like a bee sting in his hip, but it spun him and knocked him down.

He crawled immediately behind the cabin, but she stung him again, this time in the love handles.

"Reedy!" he screamed.

"What?" the man yelled.

Petey thought he'd gone nutty. He'd been shot once before, and Reedy had bailed him. Why'd he yell for him now? He pushed himself up against the logs.

"Somebody else with you, old man?"

Petey reached up and brought down the M16.

"I don't think anybody else's with you."

He laid the shotgun across his lap.

"Now look here, old man. The last thing we want is to hurt you any more. We just want to get out of here. Okay? I swear on the life of my mama and daddy. I'm swearing to God."

"He means it," the girl said. "We're sorry. We just want to go have a life somewhere else."

"See? We want to get married."

Petey didn't say anything. He thought of Reedy casting for the bass. Reedy had wanted those kids to watch their language.

"See, if you throw the gun out, just throw out that damn thing, we'll get going and we'll get some help for you, swear to God."

Petey could hear them. The man and the woman. The boy and the girl. Whatever the fuck they were.

"Come on, honey. Too many people are getting hurt," she said. "Please. Throw it out."

Her voice was sweet and milky. Petey pulled the nine-millimeter out of the holster and tossed it from behind the cabin into the jeep path. They began to laugh.

"Now that is why when they say cops are dumb motherfuckers, they ain't lyin'. You want this one, baby?"

Petey braced the shotgun into the bone of his shoulder. When she casually stepped into sight, he squeezed his finger four hard times.

"Jesus!" the man screamed. Petey could hear him running back to the truck. He threw the shotgun aside, grabbed hold of the M16, and rolled out from behind the cabin. He had the truck door open. Petey flicked the M16 to automatic and fluted out the complete twenty-round clip.

20

Miss Wilma Kirk arrived ten minutes early and pulled up close to the kitchen door. Steven had come down at five-thirty, still struggling for air. A tall young man was feeding handfuls of coffee grounds into boiling water.

"Cowboy style," he said sleepily.

"Smells great."

"I'm Jude McCormick."

"I'm Steven Kearney."

"We just grab whatever. Juice, toast, whatever. Cereal. Skyo does it better when she wakes up, but that could be late. Buck's coming in a sec."

Jude was nineteen, six feet four and a half, with a thin, hard wrapping. Without the brown ponytail that hung between his shoulder blades, he resembled a storybook illustration of a young, rail-splitting Abe Lincoln. Steven remembered something.

"Your dad called yesterday."

"They told me. New Joisey." He laughed.

Jude turned off the water and waited for the coffee grounds to sink clear of the spout, then poured the cups. "Buck'll be here soon as he smells this."

Steven sipped the bitter black brew. It was wonderful.

Jude kept talking. "Jimmy the Kid. You met Kid?"

"Yes."

"That boy lives at Antlers Ranch. He'll be over later. Got hour rides today. I'm taking the horse trailer into Del Norte and filling it with hay bales."

Buck opened the door, and the lights from the Volkswagen bounced off his back. Short and hard, the thirty-five-year-old smiled and removed his baseball cap. Steven read the inscription: LETTGO FEED 'N' SEED, WICHITA FALLS.

"Morning, Buck."

"Jude. Mr. Kearney."

"Please call me Steven."

"You bet."

"My coffee?" Bud asked with a point.

"Yes, sir." Jude answered.

"He don't call me 'sir' much."

"Usually makes me call him 'Master.' "

Buck got a serious look and ran his fingers through thinning hair. He sat at the table and turned to Jude.

"With Jimmy up on the rides, we are gonna have to bust our butts with that hay. You get your asthma inhaler?"

"Yes, sir."

"Back braces?"

"Both in the truck."

"Call your dad?"

"They're coming up on the sixteenth."

Miss Wilma Kirk entered with a knock. Red and black flannel shirt, hundred-year-old jeans, hiking boots. She wore a red baseball cap: GIVE PEACE A CHANCE.

The men stood and sat back down.

"Hey, Miss Kirk."

"Buck. Jude. Did you call your dad?"

"Yes, ma'am."

Buck said, "Grab some coffee."

"I've had my coffee, but thank you. Mr. Kearney?"

The blue Volkswagen rolled down an incline where the dirt road leveled off for a mile or so, rising slightly along the edge of the reservoir. Steven had been asleep yesterday and was thrilled now at the length and breadth of a man-made lake that stretched mountain to mountain and filled this high valley with crystalline water.

"The reservoir was a joint state venture. Colorado, New Mexico, Texas. Filled up in 1891. Fed the farms to the panhandle. In '26, Colorado assumed that the obligation to the other states had been paid tenfold and allotted a larger share to the Alamosa Plateau. Texas disagreed and sent three hundred Rangers."

The Volkswagen passed the dam and commenced a steep drop. The Rio Grande began in a tumble from under stone and concrete.

"Texas Rangers?"

"Oh, yes. The genuine article. Burned some of Del Norte. Fought a pitched battle with the National Guard. Held the dam, though."

Steven looked back with excitement. "This dam? Honest to God?"

"Now this is Ten Mile Camp."

Some trailers were camouflaged in camping areas by willow and pine. Fishermen surrounded a deep pool.

Miss Kirk sniffed. "Wormers."

From the camp the Volkswagen began to climb again. The river spread into two wiggles beneath them and disappeared into the cliffs. She pointed to the river and wiggled her finger also.

"This is where the Box begins. It travels eight rugged miles and enters the big valley at the mouth. It's where the incident began."

"With the Texas Rangers?"

Miss Wilma Kirk made a sound like a distant laugh or a horn. "We only wish it were that long ago."

She drove the valley to Creedemore, occasionally pulling over to point out the rock that Dolly Whit was supposedly buried under or the site of the Ute scout massacre or the stone foundations she believed were the conquistadors' homes during their fateful winter here. Again they crept through the two groups assembled at the Lettgo gate. Just outside of Creedemore, by the tiny Mineral Airport, she gestured to an envelope on the backseat.

"That's got your enrollment certificate in the health plan. Three months. Quite good. Also a detailed map of Creedemore and a contact sheet of members of the Historical Society. And the Creedemore Players roster, of course. Names and numbers."

Steven squeezed the envelope a little and smiled.

"Also, I took the liberty of presenting your first week's salary in cash. I knew, of course, that you wouldn't have a bank account in town. I could draw a check if you'd prefer."

"Cash is good," he said sincerely.

Cathedral Rock came into view, and she turned the Volkswagen toward it.

"Mr. Kearney . . . I hope you won't think me intruding on your artistic process, but I can't help being curious as to what methodology you're going to employ."

Steven wondered if Cathedral Rock looked more like a cathedral from another angle. Today it looked like a rock.

He turned to Miss Wilma Kirk in earnest. "I have no idea."

"Ahhh," she said thoughtfully. "Let's hit the mining museum first."

21

Two and a half weeks after the shoot-out, Petey Myers was released from Gunnison Hospital. New ball in his hip, three inches off his waist. An honor guard of eight highway patrolmen escorted the sheriff out of the hospital to the Creedemore Police Jeep pickup driven by Acting Sheriff Dan Cryer. Petey's wife, Vi, reached out to help Petey into the cab, but he waved her off and got in by himself, scooting into the middle, leg against the stick, so she could get in, too. Then the highway patrolmen saluted formally, and Dan pulled out of the hospital's circular drive.

Outside the city limits where the road to Lake City cuts over Blue Mesa Reservoir, a caravan of folks from Lake City, including Mayor Diaz and the entire school board, fell in behind the Jeep. Twenty-six vehicles honked their support in a loose, rolling symphony. Vi squeezed Petey's leg and smiled. Petey had some questions.

Twenty-one miles later, Dan pulled in to Lake City proper, turned right at the West-Best Liquor Store, and stopped in front of a small reviewing stand.

"What the hell?" Petey muttered.

The mayor stepped out of his Toyota 4Runner and mounted the reviewing steps. A crowd of perhaps fifty was gathered. Dan helped Petey from the Jeep, and Vi walked with her husband up the three steps to the mayor. Everyone applauded. A drummer rolled attention. Petey looked at his wife in utter confusion. She squeezed his trigger hand. Mayor Diaz tapped the podium microphone.

"Is this working? Can you hear me? Ladies and gentlemen, as you well know, our dear Sheriff Shari Tobias, award-winning law enforcement officer and president of the Western Slope Sheriffs Association, was brutally slain on May fourteenth by vicious cowards who were to pay dearly for their horrible deed. Well, citizens of Lake City, the most beautiful resort town the Colorado Rockies has to offer, not to mention the very site where Alfred Packer dined on several unfortunate democrats . . . well, as I was saying, to my right is the man who walked the walk and made those murderers pay the price."

The crowd burst into instant shouts and applause. Vi bussed Petey's cheek. Petey waved as if in a fog. When Reedy got it, Petey had driven Vi over to Reedy's widow's house and over to the cemetery where that tight-ass Harvard-boy commissioner laid a medal on his coffin and made a speech about being more careful. That's when he told Vi that they had to get the fuck away from Boston. Jesus. Reedy says, "Boys, please watch your language." Bang. Bang. Bang. Bang.

Mayor Diaz presented Petey Myers a key to Lake City, a certificate of appreciation, and a gift certificate for dinner for two at the Western Belle Steak and Chop Shop. Petey stepped to the microphone and smiled oddly.

"Reedy said, 'Watch your language,' and they blew his black ass away. Vi and me took Sindy, and she spelled it with an S, to the funeral, and this little Harvard cockhound says to be more careful. I mean, sometimes you have just got to slip it on automatic, if you know what I mean."

The crowd threw hats into the air and shouted their approval, and then Dan and Vi got Petey as comfortable as he could be, and they headed over the mountain pass toward Creedemore.

"Those two were out of New Mexico," Dan said.

"Staties filled me in."

Dan wasn't listening. It was important enough to repeat.

"Shot a farmer in the leg outside of Shiprock, come into Cortez in the farmer's truck. Robbed a gas station. She was a waitress, believe that? Boy was a loser."

The Jeep climbed easily past the scenic overlook of the lake. It was so blue it looked to Petey like there was sky down there. Just before the road crested and began a steep descent, the turnoff to the jeep trail that the murderers of Shari Tobias took came into view. It looked impossible, and Petey wondered how a two-wheel-drive truck with clearance of about twelve inches could have possibly gotten up and over to the sheepherder's cabin.

"Ticky Lettgo shot the shit out of that asshole from Boulder," Dan threw out matter-of-factly.

"I saw that one coming."

"Made them carry the damn rafts out of the basin in front of that fern ledge. You know, where that water gets all shallow and slow."

Petey knew and saw the orange and red and yellow of the brown trout flash in a spot just behind his eyes. Reedy couldn't trout-fish worth a shit. But with a little Rappala on the end of his bass spinning rod, the man was deadly. Petey turned to Vi.

"What was the name of that lake Reedy and me fished?"

"You boys fished a lot of lakes."

"Near Boston."

"Boston?"

"The one that little cockhound lived on for a while. Wrote a book."

"Henry David Thoreau?"

"That's him."

"Walden Pond."

Petey swiveled his head to Dan. "We fished this lake for eight hours and didn't get shit."

He remembered something else.

"What did Ticky do? When you went to get him?"

"I didn't go to get him," Dan said a little sheepishly. "I . . . you know . . . I mean, I figured it could wait till you got out of the hospital."

"I got a new hip," Petey said oddly.

Dan stopped the Jeep while a shepherd crossed his flock.

"Dirty buggers," Dan mumbled.

"So Ticky hasn't been charged?"

Vi squeezed his leg again. Dan took a deep breath and started the Jeep rolling.

"See. It gets complicated here, Petey. This guy Red Fields—"

Vi broke in. "He's the man who runs the Mountain Man Rafting Adventure Trips."

"Yeah. This Red Fields no sooner files a complaint against the old fart than he's on the phone to the *Denver Post*. They do a front-pager using that incident to get down and dirty on the water dealy."

"What water dealy?"

"Okay, now, see, if the water runs through your property, is it yours?"

"Reedy couldn't catch a trout if his life depended on it. Vi?"

"He could get the bass, though."

Acting Sheriff Dan Cryer wasn't listening.

"There's a school of thought in the cities that the water belongs to everybody. Out here it's always been you own the air above and the ground below. So if you're on the river, you may be breathing someone else's air. See?"

The Jeep crossed North Clear Creek and the turnoff to North Clear Creek Falls. Continental Divide Ranch cows spread out like dots on the high, broad meadow.

"So the goody-goodies start making noise about, 'Who do these people think they are?' and 'It's everybody's water,' and the next thing— Look!"

Dan pointed to a huge animal just outside an aspen grove.

"Moose," he said. "That transplant is taking. We got a load from Maine."

"He's beautiful," said Vi.

Petey watched the tall male turn and trot back into the trees.

"Reedy saw a bear once. Shit himself."

85

"So the very next thing, before I even had the opportunity to talk to the man, these homos have a bunch of pickets set up outside of Lettgo's gate. They got signs that say, 'You can't own the water,' and . . . Jesus . . . they had a banner that said, you saw it, Vi. . . ."

"I did."

"'This land is your land, this land is my land.' And poor old Ticky . . . Now, Jesus, the man is ninety-six."

Petey Myers thought about this. "I like that old Minnie a lot. She wears her marine pin for her dead marine. I was a marine. Remember, Vi?"

"Lance corporal."

"Reedy was in the air force."

Dan passed the turnoff to the jeep trail where Petey got them.

"There it is," Petey pointed out with a sigh.

The Jeep climbed a few hundred yards more and dropped, finally, into Creedemore Valley.

"So now there's these people carrying signs at Ticky's gate and such. Outsiders and insiders. Those people who own the outfitting store and the homos from the art gallery."

"Now, Dan," said Vi.

"Well, Jesus, you saw the pictures. Petey?"

"I saw the woman fly-fishing at the bend above South Fork. Painted, but looked real. She was casting."

"Well, okay, sure, but some of the other ones. You know."

"She was casting. Casting. Woman. Vi?"

"Beautiful."

Dan's back hurt a bit, so he scrunched tighter into the driver's seat.

"But I mean 'art gallery.' Now, Jesus. So there they are, and the woman who runs that little coffeehouse and Molly Dowie too, and her with cancer."

Petey looked lost. Vi squeezed the leg again and brushed her hand against his. "The bald hippie."

"Tall?"

"Up at Bachelor."

"She's the one, then. She's the one painted the woman fishing."

"Cancer," Dan said. "Head shines like Ticky's."

"Reedy shaved his head. Looked like a medicine ball."

"But she's there and others and outsiders, and they're all chanting, and so Jack Hill gets on the horn, and the next thing you know there are ten or so pickups between the pickets and Ticky's place. *Denver Post* had a field day. Every day it's almost war."

"Bob Marsden with that crowd?"

"Yes, sir, and the boys from the Antlers and Albert Overstreet—"

"I like Albert Overstreet."

"Standoff's got the valley cut down the middle. Nobody's seen Ticky since it happened."

"When did it happen?"

"When you did those two."

Petey was quiet for a moment, and the Jeep passed the tiny airport and turned sharply by Willow Creek. Cathedral Rock came into view, then Main Street. People were lined up and waving. Mayor Ruby Onerati waited on a small platform in front of the police station. Dave Page, editor of the *Creedemore Post*, was with her and three of the five selectmen. The Jeep stopped in front of the platform, and the 4-H Drum and Bugle Corps belted out something in the vicinity of "For He's a Jolly Good Fellow" as Vi and Petey mounted the steps. Ruby presented Petey and his new hip a huge cardboard key to Creedemore, and Val's Chili Emporium gave a dinner-for-two certificate (bring your own beer or wine). There was a moment of silence for Shari Tobias, and then the bell in the Catholic church between the Creedemore Hotel and the rock shop rang out twelve times. Vi gave Petey's hand one more squeeze, and he stepped to the squealing microphone. He looked over the gathered folks.

"Reedy pulls over these cockhounds just across the border in Worcester and they pile out like they're looking for a fight and he's got his flashlight working off their dago heads like bongos or something and he calls me when he realizes he's out of Boston and into Worcester and we just pile their asses back in their car and drive it back into the city, and then we went fishing. But Reedy could not catch the trout. He could not. I think it's a lot like that in police work, but Shari Tobias was a nice big girl and I am so, so sorry. Thank you so much."

22

oarke stepped up on the little stage and put her face close to Agatha's.
"Think. Think of what you're saying. They're not words but exten-
sions—extensions of Queen Margaret. Their losses are hers. Yours.
You caused them. You're responsible. So when you progress through the
speech, Prince Edward can't be anything but admiring. That was good, Tony.
She becomes more than your mother here."

"Thanks," Tony said softly.

"Just once more, and I promise I won't interrupt."

Roarke watched raptly, making furious little notes. The scene was classic
Elizabethan declaration, and it was Agatha Bentley's task to add humanity to
the concrete information. Roarke hunched. Stood. Swayed. Hunched again.
Tony Howard stood at attention and listened. Agatha finished the three distinct fusillades of iambic pentameter, paused, and stepped off the stage and
out of the scene.

Roarke clapped softly. The other seven students clapped.

"Excellent. Yes. You see, Agatha?"

"It's more than, I guess, just a lot of information and stuff."

"And, Tony, listening like that adds relevance. It's all detail."

She turned to the rest of the class, lounging on the metal chairs or on the
floor. There were four youngsters right out of college, two schoolteachers
from Union, New Jersey, and Sandra Tenny, who had studied with Roarke for
eight years.

"It isn't some cult method or philosophy we're working toward but exactly what took place just then. Listening. Human response. Value placed.
When it works, when we're successful on those basic levels, even Queen Margaret walking onstage full of braggadocio can be arresting. Thursday, Eugene
is going to give Williams a try."

"STELLA!" one of the girls yelled.

"No, c'mon. I'm doing *Glass Menagerie*."

"Thursday," Roarke said.

She sat on the edge of the little stage and chatted with Tony and Agatha as one by one the class left. And then she was alone. She leaned back on the black platform and stared at the ceiling. This was the pleasure of it. The serious satisfaction of her life in the theater. The pinpoint responsiveness she offered her students and the hopeful, inspiring energy they always returned.

It was 9:20 in the evening, and the stage work light was the only one on in the apartment. Roarke thought it was depressing without her "kids" around, so she shut it off and switched on the floor lamp by the sofa. She popped a beer and had gone to sit at the kitchen table when the front buzzer sounded. She pressed the intercom.

"Yes?"

"It's . . . uh . . . it's Tubby Vinitti."

"Tubby? C'mon in."

Roarke opened the door, and Tubby Vinitti rumbled down the hall. He smiled a little smile, and Roarke kissed him.

"Hey, Roarke."

"Tubby. How are you?"

"I'm good."

"How's Sarah?"

"She's good. She's good."

"Want a beer?"

"Great."

Roarke got another beer and popped it for him. "So what's up?"

"You know. Construction. You?"

"I just got finished teaching an acting class."

"I know, I saw them leaving. They looked into it."

"They are."

Roarke took a swallow of beer. Tubby did, too. They stood nodding for a moment. Agreeing somewhere on something. Tubby looked around. "Steven? You heard anything?"

"I got a letter yesterday. Postcard. He says it's beautiful and he's in the mountains."

"He'll do good."

"He will."

"Yeah."

"Want to sit down, Tubby?"

"No, thanks. I'm fine. There's your stage," he said, pointing.

He walked toward it a few steps. Roarke noticed how polished his shoes were and how out of place the tie seemed on his huge checked shirt. His hair was brushed back and was wet from sweat.

"Look . . . uh . . . Roarke . . ."

Tubby kept staring at the stage, holding the beer can with both hands.

"See . . . I been . . . I been thinking about you, Roarke, and . . . I been . . . See . . . the thing is, I really, really like you a lot, and . . . I mean . . . well . . . Oh, Jesus Christ."

Tubby hung his head, and it dropped an inch or two over his bull neck. Roarke walked over and put her arm on his shoulder.

"Tubby, I like you, too. I do. I feel very comfortable with you, but—"

"I know you do, Roarke. If I didn't think you felt comfortable with me I could never have come over. . . . I mean, something like this isn't easy for me. It's not like I've ever done anything like this before. Sarah would give me hell."

He drank his beer. Roarke took the beer out of his hand and set it down.

"Tubby. I don't want to hurt your feelings any, and I'm really flattered, but I couldn't. For a lot of reasons."

"You couldn't what?"

"I just . . . you know . . . I couldn't. Tubby, I'm a lesbian."

"Okay."

"I'm just . . . well . . . I'm inclined to feel romantic toward other girls."

"Yeah, Sarah spelled it out, but why couldn't you come to dinner?"

"Dinner?"

"See, this is what would really get me in trouble with Sarah, but she don't worry like I do. I mean, she loves Niki, everybody loves Niki, but she's not happy. I know it. I'm her big brother. We know these things."

Tubby took Roarke's amazing hands in his meaty paws.

"I don't know shit from Shinola when it comes to lesbians, but I know who I like, and I like you, Roarke. I really do. Come to dinner. Meet my sister. What the hell."

And Roarke was laughing. And Tubby, too, a little.

The lives of artists are as a rule unsatisfactory—not to say tragic—because of their inferiority on the human and personal side—there is hardly any exception to the rule that a person must pay dearly for the divine gift of creative fire.

—Carl Gustav Jung

23

Steven listened to Petey's speech from the Creedemore Historical Society on the second floor above the hardware store. This was his third official working day of the routine he felt would get him back on track yet nothing seemed to come. Each morning Miss Wilma Kirk would pick him up at Ute Ranch, extend an informal tour of the valley, and deliver him to the Historical Society office. Steven would pore over the unofficial documents of this town of played-out mines, spread his 342228 narrow-ruled writing pad on the antique rolltop desk, lay his Pilot Varsity pens in an angled row to the right of the paper, and stare. Sometime around noon he would walk across the street to the Seattle House of Joe and buy a sandwich and coffee and take them back to the office. At about four Miss Wilma Kirk would return him to the beautiful meadows above the reservoir.

He lit a cigarette and checked his watch for the third time in two minutes. The office of the Creedemore Historical Society was one large room. Throw rug of blue with a campfire woven in the center. Old photographs of mines and street scenes. Even a black-and-white rogues' gallery from 1899 with information underneath each picture of who killed whom and why. Behind the rolltop desk were floor-to-ceiling bookcases filled with every document and newspaper that ever originated out of Creedemore. Three enormous taxidermied trout, decaying in age, lay under a glass-topped display case pushed against the far wall. A microscopic blackfly was hooked to the corner of each mouth. Steven bent over the counter to examine them.

"No way, José," a soft voice rasped behind him.

Steven straightened. A thin woman wearing paint-spattered white bib overalls and a blue turtleneck was standing, hands in pockets, in the open doorway. She had on a black bowler hat slung low to just above her eyes. A long rectangular folder was under her right arm.

"No way somebody got those things out of the river with a number twenty-six dry fly. No way. Streamers, maybe. Worms, probably. Hey."

"Hello."

She took a few steps into the room and plopped the folder on the desk. She removed her bowler and rubbed her turtleneck sleeve over her hard, shiny scalp. Steven noticed how small her ears were. He noticed an arrowhead hanging from one earlobe.

"Miss Kirk around?"

"No . . . but I guess she'll be back."

"I saw you before, right?"

"Miss Kirk was showing me the mines, and we crossed the stream, and—"

"And she said, 'Hippie lives there.' "

"Actually, she did. Yes. And then you walked out."

She extended her hand without smiling, and Steven shook it.

"I'm Molly Dowie."

"I'm Steven Kearney."

"I paint. Some of those artsy-fartsy galleries around here hang my stuff. Oils mostly, although I've studied watercolor."

She pointed to the folder on the table. "When you see Miss Kirk, will you give her these?"

Steven walked to the desk and pointed also. "These?"

She kept her eyes on him. "Tell her they're my sketches for the historical mural. If the society likes them, I can start right away."

"You're doing a mural?" he repeated stupidly.

"On the side of the Western Market that faces the logging amphitheater. There's going to be some sort of historical play or something. I'm backdrop."

Steven put his hands in his pockets. "Well, I'm . . . I'm writing that play."

She stared at him a moment. Jeans, T-shirt, baseball cap. He had a two-day growth of brown and gray on his face, as if toying with the possibility of growing a beard. It was Molly's turn to be stupid.

"You're writing the play?"

"Yeah, well, I mean, I'm writing it as a kind of, you know . . . uh . . . saga . . . or something."

They rocked lightly back and forth. She put her bowler back on, tapping it low.

"Have they jumped all over you yet?"

"Who?"

"Historical Society. Or, as I like to say, the Hysterical Society."

"I haven't met them. Just Miss Kirk."

"Well, there's six of them, and they all have a different slant on things. Split right down the middle on the Lettgo thing, too."

"Those protesters?"

"Yes, sir."

"What happened?"

She took her hat back off. "You *are* a rookie, aren't you? We're going to have a range war. There's reporters from the *Rocky Mountain News*, there's the *Denver Post*. We were on CNN two days ago."

Steven nodded, then suddenly snapped his fingers.

"What?" she said.

"I just got it," he said seriously. "I mean, I just figured out where to start on this thing. I'm going to write it like . . . kind of . . . like I was painting a mural, too, only I'm gonna write a mural."

"You can look at my sketches if you want."

"Cool."

"Cool?"

"I mean, that's great."

"Who says 'cool'?"

"Me. Steven Kearney."

He could feel something now, and it might be energy.

"Listen, do you think you could go over your sketches with me and explain some things? I can go get us some coffee. I can get us some really terrific sandwiches."

She wondered how old he was. Cool?

"How old are you?"

"I'm forty-eight."

"But I mean, who says 'cool'?"

"Me. Steven Kearney."

And he was out the door. By the time she walked to the window, he was running to the Seattle House of Joe.

24

Sheriff Petey Myers eased his butt up into the driver's seat of the Jeep and switched the nine-millimeter away from his throbbing plastic hip so that the barrel pointed down in his crotch. Vi and Dan stood next to him.

"Why don't you let Dan go, or Bobby?"

"Well, now, I'm the damn sheriff."

"But your hip, hon."

"When was it me and Reedy got that Teamster mick? When was that?"

Vi thought for a minute, and so did Petey.

"You were guarding that television show."

"That's it."

Petey turned back a little to Dan. "Me and Reedy get this cush gig making sure nobody bothers the big-deal actors on this TV show."

"Shot in Boston," Vi explained. "Had that tall white man and that tall black man and the Asian woman and the Mexican."

"PR," Petey corrected.

Dan nodded with some pleasure. "*Four Cops Four.* Asian kickboxed."

"That's it. Me and Reedy got the cush assignment."

"You can still watch it in reruns. They always end up at some bar and talk about why they had to kill who they killed."

Petey smiled. "Faunce Tavern."

"That's it."

"End of the day, little snow falling, Reedy and me standing outside the warehouse where they were filming, you know, telling cars to go around, telling people to be quiet. This little mick driver, Teamster, walks over to the PR's trailer and just goes in. I know the PR is inside filming with the slant, so me and Reedy walk over and kind of just stand there by the door. Fucking mick is gabbing on the phone. Then we smell weed and open the door. Mick looks at Reedy, now Reedy's like this and shoulders like this, and the mick says, 'Close the door, asshole.' Man. We beat that cockhound half to death. I'm going to get Ticky."

Petey drove slow. By the time Ticky's gate came into view, the "free water" nuts on one side, the paramilitary yahoos on the other, a line of about forty tourist cars and trailers were close behind, afraid to pass. Petey eased the Jeep off the road and up to the closed gate. He leaned his head out the window and felt his new hip roll and scrape.

"Open up," he said.

One of the men carried a shotgun across his shoulder. He unhooked the gate, and Petey drove through. He stopped the truck and slid out of the cab, keeping the engine running. He pulled out his cane and walked past the Ticky sympathizers to the Ticky protesters. He watched them for a moment. Enough for them to feel uncomfortable. Petey's gun still hung like an outsize jock, and he hadn't shaved that morning, but everyone understood that the forensic people had a difficult time determining the sex of the woman at the sheep-herder's cabin and the man had chunks of the Dodge door in his headless body.

"Ladies and gentlemen. I'm going to ask you to keep a distance of twenty-two feet back from the gate and to stand on either side of the drive."

The group immediately obeyed.

"Thank you, ladies and gentlemen."

Petey turned and offered the same discriminating look to the ranchmen. They were more of what he and Vi had expected when they made the move. Cowboys in pickups. Gun racks. He looked back at the others. They could have come from Waltham or, worse, Cambridge. But Reedy would say even-ness was everything. Balance. Reedy did that yin-and-yang thing. Reedy knew.

"Now, I'm going to ask you boys to also observe a distance of twenty-two feet from the gate. I also want you to stand on either side of the drive, keeping it clear for operating vehicles."

They moved a little slower but they moved. The one with the shotgun still crooked on his shoulder, Mel Prophit, was the last one to rearrange his position. Petey knew Prophit as a Texas summer resident who had proved to be litigious in the past by bringing suit for a million dollars against his deputy, Bobby, for removing the remains of a bald eagle from Prophit's property. Court wouldn't hear it, but the game wardens, those Gestapo pricks, gave Bobby a hard time for months.

"Now, Mr. Prophit. I would ask you to please put the shotgun back in the pickup rack."

Prophit was Petey's age. Had the answers. His forty-three-inch belly hung strong over thirty-four-inch jeans.

"It don't have no rack. I come with Jack Hill and his boy. They got their guns in the racks."

Petey looked over to Jack. Jack couldn't hold his look. Jack had been on the volunteer rescue squad that got sent up to collect the two things at the sheepherder cabin. He knew that Petey had done that, then driven himself to the hospital in Gunnison all shot to shit. Orderly there swore Petey was listening to a Colorado Rockies baseball game when he pulled up at emergency. Petey looked back at Mel Prophit. He lifted his hand and waved him over with his index finger. Prophit kept the shotgun on his shoulder and sauntered over. Now the two of them stood by the gate, out of earshot from either group.

"I don't understand this, Mr. Prophit," Petey said softly.

"I got a right. I'm not on public land. Anyway, I can have it as long as it's displayed."

"I didn't mean that. I meant why does a cockhound like yourself think that I'm going to let myself be shown up? Now, they can see us talking but they can't hear us, so, like Reedy would say, wear the leather gloves so the bruises don't come up. You walk over to Jack's truck and you lay that piece-of-shit Kmart thing across the seat, and I don't mean no Texas drag-ass walk or I will fuck you where you live. With Reedy or without him."

Mel Prophit held his ground for a one-two count, then turned and delivered the shotgun to the pickup at a pace Petey found acceptable. Petey wondered as he drove on toward the Lettgo house if he would have actually shot him. He was thinking that he reviewed his actions after the fact more and more these days. And the idea of a simple winging with a nine-millimeter was ridiculous; Reedy would say "frivolous."

Out of sight and sound of the rival groups, Petey unlatched the second gate, drove the Jeep through, and then closed the gate behind him. He shut off the Jeep. Seventy-five feet away, the big river swirled and riffed into a slow-moving deep hole that narrowed and banked to the right in a mad rush.

"A man could fish with a nymph there," Petey said out loud to himself, pointing. "And there, by the far bank, he could throw a dry fly. Shit. A man could use streamers. A man could use the wet flies. All of it."

Sheriff Petey Myers stood quietly now and listened to the sweet flow of water.

"I guess, what it is, you don't ask them, Reedy." He sighed. "You don't ask."

Petey felt himself stiffening up and grimaced back into the truck. He drove on to the beautiful log house. He pulled off the dirt drive onto some mowed grass and for a moment watched the house, occasionally letting his gaze shift to the river. Petey thought that a man could stand on the Lettgos' porch and cast to the trout. He rolled out of the Jeep and hobbled toward the door.

"Who's there?" a voice cracked from somewhere.

Petey stopped walking. He was between the truck and the house. There were no animals around. He slid the utility belt containing his nine-millimeter away from his crotch back over to the bad hip. "That you, Ticky?"

"Petey? Petey Myers?"

"Yes, sir."

Petey could not tell where the small, pointy voice was coming from.

"Jack says you killed those two good. I liked that Shari Tobias."

"Yes, sir."

"I had some gunfights."

"I know that."

"Never shot no one dead, though. Got a couple of boys in the ass by the Feed 'n' Seed one night."

They stopped talking, and Petey could hear the river again. He thought about Minnie Lettgo and her marine pin and the big clothes she always pinned it on. Did they ever fit?

"How's Mrs. Lettgo doing?"

There was no answer.

"How's Minnie?"

Ticky came around the corner of the house in tiny, careful steps. The big Colt .45 strapped to his thigh. A Winchester in his spindly arms.

"Minnie's not too hot. She's in bed, and she's not talking."

Petey cocked his head and squinted at the sun reflecting off Ticky's Lettgo Feed 'n' Seed belt buckle.

"She wear her marine pin to bed?"

Ticky did not seem surprised at the question. "What I did, I pinned it next to the pillow."

They both thought about this and looked across the yard to the river at the same time.

"That's my land and that's my water and that's my air."

"I come from Boston, Ticky. Reedy used to say we don't have anything that's ours. In Boston anyway."

Ticky turned back to Petey and put the Winchester on the ground, then moved away from it, hanging his fingers close to the handle of the Colt. Petey watched him. He was sorry now that he'd set the nine-millimeter on automatic. Reedy would have loved this old man.

"Minnie's under the weather, then?"

Ticky was rubbing those little Popsicle-stick fingers together next to the Colt. Petey smiled at something he remembered.

"You laughing at me?"

Petey stopped smiling. "No, sir. I was smiling at something my partner did one time."

"Policing?"

"Reedy had his head shaved because he thought it made him look sexy. Jesus. We had this hooker in the Combat Zone. Big Afro. High as a kite. Skinny thing. Pathetic as shit. AIDS, probably. Only she has this asshole by the hair and she's got a razor up to his Adam's apple."

"Jesus."

"Asshole's all crying and shit, but Reedy—and I could tell because he was my partner—"

"I seen the shows."

"Reedy didn't give a rat's ass for the john, he just felt so bad for the girl. Lipstick all over her mouth, teeth. AIDS. Reedy . . . man . . . Reedy just walks up to her and gets this close to her and kisses her, here, forehead."

"Jesus."

"He just kisses her. She starts all crying and drops the razor. I asked him why he did that. I mean, she could have taken that razor and sliced off his balls, but Reedy says he just had a feeling that she needed that kiss."

They were both quiet now. Ticky had stopped rubbing his fingers.

"Now, what has to happen here is that you come into town with me so we can do this business about the raft shooting. Of course what I'll do, now that I know Minnie is not feeling well, I'll call Vi—you know Vi?"

"Wife?" Ticky asked weakly.

"Yeah. I'll call her, and she'll come out and sit with Minnie. Vi's great. I'll call her, and we won't leave for town until she's here and all set with Minnie. I better call her from your place."

After a few seconds, enough time for a lonely cloud to put them both into shade, Ticky nodded and turned toward the house. Petey followed him, adjusting the nine-millimeter back to his crotch.

25

Molly Dowie was unhappy with her scale drawing on the wide rectangular parchment. For one thing, the specific hues of western Colorado were enormous. Big colors in blues and golds and browns and greens and fires in the clouds and the shades of the seasons that altered and flopped onto each other. The history of Creedemore sprawled uncomfortable and rough, even in the pieces that time caresses and softens. Whenever she thought of it, which was always, it was never in the terms of contained paper but rather a wall, and the wall became sky. She felt that her drawing proposals were woeful. Steven Kearney thought they were dumbfounding.

He found himself looking out the windows facing Main Street, hoping to see her. He had more questions. About the Ute, about Carson, about the familiar Irishy conquistador. And if his historical-drama pageant was a new form, how could he begin? How could he know? Miss Wilma Kirk would ask him each morning the thrust (her word) of his spectacle, and he would answer, as they bounced past the reservoir and beaver streams and meadows, that once he had decided on the structure, the rest would be a breeze. But he *had* decided, really. He had chosen the cluttered form of the mural and in the choice found more confusion.

He was staring at her astonishing drawings when she finally came by.

"Molly Dowie," he said. "Cool."

"Cool?"

"I mean, you know, I didn't know how to get hold of you."

She took off her bowler hat. "Hot."

"I didn't think the mountains got this hot. But we're closer to the sun, right?"

She stepped past him to her drawings. Steven noticed that a small tooth earring hung where the arrowhead had been and that she had orangey lipstick on. Her big overalls rubbed together at the knees.

"Miss Kirk see these?" she asked.

"I told her about them. I think she saw them. They had some kind of meeting last night, but I was up at the Ute Ranch."

"How do you get here?"

"Miss Kirk picks me up."

"Every day?"

"Uh-huh."

"You don't have a car?"

"No."

"You don't have a car? How are you going to know what you're *writing* about?"

"You need a car to know what to write?"

"If you want to get it right, you do."

Molly Dowie faced him. Her eyes were green. The skin underneath them and above her high cheeks was pushed back and gray.

"How are you gonna meet the people who know the secrets?"

"Secrets? I just want . . . I don't know. . . . I just . . . I have no idea."

Now she noticed his eyes. His thin hair. His sprout of a ponytail. He looked out the window and said it again. "I have absolutely no idea . . . what I'm doing."

"You're doing—you said it the other day—a mural with words. I have to sit down."

He grabbed the chair by the rolltop desk and carried it over to her.

"Are you all right?"

"I'm just tired. I get these treatments in Pueblo every couple of weeks, and I had one on Monday. They just beat the shit out of me."

"Water?"

"I'm fine, just getting a load off the feet."

"You think a car would help, huh?"

"Got to have a car or something. You don't have to go far, but you got to get them."

"Get what?"

"The secrets."

Steven thought how Roarke had the ability to hang odd thoughts above him. Molly Dowie had it, too. Secrets?

"Every picture I draw for the mural—and I want to say I'm no muralist, certainly no expert, so I'm crude—but every picture or frame is part of a story. It's not complicated, any more than the paintings on a cave wall or an Egyptian tomb are complicated. They tell these simple stories about fighting or loving or working or even dreaming. There's a sense in a mural of moving. Going on."

Molly Dowie raised her fingers to the side of her face. They were long fingers. Steven Kearney saw that each nail was painted a different color.

"Your fingernails are very pretty."

She looked up at him with a smirk and then smiled when she realized he wasn't being a wise-ass.

After a moment Molly plopped her hat back on and gave it a pat. "Tell Miss Kirk I'll be at my house. I'd like to get started."

"Cool," he said absently.

She walked to the office door and turned at the frame. "I've got a motor scooter. Was Willie's but he's mostly in Denver now. Can you drive a motor scooter?"

"I don't know. I guess, sure."

"You remember where I live?"

"Up the road to the mines. Behind the sheriff's office."

"And you cross Bachelor Creek. I'm the second house in the rock."

"I saw you there."

"After you finish, you can walk up for the scooter. It's red and black."

"Cool."

She almost asked him again how old he was.

26

J acob tapped his china plate with a fork.

"Yo. Any risotto left?"

Tubby looked down the table to his sixteen-year-old. Like the rest of his boys and girls, this one was tall and beautiful, with olive skin and a big face, and in no way resembled himself. A rich black ponytail tied with an elastic band hung off his neck. His T-shirt had BACK OFF printed front and back.

"I'll risotto you, you little toad," Tubby said, passing the blue bowl.

"Who made this? You or Ma?"

"Who makes the risotto in this family?"

"You do. I was just wondering," Jacob said, scooping a small mountain of arborio onto his plate.

"Save some for Niki and Roarke."

Jacob looked hopefully. "Niki? Want some?"

"Scarf it."

"Roarke?"

"I'm stuffed."

Jacob tipped the bowl, and the mountain grew.

"How big are you now?" Niki asked. Like Tubby's children, his sister was tall. She was quite thin, and her long Italian face was topped off by a thick black pageboy. Her voice was soft and a touch nasal, almost a buzzy whisper. She wore a green pantsuit with an olive T-shirt.

"They don't call me Mule Man for nothing."

Everyone laughed but Tubby.

"We got company," Tubby reminded him.

"Niki's not company."

"We got Roarke, you little monster."

"I'm six-six, Niki."

"Big deal," said his father.

"The doctor says he's going to grow maybe two more inches," Sarah said.

103

Roarke and Niki and Sarah and Tubby watched the thing joyously con-
sume the risotto, huge scoops of the savory rice rhythmically zooming into his
mouth.

"Good," he grunted. "Pop, can you help me out a little?"

"How much?"

Jacob looked at his mother and raised his eyebrows. "Twenty?"

"Ten," Tubby countered.

"Twenty."

"Fifteen."

"I'm taking the subway into the Bronx."

"Where?"

"Yankees."

"Who they playing?"

"Angels."

"He'll give him the twenty. Tubby's a spoiler," Sarah said, looking across to
Roarke.

Tubby reached into his back pocket and pulled out an overstuffed wallet.
He ceremoniously took out a twenty and waved it at his son.

"Eleven-thirty."

Jacob reached for the bill, but Tubby held it back. "What time?"

Jacob looked around the table with feigned exasperation. "Eleven-thirty."
And he was gone.

"He's beautiful," Roarke said.

"You ought to see the other ones. Thank God for Sarah's genes."

"I got the genes, too," Tubby rumbled.

"You just ain't got the willpower," Niki said.

Sarah stacked the plates on her side of the table.

"They fight," she said to Roarke.

"Niki fights. I don't fight. Niki picks on me."

"I don't."

"No willpower?"

"I worry about you, that's all."

"I worry about you, too."

"I worry that you're one hundred pounds overweight, and I worry about
your heart giving out."

"So don't worry."

"Well, I do. I can't help it. You're not that much, but you're all I've got."

"And I can't help worrying about you, too."

"But you worry about the wrong things."

"Then you do, too."

"Uh-uh."

Niki carried a pile of dishes into the kitchen and returned.

"Niki wrote a book," Sarah said.

"Textbook. No big deal." Niki looked over to Roarke. "Mary Cassatt. It'll be done for fall."

"I love her," Roarke said, "the one with the mother and the baby playing."

"Patty-cake."

"That's my favorite."

"Do too," Tubby said.

The three women stopped and looked at him.

"Do what?" asked Sarah.

"If I worry about all the wrong things, then all I'm saying is that Niki worries about the wrong things, too."

Niki turned to Roarke and looked at her across the table. She noticed her hands and fingers and the way she drummed them lightly on the mahogany table. The hands seemed separate from her. Roarke felt the look and returned it.

"Roarke, I'm speaking as an art historian now. Seriously. Tubby had a body like the *David*."

"Jesus," Tubby said.

"Sarah?"

"When I met him, he was like a *big* David. But very cute." She kissed his scowling face. "I still think he's cute."

Niki walked behind her brother and wrapped her arms around his enormous head, resting her chin on top.

"When I was a baby, or five or six, this guy looked like the *David*."

"It's true," Sarah said. "I got the pictures."

"He won the New York State amateur middleweight boxing title when he was sixteen."

Roarke sat back in her chair and stopped her beautiful fingers. "Get *out!*"

Tubby smiled. "This big fireman. Mick. Sorry, Roarke, but the mick would push with his left and set up the right. Every time he pushed, I would slap his meat hook outta there and pop him."

"Why didn't you turn professional?"

"I was . . . you know . . . I was advised against it."

"Now he's a construction mobster."

"Listen to her."

"It's better."

"I gotta get back in shape. What's in the dessert department?"

Later, Tubby watched from the step as Roarke and Niki walked to the subway stop. He watched them all the way up Thirty-sixth Street and couldn't tell if they were talking or not. They were not.

The ladies walked silently by the prim brick homes, turning occasionally to the night growls of Queens. When they cut onto Broadway, Niki said, "Sarah told me you direct."

"I try."

"That's difficult, isn't it? The theater, I mean."

"I don't know. It's fifty-fifty."

They crossed Thirty-second Street and climbed up to the N train platform. Across the low houses and shops of Queens, Manhattan blinked clear as a runway.

"I like the impressionists the best. Flat-out," Roarke said.

"I like the Hudson River school the best," Niki said. "I mean to say, as far as flawed subjects and techniques go, those old men were right up there, but I know the material. I grew up in Newark. We saw the cliffs about every day, and when Sarah and Tubby got married, they'd always be taking me on picnics and drives up the Hudson Valley."

"It's something you recognize."

"It's soothing."

"I hear you. O'Neill does that for me. It's old. It's dated. It's heavy-handed stuff. But it's common to everybody. He writes for actors things that we all think about."

The N followed a ball of light on the elevated track, and they watched it all the way into the station.

"Where do you get off?" Roarke asked.

"Prince. I live on Mulberry."

"I can get off there, too. I ate like a cow. I can use the walk."

The N dove under the East River.

"The depressing thing is the perception that art is elite," Niki said. "My students are divided into the ones passionate about the survey or electing to take it because it appears to be an easy credit, which it's not."

"I feel guilty sometimes with my students," Roarke said, surprising herself. "Guilty?"

The train began to rise from beneath the mud. Lights flicked on and off.

"Well, my students are *all* passionate. This is what they want. They see themselves as actors. They define themselves as performers. But stage acting today is often seen as a kind of poor cousin of TV. And TV doesn't challenge. Film doesn't challenge."

"French films challenge."

"Okay, French films, but the others." They both nodded.

At Fifty-seventh Street, Niki said, "I get mad at Tubby. I don't want to lose him. He's got to drop some weight. I shouldn't, but I feel a big responsibility."

Roarke nodded and smiled. "But it's good to feel that. If I didn't have Steven to worry about, I'd spend all the time worrying about myself."

The train made Prince, and they walked upstairs to Broadway.

27

Jude drove it around the Ute Ranch pasture, and Jimmy the Kid worked a rope trying to lasso him. Skyo came out and tried it, too. The little motor scooter bounced wildly through the grass and prairie-dog hills. Steven watched them with Buck. Albert came out the kitchen door.

"Do better with a horse," he said.

The sun had fallen quickly, and a dry wind came. The aspen shivered around them. Albert spoke to Buck but kept his eye on Skyo, screaming over the high meadow.

"Who's taking Rat Boy and the Greaser tomorrow?"

"Jude and Jimmy."

"I'm thinking you ought to go with 'em."

"We got two day rides and a Ruby Lake trip."

"Why don't you leave Jimmy? Me and Skyo'll take the Ruby. I don't like those two."

As if he needed to explain, he turned to Steven. "Those two come up for the Lost Diablo Mine."

"I don't know it," Steven said.

"Attracts all manner of crazies."

"Rat Boy and Greaser are okay. Just weird," Buck said.

"That's the word. Come up every year like they know something."

"They all come up like that."

"True."

"Anderson family drew on me last year," said Buck.

Albert shook his head. "Idiots get packed into Pulchry Gulch last . . . when?"

"August."

"Father and his daughter and son-in-law. Buck packs them in for two weeks, and when he goes back in for them, the old man pulls a gun."

"Jesus," said Steven.

"I about filled my pants. They had eyes like this. Wild and crazy," Buck said.

"Gold fever," said Albert, spitting.

"I think the altitude got them. It's two thousand feet higher than here. Andersons were coming from Kansas City."

"What happened?" Steven asked.

"Buck does good. Hands up. Backs off. Comes back down, gets me. I get the Bakers at the reservoir, and old Petey Myers comes up."

"He's the sheriff," added Buck.

"We horse up to Pulchry in the middle of the night. Petey's mad as hell. Comes from Boston. Bad rider."

"Tough, though."

"Oh, God yes. He'll stand in. We get there at sunup and pull 'em out of the tents. Take their guns and make 'em walk back down."

"Thought the old man'd die."

"Kicked their butts out of the valley. Then we went back up the next week, but there wasn't anything."

"They're coming in July this year."

"They're coming back? Here?" Steven asked.

"I think they learned their lesson. Girl was barefoot when we walked her down."

"Cute, too," Buck said.

"They dig for gold?" Steven asked.

"They *look* for gold. The rumor is the Lost Diablo Mine was part of the conquistadors being up here."

"I heard the Spanish were here."

"They're here, all right." Buck laughed.

"I mean, the conquistadors."

Janice came out of the kitchen door and yelled across the field. "Skyo! You and Jude come help me now. Somebody's got to set the table."

"I'll get it, Mother," Buck said, and walked to the kitchen. Albert and Steven followed.

"I don't believe it myself," Al said. "Like the movies? The mountain men? Hell, even the Indians went down below, Albuquerque area, around there. How could those Spaniards stay a winter or two? Impossible, if you ask me. But they say they were a lost group of soldiers who had set out from Mexico City with Coronado looking for the Seven Cities of Gold. Pueblos. They got lost, came into the mountains around Pulchry, and found gold. Smelted it into blocks and such. Then they vanished. Some of these nuts believe it's in a cave or that the Utes killed them and hid it so no more Spanish would come."

"What are the Seven Cities?" Steven asked.

"Don't get him started," Buck said at the door.

"It's all in the arrowheads," Albert said mysteriously.

They all took their places at the table

"Steven. What say you offer it up to the Lord?" Albert said.

"Daddy," Skyo said quickly, "that's not fair."

Buck laughed. "That's what college will do to you."

Albert was bewildered. "What's not fair?"

"Well, what if Steven is not a believer?"

"Then that's okay. People don't have to believe."

"Yes, but it's embarrassing to have to say it."

"Say what?"

"Say, 'I don't believe.' "

"It's fine. I believe," said Steven.

"You do?" asked Skyo.

"Well, yes I do. But I don't really know graces and things."

"I imagined artists didn't believe in anything except what they're doing."

"Where'd you hear that?" asked Janice.

Buck shifted loudly in his chair. "Let's get on the old feed bags."

Albert lowered his head. "Lord, thank you for all of your good blessings on our little family."

Everyone mumbled an amen, and Albert added, "And please make Jude cut the ponytail before his dad gets up here."

Buck laughed. "New Joisey."

It was chicken-fried steak and white gravy. Steven listened to the wrap-up of a western day. He felt a fullness, and it was more than the savory food. An odd feeling connected to Skyo and Albert and Janice and Jimmy the Kid and Jude and Buck. An easy, good feeling.

He helped clear the table and followed Albert into the lodge room.

Albert gestured to the frames of arrowheads and patted his tight belly. "Here it is, then. Like I say. It's all here. This is the Folsom head. These are the oldest. I only got a piece, some pieces of it. See the grooves there?"

Steven got close. "Here?"

"Those grooves. What those little people did was put the Folsom head on a spear and stuck it in the saber-tooth or woolly mammoth and followed them till they bled to death through the grooves. Pretty smart little people."

They moved to a frame of beads, then one with a circle of red and white beans.

"Now, this is something. Janice and me were up to Blue Mesa when the kids were little, and I'm looking in the rocks, and I come up with a petrified leather pouch, and the beans were inside. I plopped some of them in water and, Steven, they sprouted."

"Wow."

"And these little cuties are two or three thousand years old."

"Thousand?"

"Honest to God."

They walked frame by frame. Sandstone spear points. Obsidian and flint.

"It was a hard, short life for them. And they moved constantly. They weren't like the Indians we know of. They were sort of in between. Cave people and plains people."

"And all this was from the valley?"

"Some of it was from the valley. I collect all over. They were the first Utes. These critters could squat down and chip one of these things in a minute."

"They're beautiful."

"That's the truth. Now, see, what we figure, scientists and such, we figure they all came from Mongolia and crossed the Bering Strait up by Alaska."

Albert held up his hands as if pointing to an enormous wall map.

"So they come across here, but now here's my theory, and I am no scientist, but I think instead of all spreading out across America over twenty thousand years, I think they moved down the Pacific coast into Mexico and into South America and scooted up into the Southwest later. See, when the Spanish destroyed the Aztec culture—"

"Cortés," Steven said.

"Cortés, right, after they got rid of the Indians in Mexico City, they went out in search of these Seven Lost Cities of Gold. That's a historical fact, Steven, and guess what? The Spaniards took Aztec Indians with them to serve as interpreters, and when the conquistadors came to the Pueblos, the Indians inside spoke a kind of Aztec. Which is why I think they originally came from Mexico."

Steven thought about cities made out of mud. "And people think the conquistadors got all the way into Creedemore, huh?"

"That's a theory. I think it's a lot of you-know-what, but you can check it out for yourself."

"I'll ask somebody on the Historical Committee."

"Except for Miss Kirk, those people don't know spit. They just make things up for the tourists. Evan Santi and his wife in Barnegat Meadows up the road. Used to run the San Antonio Camp below Box Canyon. Those folks have collected lots more conquistador stuff. One time they traced them from Mexico City to Albuquerque. Gave it all to a museum in Santa Fe. They're the ones you talk to."

The idea formed in his head entirely on its own, and hours later, as he sat on the side of his bed, it flowed into his conscious mind, complex and complete, tingling the hairs on the back of his neck.

111

Interviews.

A series of in-depth interviews.

The word-mural would encompass the historical reality and life and times of Creedemore.It would actually spring from the mouths of the history keepers. The stories, the traditions, the secrets of place composed by the keepers themselves. He sat at his small bedroom desk and wrote in longhand on a yellow legal pad:

1. Evan Santi and wife	—Conquistadors
2.	—Utes
3.	—Miners
4.	—Ranchers
5.	—Fishing
6.	—Hunting
7.	—Etc.

Tomorrow he would fill in the blanks and make an interview schedule. He opened a window. He smoked a cigarette.

28

ostly it was to show everyone that he had it under control. But there was more to it. There was a little of the precaution, too. Petey Myers knew that a volcano had to vent somehow, and having Ticky arraigned and getting that asshole rafter to back off would maybe offer some relief. That was a best-case scenario until Bobby came in from South Fork and told Petey about a rally at the Pancake House by the Liberty Society of Colorado. Bobby was taking some breakfast buffet with Larry Holstedt, deputy in South Fork, when they all walk in, take a long table, and start toasting Mountain Man Red Fields with juice and coffee.

"He there?" Petey asked.

"Yes, sir."

"Alone?"

"No, sir. He was being toasted."

"Anyone from Creedemore?"

"I don't think so."

Petey thought for a second. Outsiders. Reedy would say "also-rans," but that wasn't the right term. Reedy didn't really care, though. Once he said something, that was the word for it. Petey smiled inwardly and remembered the busload of johns they had collected one by one at the bottom of Boylston Street. Rookie cop says, "Now, you can't just stop every car. How do we know what they're looking for?" Reedy says, "At three o'clock in the morning down here, any car going five miles an hour is on a Poseidon Adventure." It was wrong. It was crazy. But everyone knew what he meant.

"So they think it's a cockarama, huh?" the sheriff asked.

Bobby had no trouble with that.

"Yes, sir, I guess they do."

Petey walked behind his desk and sat down. His hip hurt. His butt ached. Calf kept going charley horse. Ticky had been cooperative, if a bit sullen. Vi said that Minnie had seemed all right and it didn't look like a stroke or anything, she'd just clammed up. Well, Jesus Christ, she was ninety-six. And she was so small. He thought of the marine pin and how Ticky had said he pinned it on her pillow.

"Bobby, I'm getting a little racing in the Jeep. Take it down to the Standard. Would you do that?"

"I'm on it."

Petey watched the deputy refill his coffee mug and walk out to the parking lot. Then he called Cal Murray in Monte Vista.

"Colorado Highway Patrol."

"Cal? Petey."

"Not Two-Gun Petey Myers?"

"I had three. I gave them one."

Cal Murray was a man whose name came up in Petey's very first class in Colorado certification. A wheelchair-bound regional dispatcher for the staties, he was considered a vital first choice for information concerning any question of law or crime or person or groups operating in the vicinity that may or may not be valuable in prevention or crime solving. He remembered everything from his thirty-seven years at the console and augmented that by remembering everything he had ever read or heard.

"What's up?"

"Liberty Society of Colorado."

"Assholes."

"Serious assholes?"

"Started in Boulder. College professors. Grass eaters. Hippies. Assholes. Get into ecological stuff. Protesting smelt smokestacks in Pueblo. Tank shoots in the Springs at Fort Carson. Few years ago they were suspected of blowing up some construction equipment used in building a development they were protesting. By then their literature was something like, *The Liberty Society of Colorado. A—*I'm pretty sure this was it—*A Preternatural Organization*."

"Beautiful." Petey sighed.

"So . . . serious assholes. Why?"

"They're around here."

"Really?"

"I shit you not."

"You? Shooting those kids?"

"Me?"

"*Denver Post* made it seem like they were unarmed."

"Jesus."

"Not you?"

"Ticky Lettgo."

"That raft thing, huh? Yeah . . . fits. One of their main things is that private property is evil. Sure they're in town?"

"No, sir. They're in South Fork."

"Got a trial date? I know that rafter's making a deal. Been here, you know. Making a big deal."

"What's-her-name from Gunnison—"

"Marge Klinger?"

"She's the one hearing it. She's coming over to Creedemore on Friday."

"Ticky arraigned?"

"Yesterday. He's home now. He knows he's got a Friday date. One-fifteen."

"Hold a second, Petey."

Petey took a big sip of cold coffee and about spit it out. He stood to ease his butt, and the calf charleyed back up. He would say to Reedy that he'd had it with Boston and he was ready to pack the whole caboodle in, and old Reedy would rub his black neck and laugh that deep, comfortable laugh and say the grass was always a different shade of shit. Jesus. Was Boston possibly looking better? Cal Murray came back.

"So one-fifteen Friday."

"That's when the judge'll hear the mess."

"Well, old pal. I would expect you'll be seeing a caravan of Liberty Society sometime Friday morning."

"Assholes."

"Serious assholes."

Creedemore
Colorado Postcard

Roarke—

An artist with no hair

is helping me and so

is Albert at the ranch.

I have a scooter now so

I can get the secrets.

How are you?

xxx
Steven

Roarke
622 Vendon St.
New York, NY 10029

29

S he received the card on Tuesday, and for some reason it rattled a vague connection to her scene-study class. Of course, on Saturday night she would review their projects on her tiny stage and had always relied on having at least one impartial audience member, not an actor. Steven had usually been that member, but now he was with bald artists and riding scooters somewhere in the Rocky Mountains. He would have liked this particular group, paired off and asked to take a scene of any length from Shakespeare and play it out in the most contemporary of accents, movements, and intent. Rosencrantz and Guildenstern as three-card monte dealers. Antony and Cleopatra as Upper West Side computer moguls. Kate and Petruchio as stalkers. And more. Seven in all, and some of her darlings doubling in scenes.

She picked up the phone and put it down. Erroll Garner played *Concert by the Sea* in a small cassette deck on top of the refrigerator. She listened for a few seconds with her eyes closed and picked up the phone again. It was a little after 7:00 P.M., and no one answered at the Hunter College art department. Roarke hooked up with Niki Vinitti's voice mail.

"Uh . . . Niki . . . Hi. . . . This is Roarke, that . . . uh . . . friend of your brother's, and my acting students are doing a presentation on Saturday. . . . Anyway . . . I'm at 555-5252. . . . 'Bye."

The phone rang two minutes later.

"Roarke here."

"Roarke? Niki Vinitti."

"Hi."

"Hi."

"That was quick. I just called."

"I teach nights on Tuesday. I was unlocking my office. Your students are doing a show?"

Roarke paced a little in front of her small kitchen table. Amazing fingers traced invisible lines as she walked.

"It's not a show, really. . . . Well, it's like a show, but it's pretty informal.

The scenes each set up during my critique of the previous scene. There's no entrances and exits. It's at my little living-room stage."

"That sounds like fun. Saturday?"

"Eight, but why don't you . . . you know, come over around seven, and I'll cook something up."

"I'll bring the wine."

"Cool," Roarke said, and immediately felt like an idiot.

Niki laughed. "I haven't heard an adult say 'cool' for a long time."

"Steven says it. That's his word. It's starting to rub off."

Roarke laughed now, and when she stopped, there was a silence. It felt uneasy even in the tiny space between the words.

Niki coughed softly. "Excuse me."

"Sure."

"Will Steven be there on Saturday?"

"See, that's the thing. He's got this gig in Colorado. He's a writer, and he's doing a commission job, only he hardly ever leaves New York, and I've always had him . . . you know, around. Sounding board."

"Like I always run things by Sarah."

"Yeah. I run things by him. But Jesus, just between you and me, the guy's been driving me nuts since he moved in."

"He moved in?"

"Don't get me wrong. I love him to death, but when he gets the Irish black ass on, like he's had for a while now, he just can't get himself out of it."

Another space. A beat. An empty, spreading range.

"Roarke?"

"Still here."

"Look, maybe I can't make it Saturday."

"Oh."

"I mean, I'm not sure, but it's hard to plan . . . ahead. I don't know. I can't say."

"Oh, well, that's okay."

"If I can . . ."

"Sure . . . sure."

"Well, I'd better . . ."

"Yeah, 'bye."

Roarke clicked off softly with her finger. Well, she thought, you are a big fuckhead, aren't you?

Niki answered on the first ring.

"I'm glad you didn't go to class yet. Steven Kearney is my very best friend in all the world and I love him deeply and feel it when he's away and just miss him miss him miss him especially because he knows me and makes no judgments about me and I can say anything and do anything and it won't make

118

him change his feelings and understanding about me in any way. And if I were a woman that felt romantic toward men, I probably would be out there with him now or I wouldn't have let him go, but I'm not."

Another phone space, only this one defied a simple interpretation. Erroll Garner made bold little sounds over his joyous keyboard.

"Saturday?" Niki asked quietly.

"The scenes start at eight. Come at seven, and I'll cook us something up."

Another pause. Another good, clear space.

"I'll see you at seven, then."

Now Roarke waited.

Then she said, "Cool."

30

By ten-fifteen the sun had heated up the little office of the Creedemore Historical Society enough for Steven to notice. He'd worked steadily on his wall chart for nearly two hours, and not until some sweat dripped off his nose onto the section titled "Religious (formal)" did he stop to open the windows. He looked over the two-story brick Municipal Building and up toward the played-out mines and the tiny bridge over Bachelor Creek that led to Molly Dowie's home in the rock.

Steven Kearney had found that the scooter ride down from Ute Ranch, high above the big reservoir, took quite a bit longer than the trip in Miss Kirk's Volkswagen. The first day Jude had loaded the scooter in the back of Buck's pickup and took him all the way down to the Creedemore–Lake City paved road, but today he had been on his own. His ass felt as if sharp pebbles were fastened to it. He returned to the wall behind the desk where he had taped up enough typing paper to cover a space about four feet square. In big block lettering, he embellished the dramatic arc he drew end to end with the general frame of events as he understood them, recognizing that in all likelihood the arrangements would grow or change completely. But he had his starting place.

"Good morning, Mr. Kearney."

Miss Kirk moved importantly into the room.

"How goes the battle?"

"Good . . . I think . . . I mean . . . pretty okay."

"Well, I admit I'm glad to hear it. What with the presentation Friday evening."

"Presentation?"

"To the Historical Society over in the Creedemore Hotel. Surely you remember the presentation?"

"I'm . . ."

"It was on your syllabus. Eight o'clock, give or take the time Carol White uses to read the minutes from last month's meeting. Mrs. Dowie will deliver her mural projection and answer questions first, and you will follow."

"Mrs. Dowie?"

"She's very anxious to get a go-ahead for the backdrop. Exciting concept, don't you think?"

"Mrs. . . ."

"Then the board will hear from you on concept, time frame, casting, re-hearsals, et cetera. Have you given consideration to a director, or will you be doing the honors?"

Steven looked back over to his arc. *Mrs.?*

"Directing?" he said.

"Well, not to worry, we have at least three weeks to complete the writing and begin to get it on its feet."

Steven's brain did not comprehend "three weeks." It was missed even though he heard it and saw it on the syllabus she had produced. So much land. So endless the western horizon. So constrained the contemporary artist. He gestured toward the dramatic arc of his with a shrug, and Miss Wilma Kirk moved in front of it.

"Ahhh," she said quietly. "The dramatic arc. Classic."

Steven looked again, out the northern windows and up toward the mines and the forever mountains beyond.

"Mrs.?" he said again.

. . . fire started at the Santi annex and spread all the way, on one side of Main Street to the Mineral Bank, then went back up the other side of the street to Cathedral Rock. Dago and mick miners entered into a wild, all-night debauch with looted liquor.

Creedemore Post, May 1891

31

Petey Myers and Vi left for the Lettgo place at 6:30 A.M. on Friday. There was no one at the gate from either side of the river conflict. Minnie was still in bed and not talking. Ticky was agitated and dangerous. Vi heated up some chicken broth she'd brought from home.

"You two go on. I've got the broth that's going to perk Minnie right up."

Ticky strapped on his big Colt .45.

"Now, that's chicken?"

"Yes, it is."

"It's not beef, is it?"

"No. It's chicken."

"She'll maybe pee the bed if it's beef. Even a little. Beef always never sat with Minnie."

"It's not beef."

"One time the folks in Wichita Falls had the library dinner at our house, and they supplied the food. Steaks like this. Gravy. Minnie damned near drowned us out."

"Well, it's chicken."

At the Jeep, Petey stopped before they got in. "That Vi. She's so bossy."

"I don't think she's bossy, Petey. She's a fine woman."

"Oh, I know that, but sometimes she bosses me around."

"Minnie tries that, too."

"What do you do?"

"I let her know what's what."

"Like what?"

"Well . . ."

"Oh, I see. You let her know she can be the boss of the house but you're the boss everywhere else."

"Well . . ."

"That's smart, Ticky. That's real smart. So by your rules it really depends on where you are that decides who's the boss."

Ticky squinted at the sun coming over the mountains. "Exactly."

"Thank God. Because I didn't want you to get all hot and bothered when I tell you as the boss of the court that your Colt has to stay under the seat of the car."

Ticky thought about this. "I can't check it at the door?"

"No, because I can't have you wearing it in town when you're free on your own recognizance."

"What if I'm jostled?"

"Jostled?"

"At the courthouse."

"I'll be there with you."

"That won't stop the hippies. They'll jostle the shit out of me."

"If anybody jostles you, I'll arrest them."

"Sure, but I'll already have been jostled."

Petey looked away from the old man in the direction of the river. Deep and slow near the ranch gate, it made no sound. Ticky looked, too.

"I named the biggest one in there Nolan Ryan. It's a brown trout. Got a hooked nose. Stays in the stretch between the gate and the barbed-wire pole above. Course, there's 'bows and brookies and some cutthroat, but Nolan's the big one. The big boy."

Petey kept watching the river. Something swirled. Maybe. "Nolan Ryan, huh?"

"Big German brown. Maybe you ought to come out one Sunday and try for him. Bring Vi. Whatever."

Petey turned back again to Ticky Lettgo, who seemed shorter than last week. "Just say you had the Colt and you were gonna turn it in at the door, and just say one of the people there jostled you."

"One of them jostled me?"

"Just say."

Ticky spit, only nothing came out. "Just a regular jostle or a 'shit out of you' jostle?"

"A 'shit out of you' jostle."

"A 'shit out of you' jostle. Well, I might pull it, but I would never in a million years fire the damn thing. Unless I got a few squeezes off in the air. Just to scare 'em."

Petey turned again to the river.

"We might come out some Sunday. Try for Nolan Ryan."

*　*　*

Steven watched from the Historical Society. Since seven-thirty the municipal parking lot had been filled. Cars and trucks parked up the mining roads and out of sight around the curving dirt trail. People spilled onto the main street and lined the porches of homes across from the sheriff's office. Many carried signs. Arguments and chants ricocheted off the signs and banners. One read LETTGO OF OUR RIVER. Another, THIS LAND IS YOUR LAND, THIS LAND IS MY LAND. Another, THIS LAND IS OUR LAND, ASSHOLES. Off to the side and standing in almost marching order were about thirty men, women, and children dressed in green and brown under a banner that read THE LIBERTY SOCIETY OF COLORADO: A PRETERNATURAL ORGANIZATION. Tourists crept by in cars and trailers or milled generally off to the periphery of county conflict. A loud cheer went out from one faction. A tall, redheaded man wearing a leather cowboy hat and a red woolen jacket that had MOUNTAIN MAN printed in black across the back strode purposefully to the three steps of the Municipal Building. A young woman clung to his arm. A deputy was standing at the door and moved aside for the man, who turned and waved. Boos rose equal to the cheers. After a moment Mountain Man and the woman moved past the deputy and into the building.

Steven picked out Jimmy the Kid and Albert and Buck. Skyo, dressed in jeans and an army jacket, appeared to be in an opposing camp. He saw the bowler hat now. Molly Dowie had on her paint overalls and a sweatshirt pulled down over the shoulder straps. A faded drawing of Jerry Garcia on the front. The redheaded conquistador, the model for the mural, stood next to her in gray slacks and a blue blazer, his hair parted in the middle. They held hands. Molly Dowie looked up to Steven's window and smiled. She said something to the young man, and he looked up also. He seemed to be laughing. Steven pretended that maybe he wasn't looking at Molly. She took off her hat again, still looking up, and patted her shiny oblong head as if it had become a ritual to show it to him over and over. The paint muralist to the word-muralist. The young man said something, and she kissed him and stared as he walked away through the crowd. Steven stared at him, too.

"Jesus Christ," he said out loud.

Molly Dowie looked up again and waved. He weakly waved back.

Now Petey Myers's county Jeep, its red lights flashing, moved jerkily into the parking lot. Bobby removed an orange cone from the parking spot marked SHERIFF, and Petey maneuvered in. New signs appeared under the Liberty Society banner.

SHERIFF MYERS IS A BABY KILLER
and
DOUBLE MURDERER

Petey limped out of the Jeep and walked around to get Ticky. The old man was energized. He eased himself down to the ground and made a deal of adjusting the leg tie of the Colt holster. Men in cowboy hats greeted him, and he appeared to nod. A disapproving roar went out from the other side. Ticky made a gesture for his gun, but Petey moved him into the Municipal Building without incident. As soon as the old man was in the building, Petey turned to the crowd and raised his hands for quiet. It was slow in coming, but it came.

"Ladies and gentlemen, I know—"

One of the green-and-brown women screamed, "Are you going to shoot us like you shot those two unarmed children?"

Petey turned to look at the heckler. "No, ma'am, I'm sure not going to. However, you will not be going into the auditorium to witness the proceedings. Is there anyone else who wishes not to witness the proceedings?"

The parking lot grew remarkably quiet.

"Ladies and gentlemen, there is an opportunity here to orderly enter into the auditorium. Remember, we have a small town and a small auditorium. However, I am not averse to waiving some occupancy rules and allowing standing room if codes of conduct are followed. Now, I'll try to accommodate as many of you as I can. Let's have a line in front of my deputy here. One line."

There was a measured rush from the factions, but soon a distinct single line snaked from Bobby around the rock store and up the road. One by one they entered the building under Petey Myers's significant eyeballing. When Molly Dowie was in the building, Steven pushed the society's pocket tape recorder into a small backpack and scootered to the first of the day's interviews.

Two and a half miles out of Creedemore, he turned off the pavement and puttered across the flat plateau toward a lonely white adobe building at a fork in the big river. The high air felt dry. He was unnerved by this enormous western vagueness. He needed specifics. He knew that every scene had to be qualified. And that's what he would try to relate tonight at the presentation before the Creedemore Historical Society. The specifics of place in a qualified context. Or something like that.

The First Episcopal Church of Puerite County was identified only by a small sign next to the entrance. There was no parking lot. No paved paths. Steven knocked several times, then let himself in. A small vestibule opened into a deceptively large room. Folding chairs were semicircled around a low altar. There was an Indian blanket in faded reds and blues covering it and a Communion pyramid on top. A door opened at the back of the church. A blond young man stuck his head out.

"Hey! C'mon in."

Steven walked over to the door, and the man waved him into a small kitchenette apartment.

"Hey, man. Eli Nott. How're you doing?"

"I'm Steven Kearney. I called about—"

"You're the writer. Okay. Yeah. Writer. I got some things here about the different churches. Missionaries to the Indians. Miners. Here it is."

He handed Steven a fat manila envelope, then hopped over to the refrigerator and brought out a tall six-pack of Budweiser.

"This is the King," he said. "C'mon."

Steven followed him outside toward the river. The young man reached into his back pocket and unfurled a Yankee cap.

"Yankees," he said, grinning. "Yeah."

He seemed to bounce when he walked, like a fourteen-year-old. Steven half ran to keep up with him and hear what he said.

"You can't count the padres—I don't think."

"San Diego Padres?"

"Conquistador padres. I really don't think they got up here. First group in were the Franciscans around 1810, but they were all fucked up with the gold fever. Also, they were just sort of there to absolve the soldiers for killing so many Indians."

Eli Nott turned and grinned again as he walked.

"At least that's my interpretation. Then there were the missionaries following the miners in for the gold and silver. Con men, by and large. Couple were okay. Let's climb down here to that spot. See it?"

He moved like a goat down the winding slope. Steven fell in behind him.

"It's the argument in miniature, all right. Who knows? Sometimes the conflict that's supposed to be resolved by articles of faith, formal religion . . . well, sometimes they seem exacerbated by the process. Faith in somebody else's myth. Shit. I don't know. The whole fucking question is a bitch. I'm Reverend Eliphalet Nott, by the way. You're Steven Kearney. Did I say it right? Like Art Carney? 'Norton. Get over here.' "

"Steven Kearney. Right."

"Yeah. Here we are."

The footpath had ended in a lush green bank of grass. Beyond it the river rolled.

"Cool," Steven said. Reverend Eliphalet Nott looked at him.

"Cool." He laughed. "Yeah, man. It's cool."

He pulled a beer off the plastic stringer and handed one to Steven. He took one himself and put the others in a pocket of cold river water.

"Are you an actor, too?"

"No, I'm just a writer."

"That's wonderful. Being able to express yourself like that. It must be astounding to sit there and see your work come to life."

"Well . . . it might be."

Steven took out his notebook and pen.

"See . . . I'm trying to touch the general tone of the area and then . . . and then . . . get some . . . specifics, I guess," Steven said.

"So you need the specifics of the spiritual movement in Creedemore?"

"Well, I was hoping for some . . . you know, some general background."

Reverend Eliphalet Nott lay back on his elbows. "I'm thirty-two."

"You look younger."

"Yeah."

They sipped their beers.

"*General* background, huh? Okay. I guess you could say religious types flowed in here one after another for a variety of reasons. Some had faith. Some worked an angle. Spiritually, the Utes were a vastly superior people to the Europeans. They had grounding. They were always thanking something higher than themselves on the food chain for what they saw as their many blessings."

He took out a pipe and began to pack it with tobacco. "I'm going to smoke."

Steven took out a Marlboro. "I'm going to smoke, too."

Steven leaned against a boulder, and the Reverend Eliphalet Nott settled onto the grass, puffing out a nutty cherry aroma.

"This is not Episcopal territory. I've got nine regulars in my congregation. At any one time during the tourist season, it swells to between seventeen and twenty-five. I don't know why they keep me open. I suppose I'm a little embarrassing to the diocese. But you probably heard that."

"Uh . . . no . . . I just . . . well, I sort of just picked you out of the little Creedemore phone book."

The Reverend Eliphalet Nott sat up smiling. "I love that. I'm out of the phone book. See it's a—and I'm not being snide or putting it down—but it's a kind of silly thing, at least to me, this whole Protestant, Catholic, Jewish, Muslim, Buddhist, Hindu, on and on thing. I'm a soulist. A soulist. I've reached the conclusion that soul is life force or universal force and my calling is to minister to soul, without—and this is where the church goes nutty on me—without an actual belief in God. Or a literal interpretation of God. See? I worship the soul of Steven Kearney. I worship the soul of Eliphalet Nott. I do not worship God."

Steven popped another beer and sat next to him. Horses crossed the river above them where riffles proved shallow water, and he watched them. Reverend Nott lay all the way back and saw clouds.

"But you *are* a priest?" Steven asked.

"I am. And my father was and my grandfather, too, although he was more or less a slash-and-burner. Father's faith never faltered. His plan was to go to God in his own backyard. He taught that spiritual life was interwoven with these mountains, those aspens, the big trout, the bull elk. Pop had a . . . I guess a pastoral view. Now Papa, my grandfather, was your basic ball-busting ass kicker. A genuine prick by any account, although he was sweet to me and developed a genuine ministry here. He wasn't an Episcopalian. The original Reverend Eliphalet Nott was a little too rough around the edges, and he never skirted the issues. He'd say, 'Get the shit together, young men.' He'd say, 'Any damn ass can talk about God's way. It takes a man with cojones to follow it.' Papa was nondenominational. Kind of Puritan and Congregational. Tough mix. More Indians in church than miners."

"But you're Episcopal."

Reverend Eliphalet Nott puffed rapidly until tiny smoke signals popped out of the black briar. "I'm an Episcopalian. Although, as I say, I'm really a humanist—soulist—without portfolio."

"Can you be a minister and a . . ."

"Humanist-soulist?"

"Yes."

"Sure. That's exactly what I am." He puffed a little more and sat up. "Only I don't believe in God."

Steven noted this in blue ink. Somewhere, sometime, men rode into valleys on horses. Some believed and some did not. Some ministers were thieves. Some were real, at least in faith.

Reverend Eliphalet Nott watched Steven read what he had written. "Helpful?"

Steven shook his big fat face. "I guess even God up here isn't black and white."

"It's a fucking bitch, all right," Reverend Eliphalet Nott said, and the whole river smelled like cherries.

Miss Cassatt a autant de charme, mais elle a plus de force.

—Paul Gauguin

32

The young woman was nude. Her head was shaved completely on one side. The other was dyed gray. A harness she wore around her back and strapped to her waist and thighs was attached to a thick length of tugboat rope. She was suspended several feet above the observers, who struggled to see and not ogle.

"COCKSUCKERS!" she screamed.

The group of perhaps thirty people of varying ages mentally recorded her comments and moved to the next exhibit.

"MOTHERFUCKING ASSHOLES!" the swinging young lady screeched after them.

Roarke and Niki followed suit with the rest of their group, keeping their expressions passive.

"What was that one called?" Roarke whispered.

"That was . . . here . . . *Venus. Goddess of Love.*"

"What if she has to pee or something?"

"I'll bet she'd incorporate it into the piece."

"That's what I was afraid of."

Roarke wore chinos and a blue turtleneck. Niki dressed a little more formally in a MacGregor kilt and white blouse for their Saturday-afternoon excursion to the Tri-Annual New York Science of Art Exhibit at the Hunter College gymnasium.

"Who picks this shit?" Roarke asked out of the side of her mouth.

"Shhh."

The next display was a simple red telephone. Roarke stood behind an elderly, well-dressed couple. The man listened soberly for thirty or forty seconds, then handed the receiver to the woman, who nodded calmly at whatever was said. She smiled sweetly when she handed it to Roarke, who held it to her ear.

"You have your button on, don't you?" something rasped.

Roarke looked at the button that had to be pinned prominently on an article of clothing as a requisite for admission. It read I AM ASHAMED TO BE EUROPEAN-AMERICAN.

"How does it feel? You fucking piece-of-shit oppressor. We are going to kill you and eat your babies," a voice raged. Roarke held the phone out to Niki.

"Phone for you."

"Take a message," Niki said, and walked to the next exhibit, entitled Three Hundred Photographs of a Urine Trough at Yankee Stadium.

33

Marge Klinger listened with her head cradled in her left hand as Mountain Man Red Fields described the incident in the barbershop where a gun was pulled and the ambush on the Rio Grande. Her eyes shifted to Petey Myers, leaning against the auditorium wall to the left of the prosecution table. He had tried to separate the factions into a more homogeneous grouping by alternating admission to the building, but as soon as they were inside, they divided so that they were seated evenly on either side of the county court.

". . . and . . . well . . . it's like I told my fiancée, Felicia . . ."

Ticky's lawyer, Les Vallejos, jumped up. "Your Honor, can we have the facts without the romantic interlude?"

Ticky's side chuckled.

"No, Mr. Vallejos. I enjoy romantic interludes."

Mountain Man's side chuckled.

"Anyway . . . I said to Felicia that it was the most cowardly act of environmental sabotage I had ever—"

"Objection!" Les yelled.

Marge Klinger said, "Overruled."

Now there was a scattering of applause from Mountain Man's people.

"Who applauded?" she asked evenly.

No one raised a hand.

"No one applauded? Okay. Sheriff Myers, remove the back five rows of people from this side of the auditorium."

A rumble swelled from Mountain Man's gallery.

Marge Klinger banged her gavel twice. "Are you shooting for the clearing of the entire court?"

They grew quiet, and Petey and Bobby and Dan hustled the back sections out. Marge Klinger allowed the silence to settle as Petey closed the door after the last person.

"Quiet, isn't it?" she said, arranging some papers on her desk.

Some of the people nodded. No one made a sound. She folded her hands in front of her.

"If this were a civics class, I would point out that although the Creedemore Town Auditorium does not much resemble a courtroom, it is. It has become one. The state flag. The nation's flag. The right hand to God. We may observe but not disturb. We can do without game-show techniques, and indeed if you cannot play by my rules, then you will not play at all. Mr. Hockney?"

County Prosecutor Roger Hockney, an émigré from the Denver area, loathed the position fate had deposited him in. He was charged to bring the measure of the law against old Ticky Lettgo, a fellow landowner who maintained an immaculate property, and defend the rights of the yuppie John Wayne to float down any stretch of river he damned well felt like.

"Thank you, Your Honor. Continue, Mr. Fields."

"Yes . . . I was just saying how the Mountain Man adventure trips are geared toward protecting our environment. And then . . . well . . . then he tried to kill us."

Marge Klinger could actually hear teeth grinding among Ticky's supporters, but no one spoke. Prosecutor Roger Hockney about gagged.

"Thank you, Mr. Fields."

Petey Myers looked over at Ticky's table. He had fallen asleep, and Les Vallejos was deep in conversation with his secretary and wife, Marny. Petey scanned the auditorium now, drawn to the shining head of Molly Dowie, looking tiny at the end of one of Mountain Man's rows. There was Albert's girl, Skyo, next to her, and her dad across the aisle. Miss Wilma Kirk stood in the back. Maybe she wasn't taking sides, or maybe she had bigger fish to fry. Petey always thought there was a bigger picture to everything, and Miss Wilma Kirk saw it. Reedy spoke of an overview. Reedy had the overview. Him and Miss Kirk.

Roger Hockney called his string of witnesses for the prosecution, and Les Vallejos made notes, occasionally conferring with his pretty wife. Ticky slept with a disconcerting deadness. By the time the fourth young man from the Colorado Springs Zion Bible Institute told the exact same terrifying tale of loss and redemption, it was twelve-thirty, and Marge Klinger thought this would be an excellent time to pause.

The cowboys sauntered out damp and sluggish in that easy gait Petey knew as real and dangerous. Reedy would love these guys. Skyo and Molly looked out of place with the Boulder crowd. Petey stood left of the top outside step and watched them. The Liberty Society of Colorado, formed again into ranks in their green-and-brown uniforms, and immediately the banners appeared. How, Petey wondered, could these cockhounds come to the conclusion that he had "murdered" the "two unarmed children" up by Brown's Lake? Not that it bothered him, really, or Vi either for that matter. After Boston, after that abortion parade with the jars of babies, nothing could upset you, but it still amazed him to realize that these people really believed this shit. He shook his head.

Most of the free-river group had brought picnic supplies, and in a few minutes the parking lot and slopes around it resembled state fairgrounds. The cowboys stood sullen and chew-filled by ratty pickups. Ticky had extended his nap inside the courthouse, while Mountain Man lunched under the banner of the Liberty Society of Colorado. Skyo brought some sandwiches and soda over to Albert and Jude. Molly Dowie walked over with her.

"Mom made some sandwiches out of the pork roast," Skyo said.

Albert and Jude took them.

"Thanks, Skyo," Jude said. "Hi, Mrs. Dowie."

"Hi, Jude. Hi, Albert."

"How are you, Molly?"

"Okay. Hey, I just told Skyo I was thinking of coming up to Ute Ranch to sketch that view down to the reservoir."

Albert held up a finger and chewed his food until he could swallow it.

"Janice would love the company. Call her first so she can plan to go with you."

"I will."

Mel Prophit and his lug of a son, JoJo, slid over next to them. JoJo was a tall version of his pop, without the signature belly. Petey watched them looming. Jude took a big bite of sandwich and nodded at the men. Albert ignored them.

"No fraternizing with the enemy," Mel said.

"What?" Jude asked.

"Daddy wasn't talking to you," JoJo clarified.

Jude shrugged and smiled at Skyo.

"Mel, this is my daughter, Skyo, and Molly Dowie. This is Mel Prophit," Albert said.

Mel kept his hat on and thumbs locked under his thick brown belt. He didn't look at the women. Jude thought he might have heard JoJo snicker at the name Skyo. Maybe not. Petey wished he could hear what that cockhound Prophit was saying.

"I'm dead serious."

Albert watched him. "About what?"

"About fraternization. Now, we all got people we know over there, but if we give an inch, these bastards gonna take a mile."

"I'd appreciate a man watching his language around womenfolk."

"And I'd appreciate the womenfolk going back over to their own side, JoJo."

JoJo had a look of high authority as he reached past Jude and took Skyo by the arm. As he tried for Molly Dowie, Jude took JoJo's thumb, bent it back to the wrist, slammed his heel onto the toe of JoJo's alligator boots, and delivered a short, mean right-handed punch that turned him around before he fell. A second and a half had passed in Jersey time.

Petey had seen it coming from the step and was pushing past the crowd to get to the confrontation.

"JoJo!" Mel screamed.

"Aww, man," Jude said.

"He attacked my boy!"

"Aww, gee."

Jude bent down.

"Don't touch him! You hit him with a sucker punch! You're a bad boy!"

Albert saw Petey coming. "Skyo, you and Jude go back to the ranch now."

Jude was reluctant but allowed himself to be led away. Molly knelt next to Mel and his semiconscious boy. The cowboys crowded in closer to the scene, and, like a general law of physical science, this brought a reacting surge from across the parking lot. The Liberty Society rushed out from under their green-and-brown banners, drawing the rest of the free-river group with them.

"They've damned near killed my boy," moaned Mel.

The cowboys assumed the worst, and a protective barricade of jangled western nerves encircled the fallen Texan. The Liberty Society saw Molly corralled and huddled on the enemy side.

"Someone's down in there!" a bearded man, about sixty, in the colors of the Liberty Society, shouted.

"It's a woman!" someone shouted.

"For God's sake, it's a woman!"

"My boy! JoJo!"

Petey pushed through to Mel.

"They half near killed him!" screamed Mel.

By now the members of the Liberty Society were nose to nose with the cowboys.

"Now, everybody just back off!" shouted Petey, raising both his hands. "Bobby, get these people back."

Before Bobby could move, someone on some side threw some punch. Now both groups closed in a communal push and pull and punch. Screams rang out, and dust puffed up from the parking lot. Petey was dumbfounded. Fights were everywhere. Tourists looked out their windows the way they'd look at foraging bears in Yellowstone. A car was tipped on its side. A trash bin was set on fire.

"Bobby!" Petey shouted over the din. "Get some staties. Get the sheriff at South Fork, too. Jesus God Almighty."

Albert was knocked woozy by a rock and went down on one knee. Petey got him onto his feet and sat him in the county Jeep. Molly tried to back out of the brawl, but a surge of upwardly mobile supporters of Mountain Man pushed her back as they moved to outflank the enemy.

"Molly! Over here!"

She turned and saw Steven Kearney straddling the motor scooter.

"Over here!"

She squeezed her way to him and held his shirt while he walked the scooter to the head of the mining road. Then he started it and puttered Molly and himself up Bachelor Creek. They could still hear the battle over the sound of the little motor when they turned onto the jeep trail.

It wasn't until they pulled in front of her house in the rock and Steven shut off the motor that he realized her head was lying between his shoulder blades. She did not move for a long moment, and then he felt her push herself up and off the back of the scooter.

"Tired," she said, steadying herself with one hand on the scooter seat.

"You didn't get hit or anything?"

"No." She smiled slightly. "I'm just all beat-to-shit tired, I guess."

Molly Dowie put her arm around his shoulder and closed her eyes. "Just help me to the door."

The door opened before he reached it, and the young redhead came out.

"Molly. Jesus."

"She's . . . tired," Steven said.

"I'll take her. Jesus, Molly."

Steven let him slide his hand around her waist and walk her in. He stood at the door and watched the young man ease Molly into a blue recliner. He glanced up at Steven.

"Thanks. I've got her."

Steven stepped back and closed the door, wondering exactly what could have made her so exhausted. He wondered if it was the treatments she

137

mentioned and if her shiny head was part of it and if the young conquistador was her husband and how old she was. He walked to his motor scooter and sat thinking for a few minutes. Then, over the muted sounds of the distant fight, over the burble of Bachelor Creek, Steven heard five distinct gunshots.

34

Micky had slept well, bolt upright in his chair in the court. He dreamed of walking a line across his daddy's lower pasture with his brother and Uncle Phil on his right and Daddy on his left. The men had shotguns. Ticky at twelve and George at nine had birdshot in their .22s. They were two hundred feet apart and scuffing as they walked to shake up the grouse and see if they'd rise. Daddy had said, "Here it is," and maybe half a dozen come up, and Ticky got two. That night Mama got all the birdshot out and cooked them all in a clay pot, with greens and Mexican rice. And then Ticky came back and was old, and was alone in the court. It came to him that he was on trial and there was no one here. Outside, muffled by the heavy auditorium doors, he picked up a rumble, a bellow, the faintest smells of Mama and her kitchen. Then the smells were all gone, and the in-between was now. He turned in the direction of the doors. After a moment he turned back and remembered that Petey Myers had removed his Colt, put it in a paper bag, and placed it under the Mexican lawyer's chair. Ticky squatted down and brought the bag up to the table. It was heavy. Heavier than he remembered. But everything was. Smells. Air. Hats.

"Minnie," he said loudly, and turned. "Old girl?"

He blinked dryly and nodded to himself. Minnie was with Vi. Minnie wasn't saying much. In fact, Minnie was in bed with the marine pin he'd put on the pillow, and she wasn't talking at all. He took the brown-handled Colt .45 out of the paper bag and slipped it into the holster he still wore. Slung low, the tip of the barrel seemed thicker than his thigh. He walked to the doors. He took a deep breath, and oxygen squeezed into blood and flowed to things remembered and things forgotten. He pushed with difficulty through the high doors.

The parking lot was undulating in conflict like a breeze over cornstalks. Ticky swayed with them. From the auditorium steps, the entire parking lot heaved anarchy.

"What the hell?" he yelled weakly.

Now the sounds of struggle exhaled into a single wafting moan.

"What the hell, I said."

Ticky Lettgo pulled the old Colt out of its holster, pointed it into the air with both hands, and fired it five times until the chamber was empty. The parking lot became still, and in an instant only the crackle of burning trash bins filled the high mountain air.

Ticky looked out to where Petey Myers stood with Bobby.

"What the hell?" he said.

Most history is guessing and the rest is prejudice.

—Will Durant, *Our Oriental Heritage*

35

At 7:50 P.M., Steven left the Historical Society's offices with the drawing of the dramatic arc and a folder of notes and crossed the deserted street to the Creedemore Hotel. Built in 1895, the creaky, four-story wooden structure was the centerpiece of Creedemore society.

Terrible Linnet Colton, the poker cheat reputed to have five nipples, lived on the top floor until her death in 1911, and Bat Masterson killed the Chinese assassin Ling Lo in the kitchen in '05. Katharine Hepburn was rumored to have dined there, as was Howard Hughes. Joe Namath's picture hung over the reception desk. A heavyset woman with a big smile and a rawhide skirt met Steven in the foyer.

"Dinner? Check-in?"

"No, ma'am, I'm supposed to go to a meeting here."

"Historical, right?"

"Right."

"Through the double doors, other side of the dining room. And you have yourself a nice meeting."

The room was wallpapered a grayish red. Six round tables were arranged on a crimson rug. Each table had six chairs. The farthest one from the doors, set right in front of a small podium, was occupied by four people. Miss Wilma Kirk in her khaki safari outfit was one of them.

"Mr. Kearney, come in, come in. We were just talking about you."

She introduced Tom Zaleski of the Creedemore Hardware Store, Les Valle-jos, a Puerite County attorney with offices in Lake City, and Peter Walloon of the Orvis Fly Shop.

"There's more, but with less commitment to the cause," Miss Kirk said with a shrug.

The Historical Committee sat back down. Steven remained standing by Miss Kirk, who gestured for him to begin. He unfolded the dramatic arc and held it facing the committee.

"This is a dramatic arc."

"Ahhhh," intoned Miss Wilma Kirk.

"It's a sort of general arc. It's got the . . . you know . . . various things that happened in Creedemore. Actually, some things that happened before it was Creedemore."

"Before what was Creedemore?" Tom Zaleski asked.

"The . . . land."

Les Vallejos got to the point. "So it's general?"

"Yes, sir."

"And you're going to fill in the blanks?"

"Yes."

"I see you have conquistadors mentioned."

Tom rolled his eyes. "C'mon, Les."

"I was just curious as to how they will be portrayed."

Steven looked over to Miss Kirk. "Well . . . I'm not sure."

"You're not sure?" Les asked lawyerly.

"I'm in the process of discovering the conquistadors."

"So it's an ongoing process, then?"

"Yes."

"I'm sure you will find them noble. True believers. Perhaps the greatest adventurers who ever lived."

Tom Zaleski guffawed. "Ask the Indians how noble they were."

"What Indians?" Les asked pleasantly. "The great Kit Carson slaughtered them all."

"Not true."

Les turned back to Steven. "The town of Del Norte had been inundated by a tent city of miners in the late 1800s. They couldn't enter this valley because of the Utes."

"Baloney."

"It's in the history books. Of course, Mr. Zaleski's people were still in Poland."

"Yugoslavia."

"Anyway, Del Norte promised Carson and his vigilantes twenty dollars an ear."

"Really?" Steven asked stupidly.

"So they come slaughtering in—"

"Les?" Miss Kirk said.

"One sec, Miss Kirk. They come into our valley and get every Ute left that Meeker's people hadn't gotten five years before."

Tom jumped up. "The damn redskins butchered the man's family."

"He was an evil man."

"Who says?"

"I do."

"Well, there you go."

"When is Ute Days this year anyway?" Peter Walloon from the fly shop asked sleepily.

Miss Kirk checked her notebook and closed it with a slap for emphasis. "The Saturday before the pageant."

"What pageant?" Tom asked.

"The play."

" 'Cause a pageant's about Christ, right?"

"That's a passion play," Steven said.

"Ute Days was great last year," Peter said. "I moved just about every fly from my factory."

"It's your basement, Peter," Les corrected. "Hardly a factory."

"You know what I meant. Say, Les, I heard the judge has ordered in the National Guard."

"I heard she's moving the trial to Denver," said Tom.

"Wrong and wrong."

"How is your wife?" Miss Kirk asked Les.

"Marny took a right cross from one of those environmentalists. Eye swoll shut. She says she connected on two good kicks. Evened out, I guess. No, Marge Klinger asked for half a dozen state troopers and is closing the court to the gallery. Where were we? Yes. Carson takes the ears into Del Norte for his twenty dollars per, and the mayor tells him that he misunderstood the deal. It was for two dollars an ear. Carson burned Del Norte to the ground and killed the mayor."

"Says who?"

"The history books say."

"Well, there you go."

Molly Dowie hurried into the room. She had an old, torn cardigan over her overalls. "I'm sorry. I fell asleep. I can't believe it."

"Molly, you know everyone?" asked Miss Kirk.

"Hi, Les. Hi, Tom. Hi, Peter. Hello, Mr. . . . ."

"Kearney," helped Miss Kirk.

"Hello," Molly said.

"Mr. Kearney was giving his presentation. We've looked at your planned montage for the side of the market, and we unanimously give you the go-ahead."

"Oh, great." Molly smiled. She looked at Steven and, taking off her hat, patted her bald head. The committee applauded and smiled.

"Of course, your wonderful mural will have the needed technical adjustments, but we're all excited to see it realized," Les said.

Molly watched the lawyer carefully. "What technical adjustments?"

"Well . . . the conquistador, of course." Les Vallejos took up the largest drawing from the pile in front of Miss Kirk. "He's not Spanish."

Tom Zaleski groaned.

Molly studied her drawing as if seeing it for the first time.

"You know what, Les?" Molly said finally. "You're right. What I was going for was the youthfulness. A vibrancy. It's the model I used. But yeah, I'll find a Hispanic kid. Good point."

Les bowed. Steven stared at the conquistador. Miss Kirk smiled.

"Would you care to continue, Mr. Kearney?"

Steven thought, No, I would not care to continue. I do not like towns that beat each other up and girls that do not remember my name. He wished Roarke were around. Another stupid thing. Coming here. Another mistake.

"I'm forty-eight," he said.

"What?" Miss Kirk asked.

"I'm . . . uh . . . what I'm planning to do and . . . what I've been doing a little, actually, is . . . is interview a bunch of people and get an overall perspective of your valley and write it . . . up. And write it up, you know, in dialogue. Maybe, I don't know, maybe a narrator and . . . uh . . ."

He hung for a moment, his brain waves in mountain doldrums.

"Mr. Kearney calls it a 'word-mural,' " Molly said.

Steven looked up at her.

"Mr. Kearney's been experimenting with a new form. I think I've got it right, Mr. Kearney, so you stop me if I'm explaining it wrong, but against the backdrop of Cathedral Rock and my mural on the side of the supermarket, the story Mr. Kearney will tell unfolds as a marrying of fine art and performing art."

"Brilliant," Miss Wilma Kirk said. "Any questions for Mr. Kearney?"

"Who have you chosen to interview for the Hispanic perspective?" asked Les.

"Nobody yet."

"Well, I will make myself available at your convenience."

"Okay. Great."

Tom Zaleski stood and hitched up his jeans. "I can give you some skinny on the cowboys and the . . . hardware that tamed the valley."

"Thanks."

Peter Walloon yawned. "I'll take you fishing."

"Well, that's great."

Miss Wilma Kirk gathered the mural drawings, handed them over to

Molly, and the meeting adjourned. A few minutes later, Molly, Steven, and Miss Kirk stood on the plank sidewalk in front of the Historical Society. The acrid smell of still-smoldering trash bins overwhelmed the sweetness of mountain air. Miss Kirk looked grave, and her voice took on a confidential tone.

"I needn't tell you both that today's disaster has raised the stakes considerably. Is it the rule of fists and guns? Is it legalese and politics? Is it true that art has become irrelevant?"

She let the questions go out into the stinky night. "I believe," she said with a squeeze of their arms, "that art can save the world from itself."

Miss Kirk held them in her hard little hands for a moment and then walked to her Volkswagen. They watched it roll out of the parking lot that hours earlier had been a battleground.

Molly Dowie looked up. "Stars."

Steven looked at her. Her head was flung back so her face flattened to the sky. Holding her drawings with both hands made her seem even more waifish. He looked up again.

"You don't see stars like that in New York. I've been there in the fall, and you don't see them," she said.

"There's some. Roarke thinks that every plane she sees is a star."

"Is Roarke your wife?"

"No."

"Girlfriend, then, huh? She say 'cool,' too?"

"How come you forgot my name?"

"What?"

"It's Steven Kearney." He fumbled a cigarette out of its pack and lit it.

"I know your name," she said.

He was embarrassed and looked up at the stars in a silent change of subject, but he felt her watching.

"Miss Kirk jumped in before I said it. What's the big deal? I got to sit."

Molly sat on the wooden sidewalk with her feet in the street. She pulled her bowler hat down lower. Steven thought she could disappear under it. She leaned a little into his leg.

"Tired," she said.

He looked down at her bowler.

"I'm done with it now, but it still knocks me out."

"Done with what?"

"Chemo."

"Chemotherapy?"

"Breast. This one here," she said, brushing the back of her hand over her heart. "They took it off."

Steven watched her hat.

"That's my story."

She stayed against his leg, and they were quiet together. A bark rang sadly above Cathedral Rock.

"Coyotes," she said.

"I like the way the conquistador looks."

"Les was right. He doesn't look Spanish."

"He looks Irish."

"You think?"

"Uh-huh."

"He worries about me with the chemo. He's been coming up every weekend, sometimes during the week. I figured I'd use him for the model. I bet I've drawn him a thousand times."

She smiled to herself.

"I had him there," she said, pointing to the Creedemore Hotel. "Room 216. My boyfriend had split. I was alone in the rock house. It was February. Snow. Cold. I was ashamed to call home. I-told-you-so's. That stuff . . ."

Another coyote. Then more, until they echoed things he had never heard.

"I had no idea what was going on. I'm in the rock house. Others all gone or not friendly or passing through like my boyfriend. Scary. I bet there's maybe twenty coyotes singing up there."

"Singing?"

"Hey, man, that's a song. Listen."

He did.

"Cool," he said after a crescendo.

She looked up at him and shook her head. "So here come my folks."

"Where?"

"I mean then. I'm in the rock house. Before I figured how to heat the thing. February. Out to here with Willie. And here they come. Moved me down to the hotel. All smiles and kisses. I was pretty stupid."

"Well . . . lots of . . . I know lots of girls who . . . you know . . . got pregnant when . . ."

"I don't mean that kind of stupid. That was the best thing I ever did. Willie's . . . he's Willie, but making all those assumptions about my folks. I was stupid."

Molly shifted away from his leg, and he sat down next to her. When he spoke, he surprised himself.

"My father had another family after me. He left Mother. I never made assumptions about them. But I think I've been stupid about almost everything. I mean, I'm kind of a failure, although I still write, and I guess that I still write means I'm not a failure. I tell myself that. When you finish a painting, it stands there. It's there. How people react to it is their business. I can't get my writing to stand there. Other people have to help it stand. Poetry and novels and plays and stories. I mean, I just don't know."

"Maybe we're not supposed to know."

He thought about that and said, under the coyotes' refrain, "Cool."

36

By 10:00 A.M. Saturday, the ABC and CBS news affiliates from Denver had set up broadcast positions in the parking lot of the Creedemore Hotel. PBS in Colorado Springs assigned two reporters, and the Egalitarian Radio Network sent a radical Marxist feminist with green hair and a pierced tongue. Six highway patrol cars were stationed in the county parking lot, with two troopers in each one. Petey Myers parked his Jeep, nodded to the officers, and walked into the station. Bobby handed him a cup of coffee.

"Hey," Bobby said.

"Hey. How long have they been here?"

"Hour, about."

Petey sipped the triple-boiled brew. Peeked through the blinds.

"You offer them some coffee?"

"Yup."

"And?"

"Had their own."

Petey sat down. "Staties are all the same. Keep to themselves. Once, in Duxbury, maybe '79, maybe '80, me and Reedy by pure accident pull over this blue van. Didn't have inspection stickers. While I'm writing this cockhound up, Reedy thinks he hears someone in the back. He says, 'Open the side door.' Cockhound says he knows his rights. Reedy pulls the guy's sorry dago ass through the side window. I open up the panel. Two little boys. Hog-tied. Now, the staties were looking for the cockhound, only we got him. Still, they make a big deal about him losing the eye and the punctured lung and the ruptured nuts and how Reedy and me almost compromised their case. Well, that fucker did not do as ordered. We only told the bad guys once. But see, the staties wanted credit themselves. Tough, though. Make a new pot of coffee."

Mel Prophit swaggered in and stood at parade rest in front of Petey's desk. Petey leaned back on two chair legs.

"Good morning, Mr. Prophit."

"I'm here to press charges. And I shouldn't even have to. That little bastard attempted to murder JoJo."

"Jude McCormick."

"Albert Overstreet's hired hand. I'm here to press the charge of attempted murder."

Petey looked over to Bobby, standing next to the coffee machine.

"Bobby? Make it half decaf and half high test."

"Yes, sir."

"Mr. Prophit, I talked to the rescue squad and the emergency-room physician in Del Norte, and they both say he'll live."

"Well, hell, sure he'll live. If he wasn't going to live, it'd be flat-out murder."

"I mean, he's got . . . what? Couple of loose teeth and a torn ligament in his thumb."

"The boy's foot's all swollen. Here. And here. Now, are you going to let me press charges or what?"

Petey looked at the angry Texan, then walked over to a file cabinet. He came back to the desk with two forms, white and blue. He handed them both to Mel.

"Fill the white one out now, and I'll send Bobby over to arrest him."

Mel leaned smugly on the desk and began to answer the questions in ink.

After a couple of moments, Petey said, "Then you take the blue one home to JoJo so's he can give his side to the sexual-assault charges being filed by Mrs. Dowie and Skyo Overstreet."

Mel straightened up. "Sexual . . . what the hell . . . ? What?"

"I'm going to be straight with you, Mr. Prophit. I know JoJo's a good boy, but he did touch those women. I saw it. Now, I've talked to them early this morning," he lied, "and I just gave them hell about it, and they both backed off, but when Bobby takes that McCormick kid off the ranch in chains . . . well . . . it's going to happen."

"He never . . . Jesus, now . . ."

"I don't blame you being upset, but it's a woman's world."

Mel looked down at the white report form. He picked it up, crumpled it, and left.

* * *

Saturday, late afternoon, after the second interview of the day, Steven rode the motor scooter to the Historical Society, put the small tape recorder on the desk, and listened to what he had.

First, Brian Trujillo, seventy-nine. Retired truck mechanic and legendary county trout man. Albert had told Steven that the old man could be found every morning, precisely at 5:30 A.M., parked in his blue Chevy pickup at the public fishing water next to the Lettgo property. He didn't fish anymore, but he knew the big river and watched it closely. Steven fumbled with the recorder before capturing Brian's hard-cut Anglo-Hispanic accent:

BRIAN TRUJILLO
. . . and . . . uh . . . but you'd have to include Ray Highridge in that . . .

STEVEN
Highridge?

BRIAN TRUJILLO
That would be Highridge. Yes. White man's name applied to the last—strike that, son—*our* last Ute. But this is a fishing recounting, and I'm swearing it's the truth.

STEVEN
Can I record this? I'm recording this.

BRIAN TRUJILLO
If you want.

STEVEN
Great.

BRIAN TRUJILLO
Ready?

STEVEN
Yes, sir.

BRIAN TRUJILLO
Nineteen thirty-one, it was. I'm pretty sure because that was the year Armando Feiccabrini, who was in the payment department of my dad's Chevrolet dealership, absconded with almost eighty dollars in receipts and was killed a day later in Latimore. That summer my dad and his dad and brother Roberto and Wawa, his girl who he later married, and me, too, had come up into Creedemore for the trout. Wawa did the cooking, and the boys fanned out across the Rio Grande probably around where Texas Creek comes into the fat pool by Camp's Lower Ranch. Know it?

STEVEN

No, sir.

BRIAN TRUJILLO

Don't you fish?

STEVEN

I'm planning on learning.

(A long pause.)

Sir? Is there anything the matter?

BRIAN TRUJILLO

Don't you have to know what you write about?

STEVEN

Well, there's several schools of thought on that. Some pretty accomplished writers work solely from their interpretations or ideas of how things work.

BRIAN TRUJILLO

No matter. So we fan out across the big river, as I say, and start fishing up. We go up in crossover casts, one throw at a time. Dad and his dad and his brother Silvio were fishing western. Okay? Are we . . . ? Is this picking me up? Should I have a microphone?

STEVEN

It's very powerful.

BRIAN TRUJILLO

Where was I?

STEVEN

Uh . . . your dad . . .

BRIAN TRUJILLO

They're rigged up western. A nymph trailing a dry fly. I'm pretty traditional, even then. I've got the predecessor of the House and Lot. Some rises. Swirls. When, honest to God now, Silvio stops and says, "I'm gonna fish downstream," only he said it in Spanish. My old grandfather, now—

Oh, Jee . . . sus, I was wincing, I'm telling you, and over my bookcase now is his rod. He gave it to me. Montgomery Ward Bamboo. Anyway, old Grandfather says, "Why, Jee . . . sus, what a thing to say, and Brian is only a kid. Downstream? Kid shouldn't hear that. 'YOU CANNOT CATCH DOWNSTREAM!' " Now, Silvio and my dad were not ever disrespectful to the old man, but Silvio says, "Here I go."

(A long pause.)

I see it like yesterday. He'd have to use a loop-de-loop cast instead of the crossover cast and the rocks all disturbed. But he does it. Dow stream! Wow! You make sure you get that in your play. Nobody'll believe it!

(End of interview.)

Steven switched off the recorder and reflected on Brian Trujillo as a kind of Everyman speaking in tongues. There was in the rich cadence of his voice a surety, a specific identification with the pivotal river. If only he could have been slightly clearer, perhaps his metaphor had a place in the drama. Steven made a series of notes and switched the recorder back on to his interview with John Torrey of Torrey's Rocks and Things.

STEVEN

It's . . . it's on, I think. Testing—one—two . . . I'm pretty sure it's on. It's turning.

(A long pause follows. Some noise.)

JOHN TORREY

My name is John Torrey of Torrey's Rocks and Things, located between the Municipal Building and Norm's Standard Oil. I will . . . I will now read a brief history of the Weminuche Range and environs. I will condense the Mesozoic era, skip the Paleozoic era, and illuminate the Cenozoic era.

(A long pause. Papers. Noise.)

Could we shut it off a second? I can't find— Shit. Where is the fucking paper? I delivered a similar lecture at Rockhound West, and I can't believe I've lost the fu—

(The recorder is snapped off. Then on.)

STEVEN
It's on.

JOHN TORREY
It's on?

STEVEN
It's on.

JOHN TORREY
Uh . . . except to point out the flatness as the oceans approached and the softness of the sedimentary rocks it brought, not to mention the falling back of the seas, leaving giant marshes and sea sponges . . . here . . . see? Fossil proof.

STEVEN
Cool.

JOHN TORREY
Unisex flowers and . . . oh, no trees or vegetation . . . and that's like five hundred million years, and then we're in Mesozoic, which was, like, a hundred million years. The Colorado Plateau rose up, and dinosaurs were all over the place. And giant ferns and cycads and horsetails and cedars and yews and . . . Now volcanic eruptions signaled the Cenozoic era . . . sixty or so million years long—I'm condensing the report. . . . I dwelt . . . I dwelt . . . on the Paleozoic era in it, and I'm . . . I'm condensing. . . .

STEVEN
Cool.

JOHN TORREY
So the volcanoes and the ice sheet cut valleys and killed everything, and we start over again—not an era, mind you. A period, more or less. A Tertiary period. I mean, the land hasn't changed at all from when the Indians . . . the Native Americans . . .

(A long pause.)

Rocks are my passion.

STEVEN
Cool. It's really interesting.

JOHN TORREY
Quartz, feldspar . . .

STEVEN
Cool.

JOHN TORREY
Crystals . . .

STEVEN
Uhhh . . .

JOHN TORREY
Fossils . . .

(Sound of recorder switching off.)

Steven tapped his pen against his fat head. A swirl of images bounced around the tight parameter of his brain. He left the office and scootered up Bachelor Creek, letting the engine run in front of her house, as a kind of announcement. He had never beeped the tinny horn of the scooter. Now he did. In a moment she stood in the red-framed doorway. She had a white-and-blue flannel shirt on under her baggy overalls. She wore no shoes or hat.

"Kearney!" she shouted. "I wanted to get your name out."

He laughed and shut off the engine but remained straddling the scooter.

"I didn't forget it, you know. Really. What's up?"

"I just . . . you know, I did some interviews today, and then I started to take some notes—plot notes—and . . . I mean . . . I'm feeling good about the work."

"That's great."

"How are you?"

"I've been resting up. I'm starting the mural on Monday."

"All alone?"

"Sure."

The narrow canyon fell into semidarkness. She appeared smaller in the doorway.

"It gets dark quick, doesn't it?"

She shrugged and pushed her hands into her pockets.

"Want to have dinner with me?" he asked.

"I've got beans on."

"That's cool. Maybe we can have dinner tomorrow."

"You mean, like a date?"

"Well, I was . . . going to pay for it. Although we could go dutch treat."

The creek grew louder. Coyotes were singing again, only closer.

"I've got cancer. I've got one breast."

"That's cool."

"Who says 'cool' anymore? I'm all beat to shit. How old are you again?"

"I'm forty-eight."

She walked onto her tiny lawn and said too loudly, "You're forty-eight."

One coyote hit a high note and held it until the others reached for it, too.

"I'm pretty mad," she said.

"Why?"

"Why do you think?"

"One breast?"

"Jesus."

"Oh, the cancer, too, I mean."

She watched him a beat and then walked back into the rock.

The coyotes dropped their sorrowful call a full octave. Suddenly Steven slung his head back and joined the instinctive moan, the essential sad song.

37

icky finished the cigarette, hacked once, and dropped the Camel butt into a #10 can he kept on the porch filled with sand. He looked across to Blade Rock, made orangey by the morning sun, and listened to the shimmy of the river below, where it rushed in a quick four-foot drop. He fought the urge to talk out loud to himself. He had so much on his thinker that if he didn't watch it, he'd be having five conversations at once with just himself, like some nutcases he had known.

Minnie was still not talking. She watched the window from the bed, and she sipped the nice chicken and rice soup Vi brought over. Ticky kept talking to her when he was there. He kept talking as if nothing were odd about all this goddamn not-talking business. That was okay then, to talk out loud when he was in the bedroom with Minnie, even if she didn't answer back. But porch talking was wrong. That was for the nutcases.

Ticky moved into the house, across the living room, and up the clean pine stairs like a man in a hurry. These days he found he had an ongoing discussion with his legs to get them going. To move with authority. He called it "noggin energy" and was getting and going by order of Mr. Gray Brain. Otherwise he imagined himself stopping in midstep and just standing there until he keeled over. He slipped off his quilted bathrobe as he entered the bedroom and went directly to his closet. Minnie watched him.

"Good morning, Mrs. Lettgo."

He pulled pressed jeans, blue work shirt, red bolo tie, and the white Lettgo Feed 'n' Seed jacket and laid them on the foot of the bed.

"I'm gonna let Vi poach you up your eggs. Soon as Petey brings her."

Minnie watched him, cocking her head to the left on the pillow and then to the right until she got comfortable. Ticky pulled off his Batman pajama top and put on a fresh T-shirt.

"The little Mexican, that Les Vallejos, thinks that they'll get finished telling their side and maybe I can start telling mine today or tomorrow. I don't know."

He turned his back when he dropped his Batman bottoms. Minnie thought how there was no rear in his end, and she smiled. He pulled up fresh cotton boxers.

"Petey Myers was a marine. Did you know? He told me on the way into town. Out of town, maybe. I told him, I said, 'My Jefferson was in the Corps,' and he said he knew because of your pin. He said he knew other marine mothers."

He put on his blue shirt and buttoned it all the way up to the neck. She felt for the pin on the pillow and pinched it.

"If I get the opportunity—and Les Vallejos thinks I just might—then I am going to give them holy hell today."

He pulled up his fresh jeans and hitched them for battle. Somewhere, in the heavy, faded blue cotton, his old legs floated. His knees dryly swiveled. His waist rising to the armpits. He turned toward her and slipped on his Feed 'n' Seed cap.

"All's I need is opportunity, old girl."

She felt she was letting a little grin out of a box but wasn't sure what her pillowed head showed. Finally she decided there was a flatness to the grin, so that maybe nothing played across the small gray mug. He fidgeted with his string tie, and she knew he would never slow down enough to consider half of the things she'd been considering in her soft retreat. She saw his feet going even at a standstill. His spindly fingers opening and closing as if motion itself were the answer to all paramount questions. The answer being not to think of them. To be in the today of things. But today seemed remote to Minnie.

"Okay, Mrs. Lettgo, I'm going to scout out Petey on the porch."

Ticky turned in the doorway, and their eyes held. He stood as still as he could and knew somehow where she was and how easy it would be to go there, too.

"I still got some hell to give, old girl. I love you."

Minnie smiled, and this time she knew it was on her face.

* * *

Twenty minutes later Petey Myers dropped off Vi to Minnie-sit and drove Ticky into Creedemore. A convoy of eight pickups fell in behind them.

"Jesus," Petey muttered, checking his rearview.

Ticky was silent.

"What I'll do now, Ticky, is come up behind the Western Market and park behind the Municipal Building."

Ticky looked straight ahead and was still except for his fingers moving in a separate life.

"It's a zoo. Reedy would say we've got a 'nonsectarian day at the beach.' Staties. TV boys. Green-haired women. Don't let it throw you. Marge Klinger's not letting the cockhounds on either side of the fence in, but they'll all be around, so you should know."

Ticky thought that maybe Minnie needed to get back to the Feed 'n' Seed. Maybe vacation time is over. A small red motor scooter came into sight going in the other direction. A large man with a knapsack straddled it ridiculously. Ticky and Petey watched him.

"Anyway," Petey said, "just don't let it throw you."

Petey snuck the county Jeep behind the building, but the back door was locked and he couldn't get anyone's attention on the inside, so they had to walk around front. Cheers and jeers rang out at the sight of Ticky and the sheriff. The Liberty Society's banners sprang up passionately, with a tangential chant of "Baby killer." The Liberty Society had markedly dressed down for the cameras. They still sported the green-and-brown combinations but now favored ripped or faded cords and jeans and the dirty, raggy T-shirts of the oppressed. The cowboys had gone to their finery, many even wearing black Sunday waistcoats and their best hats and boots. As Ticky concentrated on a purposeful stride up the Municipal Building's steps, he was met by the press. Ticky looked startled and furrowed his eyebrows and felt for his .45. Petey had left it under the car seat. Marge Klinger's orders, he had explained.

"Mr. Lettgo. Is that really your name?" a pretty blonde holding a microphone asked.

"What?"

"Were you trying to kill them?" a man yelled.

"Trying . . . ?"

Petey pushed in. "Folks, please. This is—"

"What the hell . . . ?" shouted Ticky.

"But you were trying to kill them."

"If I—"

"Those were real bullets. You're reputed to be a great shot."

"Reputed? What?"

"National Public Radio, Mr. Lettgo. You say it's all yours, then? Yours alone."

"Petey?"

"You say even the air is—"

"Folks, we have to—"

Now a green-haired reporter leaped in front of Petey. Pearl pins flashed on her tongue.

"Hey, asshole. If they weren't both black, you'da never shot them. Racist! RACIST!" Bobby pulled them inside.

"Who the fuck locked the back door?" Petey shouted.

"Me. Those TV guys were putting on disguises and trying to get into the auditorium."

"Jesus. Get Ticky some coffee. Les here?"

"Everybody's in with Judge Klinger."

"Okay, you stay with Ticky, I'll go see what's up."

Marge Klinger was in her temporary chambers in the county registrar's office. Roger Hockney and Les Vallejos were with her.

"He's here," Petey said.

"We heard," Marge said dryly. "I was just saying to Roger and Les how I wish I hadn't let them talk me into a non-jury deal."

Les laughed. "We talked you into it?"

"Whatever. Tell me again."

"Well," Roger said, "I've got six more of the ZBI."

"The what?" asked Marge.

"Sorry. The Zion Bible Institute. Six of them. Then I've got John and Lorraine Ferrini. I've got the Handlemans. I've got Ronald DeFreeze. Then I'd like to get Red Fields back."

Les groaned loudly.

Marge nodded. "Good point, Les. Aren't they going to be repetitious?"

Roger tapped his head and studied a note card. "Ummmm . . . let's see. How about I go with three of the ZBIs. One Handleman. One Ferrini and DeFreeze."

"Fields?" Les asked hopefully.

"C'mon, Les, I've got to put the guy on. He's the guy Ticky shot at."

"Ticky shot at all of them," explained Les.

"But he's the guy who brought the charges on behalf of the excursion itself."

"Will you finish up today?" Marge asked.

"Possibly," Roger said.

"Let's do it, then."

Six hours later Roger hadn't finished with the young men from the Colorado Springs Zion Bible Institute. First Les got into it on procedure, and Marge almost came out of her chair and clobbered him. Then, when the first towheaded true believer was in the middle of quoting Scripture on Daniel and the lion's den, a disturbance broke out in front of the Municipal Building. Petey Myers and Bobby rushed outside to find a pushing match going on. It was not lost on him that the staties smugly watched from their vehicles.

✳   ✳   ✳

On the far end of the valley, before it arched up toward Lake City, Steven Kearney was having better luck as he carried a mug of good coffee onto the deck of Evan and Carla Santi's retirement home in Barnegat Meadows.

"Now, we don't make claims to being expert," said Evan, a big, ruddy man with white hair and beard.

"We're amateurs," added Carla, a compact woman in her seventies.

They settled in at a red picnic table.

"We've heard about the play," said Evan.

"Very exciting," Carla added.

Steven looked across at his hosts. Behind them a spectacular ridge rose up out of the big river.

"Well, what I'm trying to do is create a montage of events and actions. Of course, the conquistadors were pretty pivotal."

Evan nodded. "Now, you know there's plenty of folks say they did not get up into the Shining Mountain People's valley, but they did."

"Oh, yes they did. Remember that awful man, Evan? That Dell Phillips?"

Evan chuckled. "This ass from Colorado State University writes a book and actually gets it published claiming that the Spanish got no further than Albuquerque."

"Absurd."

"Right now, today, I can drive thirty minutes and show you a Spanish well. A goddamn *well*! Lined with goddamn rocks. If it were a goddamn Indian well, it'd be lined with clay."

"So Evan wrote him."

"A nice letter. You proofread it, honey. It wasn't a challenge or anything. I simply mentioned the well and some other structures we found during our tracing of the Coronado expedition out of Mexico."

"We traced it in '72."

"Found helmets. Armor."

"In '72."

"Anyway, this ass writes back. In the middle of this piece of typing paper was one word."

"Amateur," they said in unison.

They both looked at Steven, and he shook his head.

"Okay," Evan said, spreading out his hands, "this is what we pieced together and what we know. In—"

"Can I record this? Can I just put this on tape, because I'll—"

"Absolutely."

"Absolutely."

The little recorder clicked on, and Steven nodded.

EVAN

Honey? Would you like to . . . ?

CARLA

No, no, sweetie. I'll help.

EVAN

After the Spanish finished with Mexico, they struck out by land and sea. Ponce de León to Florida, Alabama . . . We followed Coronado because it's got the best markings.

CARLA

The maps and things. And letters. And the little Franciscans who wrote diaries.

EVAN

We know a lot about Coronado's trip.

CARLA

Names.

EVAN

We know names. Dates.

CARLA

Juan de Jesús, Julio de Méndez.

EVAN

So Coronado puts together about three hundred conquistadors. They bring women. Extra horses. Cows. Chickens. They all move up into Texas, then Arizona, New Mexico over by Antonito. They're looking for gold.

CARLA

Seven Cities of Gold.

EVAN

You see, Coronado would send out scouts, and the scouts would come back and say they saw glimpses of these cities . . . even though they—

BOTH

Never existed.

STEVEN

    Never, huh?

EVAN

    Here we have to say a word about the conquistadors themselves. Most people think they were these grizzled veterans—

CARLA

    Big beards and such.

EVAN

    Our research shows them to be usually the second sons of the Spanish privileged. In Spain all the property and money were inherited by the firstborn male. The second sons had to make their own way. So mostly they were eighteen to twenty-five, which explains how savage they were.

CARLA

    Oh, but they loved to fight.

EVAN

    Fearless. Out to make their fortunes.

CARLA

    Except Juan Carlos de Moreno, of course.

EVAN

    We know—

CARLA

    He was there for love. Or because of love. We—

EVAN

    We know from letters we traced to Spain. Had a girl in Barcelona. Good family. He had nothing. . . .

CARLA

    He was a poet. He wrote Teresa letters. He sent poems. Sometimes they took years to get there. From Mexico City and such.

EVAN

They would send couriers to the ships in the Gulf. From the Pueblos. From the Indian cities in Arizona, New Mexico.

CARLA

And one letter had to have been from here. Had to have been from the valley. The river is so clear.

EVAN

Described Cathedral Rock. Bachelor Creek.

CARLA

Still, it was mostly love.

EVAN

Oh, it was love. Yes it was.

CARLA

By the time he had gotten here . . .

EVAN

Love.

CARLA

. . . He'd had that gold lust just knocked out of him. He wanted to get back. Where are those translations of his letters?

EVAN

Well, see, we gave our collection to the state university.

CARLA

I thought we kept—

EVAN

No, no, hon. We decided.

CARLA

Shit, I wished we'd kept the translations. Something like:
    I would be the poorest soul

behind wagons, under bridges
. . . something about . . .

EVAN

He didn't need gold. He didn't want property. He just wanted Teresa.

STEVEN

That's very beaut—

EVAN

And when he was writing that, he probably realized he'd never see her again.

CARLA

Juan Carlos de Moreno. Teresa Herrera.

STEVEN

Sad.

CARLA

Love.

EVAN

Most likely killed around Ute Ranch.

STEVEN

I'm staying there.

CARLA

Described the meadow where the five brooks run together.

STEVEN

Ute Ranch? Juan Carlos . . . de . . .

CARLA

Juan Carlos de Moreno.

EVAN

Teresa Herrera.

CARLA
Love.

EVAN
Love.

STEVEN
Yeah.

38

Roarke picked up on the second ring. "Roarke here."

"Roarke? Roarke?"

"Steven."

"Hey, Roarke. It's so good to hear you. I miss you."

"I miss you, too. How is it?"

Steven switched the phone to his other ear. He sat in the big kitchen at the Ute Ranch, his work spread across the oak table. The sun was leaving the kitchen window.

"I'm trying hard. . . . I don't know."

"What's the matter?"

"Nothing. I'm just . . . I don't know . . ."

"What's with the bald painter you wrote about? How's she doing?"

"She had a breast removed. Chemotherapy. She's pissed."

"I'll bet."

"Now she's kinda pissed at me."

"Why?"

"I wanted to buy her dinner. Or go to dinner with her, and she said she had the one breast and everything, and then she went back into her rock, which isn't an actual rock but a house built up against this rock. I don't know. She's still doing the mural, which is amazing. I don't . . . I mean, I'm forty-eight and—"

"Cut the shit. Are you homesick?"

Steven thought for a second and lit a smoke. "I don't think I'm homesick. Jesus, listen to me. How are you, Roarke? Are you okay?"

Twenty-five hundred miles away, Roarke sipped a beer on the edge of her stage. She watched Niki working on her Cassatt manuscript at the table. Two writers, she thought. One so confident and clinical, one saturated with doubt.

"Well . . . I guess I'm great. I'm working on the scene-study group. The class has grown to thirteen. I'm in love."

"How many in your class?"

"Thirteen."

"Who?"

"Kids."

"No. Who are you in love with?"

"Tubby's sister."

"The daughter of Sappho?"

"The very one."

His laughter bounced off the satellites, and she smiled thinking of that fat face.

"Now I wish I was there so I could meet her."

"I wish you were here, too."

Roarke could feel the laughter float backward and stop. She read the silence. "What else, Steven? C'mon."

"I don't . . . I mean, you're going so good you shouldn't have to listen to me."

"Jesus, it's hard having a complete asshole as a very best friend. Where are you?"

"I'm at the big oak table in the Overstreets' kitchen. They own the Ute Ranch, where I live."

"Is it the bald-headed woman?"

She sensed his brain lining up thoughts in the high mountain air.

"It's that this whole thing means something, Roarke. I'm not sure what it means, but there's a need for this to be right, and I wish I was more . . . equipped for it."

"The play or the girl?"

Roarke did it again. She hung the oddest little question, and it floated through the phone lines and popped over his head like a firefly.

* * *

Jude McCormick slid out the passenger side of the ranch's pickup and stretched.

"I'm a stiff young man, Kid," he said.

Jimmy the Kid came around from the driver's side, checking the tires on the four-horse trailer.

"Yes, you are," he said.

"Let's have some ice cream before we get back to the ranch."

Jimmy checked his pocketwatch and tilted his gray cowboy hat back high on his forehead.

"Guess we can take a break. Man, that was an ornery group."

"Well, Kid, they were up there two days and didn't catch any fish."

"Ain't the fish's fault, worm-throwin' morons."

Jude and the Kid hitched their belts and rolled across Creedemore's Main Street to Ray's Ice Cream Parlor, situated between the hardware store and the Earrings and Feathers Craft Shop.

Jude watched Kid out of the corner of his eye but spoke straight ahead. "You are the skinniest son of a bitch I ever saw, Kid."

Kid answered straight ahead. "Ever get your butt kicked into the middle of next week by a skinny son of a bitch?"

Jude laughed. "Just making an observation."

"You make a lot of them for a nineteen-year-old New Jersey peckerwood, but I'll tell you now, I don't know. I do eat large."

"Yes, sir, you do."

One hundred yards up the road, in front of the Creedemore Municipal Building, JoJo Prophit stood with his dad and his buddy Larry Porfle alongside the other smartly dressed cowboys.

Larry nudged JoJo. "Look," he said, pointing to the ice cream parlor.

JoJo watched as Jude and the Kid disappeared into the store. A sneer played over his porky lips.

"C'mon," JoJo said.

Larry followed JoJo out of the cowboy mix and into the middle of the street. Larry wore jeans and a pressed jean jacket, an aqua T-shirt with George Jones looking out, and a clean brown Stetson. JoJo had pulled out the stops for his first day up and around since the infamous sucker punch and stomp. He sported green snakeskin rodeo boots, snug white jeans, white shirt with bolo tie, the same jet-black waistcoat he wore to take Becky Lawrence to the senior prom, and an enormous white flannel hat formed especially to grace his oversize noggin. He felt he would be the perfect Old West gunfighter if his stupid dad would only let him wear his gun. They stopped in the street in front of the parlor. JoJo dug his thumbs John Wayne style behind his wide leather belt on either side of his Confederate-flag buckle. Out of earshot, up the street, Mel Prophit watched his big boy with some serious pride.

"McCormick! Jude McCormick!" JoJo boomed. "I'm calling you out!"

JoJo's heart beat faster. It was like a gunfight. He sensed his dad's eyes. He motioned for Larry to step more to the side.

"McCormick! Hey, Jude McCormick! I'm calling you out!"

Now the cowboys heard it, too, and watched. The Liberty Society turned warily and waited.

Jude opened the door and walked onto the plank sidewalk, a double sugar cone of butter pecan in his hand. Kid followed with Rocky Road.

"Hey, JoJo," Jude said, taking a slurp at the ice cream.

JoJo regarded him with a sneer. Jude had taken his hair band off. Black hair danced down to his shoulders.

"You look like a girl!" JoJo said too loudly.

Jude smiled over to Kid. "Not a Jersey girl, I don't. Jersey girls are some hot things. Man, on the shore they got these little skirts they wear up to here."

Jude touched his upper thigh, and Larry Porfle thought he would surely like to see these Jersey girls.

"You know what I mean," JoJo snarled.

"Sure. You're all pissed off at me. I'm sorry, JoJo. I really am sorry. I thought you were gonna get rough with the girls."

"The only girl I'm gonna get rough with is you."

Kid, all 124 pounds of him, crossed over to Larry.

"You in this, too, Larry?"

Larry had heard one of the men who worked for his dad in South Fork refer to Jimmy the Kid as "that scary little wolverine."

"No."

"Okay, then, I'm going back to check the horses."

Kid turned to Jude. "I'm warning you now, Jude McCormick. You kill this poor slob and I will personally kick your butt."

"Yes, sir," Jude said seriously.

Now JoJo felt the full bore of his dad's eyeballing. He felt his dad's friends.

Jude stepped off the sidewalk and shifted the butter pecan to his right hand. JoJo quickly decided he had him by maybe forty pounds. He wasn't sure. He stepped forward, almost nose to nose. "Aww, c'mon, JoJo. Let's be friends."

Jude extended his hand. JoJo looked disdainfully at it and, dipping ever so slightly on his heels, brought up the sucker punch. Jude's head flicked to the side, and as it sailed past him, his tight, bony fist, the one not holding the butter pecan, jackhammered seven times under the big boy's diaphragm. JoJo looked at Jude for a fraction of a second, then crumpled to the sidewalk.

"Aww, gee. Aww . . ." Jude mumbled.

He got behind JoJo, rolled him to a sitting position, put his hands under his armpits, and raised and released them several times with the arm not holding the ice cream.

"Breathe in. Push it out. Better?" Jude extended the butter pecan. "Butter pecan?"

JoJo leaned over and took a nibble.

By now Mel Prophit had covered half the distance to his fallen son, moving quickly behind his astonishing belly.

"My boy! He's killed my boy!"

As surges will, the cowboys dragged along the jittery, conspiracy-minded Liberty Society, which in turn had the press firing up the video cameras.

Jude raised JoJo to his feet and saw the horde roaring toward him.

"That's good ice cream," JoJo said sincerely.

"I got to go now," Jude said.

Mel Prophit attempted a flying grab for Jude at the instant JoJo turned. Their Texas-size heads bongoed together in a dull, thuddy *boink* that ricocheted sickeningly off the storefronts.

"Men down! Men down!" Jack Hill shouted.

"Men down!" one of the other cowboys yelled.

"How many men?" someone yelled.

"I can't tell!" another answered.

Professionally aloof network news photographers and video men stood on top of their vans. A PBS reporter watched from her second-floor hotel window. The pierced and green-haired radical reporter waded fearlessly into the fray, holding her tiny tape recorder in front of her like a crucifix.

"Get the hell back! Fucking press!"

Creedemore Mayor Ruby Onerati, who had carefully avoided taking sides, rushed out of her real estate office adjacent to the ice cream parlor and attempted to calm the crowd, but she stumbled in the street, fell to her knees, and tripped up half a dozen members of the Liberty Society, who landed on top of her. Yale Strong, foreman at the Norgan Ranch, lost his legendary cool.

"Goddamn it! They've got Ruby down!"

*　*　*

That evening all but one network opened with footage of what ABC darkly noted was "an epic melee over the West's lifeblood—water." On *The NewsHour with Jim Lehrer*, PBS played Jane Carlisle's three-minute essay about the failure of small-town government to resolve the most basic differences. The *Rocky Mountain News* published a photo of the battered Mayor Onerati with her middle finger waving at the world, and the green-haired Egalitarian Radio reporter deemed the proceedings "a pukebag of sordid unreality" but concentrated on its long-term coverage of the "cold-blooded killing of the two unarmed children by Petey Myers, sheriff of Creedemore."

Roarke leaned in to the TV. It was the fourth report of the night, and she looked closely at the faces of the snarling, punch-throwing, feet-swinging men, women, and children. She tried to remember the conversation with Steven. Had he mentioned this? She moved across Niki's living room to the windows overlooking Sheridan Square and stared out.

"You okay?" Niki asked, still watching the news.

"I don't know."

"Yeah?"

"I'm thinking."

"About what?"

"Steven."

Niki moved next to her, gently brushing some mad hairs away from Roarke's ear.

"What are you thinking about Steven?"

Roarke turned to Niki and held her free hand.

"I'm thinking he'd better write a fucking great play."

*　*　*

Steven recorded Angela Lopez on the Spanish influence, or "Hispanic passions" (her term). He had decided against Les Vallejos's offer to be the representative soul of his culture, because Les was obviously too busy with the court thing and he was perhaps a bit too chauvinistic.

Angela proved down-to-earth. She sprinkled enough fact and spice on each era and story for Steven to sense reliability and honesty. He used both sides of a sixty-minute tape.

Before he left her small white home behind the post office, he called Ute Ranch and informed Skyo he'd be missing for supper. It was time to fill in the blanks. Get it down on paper. He loaded up his knapsack, thanked Angela profusely, and puttered over to the Historical Society.

Steven leaned the scooter against the outside stairs. He lit a cigarette and sat on the cement landing, legs folded under him. Down the street, workmen fitted new glass onto the ice cream parlor's storefront. A state patrol car was parked in front. Another was parked in front of the craft shop, while still another was in front of the Creedemore Hotel.

Steven started up the stairs but changed his mind. He threw his pack over one shoulder and walked down the street to the Western Market. He walked through the parking lot and around the corner to where the market's wall faced the Lumberjack Amphitheater. The surface of the wall had been whitewashed. A tall aluminum extension ladder leaned against it, and at the top, looping and arcing the outline of Creedemore's mural, hunched Molly Dowie. Her head was wrapped in a red bandanna. She wore a white T-shirt, baggy overalls, and black army boots. Steven watched her closely. To the top rung of the ladder, she had taped a scale drawing of the mural itself, and she referred to it often. About a quarter of the mural seemed to be outlined. Steven sat behind her unnoticed in the stands and lit another cigarette. Cathedral Rock burned gold from the low, red sun. Even though it was not dusk yet, a star blinked in the clear sky.

Molly pulled back a bit from her perch and looked at the completed lines and grids. She pushed her charcoal bits into a canvas bag, folded the drawing and put that in also, and then climbed down the ladder.

"It looks wonderful."

172

Molly turned to Steven in the stands. Then she turned back to the ladder. Steven stood and put out his cigarette.

"I mean, I know it's got to be filled in and everything, but the drawing part looks wonderful itself."

Molly put down her bag and tilted the ladder to the right. She walked the length of it, hand over hand, until it lay on the ground. Steven ran over.

"I could have gotten that down."

She looked at him, and he stepped back.

"I did . . . I did a lot of construction stuff in New York. I have this friend of mine . . ."

"That dinner thing?"

"Dinner?"

"You and me have dinner?"

"Oh . . . yeah. Dinner."

Molly walked around through the Western Market parking lot in long, strong strides. Steven kept off to her left in a sort of lope.

"And I can treat," Steven said. "I mean, it can be on me . . . or it can be . . . whatever."

Molly crossed the street and stepped up on the wooden sidewalk. She passed the gem shop and gallery with Steven a step behind her and walked into the Creedemore Hotel dining room.

They sat down in a corner under a photograph of Herbert Hoover sitting at the same table. Steven pointed to the picture. "Hoover."

Molly nodded.

They were the only ones in the dining room. No one passed in front of the window. Molly and Steven ordered hamburger pie and beer. They were silent while they waited for their order. When the food came, they shifted it and formed it and took tiny halfhearted bites every so often, and after a while the waitress took the food away and brought coffee. Molly removed her bandanna and patted that shiny bean. Steven looked at his coffee.

"I wrote a play. I wrote it a long time ago, about this guy I knew when I was in high school."

Steven waited to see if she flickered or something. See if she was listening. Now he was hungry and was sorry he didn't eat that good-looking hamburger pie with the browned mashed-potato crust. Now he was sorry again that he was forty-eight.

"Guy's name was Champagne. Bobby Champagne. In my play I couldn't use his real name because it was his actual name, so I used Almaden. The wine thing like the champagne thing . . . even though there are . . . I mean, bubbles and . . . Anyway, he comes home from Vietnam (and he really did), and he lost a leg there. Now, the real Champagne had been a star athlete and had lots of girlfriends and things. But see, he loses his leg. Here. Right below the knee part, and that was it. I mean, he got a beautiful artificial doohickey that let him walk normally. Even run. But all he thought about was how he wasn't him anymore. Want some cake?"

"No."

"Pie?"

"Uh-uh."

A state trooper walked over to the restaurant window and peered in, sighed, and walked back to his patrol car.

"So . . . uh . . . so, yeah, Bobby just . . . gave up. Still lives with his mother, or did the last time I heard about him."

Steven now joined the silence. He was glad to at least hear her china coffee cup clink onto the saucer as if it signaled some shared act.

"Mmmmm," he said, finishing his coffee.

Molly Dowie looked at the tabletop.

The waitress brought the tab, and Steven paid. They walked outside slowly into a new night.

"I have never seen this town so empty," she said suddenly. "They're all home nursing their wounds."

She turned and looked at Steven as though it were his turn now.

"Cool," he said. "I mean, it's very good to do that. Everybody beating each other up. Calling names. You don't see that in New York. Lots of murders and stuff. Lots and lots of those, but we don't give a shit about water. We think that the water is just . . . there. You *know*, I guess. You guys *know*."

Molly Dowie looked over his head to the front stars and the layers of stars starting behind them.

"I'm feeling very sorry for myself. I hate that. Willie comes up, and I say I'm great because I am, at least the doctor says I am, but I overdo the happy part on account of Willie. So he comes up, and I say 'Oh, I'm so great! I never felt better,' and all that shit, but I don't feel any good and I don't have many friends—any friends—because I've been selfish . . . between Willie and being this big artist. And I'm not any good, and I don't have . . . I don't know."

"I say that, too."

She looked down from the stars at his big face. A pen dangled behind his ear. A cigarette rode it, too. He smiled, but his eyes were saturnine and parts of the Milky Way fell behind them.

"I say, 'I just don't know.' Sometimes when I say that, Roarke says, 'Ain't that the truth?' "

"You been together a long time?"

"It's like I've always known Roarke."

Molly looked back up to the stars, then turned and watched them over

Cathedral Rock. Steven patted the top of her head. She did not react and watched the stars as though she expected the pat. He put his hands back in his pockets.

"I wish I had a cigarette," he muttered.

"On your ear," she said without turning.

He found it and lit it. "Thanks."

Now they both watched the stars, and the state trooper watched them.

After a few minutes, Steven said, "I'll give you a ride home."

"I got my truck over by the Western Market."

"I'll walk you over to your truck."

They walked down the main street of the embattled little town. Molly opened the passenger door and got in and sat staring out the window. Steven gently closed the door and stood back.

"I'm forty-four," she said.

"That's cool," he said.

Now she looked at him again.

He stepped closer to the car. "I don't care, you know."

"You don't care about what?"

"I don't care that you don't . . . It doesn't bother me. . . . I mean . . . the breast stuff."

Coyotes sang in the hills.

"What I'm going to do is go up to the Historical Society and just write all night. I have a lot of good stuff to get down."

Molly Dowie looked him over again and started up the truck. She backed out of the parking space, looked at him once more, and pulled onto Main. Steven listened to the truck burp and shift out of sight. He walked up to the society's second floor and entered without turning the lights on. At the window over the county parking lot, he looked up the narrow road to Bachelor Creek and her rock and the mines beyond. Somewhere there was a story, and that story held the secrets that Molly mentioned, and those secrets, mossy and cold and layered like an archaeological dig, seemed suddenly somehow within his reach.

* * *

Across the valley, children ran into Minnie Lettgo's bedroom. Jefferson was one of them. It wasn't a dream, because Minnie wasn't sleeping. It wasn't a daydream either. This thing flat-out had a feel of real. It was as if she could reach right out and caress Jefferson's little blue jeans and behold his little blond head bobbing among the other children.

Minnie pushed up in bed, and Jefferson squeezed away from the other kids and plopped down with her like he used to and put his funny face on part of her pillow. She slowly swiveled her head until she felt him, really felt him, touching a part of her forehead and nose. He was soft and wonderful against her ossified skin, and he carried feelings that flowed into her and began to overwhelm her. Minnie raised her forearm and wiggled macilent fingers in some forgotten signal, and Jefferson wrapped his cool, bitty paws around them. They lay considering things, their hands bound as they were in the air.

39

Now that the question of water rights and water usage had taken center stage on the American media scene and people across the country who never considered the issue at all were being harangued by commentators and editorials, Mountain Man Red Fields was losing interest. He felt uncomfortable being privy to the secret grand council meetings of Bill Clinings's inner circle. Clinings, a forty-year-old associate professor of psychology at CU, had started his Liberty Society almost fifteen years earlier and still seemed to Mountain Man to be some arrested adolescent. And the media. Jesus. While Cia appeared to enjoy the attention, Mountain Man had become fearful of looking like an unabridged asshole. He just wished somebody else were on his side. Somebody he could respect. He let out a huge sigh, walked past a full bicycle rack, into the rental-shop office. All his life, from his Chicago childhood to his Boulder education and climb up into the rugged Colorado Rockies, Red Fields had wanted to be like the cowboys on the opposing side of the court.

He wanted to dress in that cursory, "not give a hell" way. He wanted to talk that easy patois of the breed. More, though, he wanted that casual respect, even admiration, these men seemed to afford each other with a nod or a word. He ran his fingers through his red hair and sighed again. At the last Liberty planning session held at the Holiday Inn in Monte Vista, Bill Clinings's wife, Pamela, had entertained with espresso and white wine while all those dicks talked revolution. Jesus. Mountain Man Red Fields closed his eyes and visualized those cowboys at the Log Bar, enjoying Coors Light and talking elk and girls, and not necessarily in that order. And Christ, the way those pussies from the Liberty Society were dressed the other day. Now all the world thought he was a pussy, too, and not . . . well, shit. What was he?

He stood and bounced on the balls of his feet and sighed himself over to the small window that faced Main Street. Some tourists had returned, but they seemed more like gawkers than vacationers. Nobody would be riding his mountain bikes today. He walked outside and sat on the bench in front of his shop. The sun had popped up beautifully a few hours before, and that clean, dry look the surrounding hills took on only added to his frustration. An old truck turned in to the Western Market parking lot, and the skinny hippie woman got out, grabbed some buckets, and disappeared around the side of the building. Sheriff Petey Myers slowly drove by in the county Jeep. Red Fields was almost joyous when that old boy nodded in his direction. Mountain Man Red Fields stood and waved until the Jeep cleared the corner by the pottery shop. He sat back down and thought to himself that maybe the West was a for-giving place after all. Maybe, just maybe, with a little luck, he could ride out this horrible hand he'd been given, and everything would be all right.

That's when Ticky Lettgo's Mexican lawyer came out of the Seattle House of Joe across the street with that goddamn fucking volcano bitch Ferrini.

They were laughing.

*　*　*

Petey Myers nodded at the forlorn Mountain Man Red Fields, said, "Good morning, cockhound," under his breath, and drove on out to Ticky's place. Another day, another kick in the weenie. Alone in the cab of the Jeep, hip burning, stomach on fire, Petey did not stand on ceremony and talked out loud.

"Now, c'mon, Reedy, you know me. When was that gang thing with the Meehan brothers? When was that—1970 or '72 or something? Christ, those cockhounds took old Billy McGinn over to Southy and cut his balls off and cut his feet off. Now, I grew up with old Billy, and he was a little prick, maybe, but that Mr. and Mrs. McGinn did not need that. You remember how I got one Meehan to tell on the other and we were over by the projects at Bunker Hill? I could've shot the fuck out of them, but I did not. I took them in and they de-nied squealing and they got off and got away with it, but I did not shoot. And if I fucking ever had a reason to put those Meehan morons down, I had it, but I did not. Now, last night that TV news guy says that along with the water shit I'm a baby killer or something. What do you think, Reedy? What would you say? Would you say old Petey Myers has himself a 'shit sandwich on whole wheat'? Jesus!"

Petey turned off onto Ticky's property. The Liberty Society had replaced the yuppie irregulars on their side of the fence. Banners flew proclaiming their dedication to ecological warfare and anti–property rights. When they realized that Petey was driving, some of them unfurled their BABY KILLER banner. The cowboys on the other side of Ticky's gate leaned casually against their trucks, several of them slipping their rifles onto the trucks' seats when they saw Petey turn off the road. Petey honked for the Liberty freedom fighters to clear the

178

way, but they stared back at him in some academic defiance. Petey sighed. He would have liked to just back out of there and say fuck this, but Ticky didn't answer his phone last night when Petey rang to tell him that Marge Klinger had canceled today's court session on account of the ice cream parlor skirmish. And he didn't answer this morning. Petey honked again.

One of the men stepped forward, away from the others. Like them, he wore the uniform of torn jeans, T-shirt, sandals, and a headband of green and brown. He held up his hand, palm out.

"No one passes," he said.

Petey leaned his head out the window. "What?"

The man looked exasperated and peeked back at his compatriots with a smirk. He turned to Petey again.

"I said, 'No. One. Passes.' "

Petey sighed once more. He patiently reached under the seat of the Jeep and brought up five pairs of plastic handcuffs. He unhooked his shotgun from the bracket between the front bucket seats. He took out his nine-millimeter and checked the stock. Outside, the lead warrior watched him through the window, but the sun played off it and all he could make out was a quiet sort of sway. He concentrated on the glittery glass, and the smirk drifted off his face. Petey opened the Jeep's door and eased himself down.

When the spokesman saw the shotgun, he screamed, "Videotape! Videotape! Videotape!"

No fewer than fifteen camcorders whirred from every angle. The smirk returned to the leader's face. He adjusted his stance so some of the tapes would have his profile and some his full-front hard glare. If need be, he could have them edited before giving copies to the news stations.

Petey came around to the front of the Jeep and sauntered in a half-healed limp the twenty-odd feet to the man from the Liberty Society. The man held up his hand again and leaned back on his Boulder haunches.

"My name is Bill Clinings," he said, slowly and loudly enough for the small microphones on the camcorders to pick up. "I am president and founder of the Liberty Society of Colorado: a preternatural organization dedicated to environmental anarchy. I am ordering you, baby killer, shooter of unarmed children, to return to your killing machine. You shall not pass."

A loud cheer and applause rang out into the hugeness of the valley. Petey looked at this Bill Clinings with a levelness that surprised even him. He remembered Reedy's maxim: "Talk while you move. Talk nice and hard. That way," Reedy always said, "you're telling them what you mean, not what they want you to mean." Petey thought about this in the cool Colorado-morning sun. If Reedy was right about the bad guys, then he was more than likely right about the new anti-cop ballistic missile, the video camera. He smiled and pushed off on his bad hip in a loop of the cameras, giving them a good look and talking the Reedy shit the whole nine yards.

"Now, you people I'm sure feel you have a perfect right to block private driveways, impede police work, and in general bring a great disturbance to every facet of life in our poor little town. I say you *feel* that way, but of course you *know* you don't, because in this country it is still the rule of law that's been handed down for a long, long time. Now, I'm not going to get into it with your taunts about me being a 'child killer,' 'cause I do not give a good rat's asshole what you think, but those 'children' murdered a Mexican American farmer in Cortez and shot my friend Shari Tobias in the face, the first female sheriff in western Colorado and a legendary law enforcer. They shot her down and laughed at her, and then they shot me. Look it up. Any woman- and minority-murdering man or woman out there better make sure they get it right the first time. They only blew me half in half. They did it wrong, and I got them. Yes, sir, and I'd do it again if it could save other señors and señoritas out there."

Petey had now come full circle in front of Bill Clinings, who was trying unsuccessfully to get a word in.

"Now, I got a ninety-six-year-old gentleman down that road, whose son gave his life for his country and who has been the kind of neighbor and citizen we all want to live next to, and that man is not answering his phone. Now I am going to pass, you flip little son of a bitch, and I am going to arrest you, too. For that knife you're carrying on your belt."

Bill Clinings had wanted to be arrested. Manhandled. Martyred. But not for his Swiss Army knife.

"Put 'em out, pal, or we can do this the hard way."

Clinings was near tears. He held out his wrists. Petey attached the plastic cuffs, led him to the Jeep, leaned him on the hood, and frisked him. He held up the Swiss Army knife.

"Anybody else? Okay."

Petey put Bill Clinings in the back of the Jeep, then pointed to a round man with a gray ponytail and a Joni Mitchell T-shirt.

"Open the gate, fat boy."

He did.

* * *

Steven Kearney looked at the big clock above the elk head. It was just past five in the morning. He had written all night at his desk in the Historical Society and with a disembodied narrator had taken Creedemore out of the heaving, icy, oceany past and into life as the Indians knew it, and then segued into Juan Carlos de Moreno, the conquistador poet and lover of Teresa Herrera. Juan

Carlos had now become narrator and guide. A romantic figure and yet tragic enough to balance on the fine wire between drama and presentational history. Steven stood and stretched. He walked to the windows over Main Street and looked across to the Seattle House of Joe. It was too much to hope it would be open this early. He turned around, sat on the window ledge, and scanned the society's big room. He thought about the night's work now and its cleanness of line. Was it that cleanness he wanted? Did he want that uncontaminated arc of story for all his work? Or was it becoming clear, was it a slowly ripening perception, that he had constricted his life's work from the start by demanding a sort of symmetry? A cowardly line, a path that he could always follow back? A lifeline? He stood and shook his head like a cartoon character. Tired. That's it, of course. Do not think of anything when you've been up all night. He walked over to his desk and leafed through the last sixteen pages of the word-mural. The pages where Juan Carlos de Moreno had assumed the narration. Steven felt a correctness about the language of the young conquistador. That was not the problem. The language was right. Juan was simply saying it to the wrong— Stop, he told himself. Don't do this. It was a good—no, it was a wonderful night's work. He had not felt the juice flow through him like this in a long, long time.

Steven pushed the assemblage into his knapsack, shut off the lights, and walked down to his scooter. He puttered onto Main Street and toward the road out of town and Ute Ranch high above. A minute later he turned a semicircle. Sun had popped up in several places where its beam had squeezed through mountain crags, and Steven rode in and out of the lines of light until he stopped in front of her house. He shut off the little motor and lowered the kickstand. More sun flashed off the bits of silicon in Cathedral Rock. He walked quietly over to the small strip of grass in front of her rock, bordered by white quartz and wildflowers. He put down his knapsack and lay with his head on it. He was asleep in fifteen seconds.

*   *   *

The ice cream war upset Ticky Lettgo in more ways than one. Those crybabies kept finding ways to disturb things. Those damn reporters jostling him. And now, damn it, not getting a chance to have his say. He had to sit tight while Petey and the state troopers straightened out some butts before he could get his ride back to Minnie. Oh, and Jesus, her not talking. But that Vi was a good woman. Petey Myers was a lucky man to have old Vi. Good-looking gal, too.

On the drive back to the ranch, after they turned off to his road, he had Petey stop at the biggest bend by the fern ledge. He thought the water looked high, too high, and wondered out loud if maybe those pissers from the reservoir were sneaking that water out at night. Happened before, the bastards.

Things seemed to get done more and more that way these days. All these new guys doing business out of the sides of their mouths.

Ticky watched his fingers go on his jeans. They felt unconnected. Damn things just set there drumming against his thigh on their "do as you please" own. He opened and closed his ninety-six-year-old hands for no other reason than to prove to himself he could. It was surely an interesting proposition, all right. He was connected to everything okay. Legs. Feet. Arms. He just had to issue the marching orders more firmly.

"What I'll do," Petey said, "I'll come out in the A.M. tomorrow unless old Marge has something else in mind. I'll ring you up tonight."

Ticky nodded. Maybe tomorrow he'd get to have his say. Vi met them on the porch.

"She's resting now. I just looked in on her. Got a big smile on her face. She was humming 'Rock-a-Bye Baby.' "

"Humming?" Ticky asked, interested.

"I think she's coming around. Didn't eat much, though."

Ticky watched the Jeep with Petey and Vi bump out of sight and then ordered those diaphanous legs up onto the porch and into the cabin.

"I'm home, old girl," he announced, up the stairs to Minnie. "I didn't get my say. I guess maybe tomorrow. I'm going to take some Crown Royal, and I'll bring you up a nice manhattan."

Ticky took down two of Minnie's good cocktail glasses from the kitchen hutch, filled one with ice, and poured a healthy amount of Crown Royal over it. He put some more ice into a porcelain mug, poured some Old Grand-Dad and a squirt of vermouth over it, and mixed it up with his finger. He strained the fuscous liquid into the other cocktail glass and threw away the ice. He put a maraschino cherry in it.

"Just like the Cattleman that time in New York," he said out loud.

Ticky carried the two drinks up the wide wooden stairs. He turned in to the big bedroom.

"You remember the Cattleman restaurant in New York at that fancy hotel? That fat fella in the tuxedo mixed you up your manhattan."

Minnie lay high on the pillow, her head tilted a little to the right. Her right arm was crooked like a lever, and her forearm and hand floated somehow separate from the rest. Ticky walked over to the nightstand.

"That was that time we stayed at the Taft Hotel. It had the two-doors-in-one dealy. I put a cherry in the manhattan."

He eyeballed the drinks down onto the table and swiveled to Minnie. Her eyes were half open, and she appeared to stare at her raised hand. Ticky tried to see something there, too. He tried to see some flicker of finger or wrist. He tried to still himself to see more closely, but he could not and shifted madly in his place both inside and out, as if little pinches provoked the disconnected parts of a man holding on to something.

He heard the big river then, and across the big river he heard the horses sneeze and shiver. He heard the enormous crows and the bluebirds. Trucks on the highway. Was that a plane? But he could not hear her usual breaths swallowed and then puffed out.

Ticky picked up his Crown Royal and carried it around to his side of the bed. He sat with his back to her, looking out the bedroom windows, sipping his drink. He felt his torso crook and ordered it to straighten. Across the flatness of the river meadow, before it rose smoothly to the first of three plateaus, his horses seemed to turn and look through the window at him. Ticky looked back at them and nodded.

"Are you dead, old girl?"

There it is, okay, and I'll say it again,
That a man ought to do what is right.
Never mind the day or the naysay of friend
A good man ought to rise above fright.
For it's love of town in this crazy old world
That has come to be less than revered.
And it's got me down, like a low-minded girl,
That the pot of dissension's been stirred.

—From Cowboy Bob Panousus's address to the Colorado
state legislature, commemorating the settlement of Denver

40

S kyo and her boyfriend split up over the Ferrini woman's testimony. It wasn't precipitated by the breaking of ranks among the rafters, although Mrs. Handleman, in a confrontation on the steps with Mrs. Ferrini and her always-silent husband, accused them both of being insensitive to the rights of other rafters whose lives were in jeopardy and a couple of "fucking pussies" to boot. Ralph's mistake was referring to her as "that dumb bitch" and stating he wished "she'd get hit by a car."

"Hit by a car?" Skyo asked, stopping on the stairs of Ralph's cabin at the Outward Bound camp.

"You know."

"And killed?"

"Sure. That old man tried to kill *them*."

"I don't think he tried to kill them. Everybody knows he was shooting at the rafts. 'Hit by a car'?"

"Aren't you mad at her?"

"No."

"No?"

"It's her opinion that Mountain Man didn't plan properly."

"Whose side are you on?"

"I'm on . . . I just don't think anybody should get hit by a car because they don't agree with me."

"Well, I do. I think the car should kill her."

"Seriously."

"I really, really think she should get hit by a car or a truck or something and killed."

"Seriously."

"Seriously."

"We don't even know what she said."

"She's a witness for the defense."

"She could have been a hostile witness."

185

"Well, she wasn't. Mountain Man was over at the society's tent, and he said she was a bitch. And a fraud. She never gave him a chance. He said she was always against him."

"So she should get hit by a car?"

"She should get killed by a car."

Skyo drove her little Toyota pickup toward Ute Ranch and visualized Mrs. Ferrini being run over by Ralph in his old Volvo. To make matters worse (for Ralph anyway), she also visualized him backing up over the poor woman to ensure she was dead.

So suddenly even good people were traveling along that easy cynical highway. It was confusing to recognize a genuine willingness to be cruel among otherwise tender human beings, especially on such a morning as this. Cirrostratus clouds hovered under the high sun like fine linen buffeted by a slight warm breeze. Skyo passed the trail to Ute Ranch and continued in the direction of Creedemore. Outside the airport she turned right on the dirt road, toward the small Episcopal church.

*　*　*

Bill Clinings, founder of the Liberty Society, sat quietly in the backseat of Petey Myers's county Jeep. He watched the sheriff's eyes in the rearview mirror.

At the first gate on the dirt road to Ticky Lettgo's spread, Bill Clinings watched Petey open the gate and stand and gaze at the slow bend in the river. He seemed to be saying something. After a minute or so, Petey drove the Jeep through, closed up the fence, and continued on toward the second gate and Ticky's house beyond.

"These . . . these handcuffs are cutting into my wrists."

Now Petey looked up at the mirror. "No they're not."

"They are hurting me. I can feel them cutting me even if they're the plastic kind."

"I didn't lock them."

"What?"

"I didn't put them through the little latch there. They're just wrapped around one wrist, and I put the loose end in your free hand."

Bill felt the loose end. He unsqueezed his fist, and his hands came free. "Oh."

Now they were at the second gate. Petey opened it and again regarded a faster-moving portion of the river. Back in the Jeep, he caught Bill Clinings's eyes in the mirror and smiled easily.

"A man could stand there, where the water sort of swirls, and use anything. The wet flies, streamers, nymphs, dries. Anything," Petey said.

Clinings sniffed. "Fishing is immoral."

Petey drove on as if he didn't hear him.

"Fish produce endorphins," Clinings went on. "Any fool knows that that means they suffer pain, and that means quite probably they sense doom. One theory has a multilingual reference point between trout."

"You saying trout can talk to each other?"

"I'm saying it's immoral to fish. Obviously, many fish are more intelligent than many fishermen."

The negation of his videotape scheme had cast a pall over the academician's spirit, but he sensed a little positive refraction in the prism of ichthyology.

"Bertrand Russell says it correctly," he offered with a bored sigh. "Fishermen, not unlike property owners, not unlike the military, have no 'positive state of mind' or an 'erroneous knowledge of things.' So if one brings no 'belief' at all to an equation, as in the sense of Mr. Lettgo or your fishermen, then he therefore brings no 'decency,' which directly abides 'truth' or conversely 'falsehood.' 'If'—and it's a huge 'if'—you understand my meaning."

Petey Myers pulled in to Ticky's grassy yard, turned off the Jeep, and eased himself out of the vehicle.

"I'm going to check on Ticky. Stay in your seat or I will fuck you where you live. 'If'—and it's a huge 'if'—you understand my meaning."

Petey walked past a couple of grazing old Appaloosas that Ticky treated more like dogs than horses and climbed onto the porch.

"Ticky? Ticky, it's Petey Myers."

It was a soft day with some thin lines of clouds and enough quiet to hear the river rolling and the big horses chewing. He could hear nothing from the house.

"Ticky? Minnie?"

Petey knocked and entered. "Hello?"

The main floor of the Lettgo lodge sat unenclosed and bright. One large room with a kitchen. Couches and chairs were arranged around a huge TV to the left of the front door. White curtains moved in the breeze of half-opened windows. Petey climbed to the second floor. He stood on the landing and tried to get a feel for something ordinary or extraordinary but could not.

"Ticky? Minnie? It's Petey Myers."

All the doors to the rooms off the landing were closed except for the center one. It threw some light onto the staircase, and that light changed assiduously with the run of clouds.

"It's Petey Myers," he said again.

Petey put his hands onto his hips and breathed deeply. It was, after all, exactly as Reedy said. Rooms and more rooms. A veritable tour de force of rooms. That was Reedy. Old Reedy knew. The open doors were the best ones to go through. And he did.

Minnie was still high on her pillow. Her untouched manhattan glass twinkled in occasional sun. Her hair had been combed down neatly, and on the pillow next to her head was a photograph of a young marine, framed by an arrangement of medals and ribbons. Petey recognized some. He moved over to the phone and saw Ticky through the bedroom window. He was walking slowly from the big river. Another old horse walked with him. Petey called Vi, then went to meet him. It was perhaps a hundred yards to the river. Ticky nodded when he saw Petey.

"Sheriff. What brings you out here?"

"I got worried when you didn't answer your phone."

"Well, she's dead."

"Ticky I'm real—"

"See, Sheriff. We don't share that. Our people do not share that. She's dead. Jefferson's dead, and I'm ninety-six. I was looking for a good spot for her. I said that to old Apple here, and this old thing clomped over and stood right on the top of the ledge. What do you think?"

"Beautiful."

They walked again, and Ticky pointed to the house a long time before speaking.

"Minnie walked all over the place until she stopped right there and said 'Here,' and I built it there. When the woman says 'Here,' the man had better just say 'Okay.' Sames as other things. Sames."

They climbed the porch stairs. Petey half expected the horse to climb up there with them.

"I pinned his medals there," Ticky said, pointing again, only this time above them.

"I saw."

"Crazy?"

"No."

Ticky nodded again.

"This is what they said. 'Dear Mr. and Mrs. Lettgo. It is with profound regret that we inform you of the loss of Marine Lance Corporal Jefferson Tickeridge Lettgo on August eleventh, 1943, during amphibious landings.' Now, it was important to have that letter and to have those medals. We had the stone and such, but our Jefferson was not actually there, as they could not find him. That's the medal deal."

"I called Vi—"

"She's a good gal. She's a fine gal."

"She is. I called her, and they're sending the coroner from South Fork."

Ticky looked out again at his river and at the big old handsome Appaloosa crossing it.

"Well, she is dead, all right. I'm gonna have 'em do the oven deal and put the ashes on the ledge. Some maybe in the water. She could fish. She could fish."

Now Petey looked where Ticky did.

"I put the medals there, and then I kissed her. Here. Mouth. She was my girl."

Reedy was right again. Always. Reedy would say it's all about belt-high and thick as shit, and we all got to slog through it from the day we're born until the day the Red Sox win anything.

41

Marge Klinger shut it down for a week, although Ticky had insisted he was ready to kick ass—at least that's what he told Petey Myers and what Petey relayed to Marge.

"I don't give a shit. She died, and I'm shutting down. One week."

Petey had Vi cook up a nice lasagna for Ticky that first night and brought it out. In the morning Petey, Vi, and Bobby all drove out to pick him up and take him over to the Episcopal church on the Rio Grande, where Minnie's ashes were in a small white urn that Skyo had fetched with her new friend, Reverend Eliphalet Nott.

The church hadn't seen this many people since Reverend Nott's grandfather had buried Poker Alice Tubbs in 1928. A solid representation of cowboys moved solemnly into place, as did Buck Overstreet with Jude and Jimmy the Kid and his mom and dad. Del Pratt had driven all night from Wichita Falls to represent all the Lettgo Feed 'n' Seed stores' employees. Ruby Onerati brought Creedemore's floral display in her own car. Miss Wilma Kirk caravanned to the church with many members of Creedemore's arts and history community. Molly Dowie was there. Steven Kearney also. He hadn't seen Molly for several days since she had stepped over him when he was sleeping in her front yard, but this morning, having puttered down from Ute Ranch, he almost hit her coming out of the Seattle House of Joe. She stopped in the street as he squeaked to a halt. She was dressed in a long black skirt and a sweater. She removed her bowler and patted her head. Steven straddled the small motor scooter.

"Hello, Steven Kearney," she said, her face without expression.

"Molly Dowie," he said, as if he were alarmed. "You're all dressed up."

"I'm going to a funeral."

"All the Overstreets are going, too."

"You're not going?"

"Well . . . I didn't know them."

She nodded and started across the street. He looked behind him, then followed her.

"And I don't have any good . . . I didn't bring a lot of clothes."

Molly got to the sidewalk in front of the Historical Society, where she had parked her truck. "You look okay."

Steven glanced down at his sneakers and chinos and blue flannel shirt. She climbed into the truck. He walked the scooter into the alley, locked it, and climbed into the truck's passenger side.

They sputtered out of town, past the tiny airport and played-out mines.

"It's at the Episcopal church, right? I kind of know the minister."

"Your girlfriend might not like you sleeping in my yard," Molly said, still expressionless.

"My girlfriend?"

"It's okay that you watch me do the mural because you're writing it."

Horses, some baby ones, ran alongside the truck in their meadow.

"That was kind of your idea. The word-mural. I never would have thought of it if you didn't bring those great drawings," he said.

"So it's okay to watch me draw it and paint it."

"Cool."

Her mouth seemed to open for a long time before she spoke. "And dinner or coffee. That would be okay. I'm not saying that would not be okay."

"I was sorry I didn't eat the mashed potatoes at the hotel. I hardly ate anything. I was hungry that whole night."

Molly nodded. She got hungry later that night, too.

"I just thought when I came out of my house to paint and you were sleeping there, I thought that it was one of the things she would not like."

The line of cars appeared now, snaking toward the adobe church by the river.

"Who?"

"And that's a perfect way to get sick. It gets cold in the morning. Even in the summer. It snowed up here one summer. You didn't have a sleeping bag or anything."

"Snowed? Summer?"

"I just don't think it's a good idea."

She maneuvered into a rocky space in back of the church. She turned to him and didn't smile. "Everybody liked Minnie. Ticky's hard, but Minnie was sweet. She brought up beautiful baby things for Willie. She brought them up from Texas."

"So the reason you're not smiling is you're sad. I thought you were mad."

They got out and walked to the front of the church.

"I'm sad."

"I'm sorry."

"I'm mad, too."

The few folding chairs had been removed. Reverend Eliphalet Nott invited the congregants to sit on the floor around the altar with the small marble urn on it. Most sat cross-legged. Some of the younger cowboys squatted.

Eliphalet Nott wore a plain black cassock with a stole of woven Ute cloth. He arranged Communion articles next to Minnie while the mourners watched in silence. Finally he looked up and smiled. Light passed through the large stained glass depicting the manger of Christ. Eli seemed to speak directly to Ticky, who battled his face to attention.

" 'I am the Resurrection and the Life, saith the Lord: He that believeth in me, though he were dead, yet shall he live: and whosoever liveth and believeth in me, shall never die.' "

Ticky nodded.

"Well, Minnie believed. You know that, Reverend. And your daddy and his daddy knew that. That's three, then. So it's known."

Eli nodded, and Ticky nodded again.

"I'd say, 'In what?' She'd say, 'In the Lord.' 'You lose the boy, and you still believe?' She'd go, 'You lose the boy, you don't lose the faith.' That was Minnie. Me? Me? Well, I lost the boy, and brother, close the gates. But I like the hymns okay. I like 'Onward, Christian Soldiers,' I like 'What a Friend We Have in Jesus.' But lose the boy and lose the faith. Except Minnie. I'd take her to church and wait outside in the car. Listen to the radio. Scores. Hank Williams. Bob Wills's Big Band. But he's dead, too."

Eli waited to be sure Ticky had finished. Ticky's fingers played wild at his charcoal suit.

"Jesus said, 'Let not your heart be troubled: ye believe in God, believe also in me. In me—' "

" 'O Little Town of Bethlehem.' Minnie loved that one, too. It bothered her, really bothered her, that you only got to sing it on Christmas. I'd say, 'Well, hell, girl, pick another goddamn song.' She'd say, 'Don't you raise your voice to me, Mr. Lettgo. I'll love any goddamn song I want to.' 'Yes, ma'am,' I'd say."

The cowboys nodded. Miss Kirk nodded. Ticky watched his fingers.

"Remember thy servant Minnie Lettgo, O Lord, according to the favor which thou bearest unto thy people, and grant—"

"I have got me seven Feed 'n' Seeds, and I'm going to open the next one maybe in Paint Rock, even though it's Mexican top-heavy, but still close enough to San Antonio, and money's money. And I would not, I . . . I would not have one, not one, if that old girl wasn't my old girl. I'd keep the Colt on the counter of the first Feed 'n' Seed, and when all the chicos who used to pay when they damn well felt like it give the order, I'd say, 'You miss a payment, I shoot your dog,' and she'd say, 'Mr. Lettgo, you behave, now. This gentleman is a fine gentleman, and he will pay on time.' And almost always she was right."

"She wore the pin," Petey Myers said. "She kept that pin for her boy."

"I put it on the pillow when she got sick. You seen it, Sheriff."

"Yes, sir. One time me and Reedy have to protect these cockhounds parading through downtown carrying these, swear to God, jars, big jars of formaldehyde filled with fetuses. Just as big as you please, carrying these jars and screaming at the police who were there to protect them on account of the Irish Catholics who wanted to kill them."

"Jesus," Ticky said from the end of his seat.

"You could just about make out these little faces."

"Jesus."

"Vi? Couldn't you?"

"I wasn't there, hon."

"Now, old Reedy could phrase it up. He could put a few good words on things, but that day he could not speak. He shook his head. On the way back to the Back Bay station, I'm driving, old Reedy starts crying, and he's this big, with shoulders like this, and he's crying."

"Black fella?" Ticky asked.

"God yes."

"Jesus."

"I ask him if he's okay, and he says, 'I don't know. I just don't know.' Reedy knew. Something like that you just don't know. Same as Minnie's pins. Same as you losing the boy. Now Minnie."

Eliphalet Nott once more let the room quiet before continuing the Anglican Burial of the Dead. This time he brought it on through the homily and Communion, too.

*　*　*

Mountain Man Red Fields's only complaint was that Judge Marge Klinger didn't shut it down forever. What can a guy say about the Ferrini bitch? She's wrong? Shout it out? Sitting up there like some fucking *Jeopardy!* contestant. Klinger letting her go on and on. And anyway, who the hell cares about her volcano bullshit phony theories? What did that have to do with the old fart trying to ruin him and maybe kill him, too? Okay. He took elementary geology. Who didn't? He even checked out a book from the South Fork Library just in case they tried to humiliate him. *The Geological Evolution of the Rocky Mountains*. It was the only rock book in the entire fucking library not written by the Ferrini bitch herself. She says something, it has to be right, because *she* wrote it. Bullshit. Okay, there were a number of volcanic fields in Montana, but where else? Call me. C'mon, ask. I'll kick her ass.

These things filled his head so that, happily, most of the garbage Bill Clinings was spewing at the secret meeting of the Liberty Society had missed him completely. Secret meeting. Jesus Christ. A bunch of nerds sipping Chablis in the Piñon Room of the Monte Vista Holiday Inn. And Cia so into it, so ready to buy this Clinings's bullshit. Roughed up by Petey Myers? C'mon, Mountain Man snickered to himself, Myers wouldn't waste his time. Clinings droned on.

". . . as the key components in the moral dilemma, we come together at this delicate time to make sure that the moment—the *moment*, remember—does not pass. Property creates cruelty, cruelty creates complacency. It would be at this vector, passions waning, that some sacrifice would follow, usually in cultures more zestful than ours."

Todd Lehman from the CU music department shifted noisily in his chair. "We're zestful. I would say one of the things that distinguishes us from, say, PETA, is we're reasonably 'zestful.' "

Sandy Fiddler, an enormous woman given to Gypsy clothes and dirty talk, snorted. "They throw bombs, for fuck's sake. They set themselves on fire."

"That's being aggressive. That's not being zestful."

"Well, maybe what we need is more aggression and less zestfulness."

"Sandy," Todd barked, "a person can be zestful and still be relevant."

"Zestful is carrying signs."

"Zestful is a lot more than that."

"Aggression is what we need."

"We need zestful, too."

"Zestful people don't set themselves on fire."

"Sometimes they do."

"When?"

"Vietnam."

"The Buddhist priests? That wasn't zestfulness."

"Was too."

"That was aggression."

"It's a combination we need," Bill Clinings said in the most reasonable of tones. "A balance, if you will, so that the larger issue of the water–land animal–cultural matrix can be concentrated on and, of course, altered. We need, boys and girls, an event."

Mountain Man caught the last part of Clinings's monologue and looked over to Cia to share a smirk. She was taking notes! Writing word for word everything this joker with a broomstick up his ass was saying. An event! Jesus!

"Do you mean like the fund-raiser we had last Halloween?"

"No, Todd, but that was exceptional."

"Thanks."

"Sandy's been working on some rather imaginative scenarios. I especially like the one we discussed at length today, Sandy. Now, I'm going to go no further until we can be sure that what we say in this room will remain here."

Mountain Man was not sure why he let Cia talk him into coming. He wanted to lie low. He wanted some venue to show Creedemore he was sorry, very sorry, about the old fart's wife. She was friendly and always smiled. Maybe a sympathy card. Just because he was in some contrary position with Lettgo, he still had the right to be sorry. Now he was at the Holiday Inn and Cia was taking fucking notes.

"Red?"

Mountain Man looked up from his hiking boots. Everyone was staring at him. The entire secret council of the Liberty Society in all their preternatural resolve focused on the plaintiff. He looked at Clinings, then over to Cia, whose eyes seemed set in a kind of fierceness.

"Red?"

He twitched his eyes back to Clinings.

"Everyone else has agreed that what is said from now on in the sanctity of this room is private. Personal thoughts and ideas are not sharable."

Clinings waited. They all waited.

"Well . . . sure . . . I won't share anything."

"Secret in the strictest sense."

"Whatever."

"Or we'd kill you," Sandy Fiddler snarled matter-of-factly.

Mountain Man grinned at Sandy. He grinned at Cia, then Todd.

Todd uncrossed his legs and sat up straight. "Or, say, one of us, even Bill, shared the ideas that are for us only. Then you could kill Bill. Or Sandy. Or—"

"He won't have to kill me," Sandy hissed.

"I was being analogous."

"I might have to kill him. Or you."

"You won't have to kill me. I promise you."

"I don't think we ought to go around and around about who is going to kill whom, as long as everyone in the secret room knows that someone will kill them if they share."

Mountain Man's mouth was open, but he could not form the words. He licked the roof of his mouth with a dry tongue.

"I'll vouch for Mountain Man. And if he shares, then I'll kill him myself," Cia said.

"Well, what if you share?" croaked Sandy.

"Then you can kill me."

"And vice versa," Todd said. "It's really simple. Later on we could even as-sign who is supposed to kill whom should he or she share."

"All right, then," Clinings said. "The event. Sandy . . ."

Sandy Fiddler grunted her big body off the chair and exchanged places with Bill Clinings.

"I'll tell you one thing," the smock-coated manager of Boulder's only ag-nostic bookstore wheezed. "After the little doozy we have planned for them, those cocksuckers are gonna wish they could've pissed up a tree before they bought the land out from under the fucking rank and file."

The eight conspirators smiled wickedly. The ninth felt hot acid rise out of his stomach and splash like molten lava against the back of his throat.

—What is remembered?
What is seen must be of no fear,
Must be viewed as a snowflake clear
The mysterious heart, the elusive dream
The gathering night, the afternoon gleam.
O mistress, is memory true?
Is memory me, is memory you?

—Juan Carlos de Moreno to Teresa Herrera

42

The manuscript was completed in a frantic three-day marathon when Juan Carlos de Moreno, the reluctant conquistador, poet, lover of Teresa, and narrator of the Creedemore mural play, seemed to take over and drive the piece across the literary finish line. With a bold sweep of his hand, the young Spanish soldier rededicates himself to sustaining the majesty of the land and walks with resolve into the shining mountains, via the alley between the hardware store and the Western Market.

Steven topped his ink pen, stood, and walked to the window overlooking the Municipal Building. The trial was set to resume on Monday, and he was deeply appreciative of the weeklong grace period. Except for the shift of the Liberty Society of Colorado camped out under their green-and-brown banner, the crowds were gone. He looked up toward her rock house, then back at his manuscript. The great pile of paper seemed to weigh down the oak desk. He might have to cut a little. He couldn't be sure until it was on its feet. But cut what? All the character roles that swirled like miniature tornadoes around Juan Carlos de Moreno—from the mammoth hunter Moga to Chief Dan Snow-Too-Much and on all the way to Rick Levy, who gave the valley its first truly excellent television reception with the Levy Satellite System—were indispensable from the whole.

As with every one of his major works, Steven Kearney felt a true connection to the tools of his labor. He did not feel that typewriters held any comparison to the pencil. The pen. An order. A system. A formulation. He needed a typist. He gathered up the work and puttered to the mural. Molly Dowie wasn't there and, from the looks of it, hadn't been there for several days. Although the beautiful tableau had been sketched out fully, the flow of color had extended only to a transferring sky on either side of the young conquistador's enormous face. Steven turned the scooter in the direction of Bachelor Creek.

Again he ran his little engine a moment outside the rock house as if to announce himself. He turned off the scooter and waited another long minute,

198

then went to the purple door. When it opened, it was the redheaded conquistador.

"I'm Steven Kearney."

"I know, come in."

"I'm looking for Molly."

"She hasn't been feeling too good lately. She drove to her doctor in Monte Vista, and he got her into the hospital for a transfusion."

"She's in the hospital?"

"No. Doctor called me up in the Springs, and I came and got her. She was pissed. She wanted to drive herself back."

"I would . . . I would have picked her up. I mean, c'mon, I would've."

"I'll go see if she's awake."

Willie walked into her small alcove and tiptoed back.

"Out like a light."

"This is awful that she just drove herself."

"That's Molly. She's a nut. She's an artist, so she can be nutty if she wants to. Doctor said it's very common after the chemo. Blood count goes down, and they come in for transfusions. She's gained a couple of pounds, though. He thinks maybe they've got everything, and so she can skip the radiation."

Steven looked concerned. He'd missed many pieces of the Molly Dowie puzzle. Why would she not have asked him to drive her in? Or somebody? He heard Willie saying something.

"Anything I can do for you?"

"Uh . . . not really. I was going to . . . Are you sure she's okay?"

"Want to call the doctor?"

"Really?"

Willie wrote out the name and number. "I don't know if he'll talk to you or not. What else?"

"I'm looking for a typist. I wrote this big thing in longhand, and I need to find a typist."

"I'll type it."

They both turned to see Molly in an enormous red flannel nightgown that looked as if ten of her could have fit comfortably inside.

"Molly, get your ass back in bed," Willie said.

"I feel fine. I'm all rested. I can type pretty good. And I'm cheap. As a matter of fact, I'm free."

"I'm looking for a typist. I just wanted a suggestion."

"And I'm suggesting me."

"You got enough to do. The mural—"

"I can type at night."

"So you can type my play, but I can't take you for a transfusion."

"My transfusion is my business."

"So is my play."

"A play is communal art."

"Not until somebody starts acting and directing."

Willie waved his cellular phone at them and walked outside. "I'm making some calls."

"I finish the piece and I go down to look at the mural and I see right away that nothing has happened and I come up here and find out you just drove on down to Monte whatever—"

"Vista."

"Monte Vista—and get this transfusion and you were even going to drive yourself back, and now you want to type my play? Just like that?"

"I didn't say I *wanted* to, I said I would."

He wanted now, more than anything else in the world, to be clear. To choose a precise language for Molly. Some uncommon expression of resolve. But he felt the old familiar ordinariness gripping the important sectors of his brain.

"I don't . . . know. I just don't know." He looked at his feet.

"My hair's growing."

"What?"

"My hair. I've got some. I'm getting it all. I got brown hair."

"Yeah?"

"A little . . . a little gray, too. Which is good. Or which is okay."

They watched each other's eyes.

"I have a lot of gray. Quite a bit."

He yanked at his little ponytail. He imagined her transcribing his scrubby scrawl and judging his art word for word and sentence and paragraph.

"I don't want you to type it."

"Fine, then." Some redness drove up her cheeks.

"I just don't—"

"I just wanted to help. But because I don't call up people when I feel tired, for rides to the doctor, I don't get to type—fine. Fine with me. Maybe I ought to promise you that if I'm completely down on my sorry old ass and I need to go to the doctor at two in the morning, maybe I'll call you up at the Ute Ranch and you can drive down the twenty miles in the pitch-black on that crummy scooter and then drive me all the way to Monte Vista."

"Would you really promise me that, Molly?"

"I promise," she said like a dare.

"Cool."

* * *

Reverend Eliphalet Nott wasn't given to contemplating the profundity of the situation. Any situation. To the semi-Episcopal humanist, what happens happens. If it was spirit- or soul-wearing, then it became a serious problem, but the matter of corporeal man, compared to the higher part of the numen, seemed trivial. Still, Skyo was only twenty-four, and it worried him that he liked her as much as he did. He walked out of his little apartment attached to the church and under the impossible glitter of stars. He sipped the warm Budweiser, then walked around to the back of the church, the section closest to the big river. He lit his pipe, heard the rush of water, and tasted the good hops. Evenings like this came as an affirmation of the bigness of life force and man's powerful presence at the core of it all. There was a satisfaction that he was utterly correct and his direction fitting. Soul was God. And, of course, vice versa. He took a large swallow of the Bud and smiled over the uneven tent of peaks.

"Mr. Nott?"

Eliphalet jumped slightly. The briar fell from his mouth, but he snatched it back up in midair. Coruscating tobacco leaves joined the stars.

"Jesus!"

"Sorry."

Eliphalet looked up from the embers of cherry blend and saw a big red-headed man standing by the corner of the church.

"I'm sorry," he said again. "Jeez."

"Uh . . . no, no. No problem. I'm Eliphalet Nott. And you?"

"I'm Red Fields."

"Mountain Man Red Fields?"

"Well, it's that, too. Yes."

"I didn't hear a car."

"I rode one of the bikes. I rent mountain bikes."

"That's right. I've seen the store. Can I get you a beer?"

"No thanks."

Eliphalet felt he knew the basics of the contention in Creedemore and also felt that basics were as close as a soulist should come. His beer tasted flat.

"I'm going to grab another Bud. C'mon."

At his small fridge, he held out a cold one to Red Fields, who took it.

Eliphalet smiled. "It's the King. It's got it over the microbrews."

Red Fields held the tall can and set his jaw and eyes at a distance.

Eliphalet popped his open. "What's that one that everybody's shitting their pants about?"

"I don't know."

"Samuel Adams? That sound right?"

"Could be."

201

"Sit."

Red Fields sat in one of two small kitchen chairs. Eliphalet Nott sat in the other.

Red Fields sighed. "My . . . folks split in . . . oh, '89, I think. It wasn't ugly or anything. I think they always loved each other. I think they didn't like each other. Or didn't love each other enough. But I don't think there was . . . you know, infidelity."

"That's good," Eliphalet said quietly. "That's very good. These days everybody's running around getting divorced because the guy can't keep it in his pants or the chick's getting banged by the washing-machine repair guy. It's nice to see commitment. Even if they did split."

Red Fields nodded at his beer. "I spent time with Mother at first. Then Dad. I'd go back and forth. They tried to work it out so I wouldn't be upset or anything."

Reverend Eliphalet Nott nodded. "That's great. That's great they tried to work it out. When couples go around fucking their brains out, they get so pissed at each other that the kids suffer. Good for them. The way they worked it."

"Dad would throw the ball, and Mom took me to the Eastern Star meetings."

"Ahhh . . ."

"Then I got into graduate school. The rest of the stuff after the divorce is high crap, except I did undergraduate at Wayne State. The thing is, I really have this need to share something, you see, to share this conversation I had but have absolutely promised not to share."

"Where did you do your graduate work?"

"Huh?"

"Did you do your graduate work at Wayne State, too?" Eliphalet asked.

"Boulder. CU."

"Ahhh."

"Mathematics-sociology."

"I went to divinity school at Harvard. I'd have been better off just going to Pueblo. Old John Harvard can suck your faith right out of the bunghole."

The window curtain flopped in cool, short spurts of breeze.

"So you want to share something? Shoot."

Mountain Man stood and paced to the door and back to the chair. "I'm not Episcopalian or anything."

"That's copacetic. I'm a soulist."

Mountain Man nodded. "Mother started me out Congregational, and Dad, when I was there, took me to a Methodist church. Then Mom went a little overboard and started going around with the *Watchtower*, and Dad just stopped going. His new wife was Jewish, I think. Or something."

"My grandmother was Ute."

"Really?"

"One hundred percent. Didn't speak any English at all."

"Amazing."

"My grandfather could get a whole congregation by the nuts in ten minutes, but couldn't get his wife to learn English." Eliphalet smiled at Mountain Man. "So what is it you want to share?"

"See . . . I mean . . . I don't *want* to share. . . . I'm trying to figure out if it's ethically *all right* to share after I've really and truly promised *not* to share."

"So it's a secret."

"It's a real secret."

"And you're dying to share it."

"It could be put like that. Yes."

Eliphalet repacked his pipe with the cherry blend and looked thoughtful.

"One part of our study load in divinity school was investigating ethics by branch, nature, types, and relations. Metaethics and normative ethics, concepts of morality, shit like that. People look at ethical matters diversely, and about a million distinct ethical disciplines turn around and look at the people looking diversely and evaluate *them* according to some asshole formula usually put together by a dead guy who lived about a thousand years ago and spent all his time trying not to get eaten by wolves. Here's a perfect example: G. E. Moore."

"The mathematician?"

"I guess. The guy worked out these concepts of goodness and the significance of goodness with *formulas. Formulas!* Picture this. Bunch of tight-ass Anglican divinity-school students tested on mathematical equations about the nature of man and God. I mean, Red, c'mon."

Mountain Man didn't know what to say, so he shook his head sadly.

"*G* equals small *d* small *f* big *P.* Is it really only *PG*? Could it be just as significantly expressed as *PP*?"

Mountain Man said, "The *d* and *f*. Does that stand for 'defining terms of'?"

"Jesus Christ, Red. That's what I'm saying. I don't know. I simply do not fucking know. I'm thirty-two, and now I'm kind of seeing a twenty-four-year-old who makes me positively feel good but on the other hand cannot see the concepts of soul-God or God-man. I mean, shit, Red, I wish to hell there was a formula for that. I sure don't want her to think that I'm a big fake, because I'm fairly certain I'm not."

Mountain Man slouched again onto the blue chair. "Well, I'm having some trouble. . . . Not trouble, I suppose. . . ."

"Problems?"

"Pretty much. Problems with my fiancée, Cia. We can't talk too well anymore. Now, the trial . . ."

"Well, can you share what you want to share with . . . who?"

"Cia. Absolutely. I could share with her because she was there when I learned it, only, as I said, I had to take this really solemn oath not to share with anybody else. There were eight people that shared and agreed not to share with anybody else. Nine, if you include me."

"So you all agreed."

"Yeah, but see, I didn't know what I was agreeing to, other than the not-sharing thing."

"Did you explain to them that you have a need to share this?"

"Explain to them? Jesus! . . . Sorry."

"No?"

"I can't explain to them. The promise not to share was extremely serious. I can't even explain anything to Cia. I mean, she sat at the meeting taking *notes,* for crying out loud."

"So it's something you can share with the others but not with anyone else, and you can't even say, 'Look, I'm thinking about rethinking this not-sharing,' to them?"

"They'd kill me."

"It'd really piss them off, huh?"

Eliphalet relit the pipe and pulled hard until it capped red-hot.

"Ever read Reinhold Niebuhr?"

Mountain Man shook his sad face.

"He went to divinity school. Yale, I think. He was a pastor and a teacher, and he wrote some books based on lectures and sermons that he gave. You ever hear the Anglicans go on and on, Red? Jesus! It really is unbelievable. You have to be *conditioned* to be that dull. You could torture people with the homilies. However, as I understood it, this old bird Niebuhr was pretty remarkable. Remarkable because of the way he looked at things. He took the whole of things. Nations. Political parties. You name it. And what he did was draw hard comparisons between the morality of groups and the morality of individuals. Book's called *Moral Man and Immoral Society.*"

Reverend Eliphalet Nott waited for something and puffed the perfumed smoke high in the air.

"Who won?" Mountain Man asked.

"Who do you think?"

"The individual?"

Eliphalet grinned. "Niebuhr thought that not only was the group morally inferior, he felt it was so affected by the shitty impulses of the group as a whole that the individual was vastly better as a moral vessel. What we are, really, all of us, is bullied down by the group even though they are inferior to us instead of the other way around."

Mountain Man Red Fields was quiet for a moment, then said, "You have a copy of that book?"

*   *   *

Sheriff Petey Myers was still at his office Sunday evening going over Monday's court procedure with Bobby, Dan, Vi, Mayor Ruby Onerati, and a representative of the state police, Rosie Carnevale, who stood speaking at a kind of parade rest. Petey had never seen a woman officer wearing a bulletproof vest before, and it seemed to him that it looked even more awkward than when all the old-timers in Boston were issued those snug, heavy things in '79. Wait. Noreen O'Neill had worn one in Boston, but she had gotten kneecapped not two weeks after Reedy went down. And Reedy had said that the Smith & Wesson was *his* bulletproof vest. Petey smiled thinking about it. "Don't need no vest, Petey, if the man been given a new asshole between his eyes." Oh, God, but Reedy knew. Reedy. Petey chuckled. Rosie stopped talking.

"Sheriff Myers? Did I say something funny?"

"No. I was just thinking about Reedy."

He looked over at Vi, and they shared a smile.

Rosie continued. "For something like this, what we've done is computed stats to intersect with other similar scenarios."

"There were other things?" Bobby asked.

"You'd be surprised."

"Had that water thing over by Green River in Utah. Fifties, I think. I remember reading how the tribe shot the hell out of some ranchers. Sneaky bastards," retired sheriff Dan Cryer said.

"Actually, we view this as a much less extreme situation. Property disputes are in several categories. We don't see any bomb throwers out there."

Now Petey saw Reedy going down hard on the basketball court, calling to him. Petey shivered and drank his cold and oily coffee.

"The presence of the police should be more than enough to avoid any repeat of last week."

Ruby Onerati raised her hand and was acknowledged by Rosie. "How many is enough for a police presence?"

"We are estimating, with Sheriff Myers and his staff, we'll need six patrolmen from the state police."

Ruby nodded.

Dan raised his hand like a second-grader needing to pee. "Now, when you say Petey's staff, were you including me? I know I'm retired, but I kind of consider myself part of the staff. Unpaid. I mean, you wouldn't have to pay me, but—"

"Hell, Dan, of course you're staff," Petey said.

Miss Wilma Kirk entered the office from the hallway next to the auditorium. She nodded and sidled over to Ruby.

"Miss Kirk, this is Rosie Carnevale from the State Police Tactical Division," Ruby said.

"Oh, I know Miss Carnevale. I know her work."

Rosie looked puzzled.

"I saw the one-act festival in Alamosa. Miss Carnevale played Bertha, the title role in Tennessee Williams's *Hello from Bertha*, performed by the Alamosa Players. Excellent."

"Thank you." Rosie beamed. Her hair was dyed blond and gave an exotic glow to her Mediterranean skin.

"The ensemble performed flawlessly. I thought you were especially splendid in your interpretation, and the young women playing the other prostitutes were equally engaging."

"I'll tell them. Well, if no one has any questions, I'll see you bright and early."

"Six," said Petey.

"There's another force that is being brought to bear," Miss Kirk stated with urgency.

They looked at her.

"It's no secret, or I hope it's not, that I believe the arts community has a profound effect on our lives here in Creedemore and its environs. Tomorrow evening we get down to production meetings on Mr. Steven Kearney's commissioned work of the history of Creedemore. That's my mission."

She spoke to Ruby. "Do we have any idea when the trial will adjourn? Approximately would be fine. I'm going to need the auditorium."

"Petey?" Ruby asked.

"Around four in the afternoon. Marge wants to get home for her summer softball league, and she's over in Lake City."

Miss Kirk wrote down this information in a bold hand.

"Then we'll say, comfortably, six, and I'll make certain everything is put back the way we found it."

She paused and looked dramatic and distant.

"Mr. Kearney is putting his finishing touches to the text as we speak, so of course tomorrow will be the first time anyone sees it. I hope you will all consider joining the troupe in some capacity."

"Who's directing?" Rosie asked.

"Mr. Kearney, I presume. He's from New York."

Everyone nodded, even Petey Myers.

"When's casting?" Rosie asked.

"That will be decided at tomorrow's production meeting."

Rosie settled her state police cap high and angled. Miss Kirk said authoritatively, "Our own Cowboy Bob Panousus puts it this way:

" '—It's not for love of man or money
That makes us play the parts.
It's that the thing that saves us, honey,
Is called fine and performing arts.' "

Petey spoke to the ceiling. "Sometimes, if it got late and we were double-shifted up, Reedy would drop me at my house on the way back to the station or I'd drop him." Now they all watched Petey.

"Sindy—and she spelled it with an S—was a nice girl, although Reedy and her had their share of mess. Anyway, this being my night to drop old Reedy off, I cruise through his neighborhood over near the U Mass Boston campus. Him and Sindy had a little spat in the A.M., and while Reedy wasn't looking to apologize, he wasn't looking for a fight either. So we pull up in front of the three-family, and Sindy comes out on the porch all smiling and waves and yells, 'I'm taking acting lessons!' or 'I'm gonna be an actress!' or something like that. Reedy just turns to me and says, 'Get my black ass outta here, Petey.' But we went to some play she was doing. Me, Vi, Reedy, sat there, and it was pretty good."

They all considered this, then followed Rosie to the vehicles.

* * *

He was five feet five inches tall, with nearly three of those inches indebted to the cognac-colored, lizard Tony Lamas. His navy Wranglers were snug, pressed, and boot-cut. A western embroidered tailored shirt in plum was worn sleeves down and buttoned to the neck, finished off with a horsehair tasseled necktie, gold like the colossal oval belt buckle fitted with a genuine black onyx stone that caught the sun just perfectly as he lowered himself out of the Chevy Tahoe and down to the street. He closed the door and surveyed this town that the Denver papers and national networks called "under siege." Except for the sheriff and a state patrolwoman conversing by a county vehicle, it all seemed peaceful enough. While he technically remained a part of the town and its people, he had relocated years before. First time in his own mind and the second to a neat little development outside Denver. Now he found himself in a kind of apologetic mood. Sorry to have been so successful. Sorry to have had the last word, so to speak. He headed across the street with the gait of a man of accomplishment, the long heels of the Tony Lamas making his little butt stick out some. Stopping for a second or two in the middle of the street, he looked up toward the Municipal Building, then down, past the post office and grocery store. He continued across, bounded onto the wooden side-walk and up the outside stairs to the second floor of the hardware store, where the Creedemore Historical Society made its home. The door was open, even at this early hour. On the far side of the room, a man with a tiny ponytail stood looking out the window.

After a moment the visitor said, "Miss Kirk around?"

Steven Kearney started, some papers dropping out of his hands. "Uh . . . Miss Kirk? No . . . uh . . ."

"I was hoping to see Miss Kirk."

"I know she's doing a production meeting tonight at six. Municipal Build-ing. I'm sure she'll be in this morning but"—he checked his watch—"well . . . it's not even six yet."

"You must be the New York City writer."

"I'm Steven Kearney."

"Must be making you feel kind of silly, New York and all, writing about our poor old place."

"Silly?"

"Cowboys-and-Indians stuff."

They faced off on either side of the room.

"I think it's not silly at all. In fact, I like the history of the place."

"What you know of it, you mean." Steven watched him closely. "I don't mean insult. I'm just saying the big city comes to little Creedemore. Must be good for a few laughs."

"I'm not . . . I'm not laughing. It's getting typed up."

"Oh, so it's all ready, then? It's perfect? It's precise? It's unerring? It's matchless?"

"Who should I . . . If Miss Kirk asks me, who should I say wants to see her?"

The tight, small man draped his thumbs onto his belt. He rocked a little on the tall Tony Lamas.

"In the night's hot sky, it can catch your eye,
Like a girl with a long-legged walk.
And all that's why, I can tell you I
Have no time for a long-winded talk.

For my story's a dilly, and I say it willy-nilly,
'Cause my metaphor man can't rob.
Just a big old Gilly in our land so hilly,
I'm a pal you can simply call Bob."

208

A cool morning breeze bounced the words around the room and out the window. Steven was pretty sure there was a sneer on the man's lips throughout most of the recitation.

"I'm Cowboy Bob Panousus."

"The poet Cowboy Bob?"

"That's me."

Steven nodded. "Cool."

Cowboy Bob brought his heels almost to a click to raise himself to full height and unhooked his thumbs.

"Me? Or my poem?"

43

etey Myers walked Marge Klinger to her car at 4:55. Five minutes to the second after she had gaveled the deal closed for the day. She had changed into the red softball uniform of the Lake City Ladies and walked with her spikes hanging from her shoulder.

"Kick a little butt out there, Margie."

"Consider it kicked."

He watched her leave the municipal parking lot. A look of relief and not a little satisfaction riding across his face. The crowd had been smallish and well behaved. Only about three or four Colorado Liberty Society yuppies showed up, and that fat-ass Mel Prophit and his boy JoJo got bored and left before noon. Les Vallejos seemed not as combative with the witnesses Roger Hockney had lined up, although he had gotten into a shouting match with Felicia "Cia" Brun because he referred to her as Mountain Man Red Fields's "woman." Then, at the first recess, Marny Vallejos let him have it, too. But these were just little disturbances. Things, the sheriff felt, might just be getting better.

*　*　*

Todd Lehman unraveled the long, scroll-like paper. From what he could see, it was more a major blueprint than the easy six-step directions Sandy Fiddler had promised. He looked up from the passenger side of her Chevy Blazer.

"I'm not an architect, Sandy," he said, wagging the paper.

"That's only supplemental, for fuck's sake. The book's under the seat."

The Blazer rose out of Boulder toward Denver, passing endless housing developments. Sandy Fiddler in large jeans and mammoth red T-shirt looked hostilely at the passing town houses.

"Fuckers," she uttered darkly.

Todd reached under his seat and pulled out several books.

"*The Vegetarian Agnostic*? *The Agnostic's Bible*? *The*—"

"Cut the shit, Lehman. It's the pamphlet."

Todd put down the other books and held the ten-page booklet. "It's thin."

"It ain't a dissertation. Maybe you want out. Is that it?"

"I just said it was a thin pamphlet."

"I was reading between the lines."

"There isn't any 'between the lines.' "

Todd lowered his window and opened to page one. The air was comfortable and smelled like grass, then suddenly like burning sulfur.

"Factory. Roll up the window."

He rolled it back up and read the title page aloud. "*Guide to Bombmaking. Fertilizing the Revolution.*"

He looked at Sandy and turned the page. They rode down a flat stretch of highway, and she pointed over his shoulder.

"If I had one now, I'd melt that shit. That stucco shit."

He followed her finger out the window. A hacienda-style development surrounded by a rolling stucco wall glistened white and earthen orange.

"Well, at least that one makes an attempt at somehow integrating itself into the—"

"Integrating? Jesus. I'd bomb it."

"I'm not saying I wouldn't bomb it."

Todd went back to the manual, page two. Page three. Page four. "Seems too easy."

Sandy sniggered.

"What?" Todd whined.

"First you tell me it's too hard. Now it's too easy."

"I never said . . . I said the blueprint made it seem . . ."

"Make up your mind."

Todd closed the book and laid it on the space between them. He folded his arms. Sandy watched him out of the corner of her eye. Most of these swine, nestled in their complacent, cozy offices, did not have one ounce of the ardor needed for change. Deep down inside their minuscule beings, they were still a bunch of orthodox academics holding that umbilical cord of liturgical dogma. And that was that. They were for the most part, like this ponce Lehman, playing at change. But she was a disparate vessel altogether. An enormous and vengeful spirit spawned her senior year at Boulder when she rolled, full of loneliness, into a Christian Science Reading Room. A haven. A rest from the sense of not belonging. A respite. And to have that pious cocksucker ask her to leave because she had wandered in too late and they were open seven to seven and why not come back tomorrow. And *that,* that was the clarifying juncture of her until-then-insignificant, tiresome, and prosaic time on the planet. To be offered relief and to have it mercilessly withdrawn. Even God was in on the joke. First isolate the fat girl, break her heart with the cruelty of her environment, then set up the punch line with the Christian Science Reading

Room. BANG. BANG. BANG. Put her out on her ass. Come back later. Say-onara, fatso. Well, that prissy little prick could never, ever have guessed that the poor, huge, beaten-down girl with the ratty black curls and the Sears, Roe-buck muumuu would have the gumption to go out and start a reading room of her own. Only she'd open the Anti–Christian Science Reading Room. So in the late spring of 1979, having borrowed six thousand dollars from her mother, who was happy, Sandy was convinced, to have her elephantine eyesore stay out west, she opened Take It or Leave It: An Agnostic Reading Room and Bookstore, directly across the street from the Christian Science Reading Room. She raided the furniture warehouse of the Salvation Army and brought in an assortment of odd but unusually comfortable stuffed chairs and couches. She ground her very own mixture of coffee beans, gave the blends names like T. H. Huxley Roast, and sold porcelain cups of java at cost. She encouraged every possible assortment of artist to frequent and perform (on Friday evenings and Saturday afternoons), with the only contextual requirement that they astonish and disgust potential visitors to the Christian Science Reading Room on the other side of the street. Two years later, when Sandy arrived one morning to open her store, she saw that her competition had given up and were in the process of moving. Two hours later she had leased the space and named this agnostic auxiliary Not the Christian Science Reading Room.

Sandy's radical philosophies grew in symmetrical proportions to her girth and bawdy mouth. She became her own shock troop, her own essential cause. The objects of desire had almost never been people, so, of course it had been simple to discard any belief that held people in elevated orbit. People had al-ways let her down. People had weighed her and dismissed her. Sandy Fiddler made her establishment a focal point for mountains and rivers and pit bulls and black bears and anything, really, that, given the opportunity, men would ruin with the same base judging systems they applied to poor huge girls. Now Todd Lehman.

"Finish the fucking pamphlet."

"It's old hat. I bet they took the plans out of a *Popular Mechanics*."

Sandy slammed on the brakes, and the Blazer veered left, then right. She directed it over to the side of the road and brought it to a stop.

"Jesus!" Todd yelled, his glasses down low on his nose.

"Listen, you pansy, these fucking plans cost me a shitload of money out of my own pocket. These are the same fucking plans those dickheads used to blow up that asshole paper mill in Oregon and that fish hatchery in Massachu-setts. If they're good enough for those shit-for-brains, they're good enough for you."

"I didn't say it wasn't good enough. I did not say that. And I am not a pansy."

Todd picked up the plans and began to read them again. Sandy scrutinized him for another ten seconds, then pulled back out into traffic.

* * *

When it was finished, Molly found a cardboard box that would hold the 511-page typewritten play and taped it securely closed. She carried it to the passenger side of her pickup. She had some terrific stomach upsets and two nights ago a bad case of the sweats, but nothing more than her doctor had predicted, and this early morning she felt like a child. She had a sensation of newness that she hoped would sustain the completion of her work.

Molly parked by the half-finished mural and carried the box up the street to the Historical Society.

"Molly," Steven said.

"I've finished it, Steven Kearney."

"This is—"

"I know who this is. It's Cowboy Bob Panousus."

Now Steven could read the easy smile crossing over Cowboy Bob's small, pointy face.

"And you are . . ."

"I'm Molly Dowie."

"Hello."

"I illustrated the cover of *Arrows and Angels in America*," she said. Molly turned to Steven. "The Women's Democratic Club of Alamosa published it, and some of the money went to the Girl Scouts."

Cowboy Bob grinned hard. He hadn't done great on that one, but he got thirty-one cents on the dollar and the Scouts sold the hell out of the forty-page tome at $9.95 a pop.

"I was looking for Miss Kirk. Although I'm residing now in a different part of our wonderful state, Creedemore was my hometown. My . . . well, I suppose you could call it my launching pad to the literary life. But as I say, one does not forget debts real and imagined. I'm intending to offer my artistic services to Miss Kirk and the society in general."

Molly handed the heavy box of manuscript to Steven. "It's finished, Steven Kearney."

He took it as if she'd handed him a newborn.

"What would Miss Kirk do with your services, Cowboy Bob?" asked Molly.

"Well, in general, anything she wants. I was thinking of this retrospective, this dramatic display she commissioned. I must say I was a little surprised I was not approached about contributing. There's a tradition of poetics here, you know."

Cowboy Bob Panousus tried to seem casual in his banter, but his jeans were too snug.

"There sure is," Molly enthusiastically agreed.

Cowboy Bob nodded his smiling head once and stood at a kind of confident parade rest.

"When it's afternoon on the eastern shores,
When it's evening in Japan,
It's still A.M. in old Creedemore
And our coffee's in the hand."

Molly took the box from Steven and put it on the long, glass-topped display table with the taxidermied trout beneath. She opened the box and skimmed through the pages while they watched her. When she found what she wanted, she took off her bowler, as if she could not read with it on. She looked at Steven and Cowboy Bob and smiled, then looked back down at the manuscript. In her small voice, Molly read,

"These are the dreams that have
Come in the desert,
Come in a kind of rapture unfolding
Completely unto myself.
So I have seen you still, seen
Fingers playing at your needle,
Seen the endless caress of my soul in your stars."

Molly raised her eyes to Steven. Her expression challenging, almost dangerous. "It is so . . . so . . . beautiful, Steven Kearney."

Steven watched the corners of her mouth for a sneer, for a flicker of sarcasm, the mock, some scorn. He fumbled for his cigarettes. Cowboy Bob Panousus took a tiny step to Molly, lifted his hands, palms up, and shrugged at the same time.

"But . . . it doesn't rhyme."

*　*　*

Miss Wilma Kirk stood between the auditorium chairs about midway from where Marge Klinger had earlier dismissed the court for the day. Behind her were two large cardboard boxes from Valley Print, which had done yeoman duty copying and binding fifty complete scripts in under two hours. Miss Kirk waved her copy over her head.

"Here it is, then. Hot off the presses."

About thirty-five men and women from the Creedemore Historical Society and the Puerite County Community Players applauded politely. Dr. Lonnie Brustein, the large-animal vet out of South Fork, filled his Styrofoam cup with coffee and milk at the back of the room.

"Should we grab a copy?"

"Good idea, Lonnie," Miss Kirk concurred.

Steven noted a high seriousness amid the scraping of chairs and the quiet voices. When they had all settled back to their spots, thumbing through the heavy manuscript, he noticed Cowboy Bob Panousus making a pointedly understated entrance through the back door. Miss Kirk picked up a spare copy of the play and carried it to him.

"You all know Cowboy Bob Panousus, I'm sure."

History and drama applauded. Cowboy Bob had changed his clothes from the earlier elegant western wear. The elevated Tony Lamas had been replaced by elevated Dan Post Genuine Eastern Rattlesnake boots. An open, full-length oilskin drover coat dropped to just above Wrangler boot-cut jeans. A blue twill work shirt peeked out against a large silver buckle emblazoned with an American bald eagle. He held a worn Renegade hat almost apologetically, as if he had ridden hard to get here, his coat flaps trailing high off his back behind a charging mustang, and as a poor country cowboy poet he knew he was unfit to speak to this exalted aggregation of historians and thespians.

But he would try.

He accepted the manuscript and read the title page aloud. "*The Creedemore Retrospective: A Word-Mural.*"

A scattering of applause and many smiles, including a big one from Miss Wilma Kirk.

"We are so, so honored that you could join us this evening, Cowboy Bob," she said.

Cowboy Bob set Steven's manuscript down casually on a chair, straightened up, and said as boyishly as a fifty-two-year-old entrepreneur could muster:

"Well, it's easy to see why I keep coming back
To a place that I first called my home,
And it's better to be with a pat on the back
Than a lot of other places I roamed.
For it's love and it's smiles, and I'll say it again,
Though I don't want to seem like a bore,
Makes me camp here awhile midst the fellowship of friends,
In the sweet-smelling town of Creedemore."

Now a crescendo of applause. Standing next to her displayed drawings of the mural, Molly looked over at Steven. She did not have her bowler on, and her little noggin no longer shone, having given rise to maniacal short hairs, but when she saw Steven looking, she patted it anyway. He could not read the face. He felt she probably became unreadable on purpose, wearing absolutely nothing in her eyes. A mystery, all right. He returned her head pat, like ships communicating at night with flash boxes.

Miss Kirk moved back to her central position by the remaining manuscripts. For a moment she held her plump head by the chin, the very picture of poignant resolve. She looked up as though she might offer grace and drew a deep breath.

"I spoke with Sheriff Myers earlier, and he was rather pleased that today's court session did not meet with any disastrous results. But make no mistake, friends, the fabric of community has been worn thin in the great Weminuche wilderness. Skirmishes and disenchantment. Police cars for order that only, truly, the sanity of artistic expression can maintain."

A real quiet came into the room. In the back row, sitting next to his copy of the play, Cowboy Bob Panousus ground his teeth.

"In essence, this is why *The Creedemore Retrospective: A Word-Mural* was commissioned. To remove Puerite County's uncommon fine and performing-arts community from the social sidelines and set it squarely into the contending forces of political and moral belief systems."

Cowboy Bob shifted again in his tight jeans and thought, Jesus Christ Almighty.

"Is it high purpose, then? Ladies and gentlemen, it *is* high purpose indeed that has brought us here tonight. We shall work fast and sure. There are several key groups that must be formed, and I shall put a sign-up sheet here, so please include your phone number with your name. Scenic is one. Vi Myers, who has designed in several Boston-area community theaters, has agreed to helm that department."

Vi stood and smiled at the polite applause. "Well, I'm sure it's a wonderful play and I can't wait to read it and get started. And we'll need plenty of painters and hammerers, and I bet it'll be a lot of fun."

More polite applause as Vi waved and sat.

"Tom Zaleski, owner of our Creedemore Hardware Store, who costumed one of the Puerite County Players' greatest successes, *Oklahoma!*, two years ago, has graciously agreed to assume responsibility for the ensemble's ensembles."

Tom stood also. Applause. "Haven't read it either, but same dealy . . . some rentals, some bring-your-own. Sewers. Sewers. Sewers. That's what we need."

Tom sat. Applause.

"Technicals. Techy, as we say in the 'biz,' " Miss Kirk said.

Chuckles. Cowboy Bob thought, Shit.

She continued, "It's no secret that yours truly adores the backstage. The 'drama behind the drama,' I like to say. That's where you'll find me in the capacity, as usual, of stage manager. I shall need at least three assistants and four or five second assistants, and so please sign up under 'Technicals.' Also there is a category entitled 'Auxiliary.' Box office, mailings, public relations, and, in general, pulling in the audience. Not glamorous, but decidedly significant."

Miss Kirk took another profound breath and gestured boldly in Steven's direction.

"Mr. Steven Kearney. Playwright and director of *The Creedemore Retrospective: A Word-Mural*."

Steven stood at a kind of awkward attention and put his hands into his pockets. Miss Kirk sat down. Applause.

"Well . . . uh . . . I'm really, really excited to . . . you know . . . get started."

More applause.

"Miss Kirk says that the actors are good, and . . . you know . . . we'll have a lot of good ones to choose."

"When are the auditions?" someone asked.

"Miss Kirk?" Steven asked.

"Wednesday, Thursday, Friday evenings at seven—here. Saturday one P.M. here. First read-through is scheduled for one Sunday at the offices of the Historical Society."

John Torrey from Torrey's Rocks and Things raised his hand. "How many roles are there?"

Miss Kirk looked over at Steven.

"Uh . . . oh . . . I guess about ninety or a hundred or so. I guess we'll double and triple up. We have to when the rocks are talking, because they talk in unison."

Cowboy Bob glanced down at the script and shuddered. Rocks?

Steven looked over to Molly. "Molly . . . Molly Dowie typed it up."

Molly waved and stood. "It's wonderful."

And her words pushed articulating rocks aside because history and art so wanted to agree. Applause.

✳   ✳   ✳

Ticky carried his tall Crown Royal onto the porch and beheld a starry night. He did not take his ancient Planisphere with him. It remained on the doily covering the oak side table. He wouldn't have been able to make out the connected representation of the stars or the times and latitudes anyway. The actual stars were a different story. He had learned his Planisphere by heart along with Jefferson while Minnie cleaned up supper. And the bursts of effulgence floating in their ordained spots didn't require anything special, even from his old eyes. He looked over the mountains. It was the bent cross of Aquila. Jefferson had been five or six and had shouted "Attila," and that's what it was.

"Attila," Ticky said softly, and pointed.

He looked lower and to the right.

"Sagittarius," he said, and pointed. "Crazy dog. See it, Jefferson?"

Ursa Major, they had decided, looked like either an upside-down stool or a three-legged horse. Ticky commanded those legs off the porch and onto the dry mowed grass so he could gaze high behind the house.

Capricornus came, and so did Aquarius, which Minnie had said was truly the Rio Grande's father. Then Jefferson would always say it was the daddy Rio Grande.

"Daddy Rio Grande," Ticky said, pointing with the smooth Crown Royal.

He identified Pegasus and Draco, and then certain links drifted behind new clouds, so he brought his eyes down.

"Close your eyes now, Jefferson. Daddy's got you. Listen. Listen."

"I don't hear anything."

"Nothing?"

"No, Daddy."

"You don't hear that old dog snoring?"

"I hear him snoring. He's loud."

"And you don't hear that river? Our big river?"

"Sure I hear it."

"Then what do you mean you don't hear nothing?"

Ticky smiled and spoke both sides of the conversation, and now he listened, too. Things here and things gone rebounded like keepsakes in a bowl until a Lettgo calliope trilled in his small head.

After some time he drained the glass of Crown Royal and moved those spaghettini legs across the yard and up the meadow path that led to that soft rise above the bend in the river, to say good night to Minnie.

44

Sandy Fiddler paid four hundred dollars cash for the ancient Airstream trailer in Pueblo. She had researched *Consumer Guide* for a price analysis on used trailers and beat down the overwhelmed salesman substantially. Sandy was confident that fucker wasn't so smug now, watching her hook it up to her Blazer and pull out. She gave her name as Tanya Lopez and bristled as he yelled, "Thanks, Tanny!" after her.

Todd chuckled to himself.

"What?"

"I was just thinking how stupid people look when they're pulling these ugly things. Now here I am pulling one."

"You don't like trailers?"

"They just ruin everything."

"How?"

"They just . . . they're all over the place."

"They're the weapons of the proletariat. It's earth-hateful."

"They're silly."

"They fuck up everything," Sandy said with finality.

Sandy drove under an overpass of I-25 and stopped in front of a garden store. She checked her notes.

"Okay. We go in and get six fifty-pound bags of Cadwell Nitrogen Stall. Anybody asks—and these kind of nosy fucks always do—tell them it's for our tomatoes."

"Sandy! We'll need at least ten times . . . We'll need more than ten times that. The plans call—"

Sandy pointed her stubby finger half an inch from Todd's nose. "And after you order one hundred fifty-pound bags of unstable nitrogen-rich fertilizer from those farmers, why don't you get some blasting caps while you're at it and tell them you were gonna open up the Rio Grande Reservoir? Give them your name, too, you dumb fucking music teacher."

219

Todd pushed her finger away. "Jesus. Now, I've had it with your personal attacks and innuendoes. I'm *adjunct professor* of music. Jesus!"

They put the six bags in the trailer. By the time the couple hit the turnoff to Creedemore at South Fork, they had stopped at eleven garden-supply centers. Todd's arms and shoulders ached miserably from packing the eighty-three awkward bags into the corners and niches of the trailer. Also, his allergies were going berserk with escaping dust from the pulverized fertilizer.

*　*　*

Molly Dowie redrew both the leaping rainbow trout at the far right side of her mural and the black hat slung over Poker Alice Tubbs's enormous forehead, climbed off the ladder, and backed into the middle of the amphitheater. It occurred to her that adjacent to the conquistador, now the poet-warrior Juan Carlos de Moreno, there might be room for a smokily implied Teresa Herrera. Or would that only clutter the arrangement? She had sworn to an overall sense of time and space. A length and openness that was easily a first and last impression of the valley. But the transition of the nameless conquistador from merely an attractive adventurer into a true historical nabob, who would speak Steven Kearney's sensuous narration and relate a kind of love poem not only to Teresa but to the valley itself, pushed her closer to including a dreamlike representational image. An almost cloudy interlude. Perhaps then the confined market wall could sustain everything. She stepped side to side for perspective. Clouds and dreams. A ribbon of river. Tributaries flowing out of the idea itself. She sat in the bleachers, stretched her legs, and took in the mural and Cathedral Rock shooting up above it as if out of the market's roof.

"It's perfect," Steven Kearney said, standing behind the mobile football bleachers.

"Steven Kearney. You snuck up on me. I'm thinking of changing stuff."

"That would be perfect, too."

She looked back to her mural, and he did, too. "It better be. It has to be. Your play is just so beautiful."

Steven walked over and sat next to her. "You said my play was beautiful before. You said it was wonderful, too."

"It is. It's both."

"Really? Truly?"

"I'm not a liar."

Now there was the challenge again. The fierce declaration like a small shout, a wee oath.

"I didn't mean that. I'd never think that."

220

They both studied the mural. It was early and cool, and they watched quietly as if it might begin to adjust itself. Steven lit a cigarette.

"I think you smoke a lot."

He put it out.

"I'm not telling you to put it out."

"I've been thinking that, too. It's hard to breathe up here."

"Cigarettes don't help."

"I don't know."

"I smoked."

"You don't smoke now."

A cyclist walked a tall English racer by the mural and into the market parking lot. He wore a green riding cap and bike shoes that seemed coordinated with his green jersey and tight black cycling shorts. He wore a number, front and back. Molly and Steven watched as another cyclist joined him. A white van pulled in to the lot. More riders followed. Milled.

"Race today. Not a race, I guess. Rally. They're going over to Lake City. Parking lot'll be full in a few minutes. Willie and his friends did it last year. Last year there were a couple of people in their eighties."

They watched the mural and the arriving riders. Steven took out another cigarette. He had it in his mouth when he remembered.

"Sorry," he muttered, taking it out of his mouth.

"Smoke it."

"It's all right."

"Quit when you're ready."

"I'm ready."

"Really?"

"I'll just smoke one or two more."

He lit it up. It tasted sugary and flat.

"It's flat," he said.

"That's 'cause you're thinking about it."

Steven looked at her little hands and smoked it down anyway.

"Nobody, not one person . . . nobody has ever said my stuff was beautiful or . . . or wonderful."

"I don't believe you."

"I'm not a liar, I don't think."

"Nobody?"

"Only you."

"What about your girl?"

"I don't have a girl."

"You live with a girl."

"Roarke?"

"Is she the one you live with?"

"Uh-huh."

"She never said your writing was beautiful? Was wonderful?"

"She likes some of it. I'm not saying she doesn't like some of it. But Roarke, more or less, has a sentimental—that's what she says—a sentimental reaction to my work. She won't criticize me. I understand why she won't. I don't mean she doesn't tell me to 'get it together' or 'stop feeling sorry for yourself,' but it's hard for her to separate me from my work. It's just too hard for Roarke to stop being my best friend for a minute."

"Because she loves you."

"It's not—"

"And because she knows you love her."

"It's—"

"Right? Right?"

Molly had no mystery in her eyes now. She was clear, as clear as a dare, as clear as her turned-up chin. When he didn't say anything, she got up and strode back to the ladder. She climbed it, ran her marker over the top of Poker Alice. He watched her try to arc, to spread the line, but somehow she could not. She threw the marker aside and climbed back down. Molly turned to Steven still sitting on the bench.

"Right?" she yelled, her small voice taken by the morning so only a peep reached him. Her arms hung like string, and the silly bowler looked as if it might slip down to her feet.

He started over to Molly and the mural. He dragged his unsettled character with him. The continuing crisis of his hesitant art, his poor words, washed over his big body. When he finally arrived, he wanted a cigarette badly. He felt for them but left the pack in his pocket. Laughter and energy passed through the parking lot from the cyclists.

"Nothing happened. Nothing," he said.

Now there was a hawk above them. Also crows. Deep gray Canadian jays watched from the bleachers.

"That would be until I was eleven and I wrote this story about the Flying Tigers. The fliers? John Wayne? And when I wrote it, somehow I got convinced that I had made it all up and that I invented it all myself. I got a failure on it from Mrs. Conlin. She was my sixth-grade teacher. She made a big deal about how I plagiarized. I didn't know what that meant. And at recess I got beat up by Bill McGill and Donnie Thompson, who kept calling me a plager man."

Now he took out the smokes and lit one.

"That night I sat at the kitchen table—and I don't have a lot of memory about being a boy except when I was writing—and I sat there and wrote a story that was just mine. Only mine. Nobody could say 'John Wayne' or 'plagiarize' or nothing. It was the story of Bill McGill and Donnie Thompson and how they would go around beating kids up. The story ended with them beating me up. I showed it to Mrs. Conlin. She never said whether or not she liked it, but she got those guys and took them down to the principal's office. So I saw, you know, how writing was a powerful thing.

"And I was very stupid in subjects that didn't interest me. And only English did, but not really English. Only when we had themes and things, because then I could express myself in sort of a full but secluded way. So I didn't go to college or anything and went into the army, and I kept writing. When I got out, Mother and Father had separated. It was just me and them, and they had parted about a year earlier, only no one told me. I wouldn't have been able to write about it. I didn't understand them. I never understood them.

"I wrote twelve plays in the army, and I put them in my duffel bag with some clothes, and I went to New York. I went to the McBurney YMCA. My plan was to get productions for all twelve plays at the same time in different theaters around the city. That way no matter where you were, you could easily get to a Steven Kearney play. I mean, if you wanted to. I had unemployment from the army, so I had this two- or three-week grace period before I had gone through my savings and would have to get a more or less full-time job for a while so I would be able to continue writing. Only it's hard to work all day and write at night. What I finally fell into doing was getting up at four in the morning. Work until six. Plots. Rewrites. Work. And then have a better starting point for night writing. Till twelve or one. Anyway, I couldn't get a theater that liked my work. But I was twenty-one. I had been a soldier. I had nothing but time."

He crushed out the smoke with his sneaker and stuck his hands into his pockets. He looked down and hunched a little. She found herself standing exactly the same way.

"I never felt sorry for myself. . . . Now I do, a little, even though I understand that you shouldn't hurry art. Art goes at its own pace. . . . Mine goes slow. But I wrote, like I said, on this good schedule, and I tried to view the work, the other work, the real work, as not work at all but a . . . a search for metaphors. And I had jobs that were so packed with metaphors you wouldn't believe it. I was a night skate starter at Rockefeller Center. It was a fall-winter thing, and I could do it and still have other jobs at the same time. I'd just skate around and encourage and assist the other skaters. We had to sign a pledge to 'assist and encourage.' I worked as a census taker. A hospital orderly. I worked four years at the Children's Aid Society, but . . . well, it was very sad, and I'd be there so early and stay so late that my writing fell off. . . . I hated to leave that. I'm a good unskilled laborer, too. I mean, I can work at a pretty good pace. I got a friend who gets me these jobs. But I work hard . . . and . . . and when

I get ahead, I write. I turn it out. I have a . . . I have this body of work that you might say is ridiculous . . . ridiculously big. Plays. Poetry. Short stories. Novels. Some essays, but not many. I write essays, really, to explain things to myself."

Steven swayed slightly. Molly also.

"I have developed a theory of writing that helps me a lot when I have to put one of my things aside because no one wants . . . understands the thing . . . and I have to go on to the next project. I find that the most difficult. Not that absolutely nobody wants the stuff, but to have to put aside this . . . this work . . . So what I've done is develop this theory.

"The theory is that art, any art, is an infinite thing. There's no time limit. Nobody to say, 'Time's up, you fraud, you phony, you talentless piece of . . . nothing.' Nobody can say that. Even when they do, they're wrong. They don't realize that art's life can be forever. So, see, when I put the compositions aside and have to go on, I can say that they're just aside and not things I've given up on."

Some cyclists left now for Lake City. A little dust kicked up.

"I've had two girlfriends. Girls that I lived with. Lauren Folger—"

"The movie star? The big star?"

"Uh-huh. We were night skaters then."

"The one who played the mute in . . . ?"

"Uh-huh, and then I lived with—"

"You lived with Lauren Folger? What happened?"

"She did an off-Broadway play, and I forgot to see it. She kept telling me about it. Leaving me notes. But I was writing this novel about Antoni van Leeuwenhoek, who was the first man ever to observe protozoa through a microscopic lens in 1674. He's the father of protozoology, and I was just so distracted. One day I came home—I was driving a cab then—and she had left."

"Lauren Folger left? What did you do?"

"I sent *The Lensman of Holland* to most of the big publishing houses and maybe forty small presses. I don't know. I mean, I know it was very long, but here was a guy who ground over four hundred lenses in his lifetime. *Four hundred.* Some like this. Like a pinhead. But she moved out and I had the apartment on Thirteenth Street to myself. I set the bedroom up as my study and slept on the pullout couch, and later Beverly moved in."

"Beverly?"

"Uh-huh."

"What about Roarke?"

"It's hard telling everything. I have to start somewhere."

"Okay."

"I mean, not right away. I was alone for a long time. I'd work this construction for my friend for a few months and then write. Once I wrote for three days. No sleep. Nothing. I smoked. I ate. But I didn't sleep. I wrote a play, whole thing, three days. It was nutty. There were things in the play that seemed like they were written by an idiot. It scared me. That's when I met Beverly. I went out to get some soup or something from the bodega on Astor Place, and I just passed out somewhere on the way. I woke up, and there was Beverly. She was nursing me back to health, but she also moved in. And I lost the play."

"You lost it?"

"I took it with me to the bodega, but it vanished."

"Could you rewrite it?"

"Once it's gone? I don't know. It started out pretty traditional. It was about George and Georgia Clairmont, the chiropractors who discovered the reflex points for the bladder and groin. Here, under the heel. But then, the less sleep I got, I kind of riffed out into a surrealistic full-body poetic chiropractic adjustment. It was one of the only times my writing actually frightened me."

He nodded, remembering. She nodded, too.

"But I think about it. Out there somewhere. My words. My meaning. Story. I don't know. So we had an odd relationship. Sometimes Beverly didn't speak for days. Or come home, even, sometimes. I think that was my fault, because when you wake up from passing out at a bodega and you've lost your play and there's a girl there with all her stuff, it's hard to . . . I guess, connect. I never connected. I never really talked to her about anything. And of course she absolutely despised Roarke."

Now they were all cycling away. Off the paved parking lot, through the dirt-and-grass amphitheater, and on to Lake City. Horns blasted. Several white emergency vehicles with lights rotating followed them.

"And really, a lot of it was Roarke's fault. Sometimes she would just stare at Beverly, then look at me and shake her head. I ignored it, but Beverly got pissed. Every now and then, Beverly would say, 'We're not going to that bitch's place,' or 'We're not going out with her,' but she knew I would go, so most of the time she did, too. So I wake up one morning and Beverly says she's leaving and going to live with Toby Hunter, who was very upset by the whole thing. See, I had saved some money so I could finish this thing, this poetry I had put off. I had this image of being a little boy on the steamer over from England after the First World War. And I would write from the boy's perspective a poem about . . . well, I was going to try to write about Father meeting Mother. Sort of follow the boy. Help me, actually, help me sort it out. I had just finished writing a biography of Eben Faerld, who was the last eisteddfodic poet. You know, the Eryri school, Ieuan Glan Geirionydd, Mynyddog, Islwyn, those guys, and I was pooped out and kind of frustrated because nobody wanted it, so I worked construction for around five months and saved pretty good for the poetry run about my parents, but I got bogged down, writer's block, and Beverly left, and she hadn't been paying the rent or the bills with the money I gave her. She kept the money and then took all the rest from my bank account, and Mrs. Marmar threw me out, and then I got hit by a car on my way to Roarke's, but I saved all my work. Both bags. And that's how I live with Roarke."

Molly leaned one shoulder into the mural. Steven did, too.

"Roarke says . . . Roarke thinks we're like each other's kid."

Molly looked down at Steven's sneakers.

"I don't think that's quite it, though. Although she scared me once. There was a time when she got really sad. . . . I never told this to anyone, but Roarke wouldn't mind if I told it to you. . . . She got this prescription and tried to . . . you know. . . . It was the scariest time I ever had. The doctors won't tell you a thing, and they say you're only a friend. And of course me and Roarke, I mean . . . What do you call it when you only have one friend? I'm not saying I couldn't be a good friend to other people. But I had Roarke. 'Friend' doesn't cover it. Like, if I said I wanted, I would like to be, you know, *your* friend, that wouldn't cover it either."

Now Molly watched his face. Sentences formed in his stomach, and he tried to keep them down there in the juices.

"Even if it's not two-sided. But I . . . feel good just . . . when there's even your work . . . knowing . . ."

Steven stepped back and spread his arms to the mural.

"It's not just that it's . . . glorious . . . but it's that *you* did it. And it's this . . . saying . . . I mean, 'friend'? I mean, I love you. I mean I love you."

His arms spread and his big head hung. Some breeze wiggled his little ponytail.

"I've never said that to anyone."

Steven put his hands into his front pockets. He was, and now had proved it to himself, that character lurking in the corner of all his novels, plays, and short stories. That prodigious, indiscriminating, woolly asshole. The cyclists were on to Lake City. He was watched by birds.

"You never said that to Lauren Folger?"

"No." And Jesus Christ, he hadn't. Poor Lauren. Maybe.

"Beverly?"

"Not Beverly. Never. I can't remember saying it to Mother, even. I'm sorry. Jesus."

Now she was at his face. Why had she said it was wonderful? Beautiful? When nothing ever happens, there's time, and it lets you go on. Going on. Waiting.

"You never said it to Roarke?"

226

The big Canadian jays became quiet. Even birds wanted the truth.

"Yes. Yes, Roarke. I love Roarke. I've told Roarke. I lied or I didn't think that counted. Of course, Roarke. As long as Roarke thought I had a little value, some true point of view, I could keep on. As long as she didn't condemn me. Yes. Roarke. I love Roarke. Who knows, if she was straight . . ."

Molly narrowed her brown eyes, and her ears twitched against the bowler.

"Roarke is gay?"

"You knew that, didn't you?"

She put her arms around his stomach and her head on his chest. The bowler fell off. He felt her hands on his love handles and put his hands flat on her shoulder blades. Birds still watched.

"I have one breast," she said.

"That's cool," he whispered into the top of her head.

Suddenly it was all right for him to be stupid and inappropriate, and the thin air filled him.

*　*　*

JoJo was an uneasy passenger in his dad's pickup. In the back, hacking around on the bed of the truck, were Ronnie and Brian Coolette, his second cousins from outside Huntsville.

"How come you don't ride back there with Ronnie and Brian? Fool around. Have fun."

Ronnie and Brian drained their colas and flipped the cans over the side.

"I'd rather ride up here."

"Suit yourself."

Mel pulled up in front of the post office, guessing that the outsiders had already captured all the good parking spaces closer to the Municipal Building.

"Yuppie faggots," he muttered, easing his wondrous belly out the driver's side. The rest of him followed.

In the municipal parking lot, the Liberty Society and their allies far out-manned the Ticky supporters, and the cowboys that were keeping vigilance seemed dog-tired. Mel and JoJo took their spots. Ronnie and Brian stood on either side of them like bouncers. Their twenty- and twenty-three-year-old snarls were permanent and not open to discussion. They were both an inch or two shorter than JoJo, but gutty and butty in the style of that side of the Huntsville Coolettes.

"Who're the homos with the signs, Uncle Mel?" Ronnie asked.

"They're trying to kill an old man and use his property themselves."

Mel's answer pretty much bewildered the Coolettes, but they nodded anyway.

"Like as not they'd rush the court if we weren't here."

Mel counted his side. Fourteen including the Prophit-Coolette contingent. "Where the hell is everybody?"

Jack Hill and Bob Marsden looked up from their coffees.

"We decided to do it in shifts," Jack said.

Mel put his hands on his small hips, elbows back to balance the gut. "Shifts? Jesus."

"Petey Myers asked us to. Thought it might defuse the tension."

"Why'd we want to defuse the tension? Those assholes in the L. L. Beans aren't defusing the tension. Why the hell do *we* have to defuse the tension all the time?"

"Well, we're just helping Petey out," Bob Marsden explained to Mel.

Mel spit.

Dan Cryer came out of the auditorium wearing his old brown sheriff shirt and khaki slacks. He lit a cigarette, looked at the Liberty Society, and lumbered over to the cowboys' defensive line.

"Hey, Dan."

"Hey, boys."

"What are we up to?" Jack Hill asked.

"They'll be doing lunch in forty-five or so. Marge Klinger has been real crabby, though."

"What'd she do?"

"Well, Les Vallejos—"

"Who?" snapped Mel.

"Ticky's lawyer."

"Mexican?"

Dan ignored it. "Les went at those nutsos from the Bible Institute pretty hard."

"Yeah?"

"He tried to show they were nutty, but Marge got mad."

"Women. Jesus."

"They been fighting all morning."

Jimmy the Kid's pickup pulled in to the lot and stopped in front of Dan and the rest. Jude slipped out of the passenger side.

"Second shift is arriving," Kid said. "I'm just gonna park it."

"I'm for you, Mr. Hill, and Kid is for Mr. Marsden," Jude said.

"Thanks, boy," Jack said, and they sauntered off.

"Hey, JoJo," Jude said.

"Hey," JoJo said.

Mel shot a withering look at his big boy, who looked away. Dan finished his smoke and went back inside. Mel followed his belly up alongside Jude.

"Hello, Mr. Prophit."

"You just watch it," Mel snapped. Ronnie and Brian stood behind their uncle Mel. Down the street Jimmy the Kid watched the Texans' movements. He shook his head and got out of the truck.

"Looks like another tricky day," he said in a whisper.

"What?"

The radical reporter, green hair spiked high, stood on the sidewalk in front of the Seattle House of Joe.

She asked it again. "What?"

This time Kid saw the gold stud on the tip of her tongue.

"Talking to myself."

"Yeah?"

" 'Looks like another tricky day.' That's what I said." He stepped up to the sidewalk and stood in front of her.

She wore baggy shorts with big pockets. A white T-shirt. A tiny recorder hung around her neck like a necklace.

"How come your hair's all green?"

"How come you wear that stupid hat?"

Kid took off his mangled old Bailey Crushable and held it up with both hands. The western apology for being what you were.

"Well, ma'am, I'm a cowboy."

"I'm a reporter."

"Oh." He nodded.

"A radio reporter. Egalitarian Radio Network."

"Okay."

"Know it?"

"Well, no, ma'am, I do not, but I seldom listen to the radio, so the fact that I do not know it doesn't mean much. My name is Jimmy Wells."

He held out his hand, and she shook it.

"I'm Nellie Ordoñez."

"Folks call me Jimmy the Kid."

"I'm Nellie."

He took in her smooth pink skin and long eyelashes. Her eyes were the color of her hair. He noticed things even though her pearl barbed tongue was a distraction.

"So," she said. "You're one of the landed gentry."

He laughed, and Nellie Ordoñez was not offended. He pointed to the sky.

"I'm going to be up there when I get my land, ma'am. Or down there. Might not be what I had in mind."

She smiled, and some of the radical inflexibility smiled.

"I have been called a lot of things, but I do believe this is the first time I've been called a landed gentry. Like the sound of it, though."

"So why do you do it?"

"Private property seems important."

"But you don't have any. Doesn't that piss you off?"

Jimmy the Kid looked genuinely baffled. "No, ma'am. It sure does not. A man shouldn't spend time on sour grapes."

"Or a woman," she corrected with an edge.

"Ma'am, when I say man, I mean woman, too. I always thought that was understood. My mother would have been a great president. She always said that. I'da voted for her. I mean, I mean men and women. Damn, it's a tough world."

"Especially if you're a woman."

"I can't be sure. I just don't know."

Jimmy the Kid, about to suggest more coffee, pointed to Nellie Ordoñez's cup. That's when Mel Prophit's tinny screams reverberated the length of Main Street, just behind the gunshots.

* * *

Miss Kirk gave it her third reading since she had divided the text by cues. The pages were spread out in the living room, arranged in the period context of each segment of the dramatic arc, which she used as a guide. If her calculations were correct, the epic now ran a touch over six hours, and at least one stage direction, the landslide at Slumgullion Pass that created Fork Lake, seemed impossible to realize. Also, the pauses that Steven Kearney had written and emphasized by boldly underlining them were problematical, to put it mildly. She put a pencil between her teeth and reached for the fishing segment. She nodded to herself at its clarity. Letting Brian Trujillo narrate his own tale would keep it concise and genuine. But was he up to it? And would anyone believe the downstream fishing? Miss Kirk noted in her margin to mention that. She put "Fishing" back in its place and picked up "Religious." Oh, boy. There was an area everyone in the valley had powerful thoughts on. Mr. Kearney had assigned the highest spiritual and moral bent to the Utes. Catholic missionaries and less formal Christian affiliations received a glancing bump in the persons of Friar Joaquín Santaló, who failed to protect the Utes from slavery in 1591, and Disciple Jackie Crumb, who rode into Creedemore's silver boom of 1888 with nothing more than a worn King James Bible and left two years later with three hundred thousand in gold from a gaming operation called Disciple Jackie Crumb's Lutheran Theological University. She laid down "Religious," picked up "Kit Carson," and carried it onto her deck overlooking a narrow section of Ear Grove and the Norgan Ranch. The sun would be behind the hills in fifteen or twenty minutes, and the Norgans were pastured half in light and half in shadow.

It promised to be a clear night. Perhaps she had overestimated the possibility of land and water passions rending a community asunder. Perhaps it may have already played itself out and that Art as savior, as wonderful ultimate counselor, could again be held in reserve and not be jeopardized in one great creative tableau. Miss Wilma Kirk had reservations about the achievement of Mr. Kearney. So much was not precise, seemed purposely vague, unwieldy, even esoteric. Worse, several of the narrator's love poems to his beloved, waiting forever in the Spanish hills above Valencia, were downright prurient. And while she herself found the rhythmic refrains thrilling, the rank and file of Creedemore would surely not.

Miss Wilma Kirk sighed.

"Carson," she said aloud to the pages in her hand. The Norgans called to each other, and she watched them. Kit Carson had had a dark side. It could not be held simply that his temper was short or he was intolerant or ignorant or self-aggrandized. That would not summarize the whole as she saw it.

He was the complete savage. A savage with authority who could rightly lay claim to any heroic anthologies written about him, softened as they were in the fuzziness of cowboy history. Mr. Kearney had seen this and built an uncompromising man of his times, slashing old life out of the valley so new life could come in. The Kit Carson Society of Puerite County would go ballistic.

Headlights turned off the road to South Fork and onto Miss Kirk's long dirt drive. The car moved smoothly up the slight rise toward where her cabin peeked out of an aspen grove. She checked her watch. No visitors were expected. The Chevy Tahoe reflected the last sun and early moon. Cowboy Bob Panousus eased himself out.

"Miss Kirk?" he shouted up to the high deck.

"Cowboy Bob?"

He reached into the front seat of the Tahoe and held up a fat eight-by-twelve manila envelope.

"I've got something here at the close of the day
That you might want to see for yourself.
It's a labor of love and you don't have to pay,
That is why I brought it to you myself."

Norgans mooed, and one blubbered a fart, resonating up to the solitary cabin.

"Then bring it on, Cowboy Bob."

* * *

231

This time she called herself Bernadette Ogilvy, taking the name from the Little Miss Perky Pants at the sorority rush. Little Miss Perfect. Little Miss Skinny. Standing there in front of her, wanting to say she was blocking the moon. Little Miss Flawless. She hadn't fooled anyone. She wanted to say, "You're blocking the moon, fatty." Little Miss Strawberry Hair Bernadette Ogilvy. Judging Sandy because she was large and Little Miss Cheerleader was perfect. Sandy had gone with Patty and Kate. Kate had talked her into it at the end of freshman year. It'd be fun. It'd be cool. We'd be the Three Musketeers for the rest of school. Sisters. Sorority sisters. Jesus. She knew doom when she smelled it. She knew the fix was in the second Miss Congeniality opened the door gushing how happy—"joyous," she had actually said—joyous she was to see them. And then every single piece of furniture in that fucking house was so small, so delicate, it was as if the chairs were telling her to go home. They didn't want her. Nobody wanted a fatty who blocked the moon. She pretended she was sick so she could get back to the dorm before they had to eat. Even if she had a cracker, one shitty cracker, Little Miss Skin and Bones would say, "Did you see the way she stuffed herself?" You could not fool Sandy. She knew. She got it. Patty and Kate said they would walk her home, but she knew they didn't want to. Wanted to stay. Wanted to win. She got it. And in the morning they lied. They lied. They said that the sorority girls loved her. And Kate said almost all of them thought she was great. And Patty said practically all of them thought she was great. And Bernadette Ogilvy had told them to tell her that if she would just furbelow herself a little, she was in, because she had good grades and Patty and Kate had said she was great and they were dolls. *Furbelow? Furbelow?* Kate said "primp." Patty said "beautify." Well, she couldn't. And didn't. And no more musketeers.

"Is that with two *t*'s?" Bob Lobato, asked writing down her name in the campground guest book.

"Is what with two *t*'s?"

"Bernadette."

Lois Lobato smiled broadly. "Such a pretty name."

"Two *t*'s."

Sandy Fiddler knew that the ruse was completed with a smile at her elderly campground hosts, but she could not bring it up. Even the Colorado practice of hiring pleasant retirees as hosts at campgrounds irked her. A smile was out of the question.

"We were wondering . . . my husband and me were wondering if there are any sites close to the dam," she asked them.

"Near the dam?" Bob asked.

"He's an architect. He might build some dams. We're not sure."

Lois put her hands on her hips and smiled wider. "An architect. Wow. Bob operated a Pep Boys out of Tulsa."

"I don't miss it. Lots of work," Bob said. "High volume. Really wonderful support, though, from the home office. They're located in Delaware."

Sandy thought about reaching out and banging their two heads together. She said, "It's our anniversary. I was hoping that a nice present would be the perfect spot near the dam."

Tiny, sticklike Lois Lobato gave her a hug. "Well, happy anniversary, honey."

Bob gave her a kiss on the cheek.

"Oh, God," Sandy groaned.

"Are you okay, honey?"

"Uh . . . uh . . . look, he's also . . . he's also very, very ill. In fact, my husband is not going to make it."

Lois put her hands to her mouth.

"If we could get close . . ."

Bob put his arm around Lois. "Our boy's wife got sick. Abilene. They tried everything. Depression. Finally they gave her lithium. Worked."

"Well . . . this is worse. Cancer . . . brain."

"Oh, no."

Bob made a show of looking over his clipboard with the individual camp designations neatly diagrammed.

"Okay, look. Drive up to where it says HORSE LOADING AND UNLOADING, go past that, and take your next left. It's not much of a road, but it goes to the pump house. There's space there, and I don't believe the water group are coming up until next month."

"Thank you. You're both kind."

They hugged her again. Sandy thought of squeezing them to death but didn't want to complicate the operation.

Even a thought, even a possibility, can shatter us and transform us.

—Friedrich Wilhelm Nietzsche

Put the bat on the ground or I will transform your asshole.

—Reedy, to a protester during the Boston busing riots

45

Vi made the butterfly bandage too small and had to build it again. The gash went from Bobby's temple to just above his eyebrow. Petey had put Dan Cryer on the horn to Lake City. He looked closely at Bobby's wound and shut the door to the holding cells.

"Might need some stitching, Vi."

Petey picked the processing forms off his desk and patted them into a neat stack. Forty-three arrests. Holding in a tank built for six. Reedy would have said they 'sardined the cockhounds.' Reedy would have been right, but then he might have had a different take on the situation if he knew most of the sardines. Boston had that great anonymous thing working for it. When they go crazy and their faces all go deranged on you, it's always a bonus never to have seen them with a smile or a cup of joe in their hands. Man. Forty-three, and Petey knew he could have stacked another fifty or so in there instead of giving them show-up summonses.

"Ow," Bobby said.

"Ouch," Vi said sympathetically.

"Might need some stitching, Vi," Petey said again.

"Oh, I don't think so, hon," she said hovering over Bobby. "He's young. He'll heal quickly. You'll heal quickly."

Dan Cryer hung up the phone. "That is a chickenshit town. Sorry Vi."

She waved him off.

"Can you believe they haven't finished a search yet for Sheriff Tobias's replacement? That dago who teaches criminal justice or something is still interim sheriff. Jeez K. Christopher. A goombah policing up. Wow."

"What'd they say?"

"He needs some authorization to send one of the deputies. Hell, they got three deputies. We only need two of them."

"Could use them all. Staties weren't worth a damn."

Petey walked into the hall between the makeshift court and police headquarters. Two staties milled by the door to the parking lot. Marge Klinger came out of her temporary office with Les Vallejos.

"Petey, you should be in on this. We're going to have to move the thing to Monte Vista or Alamosa. This is too much."

Petey nodded and put his hands on his hips. Pissed and embarrassed to have the proceedings cut and run on his watch. Les was talking.

"But if we retreat to, say, Alamosa, wouldn't another judge be assigned this thing?"

"Not necessarily."

"But possibly."

"Possibly."

They were quiet, contemplating starting over from scratch.

"Where's Ticky?" Petey asked.

"Sleeping. Still in the court."

"Well, I guess I'll go rouse him and take him home."

"How's Bobby?" Marge asked.

"Vi's working on it, but I think he might need stitches."

"Prophit?"

"He was still in surgery as of twenty minutes ago. They couldn't tell me a thing. JoJo's with him. I've got those other two cockhounds in a cell."

"How do you shoot yourself?" Les asked.

"Shit, Les," Marge said. "How do you shoot yourself twice?"

"Bobby says he might have been trying to shoot Jude McCormick," Petey said.

"Jesus," Marge said.

"Bobby's not sure, though. Jude and JoJo had been having some trouble—"

"That's the boy from New Jersey," Les said. "Do you know if you steal a car in New Jersey, they ask you to sign a piece of paper saying you won't do it again?"

"Anyway, they were having some trouble, and the next thing you know, that Mel Prophit brought up these yahoos—"

"Irish," Les said sadly.

He saw Marge looking.

"I mean the *Texas* Irish. You know."

"Les, you're a bigot."

"No I'm not—"

Petey cut in. "These two guys are troublemakers. Dan Cryer remembers them coming up when they were kids and causing problems. So they pick a fight with Jude, and he pops them."

"JoJo?"

"I guess JoJo wasn't involved. I don't know. But Prophit, that asshole, draws on him. First shot went into his own right thigh, second shot got him in the foot. Never got the damn gun out of his holster."

"Jesus."

"Cowboys thought one of the Liberty Society fired the shots and went nuts. Thank God for the fire hose."

"Are we going to arraign the idiots now?" Marge asked.

Petey lowered his voice. "I was thinking maybe I'd just keep them sardined for a while and then summons them so you can take your own time with it."

"I like the way you think."

"I never saw so many video cameras. Mostly Liberty Society, but some of the others, too. They're throwing rocks and setting fires and videotaping everybody else. Bobby had ours set up on the second floor."

"That's illegal, Petey."

"They're my home movies."

"Be careful."

"They all get on their cellulars, and before you know it, there's a parade to get to the fight."

"And of course the press will make it more than what it was," whined Les.

"It was plenty, Les. Hell, I got some press in the holding pen. I got a cameraman from the ABC station in Denver. Incitement to riot, for Christ's sake. I got that little Commie with the green hair. Called me a cocksucker."

Marge looked at her watch. "Miracle of miracles, if there's no more business, I'm going to make my ball game in Lake City. Let's sleep on this, then see what tomorrow brings."

Marge started in the direction of the parking lot.

"Uh . . . Marge," Petey called.

"Yes, Petey?"

"Dan didn't talk to you, huh?"

"No, he didn't."

"Well, shit, I asked him to talk to you."

"About what?"

"Your car."

"What about my car?"

"Well, Marge, it kind of exploded."

*   *   *

Mountain Man Red Fields let it ring until it stopped. Maybe twenty times. He knew it would be Cia calling from the Holiday Inn in Monte Vista, where

237

the Liberty Society was having another supersecret meeting of its leaders. It was seven-fifteen in the evening, and he knew that Cia would be waiting along with Bill Clinings and the others to put the finishing touches on some cataclysmic design. Some geeky doomsday operation. He thought of the mountain bikes. He began to think of profit in an aesthetic way. He despised his expansion into river rafting. The phone started to ring again, and Mountain Man wheeled his dirt bike onto the sidewalk. The ringing took him out of town.

The small adobe church lay under glorious stars. He walked into the main entrance and took a seat next to the altar.

"Reverend?" he said out loud. "Reverend Nott?"

Some voices scrambled inside Eliphalet Nott's apartment, and the door opened a little.

"Someone calling for me?"

"Reverend Nott?"

"Mountain Man?"

"I read that book. That *Moral Man and Immoral Society*."

"Ahhh . . . good . . . just a sec."

Mountain Man took out the book and balanced it on his knee. Eliphalet Nott came in pulling up his jeans. He sat next to Mountain Man and waited. After a few moments, he packed his pipe and filled the chancel with the fragrance of sweet cherry.

"I read that book. That book you lent me. Here it is."

"Thanks."

"It's amazing, really. He located 'original sin.' "

"He did?"

"We're all messed up. He sees that, all right, but he doesn't think we're done for because of 'common grace.' "

Eliphalet Nott puffed on. "That's wild."

Mountain Man Red Fields looked wistful, almost distant. "I've got a girl, you know. She's great. She's hot . . . that okay?"

"Hot, man, yeah."

"Felicia. I call her Cia. Works in Boulder. We used to live together until I came up here for the bikes and the . . . uh . . . the raft thing."

"Hot. That's okay."

"If it weren't that she was all gung ho over this Clinings character, I wouldn't have needed the book. But he puts it clear. It's out of our control, but we still are responsible for the supply of grace. I mean, she'll hate me, she might even have to kill me, but there's still the 'common grace' thing."

"Did you say she might have to kill you?"

"Do you have a girl, Reverend?"

"Uh-huh."

"What if she made you swear on a Bible not to tell anyone else what she was going to tell you?"

"Then I wouldn't tell."

"Just like that."

"I swore on a Bible, for Christ's sake."

"Yeah, but what if she told you something that wasn't good?"

"Well, I still took an oath."

"So even if it ruins her life, you wouldn't tell."

"Oh, well, if it was going to ruin her life . . . maybe. Is this girl the same age as you?"

"I think I'm about a year older."

"I'm almost ten years older than mine."

"Really?"

"She's pretty young. Smart. Good conversationalist. Hot little bod. A Kathy Ireland type."

"Honest to God?"

"I just want to make sure I'm not too old for her."

"She sounds like she can handle herself."

"Oh, man."

Mountain Man stood and paced slowly around the altar.

"You can't read a book like that without getting a higher sense of your responsibilities. So even if she, like I expressed earlier, has to kill me or get one of the others to kill me, I have to share this. I have to."

"Man."

"What do you think?" asked Mountain Man.

"Oh, man . . . well, gee . . . this is some heavy shit. Look, why don't you share with me?"

"Share with you?"

"We'll call it a confidential share. People in the clergy have an elevated sense of the discreet. If I think your share is something that ought to be shared in a larger sense, I'll give you my opinion, and if I think it doesn't need sharing at all, I'll tell you that, too."

"I like that."

"Heavy."

"Okay. There is this group, and they are planning something so big that it's going to ruin the valley for years to come. It's going to absolutely destroy tourism and ranching and everything."

"Man."

"It'll probably ruin Puerite County."

"Wow."

"People won't know what hit them."

"Man."

"They're having another meeting right now. I don't know. They're planning it, though. They're taking oaths."

"So what is it?" Eliphalet asked.

"What is what?"

"What exactly are they planning?"

"I don't know."

"You don't?"

"I only know it's really bad. So what do you think?"

Now Eliphalet stood. "What does Niebuhr say? What does *Moral Man and Immoral Society* say?"

"It just . . . it says so much."

"Like what?"

"We have to 'harmonize.' That's important to the masses. It's important to the individual, too."

"Ahhh."

"What do you think?"

Skyo stuck her head out of Eliphalet's apartment. "I'm going to change my oil. I'll be outside."

"Okay."

"She does look like Kathy Ireland," Mountain Man whispered.

"No shit. It's great. But sometimes I feel old."

"You shouldn't."

"Look. Here's what I'd do. I think I'd go see Petey Myers and tell him what you know. That way you've at least covered your ass."

"Then we're back to the being-killed part, because I shared."

"Jesus."

"Yeah."

"Christ."

"Yeah."

"Okay, what about this? You type out a note. Anonymously. Slide it under the sheriff's door. That way nobody'll know it was you."

Mountain Man's burden lessened. He snapped his fingers. "Thanks, man."

"There's always a way to sort through shit."

"This is great."

"Hey, man," Eliphalet Nott said with a smile. "God is great."

Skyo's car was leaking oil something awful, so Buck and Jimmy the Kid drove her, Janice, and Jude to the tryouts.

"Drive by Molly's picture," Janice said.

"Yes, ma'am."

The market parking lot was dark. Buck backed up to the bleachers and pushed the truck lights high.

"There you go."

"Look at that. That girl has some talent."

"That girl has our guest, too."

Jimmy and Skyo laughed.

"Why, Buck Overstreet," Janice said, trying to seem indignant.

"Mom, what kind of rent do you think she's charging old Kearney?"

Jimmy put a little minted chew into his cheek. "Jude's gonna audition."

"That right, Jude?"

"Haven't made up my mind yet."

"Skyo told him all the girls are going."

"Yeah? You think they got a part for Jude?"

"Sure. Gold digger from New Joisey."

"New Joisey."

They pulled out and rolled toward the town center. The lot was filling up. Cowboys and summer people. Both sides of the equation hustled into the building. Janice leaned over the double cab and put her hands on each of their shoulders.

"I wish you boys would come in. Now, don't you drink too much."

"Scout's honor, Mother."

Nellie Ordoñez, the radical reporter, walked by the truck in a surly swagger, jeans and T-shirt, smoking a brown cigarette. Jimmy the Kid watched her. She stopped at the first step and looked at him. Stared, really.

"I believe the hippie girl is staring at you, young man," Buck said.

Jimmy the Kid slid out of the truck and opened the door for Janice and Skyo.

"Where's your beau, Skyo?" asked Jimmy.

"Which one?" asked Jude.

"Ralph is history," she said.

"Good, I was getting ready to shoot him."

"Why, Buck Overstreet!" Janice said.

Jimmy the Kid watched them walk into the building. "Buck, I'm going to see what's doing."

"You best do."

He walked over to Nellie Ordoñez, who had not stopped looking at him. Her green-and-purple hair seemed blacker.

"Hello there, Nellie."

"Hello, Kid."

Jack Hill walked by them. Mayor Ruby Onerati, too, who gave Jimmy's butt a pat.

"Hello, Mrs. Mayor."

"Hello, cutie."

"Cutie?" Nellie asked with a smirk.

Brian Trujillo came in, too, with his son and a granddaughter.

"Hey, boy." He nodded.

"Hey, sir." Kid nodded back.

"So," he said to Nellie, "you still got that thing on your tongue?"

"No," she said, taking a drag. "You still chewing that shit?"

Kid spit out his pull of tobacco. "No."

They went inside.

Miss Wilma Kirk had arranged chairs on either side of the hall leading to the auditorium. This gave a sense of privacy for the auditions. Steven Kearney and Miss Wilma Kirk sat behind a long table. Vi Myers, on dispatch duty this evening, had stopped by earlier with a scale-model mockup of the Western Market Amphitheater. She had some tiny ribbons and flags to signify performance areas. The model sat in front of Steven, who occasionally glanced at it with terror.

Miss Kirk checked her watch. "Six fifty-one. We'll begin promptly at seven. Promptness is essential in the theater. Are the stage managers 'by the book' folks in the Big Apple, Mr. Kearney?"

Steven looked up from the model. "Stage managers?"

"I was wondering, you see, if they're as literal as I tend to be. One likes to think of the art of stage managing in a universal context. A shared system. A quality control."

"I don't know, Miss Kirk. I just don't know."

Miss Kirk laid her hands on the back of her chair. "Nineteen forty-one. Days, really, before Pearl Harbor, when this valley simply emptied of young men, Mother and Dad drove my brother Charlie and me down to Elitch's Gardens in Denver. Rory Campbell and Fay Scott in *Taming of the Shrew*. I was ten, and I knew that my dear mother and dad had provided me with something I would always cherish and forever believe in."

Steven nodded. "You had nice folks."

"I did indeed. I took those speech extracts you gave me and copied them. Speeches each for boys, men, middle-aged and elderly, and same such, of course, for gals. I had Les Vallejos translate a bit into Spanish for any non-English-speaking actors, although I only know of three, and the Sanchez girls won't be here until Friday's audition. Many will be seeing the material for the first time."

Miss Kirk stood, and Steven, too. She walked to the double doors and turned before she went through for the first auditioner.

"Break a leg, Mr. Kearney."

"Okay, Miss Kirk. And you break yours, too."

*   *   *

Todd Lehman had wanted to go to the meeting of the Liberty Society's secret council in Monte Vista. They'd been camped for five days under the churning dam, and that bitch wouldn't even let him make a phone call. Like she was the big cheese or something. He hated the idea of spending time with someone so bitter over his associate professorship and corner office. And his musicologist's heightened senses told him her anger probably extended to his trimness. He put his hand on his tummy.

"What?" Sandy asked, sitting in the high passenger side of the Blazer.

"I didn't say anything."

"No?"

"No."

"Something about your office."

"I didn't say anything."

The Blazer entered Monte Vista's town limits.

"Now, slow down, for shit's sake."

"I'm going the speed limit, Sandy."

"The speed limit is forty, Einstein. Now it's thirty."

"Well, it was sixty-five two seconds ago."

"Now it's fucking twenty-five."

"I'm just—"

"Yeah, yeah, yeah. Listen, Teach, these fucks don't fuck around. They ticket your ass. They pull you over. They smell the stuff."

"What stuff?"

"What stuff? Jesus F. Christ. The fucking fer-til-izer."

"Stop condescending."

"Take a left here, dickhead."

"Okay, that's it."

"What's it?"

"I am sick to death of you thinking you can walk all over me because I have a professorship."

"I don't give a shit about your professorship. I'm on a mission, and that's that. Left. Right. There it is."

Todd pulled in front of the inn's main entrance.

Sandy squeezed out quickly and stood watching the Blazer. "Well?"

"I want to go to the meeting."

"We settled that."

"You settled that."

"Look at it any way you want, jerkoff, but I'm going to the secret council meeting and you're heading over to the garden-supply store in Alamosa and pick up another ten hundred-pounders."

"Don't call me jerkoff!" Todd yelled, pointing his finger like a baton.

Sandy spread her feet into a semi-sumo stance and leaned onto the car with a sigh. The absolute worst part of anything was needing helpers. If she could snap her fingers and the fertilizer would magically appear, then she would simply reach through the window and snap this ponce's fingers and maybe his neck, too.

"Okay, I'm sorry I called you jerkoff."

"And dickhead. Swear to God, you call me dickhead once more and—"

"I'm sorry I called you dickhead, too."

"And shit-for-brains."

Sandy pressed her tongue to the roof of her mouth. "Look, Todd. I'm sorry. No more name-calling. Okay? I'm sorry, okay? Now we really need more fertilizer."

Todd seemed to be considering his finger. Then he dropped it onto the steering wheel and drove away.

"Shit-for-brains," she muttered, waving a good-bye.

They were sipping wine and munching on brie in Room 312, the one Clinings kept as his operational base. The door was partially open. She shook her head at the lack of caution, the celebratory tenor of the council. How like a college English department. Sly waves and conspiracies. Standing there, unnoticed, she felt a real sensation of pretend in the room. An invention of dilemma for the amusement of this overeducated gaggle of academicians. Something told her to back out of the room. To skip this meeting. To share with no one. To let these pathetic weenies find out the score with everyone else. Sandy rode the elevator to street level, found the bar, and waited for Jerk-off to pick her up.

*　*　*

Roarke watched the interview with Bill Clinings on ABC. First they ran clips of the latest knock-down, drag-out fight in front of Creedemore's

244

courthouse, and then the reporter lobbed softball questions at this Clinings character, who seemed a little like Fred MacMurray, only not so tall or hesitant.

"So are you saying it's a shared responsibility, Mr. Clinings?"

Clinings looked smug and comfortable. "No, not at all. People must come to respect the boundaries of their souls, of course, but not the artificial borders that the landed have erected to marginalize the working man and woman."

More shots of fistfights and out-of-context yelling followed. Clinings spoke over the videos.

"There is a brutish intimidation, of course, by the landed and their minions. The sheriff, for example, is a murderer. It's known."

The reporter nodded thoughtfully and solemnly said into the camera, "Back, after this."

Roarke clicked off the tube and called Ute Ranch.

Skyo got it on the second ring. "Ute Guest Ranch. How may I help you?"

"Hi, I'm looking for Steven Kearney."

"You are?"

"Yes, dear, I am."

"Well, Mr. Kearney has temporarily moved into Creedemore proper. Can I take a message?"

"Got a number for him?"

"I believe he's staying . . . you know, with a friend."

"Would you have his friend's number? He won't mind if you give it to me. We're roommates."

"Roommates?"

"Yes, dear."

"Oh. Well, you know, I'm looking, but I surely do not see that number."

*　*　*

They went until almost eleven-fifteen helping the efficient Miss Kirk collate the Polaroids of the actors with Steven's notes about them. It was close to midnight when he tiptoed into her rock.

"Steven."

"Go back to sleep, Molly. It's late. Sorry."

"Don't be sorry."

"Go back to sleep."

"I can't sleep without you."

245

Steven undressed to his boxers and got under the covers. She snuggled and kissed him.

"Good night?"

"Uh-huh."

"Actors good?"

"Pretty good, yes."

"Miss Kirk making you nuts?"

"Oh, no, I like her."

They breathed together.

"I have to go to the doc's tomorrow. Can you take me?"

Steven sat up. "Why? What Molly?"

"It's nothing. It's been scheduled. Follow-up stuff. Can you?"

"Of course."

"I have to be there at ten. We'll get lunch after."

"Cool."

He lay back down.

"So what?" Molly asked.

"What?"

"What is bothering you? I can feel something."

"Nothing is bothering me."

"Okay."

She snuggled again.

"The whole mural got outlined perfect today."

"Yeah?"

"I'm happy with the dimension and everything. It's gonna be pleasure now. It won't be work now."

Thunder cracked nearby. Rain started. She pushed up and listened.

"Doesn't it sound great in here? It hits the tin awnings and the metal around the chimney spaces. Listen. Like piano pings."

They listened.

"Willie's coming up on Friday."

"Oh . . . well, you know what? I can just go back to my room at Ute Ranch and—"

"I told him I love you."

"You told him you love me? I love you."

"I know."

"I do, too."

"His room is behind the kitchen," she said.

They were quiet.

"And he's glad I love you."

The rain stopped and started again.

"I'm not sure what I'm doing."

"You're with me."

"I mean about the word-mural. I'm pretty sure it's good. . . ."

"It's long."

"Yeah, but . . . Molly, I never directed anything before."

The rain fell harder.

46

owboy Bob Panousus clenched tiny hands into fists and whapped them against his thigh. He'd gone directly on to Denver after dropping off his own version of *Creedemore: The Life of a Boomtown* at Miss Kirk's cabin. He'd been efficient and clean, bordering his story between Carson and the closing of the last ore mine. More, though, even if he'd whipped it up in two days, his ninety-page tale contained some of his finest verse and intricate rhyme schemes, including:

Some of the dago men came from Naples,
Where the sauces stewed bloodred,
And the micks brought their own odd staples,
Upon which their muscles fed.

And not only had he followed Kit Carson's career with a scholar's passion, he felt he knew the soul of the man. Who could not agree that that New York homo had slandered a hero?

He stood outside the auditorium under some heavy cloud cover. He waited until Miss Kirk emerged with the big-dealy New York pansy. Jesus God.

Miss Kirk stopped at the top of the steps. "Good evening, Cowboy Bob."

Cowboy Bob nodded. Felt the veins in his neck tighten at the sight of the huge manuscript tucked under the ponytailed fruitcake's arm.

"Hi, Cowboy Bob," Steven said.

"So you're going ahead with the auditions?"

"Affirmative," Miss Kirk said with vigor.

"We've completed our third evening of casting and have seen well over sixty talented actors from as far afield as Del Norte. Tomorrow at one should wrap it up."

Cowboy Bob chortled and shook his little head. "Well, whoop-dee-doo."

If Miss Kirk was moved, she didn't show it. "Saturday night I'll assemble my assistants and we shall tape out the auditorium floor for blocking. First rehearsal Sunday."

"Gonna rehearse all what? Four million pages?"

"Was five hundred eleven," Miss Kirk corrected. "Now three eighty-three."

"And my script? Perfect length. Rhymes. *Rhyming* poetry. Real poetry. What about that?"

Now the coyotes cut into the silence. Miss Kirk stepped down to him.

"There is not a more devoted follower of your work than I am, Cowboy Bob. I am a believer," she said.

"Well, you wouldn't know it. You chose him."

Miss Kirk took a breath. Steven listened hard for the coyotes. He looked for them, too, in the hills above Cowboy Bob's head.

"First of all, the dramatic and historical communities of the county have made a financial commitment to Mr. Kearney. More important, though, is the objectivity he brings to the project."

"The massacre at Ear Grove? Making Carson look like a killer?"

"He was a killer."

"He had to be."

"I'm not disputing the times he lived in, but—"

"And he was not motivated by a *bloodlust* or a *gold lust.* Good Lord, Miss Kirk.

'As a lad his little band hunted quail,
While his family tried so hard not to fail,
'Cause the times were prepubescence
And the lad in juvenescence.
Still, it was all up to him not to bewail.' "

"Ah," Miss Kirk uttered, as if remembering a magnificent sunset.

Steven could see that Cowboy Bob realized he would not be able to sway her. He turned to walk to his car. Steven felt the words, and they were coming hard, so he opened his mouth.

"It's still a . . . a work in progress, Cowboy Bob. It's going to change. I don't dislike Kit Carson."

Cowboy Bob continued to his ride. Miss Kirk watched him sadly. Steven felt more.

"You know, you would be perfect as Kit Carson in the word-mural."

Cowboy Bob stopped in his tracks, and Steven wanted to stop also, as if all of New York were yelling for him to shut up. Already crazy and directing, too? What else?

"Would you . . . you know, try out tomorrow, and if you get it, then we could rework . . . you know . . . some things."

Miss Kirk's expression remained the same. Cowboy Bob turned in the street. A spotlight on the corner of the Historical Society Building tossed the little man's shadow long.

"Rhymes?"

"Well, you know . . . sure."

He tipped his hat back high and thumbed his buckle.

"I'd have to try out?"

*   *   *

Todd Lehman's feet were soaked. The sleeping bag he had borrowed from Harriet in Music Theory was not waterproof, but he'd believed that he would be sleeping in a section of the small trailer they had wedged up next to the base of the Rio Grande Dam below the enormous reservoir. Now, thanks to that obsessive cow, the trailer was packed completely with nitrogen-rich fertilizer and Todd was sharing a tiny tent, in this downpour, with Miss Piggy. God, he was uncomfortable. And she didn't snore as much as rumbled. Even the pleasure of the rain on nylon was obfuscated by the roar of the mountain lying next to him. She just would not let him out of her sight—even phone calls were a no-no. Like she was some big KGB agent or something. He closed his eyes and thought of a piece by Haydn. Haydn was good for sleep. Haydn. But she'd called herself Bernadette, for heaven's sake. Lying to that lovely couple. Bob and Lois Lobato. Why do we have to lie to them? Telling them he had brain cancer so they could get the trailer up to the dam. Brain cancer. God. And they were just so nice. So thoughtful. He liked how even Bob Lobato, who always seemed to shout, was so quiet and comforting around him. And how Lois brought that zucchini bread. Moist. Yes. But Todd's feet were wet, and he'd dreamed last night about bombs, and now he was thinking that maybe she really means it. Is it possible? Did he know anyone who really means anything? He closed his eyes and tried Haydn. *Orlando Paladino.* One of his last works for the stage. He felt the comic strands in his head. Felt movement and the orchestra's sway. But Bob and Lois would be swept away if it truly were not a ruse, and of course it was a ruse. To show intent but not action. Who said that? Sandy had laid out the tray. What did she call it? Her ready tray? That large porcelain jar with the rubber-lined top. Her accelerator, she said. Her Playtex gloves, like a lunatic scientist. But she had to be trying to just scare him. She had to be.

*   *   *

250

Mountain Man Red Fields parked his Jeep in front of the bike shop and took his long strides directly up to the sheriff's office. It was eleven-fifteen in the rainy morning, but he had already driven to Monte Vista and back. He knew that Clinings would be returning to Boulder until his last class Thursday afternoon, and he had planned to advise the founder of the Liberty Society of Colorado that he would be sharing, despite the consequences, what he knew about the intended tragedy with Sheriff Petey Myers of Creedemore. He had sipped coffee from his thermos in the hotel parking lot while composing his warning. Just as he was opening the vehicle's door, Clinings emerged from the Holiday Inn. Felicia was with him, holding her orange Denver Broncos umbrella over them both. At his car, a late-model gray Lincoln Continental, they kissed. Hard. Long. Mountain Man was not angry. He felt he was getting better. In fact, he could feel small genetic defects setting themselves right in his big, oddly coded body.

"Sheriff Myers around?" he asked as he entered the office.

Bobby pointed, and Vi did, too.

"He's in the auditorium," she said brightly.

Petey Myers sat alone in the auditorium-courtroom at the long table Miss Kirk had set up on Wednesday. Wearing Vi's purple bifocals, he leaned over a pile of papers. He looked up when Mountain Man Red Fields entered.

"Auditions are at one. Miss Kirk posted the time in the corridor."

"Oh, I'm not going to audition."

"No?"

"Oh, no."

"Why not?"

"Well . . ."

Petey tapped the top of the pages. "Hard to imagine rocks and trees talking, though. But it's interesting. Time goes by, and the whole place just goes up and down. Reedy's ex was an actress, although, really, she was not too good. She was . . . what? She was stiff. There's a talking rainbow trout in here. I could see her play that. But the Indians? Conquistadors? Reedy had that Carson thing. He was deep. Still water running deep. We walked into the Boylan Building one block from Southy, and it was like they never seen a black man, and old Reedy says, 'That is it, boys and girls,' only I can't do it like him. You have to imagine the voice like a brick plopping in water, and he says, 'We are going to play a game, and the name of the game is clear the fucking building or the midnight ride of Paul Revere gonna be up your Paddy assholes!' And I'm thinking I can see Carson telling old Chief Ute, 'Get your mick asses in high roll, O'Leary.'"

Petey Myers smiled to himself. Mountain Man smiled, too. Healing and lining up somehow.

251

Petey stood. "Got to go to work. Ride with me? Talk there?"

"Oh . . . yeah, of course."

They crossed back to the sheriff's office, where Petey laid the play on Vi's table.

"Going out, Vi."

"Okeydokey, hon."

"Bobby, you tell that fella from Texas, that guy who owns the map store, to nail down those loose planks in front of his store. You tell him I'm not going to tell him again to batten down the hatches. The fine is clear. Four hundred dollars."

"Yes, sir."

Vi chuckled. "Remember what Reedy would say about the hatches, hon?"

Petey laughed, and he and Vi spoke in unison:

" 'You best batten down your hatches, my man, or the shit you could have saved be flying out your ass.' "

The department Jeep headed west past the airport.

"Raining," Petey said.

"It is."

About a mile later, they passed the turnoff to the Episcopal church, its white adobe obscured by mist.

"I need to share something with you, Sheriff Myers."

"Share away."

"It's about the Liberty Society."

"The Liberty Society are assholes."

"I've reached that conclusion also."

"Serious assholes."

Lightning flashed brighter than Red had ever seen it.

"I attended some of their meetings, and I really and truly have to share this."

"Then share away."

Petey turned off the paved road, opened a gate, drove through, and closed it behind him. By the second gate, Mountain Man Red Fields had performed his share.

"Something big, huh?"

"Something really terrible, yes, sir."

"Only you're not sure what? Or when?"

"That's the thing. They talked in generalities at the secret leadership meeting. Clinings knows, maybe. The big woman, Sandy, knows for sure. Clinings said whatever it was was her idea."

"Sandy who?"

"No idea."

"Local?"

"Boulder."

They drove to a rise overlooking a beautiful log cabin. Horses roamed on both sides of the big river, comfortable even in the downpour. Petey pointed across Mountain Man's chest toward a large, slow pool that registered as familiar to the ever-healing Red Fields.

"There are trout in that pool," he said with a low fervor, "that are so wonderful they have names. I swear to God Almighty. That play has the trout, the talking rainbow trout—who's not in it long, by the way—but in the play the trout talks about how the Ute Indians preferred the small streams and creeks to the big river. They were afraid of it. Reedy would have said, 'They developed a healthy attitude to not get their assholes washed into the ocean,' but I don't see it. If I were a Ute, I would have camped right here and fished and hunted, and old Vi could make clothes and get water and that."

It stopped raining. The horses all looked up at the truck.

"It's not like they just came into the valley either, these Utes. The play says they came like the rocks and the birds and all. How's that for a thought? And then Carson got 'em, and then mines and fishermen. What I'm going to do is ask you not to tell any of this shit to anyone at all until I have a chance to chat with Clinings. I met him once. Boulder? University?"

"Through Thursday, yes, sir."

"Last auditions are today."

"What?"

"The play."

"Oh . . . yeah . . . well, I don't think I'm too interested in being in it."

"You're already in it."

Mountain Man turned from the horses to Petey, then looked where Petey looked and tried to see in the big, slow pools of water what Petey saw.

"Or somebody a lot like you. The trial thing."

Mountain Man nodded sadly. "I guess I'm the play's fool."

"Nope. You're just there with the talking rocks and trees and Carson and that rainbow trout."

Petey pointed again.

"If you stand over there on that bank, that one there, you can see the big fish. The ones with the names."

"That bank?"

"Yes."

Mountain Man Red Fields stepped out and walked to the bank. When he heard the Jeep start and Petey pull out of the place without him, he was not

253

surprised. Somehow it seemed correct to be standing alone above this gorgeous stretch of the Rio Grande looking for fish so wonderful they had names.

Earlier, in Monte Vista, he had seen Felicia with Clinings. How odd that the pain he should have felt, the anxiety of betrayal, had never materialized. Instead there was an amazing sensation of lightness, as if a weight, a dead weight at that, had been balanced on his back and had just dropped off. It began to rain again. He pulled his baseball cap lower and hunched into the weather. Above the curving pool, where the river widened and became briskly shallow, a horse and rider emerged from willows on the far bank, dropped off it, and clomped across the water. The rider's head hung as if he were asleep. His long gray canvas duster was draped over the gray horse's back, where the material blended into its skin. On the bank now, horse and rider looked up at Mountain Man, who waved a small, halting wave. They started up a steep trail, the rider guiding the big horse with his voice. At the ridge by the cabin, they stopped and looked at him again. The man swung down from the horse in slow motion. He reached under the animal's belly and pulled hard at a leather strap. The saddle gave, and he hoisted it onto his shoulders and laid it on the porch. He returned to the horse and removed his back pad and bridle. Now the horse turned his gaze away from Mountain Man and looked at the rider, who pointed to the other side of the river. The big Appaloosa actually seemed to nod as he started there.

Lightning crackled almost simultaneously with thunder, cold rain began in earnest, and the rider walked in tiny steps up the stairs and under the porch roof. Mountain Man turned up his collar in a silly gesture, hunching into himself. The rider moved back in a lean against the cabin and slowly drew a large pistol from its holster. He motioned with it for Mountain Man to come in out of the rain.

*　　*　　*

There were sixty-one speaking roles and twenty-seven nonspeaking but physically challenging and important lesser roles. Miss Kirk had arranged the chairs and benches in a circle five rows deep, with Steven Kearney's chair in the middle of the wheel. Her stage manager's table was pushed back against a far wall. She was laying out scripts with numbers and names when Steven and Molly entered.

" 'Holla, Bernardo!' " she said deeply, not looking up.

"Hello, Miss Kirk," Molly said.

"At the wall with Hamlet's ghost," she said. " 'Holla, Bernardo!' And we are at the wall with Creedemore's ghosts."

She waved one of the fat scripts at Molly. "And Molly Dowie as the Rainbow Trout."

254

"I hope I don't screw it up."

"I think you'll make a splash in the role."

Steven walked close. "What's the chair in the middle of the circle?"

"That is the director's chair, Mr. Kearney. Of course you may sit anywhere you wish. However, I feel that this arrangement says authority, leader, guider of our omnibus."

"Oh."

Molly grabbed some scripts and helped lay them on the empty seats.

"Generally, I've tried to start at the front rows with prehistory perspective and progress to the rafting battle royal. Use your own judgment."

Molly read the character that Miss Kirk had written on script fourteen. "Feldspar?"

Miss Kirk pointed to a patch of the second circle. "All minerals, Gold, Silver, et cetera, over there."

"Lava, too?" Molly said, reading script number twenty-one.

"Lava indeed." Miss Kirk winked at Steven. "The writing in that section really flows."

"But if I'm in the middle, won't I have to keep turning my chair around? Won't I lose contact? Won't people think I'm an idiot?"

"Nobody's going to think you're an idiot, Steven." Molly took his hand. "Nobody."

"Floors taped to approximate areas. Black tape indicates bleachers. White and orange, mountains and plains. Blue, the river."

Steven watched her mouth but then heard only the gurgle of his panic. He looked at the circle of chairs, at his words set bloatedly on them. It was true, then. Miss Kirk had said it correctly. They were down to it now. This community coming in a kind of prayer, over his poor words. Steven staggered and braced himself on a chair.

"Steven . . . what?"

Molly propped him up. Miss Kirk turned the chair quickly, and they sat him down.

"I don't feel so good."

"Put your head between your knees," Miss Kirk ordered.

"Breathe deep," whispered Molly.

The auditorium door opened, and a glittering figure rolled in on little legs. Removed his huge hat and smiled confidently.

"It's a glorious day in our mountains so high,
Where the heart of adventure ne'er quits,
And it's all the more special for this lucky guy
'Cause I'm the actor who'll portray our dear Kit."

They all looked up at Cowboy Bob. Miss Wilma Kirk shook her fist in the air and yelled, "Showtime!"

Steven Kearney put his head back down between his knees and vomited.

*　*　*

Sandy Fiddler squeezed out of her Blazer and walked into the Creedemore Post Office. She'd shopped for groceries earlier, cleaning the shelves of Beefaroni. What a place! Christ, she should've been able to get forty or fifty cans if she had to. Instead she managed only nine. Jesus. She got three boxes of her beloved Cocoa Puffs and sandwich stuff for El Pussy. She bought two Styrofoam coolers and ice for them to keep the milk and eggs fresh. She bought a postcard, too. It was a drawing of an Indian maiden cuddling a bear cub.

At the post office, she bought a stamp, addressed the card to Bill Clinings care of his university office. She looked up, considering what to say, what not to give away of her paramilitary operation so sensitive she could share the plan only with El Pussy because he was a needed labor force. She saw, at eye level, a poster. At the top of it was a sketch that matched one she'd noticed on the wall of the market.

" 'Creedemore,' " she read. " 'A Word-Mural, August twenty-fourth.' "

Sandy counted the days on her fingers. Twenty-one. Twenty-one. If she could keep El Pussy off the fucking phone. If she could keep those nosy old campground farts at arm's length, it would be perfect.

"Perfect," she rasped.

She looked back down at the postcard and wrote it out and mailed it.

"Perfect," she rasped again, and headed across the street to the hardware store to buy El Pussy a waterproof sleeping bag.

I say then "Love."
I say then "You are my brother."

—Chief Sapiah (Buckskin Charlie)
of the Mountain Utes, to Indian Agent Meeker

Twenty-one days and counting.

—Sandy Fiddler of the Take It or Leave It
Agnostic Reading Room, to Bill Clinings

47

He was sipping some ice water when Molly returned from the read-through.

"What?" was all he managed.

"It went fine. Everybody's sorry you got sick. Miss Kirk just had us introduce ourselves and read it through once."

"It was too long, wasn't it?"

"I didn't think it was too long. Everybody had fun. Hey, Cowboy Bob was terrific, but he added some things."

Steven shrugged.

"I'm worried about you."

"I'm all right. Juan Carlos de Moreno? Teresa?"

"Jimmy the Kid and that girl with the green hair. They were kind of edgy. They stared at each other all night. She took the pin out of her tongue, though."

"How was the Trout?"

Molly kissed him softly. "The Trout was very sexy. The Trout could use some cuddles."

What is it, Steven Kearney wondered as they crawled under the covers, that ladles such confusions over the world? He did not want the balance of art and life any longer. The search was a poor one—bogus, he would say now. He would put art below life, certainly below love. If his contentment, his joy with Molly, more complete than he had ever imagined, could be wobbled by the fear for his art, the looming terror of exposure as fraud, as impostor, then why had he spent his life doing it? The scenes in his mind at the end of the day, the actors walking away, the casual snicker of recognition that Steven Kearney was who he was. Who he had always feared he would become.

"You're not a fraud. You're not, Steven."

He pulled back and looked at Molly. Her fine gray-black hair some inches now. Her creamy skin flushed, jaw set. Had he been talking out loud?

"Art is . . . well, who cares what people think?" she said.

And she was right, of course. Always right. Who cares? Yet it was the reflection of rejection, of label, a mirror of contempt that paralyzed him now. Not that these rural actors might conclude in a twinkling of clarity that this writer was indeed specious and artificial and, unworthy, but that Steven Kearney, through their eyes, might see it, too.

*　*　*

"Because, among other things, Attorney General Tyler said the state of Colorado does not want to end up looking like shit," Marge Klinger said.

"Tyler said that?"

"Word for word. That whole grandfatherly image is bullshit."

Les Vallejos shook his head. Roger Hockney was downright angry and spoke at the moon peeking in the center window.

"They are tipping . . . I mean, Tyler had to have seen them tipping the cars over the last time."

"Hey, Rog. They burned my Toyota."

Marge had called the meeting at the Creedemore Hotel to inform the attorneys that her demand for a change of venue had been overridden. Les paced and tried to sound reasonable. "Now, point of procedure, Judge Klinger—"

"Cut the shit."

"Margie, it is perfectly within your authority . . . given the circumstances of the trial itself—that you can have a change of venue. Rog?"

"Well . . . technically . . ."

Marge waved her empty glass of scotch at the waiter.

"Billy Tyler has run things for twenty years. He's a prick, but he's not stupid. And, okay, little Margie Klinger does not want to duke it out with him. We're staying."

They thought about it in silence.

Les said, "Lake City Ladies win last night?"

"No. I was two for two, though."

Roger Hockney said, "So when?"

"I'll have a prelim on Wednesday for the ground rules. Mountain Man and Ticky don't have to be here."

"Mountain Man. God Almighty." The dapper Roger sighed.

"He's your client, not mine," said Les.

"Roger," Marge said seriously, "do not betray yourself."

"I was only groaning."

"If it happens again, I just might perceive that groan the wrong way. I'd hate to have to start this shit from scratch with Sam Plebe prosecuting."

"That dick." Roger sighed again.

"Seconded," said Les.

"Motion carried, then. We'll need some new guidelines though. I'm not sure how we'll prevent another fiasco. Where's Petey?"

Les shrugged, and they all sipped their drinks.

Marge snapped her fingers. "I forgot. Vi said he had some business in Boulder. He'll be back tomorrow night."

Roger stood. "Okay, Wednesday we meet . . . and?"

"We'll start Friday, that'll give us the weekend to recover."

Les Vallejos finished his Coors. "So, Marge, what'll you be driving over from Lake City?"

Marge Klinger smiled at that one. "Go fuck yourself Les."

"Thank you, Your Honor."

*　*　*

Ticky Lettgo fixed up some macaroni and cheese and plopped cut-up boiled hot dogs in, divided it into a couple of Minnie's everyday bowls, white with blue flowers, and carried the feast to the big room. Mountain Man Red Fields stood up when he entered from the kitchen. Atlanta was creaming the Cubs on the huge TV.

"Mac 'n' cheese and a dog," Ticky said, handing the concoction to him.

Mountain Man took it. "Thanks."

"We'll just eat in front of the tube. Score?"

Mountain Man had not been watching. "I'm not sure."

Ticky chuckled and sat. "Well, you can be sure of one thing: Cubbies aren't winning. Jesus."

They sat facing the set on the huge couch. End tables held Mountain Man's beer and Ticky's Crown Royal. The warm bowl soothed Mountain Man's cold fingers, and the smooth, artificial ingredients slid down nicely. It had stopped raining a half hour ago, but it still loomed in the darkening afternoon. Martinez bunted, and Atlanta doubled them. Ticky almost leaped up. His legs were working and the spoon on his bowl drummed out a backbeat.

"They couldn't do it with Ernie Banks, they can't do it with Martinez. When they give up Walker, they raise the flag. Jesus. Astros should have gotten him. Jesus."

Mountain Man watched him. Ticky was rapt. He was in the game. He had said nothing to give any recognition to Mountain Man, who was now sure that Ticky did not know him or thought he was someone else.

"There's some more on the stove. Beers, too. Help yourself."

"I'm fine. This is great."

Ticky pointed at the set with his spoon while what he was thinking drifted out of his brain and into his mouth.

"They don't throw easy. They go to strike them out every time. Where the hell are their coaches? Somebody's got to tell these boys that that's why they got the goddamn infield. Put the goddamn ball in play. Put it in play."

"That's the name of the game," said Red Fields, wanting to be a part of the game, too.

"Know what I mean?" asked Ticky.

"Put the goddamn ball in play."

"Strike them out when they need striking out."

"Put the goddamn ball in play when they need to put the goddamn ball in play."

Ticky nodded and set down his bowl. He picked up his Crown Royal, sipped it, and shifted it from hand to hand. The picture close-upped the Chicago bench, who all wore their caps backward.

"Jesus," said Ticky.

"Jesus," agreed Red Fields. Ticky pointed at the set again. Mountain Man Red Fields waited.

"Saw Joe Jackson in Cleveland with Father and Mother. I remember him wearing his little glove on his belt between innings. There was watermelon ices, too. Astros got ice cream, but it's so damn expensive. But, Jesus. I think 1919, maybe, me and Father and Mother. He was selling, and we were along for the ride. That's them on top of the TV. The brown frames. He's holding a fish."

Mountain Man got up and looked.

"Eddie Collins, he was with the Sox. We saw them when they barn-stormed Texas. Played at A&M. Me, Minnie, Jefferson, Mother, Father. We saw Collins. We saw . . . oh, Jesus, Dickie Kerr. Wasn't he something? Minnie swore he was a midget. All the gals wanted to be his mother. Ray Schalk. Mc-Graw brought them down. Played three games: 22–1, 22–2, 22–3. No kidding. Jefferson played on the Squirrels out of the Falls. Like Little League, I guess. Oh, Jesus, they'd scrap. Fourteen- or fifteen-year-olds. They had heroes. Now, I hated to take—"

Ticky waited for Mountain Man to turn around so he could establish this important kernel.

"—I hated to take some goddamn vacation when you are operating a feed store. It does not stop because you do. So one day she says, 'Here we go.' Well, Jesus, but I go. Me, Minnie, Jefferson. New York, Taft Hotel."

He held up the Crown Royal.

"Crown Royals. Minnie's manhattans. Jefferson had the Shirley Temple. Goddamn thing looked just like a highball. Nineteen thirty-seven. Boy was sixteen. Now, we get there on the train and we get the room, and I'm all wor-ried about— Jesus!"

Ticky pointed to the set. The pitcher had lofted one over the left-field wall.

"That's it, then. When your pitcher is getting in on the label. Your pitcher . . . Jesus . . . Cubbies!"

Red Fields sat back down, and they both watched the Atlanta bench congratulate the grinning pitcher. They called him out for a bow, and they were playing in Chicago. Ticky shook his head again and pointed again.

"I'm all nervous. . . . I'm calling the feed store, I'm worried about all this damn vacation because . . . well, Minnie had got the goddamn room for six nights. Six nights! Roll-away bed for Jefferson. She reaches into her pocketbook, and out come four packs of tickets, and she's got an elastic band around each one.

" 'What the hell?' I say.

" 'Home stand,' she says.

" 'Who?' I say.

" 'Why, Mr. Lou Gehrig's team. Why, Mr. Tony Lazzeri's team,' she says.

"Right there in the Cattleman. We had steaks and salads, and she takes out the tickets. Me and Jefferson look at each other and go, 'Whoop! Whoop! Whoop!' Right there."

Ticky smiled so hard that his legs stopped moving. He spread his arms and shook his head.

"Yankee Stadium. That was a hot dog. That was a meal in itself. We saw a play, too, but I forgot it. And Tony Lazzeri signed Jefferson's glove, and the big dago writes, 'Play hard, Jeff—Tony Lacer.' "

They both thought about it. The Cubbies and Braves switched at-bats.

"We loved Al Kaline," Mountain Man said.

Ticky smiled at the name, the Crown Royal at his lips.

"We liked Billy Williams, too, but me and my dad loved Kaline the best."

"Detroit," Ticky said with pleasure.

"We saw him. We saw him at Tiger Stadium. Me and my dad."

"I have never been there," Ticky said.

"It's small. You can see the whole field."

"Although I *have* been to Detroit proper. I visited when we bought the feed trucks. I wanted to be sure. Minnie would say that Jefferson could have been a professional if he had wanted it, but of course the store was there. I'm not sorry that he chose the store for a moment, even if there was no time for choosing. I'm not sorry about too much. Sure not sorry about that Minnie vacation. Home stand. 'Here's the tickets,' she said. 'Whoop! Whoop!' "

Rain came again, wondrous on the log cabin's blue galvanized roof.

Ticky stood up and concentrated on his disappearing Crown Royal. "One more little one, I think, before the seventh inning. Beer?"

"Sure."

Ticky nodded. "I'm sorry though, that the Astros couldn't do it with Ryan and that colored man. I am sorry about that. And I'm sorry that I never bought the fast water above my spread when Old Man Lavallee put it up. But I had to make that choice. You don't expand your ranch while you're opening another feed store, no, sir."

Ticky headed for the kitchen and the beer and the blended whiskey.

"And I am sorry," he said out loud, "that I opened that goddamn store in Pueblo. Pueblo was a loss. What do I know about Colorado feed? And that college fella running things. So I'm sorry as hell about that. But I guess that's all."

He clunked some more ice into his glass. Mountain Man had turned back to the game. The rain stopped. Sun came out, too. He heard Ticky again.

"But I'll tell you now, I'll say I am not sorry that I shot the hell out of your goddamn rafts. I told Minnie to give it a ring when she saw you, and by God if the girl didn't clang you out."

*   *   *

The postcard was on his desk along with about forty other pieces of mail, mostly regarding his appearance on ABC. Bill Clinings looked at the glossy print of the Indian maiden cuddling a bear cub and turned it over.

Twenty one days and counting.
S.

263

He glanced through some of the other mail but came back to the postcard, read it again, and tore it up. He looked out his window directly across from the Mary Rippon Amphitheater, where student technicians were erecting a set for the Colorado Shakespeare Festival's production of *The Taming of the Shrew*. On the apron of the stage, two actors rehearsed quietly. Bill Clinings watched them, but his mind was playing over the absurdly overstuffed plate he had prepared for himself. It was bad enough that his decision to accept two psych courses during the recess had failed to lionize him in the eyes of the Antichrist Doris Hutchinson, head of the department and the monster he would have to overcome for full psychology professorship, but the classes themselves were completely composed of the walking brainless who had failed, at least once, the courses during the regular school year. It was, pure and simple, remedial psychology for the cerebrally disadvantaged. And his Liberty Society, which he had formed to prod long-legged coeds into the sack, was now peopled by half-baked academicians who cramped his style. Well, at least the delicious Felicia Brun had made herself available, even if at twenty-five she was a little older than he preferred. But he had warned her up front that he had no intention of changing his marital status, as he counted it toward his moral and aesthetic obligation as both teacher and leader.

Bill Clinings checked his watch and began to assemble his class materials. He put the short lecture entitled "The Phenomena of Action" into his case. He put his index cards, the blue ones marked "Dimensions of an Act" inside also and closed it up. He looked down at the torn postcard. He dialed Jan Wilke in sociology, treasurer of the Liberty Society.

"Hello."

"Jan, it's Bill."

"Yes Bill," she said, with her usual disturbing solemnity.

"Have you heard anything from Sandy? Anything at all?"

"I haven't, no. I know that she and Todd left on a mission last Monday."

"What mission?"

"The Creedemore mission."

"But what mission? What exactly?"

"I don't know."

"And Todd went, too?"

"He's got a graduate student finishing up his summer schedule."

Bill Clinings thought for a moment. "Thanks, Jan."

He dismissed the seminar twenty minutes early before the entire roomful of slugs fell asleep, and then he walked across the corridor to his office, where Sheriff Petey Myers stood looking out the window. Petey turned and smiled at the speechless teacher, then turned back to the window.

"Now, they are going to do a play out there, aren't they? That's why they're fixing it up and those kids are all jumping around," Petey said with wonder at the beautiful outdoor stage.

Bill Clinings waited, but Petey Myers held it, lost in stagecraft. After a long moment, Bill composed himself and moved to his desk.

"The play is Shakespeare. Heard of him?"

"Hell yes."

"Well, it's *Taming of the Shrew*, part of the festival. I'm sure it could not possibly measure up to the advanced artistic activities in your Creedemore, but then again we do our best."

Petey nodded, still looking at the kids below. Bill Clinings unloaded his leather briefcase.

"We leave our office doors unlocked as a show of faith in the student body. It is an unwritten gentleman's agreement—I say gentleman's agreement— among members of the psychology department not to enter an unattended office."

He waited. Petey Myers pointed out the window. "You got a terrific view here, Mr. Clinings. When they do the plays, can you watch them from here?"

"Of course."

"That is great. Wow. Me and Reedy got to sit on the stage with Arthur Fiedler and the Boston Pops once. Off to the side, really, but man. Right there. We were on one side just off to the side of the shell, and, I think, Jackie Palmer and Hilly Dale were on the other side. We were the uniforms. There was maybe a hundred plainclothes. Nineteen seventy-six. Somebody kept writing letters and calling places and saying they were going to blow the goddamn place up. But hell, the loons were crawling out of the woodwork in '76. Fourth of July. Bicentennial. They start playing that one that goes, 'Mine eyes have seen the glory of the coming of the Lord.' "

"That would be 'The Battle Hymn of the Republic,' " Bill Clinings said with a bored sigh, arranging some papers on his desk.

"That's right. Now, old Reedy stands up with the crowd and starts to sing in this sweet, big voice along with everybody else, but I swear, now, Arthur Fiedler, up there directing like hell—Horns . . . drums . . . cheering—Fiedler looks over at Reedy with this huge smile. Looked right at him."

"Sheriff Myers. I've just taught a psychology seminar for two hours and fifteen minutes. Now it's time for me to have my lunch. Then I have yet another seminar."

"Psychology, huh?"

Now Bill Clinings stared at him.

"Are you a psychologist, Mr. Clinings?"

"Not technically."

"What does that mean?"

"That means I haven't gotten certified. I teach, in case you haven't noticed."

"So you're not a doctor?"

"I have a Ph.D. That makes me a doctor."

"What do the kids call you?"

"Look here, Sheriff. Aren't you a wee bit out of your jurisdiction?"

"I sure am. I'm just Joe Citizen in Boulder."

"In that case, Mr. Joe Citizen. Please leave."

Petey moved to the door. "Sure. I just thought I'd try to clear up some info I got from one of your members, be civilized, not get the staties, FBI, and all in on it, but sure. Sorry I bothered you."

"What about the FBI?" Clinings asked quickly.

"Every now and then, me and Reedy would have to team up with some of those cockhounds. Reedy called them Fucking Bastards Incorporated. Man, but they can be pissy. One time this guy took some kid out of Connecticut and into Massachusetts to molest him, so the feds get into the back of our patrol car and we get him out on Route 28. Jesus, me and Reedy wanted to just cut this cockhound's nuts off, but the Fucking Bastards Incorporated were so polite and businesslike. Course, they put his ass away for about ever."

Petey Myers closed the door and sat in the chair opposite the desk. He continued pleasantly.

"Now, you are a squirrelly little fuck, Clinings. Reedy would say you need a magnifying glass and tweezers to jerk off. That said, I would hope we can be cordial conversationalists on the subject of a certain big woman named Sandy and a scheduled Liberty Society event that might not be so good for our little valley. Or," Petey Myers said, leaning forward a touch, "for your squirrelly little ass."

∗   ∗   ∗

JoJo wanted them to remain in the waiting room, but Ronnie and Brian Coolette insisted on going with him.

"He's one of our favorite uncles, JoJo," said Brian.

"Mel's great. I'd put him, like, fourth favorite. Maybe even third," agreed Ronnie.

"It'd be close, that's for sure," added Brian. "Although it'd be hard not to put Uncle Dukey on the top."

"Hell yes."

Brian put his arm around JoJo's shoulders. "Uncle Dukey's got a professional Bass Buggy deal out at Possum Kingdom Lake."

"Skeet shooting, too. The whole nine yards. He's my favorite."

"Mine, too. Always got big beer in the downstairs fridge."

"No shit, JoJo. Uncle Dukey has this nigger deliver ten cases a week. The best. Just the best!"

The Coolettes stood on either side of him at the front desk. A pretty Hispanic girl finished typing something into a computer and turned to him with a smile. "May I help you?"

"I'm here to see Mel Prophit," JoJo said quietly.

"Are you a relative?"

"I'm his boy, yes, ma'am."

She looked at Brian and Ronnie.

"We're his boys too," Ronnie said.

"Room 409. Know how to get there?"

JoJo furrowed his brow. "Yes, ma'am. Elevator to the fourth floor . . . uh . . . circle the nurses' station, and it's behind that. I been here three times."

"Okay, then."

"Twice for my dad and once when I got my foot stomped."

"Okay, then, that's Room 409."

They rode the elevator up and did the circle. There were four beds, three occupied by elderly Hispanic men. Mel was watching a small TV. His leg elevated and draining.

"Hey, Daddy," JoJo said softly, touching his father's shoulder. The Coolette boys gathered themselves seriously at the foot of the bed. Mel was nonplussed.

"Looks like another week, is what they said. You feed the horses?"

"Yes, sir," said JoJo.

"You boys okay?" he said to Ronnie and Brian.

"Uh-huh," they answered in unison.

Mel adjusted himself higher. "This guy who took the chips out of my foot said the insurance company won't pay. Called it self-inflicted."

"What about the top of your leg, Daddy?"

"Went clear through, but he had to clean it up and said they're going to say it was self-inflicted, too. I told the son of a bitch, I told him it was more like self-defense. That little bastard went at Brian and Ronnie. Just went at them like an animal."

Ronnie and Brian agreed by shifting their feet and rocking back on their boot heels. JoJo remembered Jude McCormick's big bony hand going out to his father.

"Want to shake and be friends, Mr. Prophit?" he'd said.

Mel had slapped it away hard, and that's when Brian and Ronnie made a run at him. They lunged like TV wrestlers, but Jude hit Jersey style, ignoring every target not directly above the neck. Brian's busted nose stopped him fast,

267

while Ronnie required maybe six hard ones to the top of the head, and that's when Mel went for iron. Still, JoJo noted, it was only Jude who had the presence of mind to apply pressure to his dad's thigh wound, which bled mightily after he shot himself.

"Came up here with those sonsabitches Buck Overstreet and 'Kid,' too. Said he wanted to shake, but gloat was more like it. I wouldn't see 'em."

"Thataway, Uncle Mel," said Ronnie.

"Coming to gloat and all," added Brian.

"This is not over. Nobody is going to shoot me in the leg and get away with it."

"But you shot yourself, Daddy."

JoJo knew he shouldn't have said it the second it popped out. Mel pushed himself further up in the bed.

"That's the sort of thing your mother would go around blabbing. Look where it got her."

JoJo's mom had remarried last fall to the chiropractor Pat Clairborne. He sure wished his dad and mom hadn't divorced. Life would be easier, especially now.

"I just meant—"

"Well, he hit us when we weren't ready. Your daddy was protecting family," said Ronnie.

Brian stepped forward and touched Mel's good foot. "It's what families are all about. We'll get him, Uncle Mel. We'll get all of them. Me, Ronnie, and JoJo. Right, JoJo? We're going to get them."

Mel watched his big boy hard.

"Sure," JoJo said quietly. "We'll get them all."

*   *   *

"I need to call! I want to call! I have to call! I have a life outside of this! I have a classroom to monitor!"

Todd Lehman stood hands on hips in front of Sandy. She had figured at least another week before he went completely stir-crazy and she would be forced to exert a little more authority. She was sitting on a beach chair leaning over the fire, monitoring a can of Beefaroni. Comfort food in all its wondrous aroma, and now this hysterical little dickface playing rooster. Jesus God Almighty.

"Look, Todd, don't you think I want to call, too?"

"Call who?"

"Call . . . call."

"Frankly, Sandy, I've wondered if you want to call anybody or if you're simply enjoying all of this intrigue." He held his hands out and gave an uncomprehending shrug.

"Okay, so who do you want to call?"

Todd nearly shrieked. "Who? Who?"

"Who?"

"Well, for one thing, there's Jason Bataglia, who's been overseeing my Music Theory 211. He's competent, okay, but he is just a grad student, and I'm sure some of the material—"

"Who else?"

"Jan in sociology."

"Jan Wilke?"

"We've been dating, not that it's relevant, but Bill, too. I feel we have to . . . If we don't . . . The bylaws of the Liberty Society, which—I'm sorry, Sandy—you seem to be not taking seriously, call for constant reexamination of goals and actions. That's the creed. That's the story."

"What's to reexamine?"

Todd reassumed his hands-on-hips position. "Oh, grow up, Sandy."

"Really, what?"

"Well . . . well . . . this." He motioned madly at the trailer stuffed with nitrogen-rich fertilizer that was backed up against the base of the dam. Sandy acted dumbfounded and hurt.

"You mean our plan? Our plan to teach the robber barons that the people will always own the land? The people will always exercise their will?"

She stood and picked the pan out of the fire. Todd watched as she spooned some of the orange Beefaroni directly from the pan and into her mouth. He waited until she was through chewing.

"I'm having doubts about this plan, Sandy. As a member of the society's secret council, I feel I have to share my doubts with Bill. And as I say, with Jan."

"Jan's not a member of the secret council."

"Okay then, with Bill. But I still want to speak to Jan . . . and . . . and Jason Bataglia."

Sandy thought quickly. She didn't think killing Todd would be difficult, although the closest she had ever come to killing anyone was the LSD she slipped into that sorority bitch Bernadette's beer that time at the Sink & Suds, when she was waiting tables and all those Little Miss Perfects came in. But this would be different. She had reserved a heavy dosing of tranquilizers for Todd. A somewhat gentle holding pattern, and she surely did not want to waste them on his first moment of hysteria.

"You're right, Todd. Absolutely. I'll go with you."

Todd gave another exasperated hand and shoulder shake.

"You don't have to go with me. That's another thing. It's like you're always watching me."

"You know, Todd," she said reasonably, "for someone who says that I'm not taking the Liberty Society's bylaws seriously, you are being very selective in what parts of our constitution you choose to follow."

"What are you talking about?"

"I'm talking about the fact that we are supposed to work and live in *coveys* while we're in action states."

"But that's . . . wait, a covey is *five* people."

"That's right, but when there are only two or more, they can also constitute a covey under the Articles of Class Action."

"The Articles of Class Action are pretty obscure."

"So is action. That's why Bill wrote it in. It's the separation of individual oversight. It saves us from the tyranny of ourselves."

Todd thought about that. It sounded right. He may have even remembered Bill Clinings saying it. Sandy took two more spoonfuls.

"Okay, you can go with me when I make the phone calls. . . . When is Thursday?"

Sandy, chewing, held up three fingers.

"Okay, on Thursday we're invited over to Bob and Lois's trailer for dinner, and I want to go."

Sandy smiled. "Thursday? Fine. But remember we cannot give any location, even to Bill."

Todd looked puzzled.

"Wiretaps," she said.

"Oh, yeah, of course."

Sandy finished the Beefaroni, and they walked together in silence up the path to the camp pay phone. Sandy's breathing came in machine-gun gasps, and Todd experienced a wave of sympathy, sorry now he had lost his temper.

"I bet you'll love the dinner at Lois and Bob's. They're going to barbecue venison and rabbit."

The grinding of Sandy's teeth was lost in her wheeze.

48

He went for a walk early, even before the sun painted Cathedral Rock. He followed the dirt road over Bachelor Creek and turned right, away from Creedemore, to the mines above. He had tossed all night, finally moving to a kitchen chair so as not to wake Molly. He fantasized, for a while, demented scenarios where he would be crushed by a cave-in or lose his footing and tumble thousands of feet down some uncovered air shaft. Then how could anyone expect him to attend rehearsal? How could they possibly expect him to direct, rewrite, or in any way enter into the creative process? After half an hour, he reached the parking area of the Corso Mine, the largest of Creedemore's old gold mines–turned silver mine–turned magnesium mine–turned copper mine—and now turned tourist attraction. Steven followed arrows to each specific destination. He stopped at the Hoist House. He stopped at the Head Frame. The Shaft Collar. There were also mockups of underground supports. The Round Lagging was one. The Open Lagging was another. At the Waste Fill Chute, he lit a cigarette and sat on a rock. He was warming with the sun now and looked down on Creedemore and the beautiful valley beyond, defined by the Rio Grande shimmering in the early shadows of mountains.

Tonight would be the second rehearsal for *The Creedemore Retrospective*, and his first. Seven to ten. He planned another read-through. He would read it through.

"A read-through, I guess," he said out loud.

Okay, so a read-through. Then the play would have been read through twice.

"A second read-through," he said again, as if speaking to the empty mine might give him a plan.

He watched Molly's truck scoot over the bridge at Bachelor Creek, the single portion of road he could see through the rock crags. He turned his gaze down to the fire station in the old Anderson Mine, and soon the truck shook into view, puttered down Main Street, and pulled in to the Western Market parking lot.

She quickly removed paint cans from the truck and disappeared behind the market wall. Soon her wonderful project would be finished. She returned to the truck, grabbed another can and what looked like a sack of material. She stopped to look up in his direction. He did not think she could see him, but he waved anyway. Even her steps, even the way the heavy cans hung from her delicate arms, framed a kind of personal bravery that transcended doubt. In her confident art, she seemed to give herself permission to go for broke, to risk everything in the bold Molly strokes. Far away, the Weminuche Mountains' snowy peaks burned whiter in the new sun, and he thought how a sample of fire was as common to her art as it was to the Rockies themselves. There was no easy explanation of her work, except perhaps her utter indifference to confinement, to the flat inadequacy of space itself. What had she said? It was simply a story? A dream? It was nothing more or less than drawings on the wall of a cave? Whatever it was embodied in the bordered range of mountain, flow of rivers, cloudy conquistadors—timeless feeling of common experience that allowed it to be true. Real. And as complete in form as the inherent structure of one of Roarke's classes.

"Artists," he said.

And that was the mystery. He had never felt so completely unequal to the task in all of his life.

* * *

Cal Murray might have seemed out of place at the state police headquarters in Monte Vista, what with his long gray hair and Santa beard, and him all dressed like a hippie in his big wheelchair, but watch him for a few minutes at his dispatch console and he appeared to be not unlike a fax machine or computer or any other control fixture. His big, sure voice never panicked, never wavered, and the secure manner of instructions given with an almost metaphysical clarity charged the state patrol radio waves with jurisdiction. Petey Myers tapped him on the shoulder. Cal held up one finger and finished two pending dispatches, then turned to a pretty woman in a state trooper uniform.

"B.B., watch this for me, will ya?"

"Watching," she said.

Cal pointed Petey to the coffee corner. Petey poured a cup, handed it to him, and poured another.

"Now, Sheriff, I have to ask. Is it true you tied up those two before you executed them gangland style?"

Cal laughed heartily, and Petey chuckled with him but if the truth be told, he had been wondering lately if maybe there could have been some discretion in his use of the firearms. He wondered, for example, if there'd been a way to put them out of action temporarily, without literally blowing them apart, which, by God, he did.

"What's up?"

Petey sipped at his hot, good coffee, then took an eight-by-ten copy of a photograph of Sandy Fiddler standing by a storefront.

"This is Sandy Fiddler. She owns the"—Petey referred to his notes—"the Take It or Leave It. An agnostic bookstore, in Boulder."

"Don't know it. She looks mean."

"Well, I wouldn't know. I can't tell from this picture. I dropped off some copies with Captain Dix. Liberty Society shit."

"Jesus."

"I got word they were planning some kind of sabotage—they called it an 'event.' "

"An 'event,' Jesus."

"Thing is, nobody seems to know what she's up to. I talked to this guy Clinings, who's the head man or some shit, but I believe him when he says he don't know."

Cal thought for a second, sipped his coffee, too. "A lot of these cells are a bunch of wackos who just get together, Petey. Survivalists, cultural revolutionaries, militia, you know, assholes on all sides of the equation, and from what little I know about them, it looks like most are just looking to join something. I mean, they're pretty harmless slobs. But every now and then, one of these psychos takes the thing seriously and all hell breaks loose. I'll bet dollars to dimes *somebody* knows what she's up to."

"Yeah, Clinings said she's got some guy with her."

Now they sipped together. B.B. murmured low into her microphone. In another room a phone rang. Cal Murray looked above him.

"Thomas Huxley was a famous agnostic. He tried to calculate, I guess, if there was a God."

"Calculate?"

"Well, that's why they're in colleges, Petey. This is the stuff that concerns them. Genuine cockhounds."

Petey stopped drinking. "I thought I was the only one who said 'cockhound.' "

"Well, I heard it from you, and it grows on a person."

"Yeah."

"It somehow fits just about everything. But the thing is, the agnostic concludes that they just don't know."

"They don't know what?"

Cal smiled as much to himself as Petey and shook his hairy head at all the cockhounds, agnostic or otherwise.

"They don't know shit."

* * *

In the morning Ticky was not nearly so talky. He was out of cigs, for one thing, and old Mr. Gray Brain was fooling around again, this time not letting him remember that he had a guest sleeping on the couch in front of the TV. Ticky had come downstairs from his bedroom wearing his Batman jammies to boil up an egg.

"Good morning, Mr. Lettgo," his tall, redheaded guest said.

Ticky spun and reached to his thigh for his Colt. If he'd had it strapped over his Batman getup, old Mr. Mountain Man would've been OK Corralled before he remembered that invite the night before.

"Well, just goddamn Mr. Gray Brain."

"What?"

"Nothing. Sleep good?"

"Excellent, thanks."

"Egg?"

"Sure."

"Who won the game?"

"I fell asleep before it was over."

Ticky nodded. "Well, we know it wasn't the Cubbies."

After the eggs and coffee, Ticky took a pad of pink paper from a utility drawer and wrote out a shopping list.

"If I don't write it, I don't get it. I remember '37 better'n today. Got some calls to make."

He pulled a portable phone out of the same drawer.

"Minnie loved the portable phone. Jesus, but a man could talk on the river. As a matter of fact, she liked me to put one in my fishing vest so she could call me. Worked as long as I fished the big stretch near the house, but I couldn't hardly hear the damn thing ringing. Don't get that old. Or don't get too old."

He punched in some numbers and looked over the refrigerator at the kitchen clock.

"Six o'clock on the nose." He winked more to himself than to Mountain Man and waited for his first store to pick up.

"Henry? This is Ticky Lettgo."

"Why, hello, Mr. Lettgo. How are you?"

"I'm fine. How'd we do yesterday?"

"Three thousand two hundred sixteen and thirty-one pennies."

"That's the way to sell."

"Thank you, Mr. Lettgo."

Mountain Man carried the strong coffee out onto the porch while Ticky contacted his other stores. The earth was still soaked from yesterday's rain, but the morning sun had begun drying some of the cliffs above the river, and little bits of mica and feldspar twinkled. One of those big horses clopped over and put his nose on the porch rail. Mountain Man rubbed it and scratched it.

Ticky walked out without saying anything and headed to the path at the edge of the yard, the one that led to the grassy ridge over the slowest stretch. His wild, wiry arms seemed to stroke the air like paddles, his legs in a kind of crazy march. Mountain Man watched him make the short climb, take off his hat, and begin waving it and gesturing with both hands. After a bit he came back down.

"Giving my old girl the business report, is all. Saying good morning. She's up there on the ridge. What's left, I mean. Crazy?"

"I don't think so."

"No?"

Mountain Man looked up to the ridge. "Reinhold Niebuhr says it's 'common grace.' "

"Who?"

"Niebuhr. A philosopher and a minister."

Ticky looked back up at Minnie's ridge and thought about Granddad Leeds on his mama's side, the only real philosopher he had known in his long life. "Common grace, huh?"

"It's like something we don't run out of, because it's God's plan that we have it no matter what."

"God?"

"That's what Niebuhr says anyway."

Ticky nodded and adjusted his jeans so they rode comfortably just below his armpits. "Granddad Leeds. Know him?"

Mountain Man shook his head.

"On my mama's side. Big. God . . . fat fella, operated a dairy farm and made cheese and things. He was a philosopher, too. If you wondered about things, old Mr. Granddad Leeds could give you the answers in those little sayings that the big-deal philosophers say. I remember he always said, 'Watch out, goddamn it.' And that's what I'm doing for my old Mrs. Minnie Lettgo. Jefferson, too. I'm watching out! Let's go to town."

∗   ∗   ∗

Nellie Ordoñez, her green hair rapidly darkening over a quite beautiful olive face, stared hard from her seat in Miss Kirk's circular arrangement at Jimmy the Kid, a/k/a Juan Carlos de Moreno. Jude McCormick, sitting behind him and in between the gorgeous Miller sisters from Illinois, poked him. "She's staring at you, Kid."

Jimmy the Kid did not so much as blink. "I'm staring back, boy."

Actors milled by the two coffeemakers Miss Kirk had set up in the far corner of the auditorium, and some stood near the chairs trying to recall the loose but important configuration of character placement.

Mayor Ruby Onerati called out from the seats, "Miss Kirk. What if you're both a Mineral and a Homesteader?"

"Good question, Mrs. Mayor. Let me look at my notes."

Miss Kirk searched her script.

"You were straight on with Minerals at the first rehearsal. Was that a problem?"

"I think after the lava flow, my scene with Zebulon Pike was confusing."

"Let's say you get up and move over, then. After the lava flow."

"Great."

Steven joined Miss Kirk at the stage manager's desk. "Hi, Miss Kirk."

"Mr. Kearney. Excellent news. Jude McCormick and Reverend Eliphalet Nott have agreed to play the two drunken Conquistadors that cause the Ute uprising."

Steven looked around the packed room. "Great."

"How are you feeling?"

"Uh . . . you know . . ."

Cowboy Bob Panousus strode over atop elevated dark green alligator boots. He plopped his nine pages of type on the tabletop.

"Now, I'm not saying this is written in stone here, but as actor to director, I would like these items here to be considered as an addition to act . . . where is it?"

He looked through his big script, leather bound in brown rawhide with COWBOY BOB emblazoned in gold across the front.

"Here we go. Act four, scenes fourteen through nineteen and scenes twenty-nine through thirty-seven. Just a kind of embellishment."

Steven Kearney ran his hand over the pages. "I'll . . . you know . . . I'll read them."

Cowboy Bob smiled confidently.

"When you're all broke down at the end
Of your rope and are given a rowdy task,
Just save your frown and don't give up hope.
It's all that a man can ask."

He nodded, and Miss Kirk nodded, and Steven did, too.

Molly came in with Willie. She kissed Steven and held his hand. "Willie's going to listen, okay?"

"That's cool," Steven said quietly.

Miss Wilma Kirk assembled the cast and thanked them for participating. She had them all introduce themselves for the second time.

"Now let's sink our teeth into the real business of the theater, and that is action. Ladies and gentlemen: Mr. Steven Kearney."

The actors applauded, even Cowboy Bob. Steven rose from his uncomfortable center stool. After a few seconds, the clapping stopped and he faced the circularly collected cast. He saw Molly behind Brian Trujillo, the downstream-fishing actor, and concentrated on her as if this would be his last sight before he died of ignominy, but he felt his mouth moving and heard his own voice.

"Let's . . . let's read it."

"Very good, Mr. Kearney," Miss Wilma Kirk said flatly. "I'll throw in the complete stage directions."

Miss Kirk set the act and scene, and the summer people and all-year people and cowboys and Liberty Society sympathizers all jelled fluidly so that the first third of the script seemed an effortless journey through hot stone and dinosaurs. By the time Juan Carlos de Moreno, the young soldier-poet and lover of Teresa Herrera, made his first appearance, Miss Wilma Kirk called for a short break and walked over to Steven. She held a stopwatch.

"One hour and thirty-one minutes, add some for movement but also subtract when memorized—okay timewise. Yes?"

"Yes," Steven said. "But the lava flow . . . ?"

"You know what? I actually enjoyed the lava flow." She winked. "Hot stuff."

Cowboy Bob made his way over to Vi Myers and Tom Zaleski. Scenic and Costumes listened.

"Now, Mrs. Myers, I think I should spend as much time as possible positioned in front of my picture on the mural. Carson's, I mean."

"Call me Vi."

"What say, Vi?"

"Mr. Kearney would be in charge of positioning, but I'm going to just fill all the crannies with rocks and trees and even that old outhouse behind Baker's Funeral Home. Petey and Dan are moving it tomorrow. Great background."

"Outhouse?"

"It's that rustic, manly thing."

Cowboy Bob wrinkled up his face and turned to Tom. "What about Carson's raid on Ear Grove?"

"What about it?"

"Well, can I wear some leadership clothes?"

Tom checked his clipboard. Next to Cowboy Bob's name, he had written, "Bring his own clothes."

"Sure, Cowboy Bob. That's what I was figuring."

Miss Kirk was strict on the ten-minute break, and soon the poetry of the young Conquistador and his Valencia woman, read by Jimmy the Kid and Nellie Ordoñez, had heated up the room.

"Oh," sighed Vi after the lovemaking sonnet Kid twanged out. Molly, two rows behind Nellie, thought she heard the reporter growl. Then Carson charged into the valley.

Cowboy Bob stood to read it and at certain moments of conquest and slaughter would aside to Steven, "Now, right after the killing-of-the-mayor business, I'd put a poem—the one's marked, I gave you."

And:

"Now, right after he takes the farm boy's ear by mistake, I'd put a poem—funny poem, you know, to show he was sorry and a good guy."

And:

"Now, right after the skinning-alive of Chief Fern Waters's son, I wrote something that ought to be included to show the introspective side of Kit."

Later, Evan Santi, portraying Eliphalet Nott's granddad, the fundamentalist Calvinist, haltingly read his iambic sermon to the Ute Youths, and Miss Kirk again high-signed a break.

"Two hours on the nose," she whispered to Steven. "And give ten extra minutes of filler to Carson. Sorry. I didn't mean that. He means well."

Steven walked out to the parking lot and lit up. The cast avoided him. He was leader now. He was New York. Willie and Molly came over.

"Wild," Willie said, and shook his hand. "Wild."

"When Kid was reading, that girl with the green hair growled at him," Molly said.

Willie laughed. "She did not."

"She did too. She growled. I love it, Steven. It's long, though."

It was past eleven-thirty when Jimmy the Kid read Juan Carlos de Moreno's and the play's last stanza and Miss Kirk read the stage directions:

> "He turns once again to the mountains and
> Exits.
> Blackout."

Big smiles and applause from tired actors and crew. They looked at Steven, and he looked at them.

"That was . . . that was . . . cool. Cool. I know everybody's tired and . . . uh . . ."

Cowboy Bob stood next to campground host Bob Lobato and his wife, Lois, who were playing the Mayor of Ear Grove and his Wife, respectively.

"Are we going to do this by sections? Scenes? Whatnot?"

Brian Trujillo, downstream actor, seconded the questions. "Well, hell, we'll have to, it's already . . . what? Later'n hell."

Janice Overstreet looked at Zebulon Pike, also called Al, her husband, snoring in the Homesteader section.

"I guess we really need some pretty general schedule."

Steven looked for answers in rocks and lava and volcanoes, but there was nothing.

Cowboy Bob pressed. "So okay now, what's the plan?"

In the silence even Miss Kirk waited to know Steven's plan. Cowboy Bob Panousus moved to fill the void.

"Kit rode all night to the Indian camp
And attempted his bravest stand.
'Cause his greatest might was he was the champ
At having a wondrous—"

"Sorry I'm late, Steven. Hi, everybody. Sorry I only got here for the last fifteen minutes."

Roarke made her way from the auditorium doorway where she had waited, toward Steven.

"I'm Roarke," she said, waving. "I'll bet Steven didn't tell you about his assistant from New York."

She kissed him on the cheek.

"Close your mouth," she whispered.

"First thing is, let's make it the most convenient for everybody. That's what we always do in New York. Do we have some kind of a way to contact people?"

Miss Kirk did not miss a beat, although she could not take her eyes off Roarke's amazing hands that animated the room as she spoke.

"I am Miss Wilma Kirk, Stage Manager."

"Hi."

"We have an answering machine set up at my home."

"Great. So everybody make sure you have the answering-machine number. Tomorrow call in, and we'll have a recorded schedule for—" She looked over at Miss Kirk.

"Friday, six to ten."

"Friday, six to ten. We'll be specific about scenes. And . . . can everybody hear me? Okay. One important thing. It's really easy to learn lines if you learn them in the morning. Just browse them in the morning, and you'll be amazed how they stick. Okay? I'm so excited to be working with you. Get lots of rest. Energy is the key. Good night, everybody."

"Good night," they said happily.

Roarke looked at Steven, his mouth still open. Miss Kirk brought over a script for her to see. Roarke put a big hand on the other woman's shoulder and listened intently.

"I would suggest we get to the meat, which of course is the Juan Carlos sections. I didn't want to impose on Mr. Kearney, but . . ."

"That's a great idea, Miss Kirk. You've done a lot of theater, I can tell."

"Nothing akin to the New York scene, I assure you."

"Well, it's akin now." She winked.

Across the room Skyo nudged Eliphalet.

"What, babe?"

"I think that's his girlfriend."

"I thought he was living with Molly."

"He is. Oh, shit."

On his way out, Cowboy Bob stood tall in front of Roarke. His heels brought him thorax-high.

"I'm Cowboy Bob Panousus."

"Hi there, Mr. Panousus."

"Cowboy Bob."

"Cowboy Bob."

"I wanted to welcome you to our little town and say if there's anything you need, anything at all, I'm the man to give it to you."

"Why, thank you, Cowboy Bob."

He gallantly reached for her beautiful hand and, without taking his eyes off her face, kissed it.

"Ooooh," she giggled.

He plopped his big hat on and swaggered away.

"I'm Molly Dowie."

Roarke hugged her. "Molly Dowie. The bald artist. Your hair is growing."

Roarke held her hand and walked back to Steven. Miss Wilma Kirk and Willie followed.

"This is Willie. He's mine."

"Hi, Willie."

"Hey."

Now Roarke held Steven's hand, too, and kissed him again. He still couldn't speak. She shrugged.

"I saw that last fight on TV. I haven't had a vacation since I directed *Thurber's Carnival* in summer stock up at Bar Harbor . . . what? Four years ago. My classes are down until September." She shrugged again.

Steven looked concerned and found words. "Tubby's sister?"

Roarke took in everybody around as if they had all been with her and Niki since day one.

"She knows about best friends. She's a keeper."

And they nodded and smiled, and even if they didn't know what she was talking about, it just sounded right.

* * *

Bill Clinings's last seminar was a study in distraction. Ten minutes into his discussion of the dynamics of personality, he had raised his head and heard himself tell the dolts to spend the rest of the hour reading the next chapter. He simply was not there. His mind ping-ponged off Sandy Fiddler's three potential projects and Sheriff Petey Myers's threats of mayhem. And who in the name of God was this Reedy? This quoted layman philosopher whose themes were so predictably calamitous? Bill gathered his texts and notes and walked out of the room and down the hall to his office.

What was it she had suggested? One project was a bomb, but of course, although he condoned a kind of open violence in the inanimate mold, it was certainly understood by the society members that that was merely a tangential tool. Even the jar of gasoline he himself had placed on the earthmover out at that development site had only created some smoke and dents. It was, as he had made quite clear in the constitution of the Liberty Society of Colorado, the Sensation-Perception of Action. He wanted to screw coeds, not kill them, for God's sake! The second was some chemical she knew of that could kill all the game fish in the Rio Grande. Bill Clinings shook his worried head. Right then and there, instead of chuckling, instead of assuming she didn't mean it, he should have seen her nut potential. What was the third? What had she presented to the secret council? Oh, yes. A human blockade of the courthouse. Well, *that* wasn't nutty. That wasn't a big deal.

"Unless she brought her fucking bomb with her," he moaned, reaching for the phone.

"Jan? Bill."

"Yes, Bill."

"Have you heard anything from Sandy?"

"I talked to Todd last night."

"What did he say? Where was he?"

"He wouldn't tell me. He said the phone might be tapped."

"Jesus."

"He wasn't happy. He couldn't get a hold of Jason Bataglia, who's been watching his classes, and . . . well . . . he had to keep telling Sandy to please give him more room. I guess she was just looming or something."

281

"Jesus."

"He said he was going to call you."

"He did. He wouldn't say anything about where they were or what they were doing."

"Well, those pigs will be surprised, whatever it is."

Bill Clinings stopped himself. Sensation-Perception of Action was lost on them. Pigs?

"Yeah," he said, and hung up.

When it seemed as if Todd might be more forthcoming, Sandy had apparently grabbed the phone out of his hand, because Clinings's own demand to know had fallen on her big ears.

"We might be wiretapped, Bill."

"They can't wiretap us. Now what the hell is—"

"That's right, Bill. We're in a covey now and probably won't be contacting you until Operation Valley Sweep is over."

Bill Clinings found himself screaming into the phone, "Valley Sweep?! Valley Sweep? What the hell . . . ?"

That's when she hung up. And that's when Cia walked in, kissed him on the mouth, and said, "I just talked to Jan. I guess I have to kill Mountain Man, huh?"

49

etey Myers sat at his desk and ate the meat loaf, mashed potatoes, and peas Vi had cooked up and brought over to his office. She sat across from him eating hers, and Dan had his standing up, his plate on a file cabinet. Bobby took off right after the trial day had ended at four.

"Where's Bobby?" Vi asked.

"Date," Petey said, mouth full of potatoes.

"I brought plenty."

"He was going to take one of the Miller girls to Lake City."

"Good, Vi," Dan said, scooping some peas into his mashed potatoes.

"There's more."

Petey was surprised he wasn't all tired out. The day had started early and promised to go late.

The ABC affiliate in Denver did a full five minutes on the restart of the Lettgo thing, complete with the inimitable Jamie Vargas, their star weatherman, standing in front of the old Corso Mine giving the weekend outlook dressed like a gold rusher. This coverage drove the state's public television station to do a half hour, which got picked up by the big free station in Boston, which then broadcast the damn thing national, and, like baby ducks behind their mother, before Petey could say "Hold it, cockhounds," the parking lot of the Municipal Building again looked like a three-ringer. New banners unfurled all over the place, and not just from the artsy-fartsy aging-hippie antiproperty mob either. Cowboys had spread out a big one at their position, reading THIS ONE'S FOR MINNIE, and silver-taped it to the side of Yale Strong's Norgan Ranch cow freighter.

"Did everyone behave, hon?" Vi asked. She'd been stuck in the office all day and couldn't even get a second to pop her head out of the office until after four.

"They stayed on their side."

"Press gets rowdy," Dan said, dabbing some sourdough into the smooth gravy.

"Uh-oh," Vi said sympathetically.

"They think the world revolves around them. How about that little creepy one? That green-haired one? Jeez K. Christopher."

Petey sipped some coffee. "You know she called me a cocksucker?"

"I remember," Dan said.

"And she was struggling and stuff when we arrested her with the others last week. I really could've got a resist on her."

"You're a good guy."

Vi poured the boys more coffee. "She's quite the actress, though."

"The little thing with the green hair?"

"She's playing one of the leading roles. She plays Jimmy the Kid's girl-friend."

Dan smirked. Petey chewed and drank thoughtfully and looked over to Dan. "Have you seen Vi's design for the big play?"

"No, sir."

"You should. It's wonderful. It's wonderful, hon."

Vi smiled, and Petey stood up and wiped his mouth.

"What it is, is that these artists—and I'm including you, too, Vi—tend to hear a different drum and step out to that drum. Some of them do it quiet, present company included, and some of them think that because they hear the drum they can just do it out loud. That guy that wrote the play?"

"Steven Kearney," Vi said.

Dan shook his head a little.

"He's been living with you-know-who. Now he's got you-know-who and another one over there."

"Dan, you better stay out of Boston," Petey said with a wink to Vi.

"Oh, hon!"

"But now here's a guy, this Kearney, who . . . well, I thought he was like a highway worker or something."

"Got a ponytail. I mean, Jeez K. Christopher."

"But he's quiet. He's a guy."

"Shy," said Vi.

"He's not doing the big-drum walk. He's just doing what artists do, only quieter."

"How do you know it's any good?" asked Dan.

"I think it's good," Vi said.

"Sure, but Petey's saying this guy's an artist, and he don't really know if he is or he isn't."

Petey thought about that. "Okay. Only I don't think it matters if it's good. Just that it's there. How's that? It's what he does. Green-hair girl, too. When did that cockhound go onto the tracks at Kenmore station? Vi?"

" 'Seventy-eight, was it?"

"Jesus. That long ago?"

"I think so, hon."

Petey stacked his plate and silverware in the basket Vi had brought dinner over with. "This cockhound, kid maybe thirty, jumps onto the track in the morning commute. Trains coming, holds out his hands like this, like Christ on the cross, right in front of the inbound."

"Jeez K."

"Only the train stops in time," Vi added with excitement.

"It does. Engineer hammers the brake, and the thing scrapes and squeaks and stops. About two feet from the kid."

"Jeez K."

"Me and Reedy are up one flight having a doughnut when we hear all the screaming. We push down there, and he's still on the track. All these people watching. Train stopped. Watching."

"So'd you grab him?"

"Grab him?"

"Train stopped and everything."

"Well, Dan, see, there's a thing called the third rail. See, the trains are electric, and all the juice is in the third rail."

"The third rail," Dan repeated.

"Now, this kid had got his foot about an inch from it, and if anybody grabs him and he touches that rail, then it's two for the price of one. The kid's crying and screaming, and me and Reedy are trying to calm him down. So Reedy has this thing—God, but old Reedy could talk to anybody."

"He had a way," Vi said.

"Oh, God, he had a way, but the kid's a tough nut, and Reedy's saying, 'Want a rabbi, kid? Or a priest? Or who can we get? We'll get anybody.' Now, the kid, I remember, says to Reedy that he was Jewish but not a temple-goer, and Reedy knowing a little about everything says, 'Hell, you don't have to be a goer to participate. Let me get a rabbi.' But the kid says no. What he wanted was an exhibit of his paintings. I swear to God. Vi?"

"Front page said it. *Boston Globe*."

"Even Reedy thinking he's past talking now. What the hell can you say? People don't kill themselves because you can't get an exhibit. But Reedy says, 'Shit, son, I'll get you an exhibit.' The kid—and he was a nice-looking kid, ponytail, I know, but had an old dressy coat on and jeans—the kid says, 'Where?' Reedy says his church. 'Where in the church?' Reedy says they have a big basement meeting room where the Sunday schools are held. Kid says but what about light? He says his paintings are dark and unhappy, but they need light, and old Reedy says, 'Hell, we'll have it lit just so. Dark, unhappy, and lit.'

Now the kid is thinking. Reedy's letting him. He's not saying anything, and out of nowhere this cockhound on the platform says something like, 'Aww, go ahead and kill yourself. You're probably a shitty painter anyway.' Just said it loud, and I swear to God some of the other cockhounds started applauding him. Kid that far away from doing himself and the guy's saying go ahead, and some others are clapping."

"Boston. Jeez K. Christopher."

"Anyway, I get the cockhound with a kind of lateral swing of my night-stick, not full out, just a kind of one of these across the teeth. Now he's down, and Reedy's attention is back to the kid, and he tells him again how he can get his paintings exhibited, but by then the kid had heard all the cockhounds laughing, and he just looks at Reedy and steps flat on the third rail."

"Jeez K. Christopher. Does smoke really come out of their heads and eye-balls? Ticky saw an execution once and swore that flames were shooting out of this guy's ears."

"Well, see, while Reedy was talking, some smart MTA guy had all the rail power shut right down. So nothing happened. We're expecting a french fry, and what we get is a disappointed kid. We take him over to the prison hospital at Charlestown and give him up. That night Reedy goes over to the kid's mother's house because . . . See, you had to know Reedy. . . ."

"He was just so nice," added Vi.

"Kid lived with his mother, so Reedy goes out to Newton to get the paint-ings so he can have the exhibit he promised the kid. He gets there, and the old gal says, 'Well, you can look around, but my son didn't paint. He didn't do anything. He might have thought about it, but he didn't do it.' "

"He was lying?"

"Reedy said he was dreaming. And that's it with the kid. You either do it or you talk about it. Either way I guess art is tough. Now, Dan, I gave you those posters of the fat girl, and I want them put up all over the town and up at South Fork, too. And ask the questions. I know I don't have to tell you."

"You know I know."

"I know."

Petey put on his Boston Red Sox cap and took the shotgun down and checked his nine-millimeter.

"I'm going to walk around Lake City. Put up the pictures."

"You be careful, hon."

"I will, hon. Dan, hold down the fort."

*   *   *

286

Roarke powered the rehearsal with an enthusiasm that propelled everyone. She had diagrammed the word-mural into three divisions and each division into three sections. It amazed even Steven how her rapid rehearsal outlines seemed to have balance and symmetry.

"It's because the *piece* has symmetry," she said.

She had promised a schedule to Miss Kirk for inclusion on her answering machine at 7:00 A.M., and by noon all seventy performers had their weekly time frames. By Friday's break, at 11:15 P.M., "Prehistory" had a sense of shape. A contour that the actors could see and understand. They hung on her words and found creative strength. Even lava flows smoother when its worth has been affirmed.

The Quartz Crystal that was Janice Overstreet approached her.

"Thanks, Roarke. That was just so . . . well . . . I wasn't sold on playing a rock, but . . . thanks."

"It's going to be wonderful. Now, can everybody hear me before you scoot out?"

Miss Kirk was charged by the cast's intensity. Roarke stood on a folding chair, her khaki shorts rolled once, denim shirt, Yankee cap on backward.

"We see how it's shaped? Play it over and over in your minds. We're going to go on to the next division, and we won't get back to this until . . ." She looked over to Miss Kirk.

"Tuesday. We're dark Monday."

"So I know most of you are doubling up and some are even tripling. Skyo's tripling. Janice. Are you tripling, Jude?"

"No, ma'am, I'm Graphite and a Bad Conquistador."

"Everybody remember what we worked on. See ya."

Miss Kirk immediately began resetting the auditorium for the trial. Vi was moving her designs to a far corner.

"You can just leave that up, Miss Kirk," she said. Miss Kirk was about to remind Vi of the trial, but Vi said, "Weekend. No trial till Monday."

"Where is my brain? Mr. Kearney, did you have any running notes?"

"Uh . . . no, Miss Kirk."

Roarke came over to the director's table where Steven sat. She put her arm around Miss Kirk and gave a squeeze. "You really know your stuff."

"Thank you. Needless to say, your first rehearsal was a revelation."

The three of them walked outside under the usual cover of stars. They all looked up.

"See?" Steven said. "It's only in the city we can't see the stars."

Roarke laughed. "I know about stars, Steven. I'm from Kansas. You know that."

"I know."

"Auntie Em! Auntie Em!" Miss Kirk cried playfully.

They kept looking at the sky.

"That, too," Roarke said. "That, too."

*   *   *

The enormous motor home was parked on a small rise above a one-lane log bridge that crossed the Rio Grande some three hundred yards below the dam. It was turned so that the entrance was shielded from the dirt road. When the tent tarp that extended out from each corner of the vehicle for twelve feet was unfurled, it was as though Bob and Lois Lobato's road home was completely alone in this canyon and not one of thirty-two trailers and tents in the packed campground.

A full moon popped over the ridge of the dam. Bob lit a White Owl cigar and poked at the beautiful fire just outside the tent fly. Sandy, Lois, and Todd sat in director's chairs around it. Bob had a rocker and leaned into it.

"Really we live in Owasso, which is a half hour or so from Tulsa, where the shop was."

"Bob doesn't miss it," Lois said, turning to Sandy. "Are you cold, honey? I've got sweaters."

Sandy could imagine the sweaters. What do little old ladies from Oklahoma wear? Jesus.

"I'm fine."

"We've got them big," Lois said warmly.

"I'm fine."

"I don't miss it, but you got a hell of a lot of support from those Pep Boys people. I miss that. They didn't leave you hanging. But the other stuff? Getting reliable help?"

Sandy nodded and looked at Todd. "I know exactly what you mean."

"Now, do you do the whole shebang, Todd?" Bob asked.

Todd looked confused.

Bob continued, "When you do your architecture thing. Do you just draw it up and walk away, or do you do all the hiring, too?"

Sandy laughed. "Oh, Todd does the whole shebang. You do the shebang, don't you . . . honey?"

Todd glared, then caught himself. "Dinner was wonderful."

"Why, thank you, Todd," Lois said. "But really, it's the quality of the game. Wouldn't you say, dear? Quality of the game?"

Bob nodded. "Took the elk here last November. Good winter, so the thing had lots of good grass. That's why the texture's so tender. You get 'em when they been lickin' lichen off the rocks. Al Overstreet guided us with his boy, and those people know how to hang a piece of meat."

288

"Get your album, dear."

"Okay."

Bob got up to get his album.

Lois turned to Sandy. "The elk dish is called cotelettes de chevreuil poivrade," she said, concentrating on her twangy pronunciation. "A good pepper sauce is the key."

Sandy showed her teeth.

"The rabbit ragout takes time, but it's worth it. Bob took the rabbits near home. They're clever little devils, but Bob says they're no match for his Browning shotgun."

"Here we go," Bob said, returning to the campfire. He squatted between Sandy and Todd and opened the album with some ceremony. Dead deer and elk and quail and rabbits and ducks lay over the hoods of cars, hung by hoofs on limbs of trees, held in the mouths of slobbering Labradors or displayed by the ears by proud grandchildren. Sandy felt the digesting rabbit hopping in her gut.

"Look at this one. It's from Ute Point up above the timberline. You can almost see Creedemore at the end of the valley."

Sandy took the photo and studied it. There it was, all right. The edge of the dam and into the valley and beyond. She could just see the wall of water coursing down, spreading out, carrying trees and rocks. She nodded. This will most likely be the last little deer you ever kill, asshole.

She smiled up at Bob. "Beautiful," she said.

"Of course, I don't hunt," Lois said.

"I offered."

"Bob offered to teach me, but . . . I don't know. I keep thinking of Bambi and Bugs Bunny and such. It's easier to have Bob kill them."

"I never was much for cartoons," Bob explained.

"I just cook 'em up."

Now they were all quiet. Bob poked at the fire some more, and Lois put her head back and looked at the stars. Sandy reached over and squeezed Todd's knee hard.

"Ow. What?"

"Why don't we turn in, hon? It's getting late."

"Hell, don't leave on our account. We're night owls," Bob said.

"We are," Lois said. "We are owls. That's one of the reasons we applied for camp hosting. We stay up late and get up early. We are people persons. Aren't we, Bob?"

Bob reached over and put his hand on Todd's other knee. "Son. What old Lois is saying is that we're here if'n you ever need to talk about . . . you know . . ."

"About what?"

"The cancer, hon," said Sandy sadly. "The brain cancer that is eating your brain cells."

Todd looked momentarily stunned, then smiled. "Oh, the cancer."

Lois began crying and hugged Todd. Bob also joined the hug. After a few seconds, Todd began crying, too. Sandy watched them. She imagined the three of them tied together, rolling on crazy waves toward the little town at the end of the valley.

* * *

Bill Clinings called his wife to say he would be driving up to Monte Vista alone. Given the turn of events and the intricate hostilities he was facing, he wanted his partner of twenty-two years out of harm's way and to not expect him home until next Thursday. He taught his last class, threw his camcorder and his Liberty Society executive wardrobe of torn jeans and T-shirts into his new Land Cruiser, and drove over to pick up Cia.

He was distracted as the unit climbed out of Boulder toward Denver.

"You're awfully quiet," she said, rubbing his thigh. "Want me to put on some music?"

"Sure."

"Beastie Boys okay?"

Bill looked over at Cia and smiled. Beastie Boys? Jesus. He noticed her braless T-shirt and the drawing of a fist with the middle finger up.

"Sure," he said.

She slid a CD out of a small portable pack, and the rhythmless, punchless sound hit the air like water balloons. Bill sighed. What he had to endure for a visit into a young disciple's pants. It wasn't fair.

He listened for a moment, and then he tuned them out and played a vinyl Pete Seeger in his mind. He didn't notice, after a while, that Cia had turned off the CD.

"Blow job?"

"What?"

"Want a blow job? You seem uptight."

"A blow job?" he asked.

"Yeah."

"Okay."

Cia unbuttoned his suit pants and unzipped his fly. Twenty minutes later she gave up and looked out the window with a little pout. He patted her leg.

"I'm . . . I'm just distracted, dear. I have—you understand—I have a lot on my mind."

Cia reached for his hand, squeezed it and kissed it. Here was this great man, she thought, doing the masses' labors, daring them to dream the heart-felt dreams of revolution, unable to get a boner because bastards like Mountain Man were distracting him. It was all too unbelievable.

"I know you do, darling. I know you have a lot on your mind. But I know how to help."

Bill Clinings smiled and felt himself loosening. Maybe she could. Maybe when they got to the Monte Vista Holiday Inn, this delightful thing could help him. He gave her hand a playful squeeze and wished she were nineteen.

"I brought my video camera. Can I take some pictures of you with no clothes on?"

She laughed. "Sure."

But she was thinking of Mountain Man. That he had shared. She knew because Bill Clinings had told her about the killer sheriff's visit. Mountain Man had shared with an outsider. And then she was thinking about her solemn oath.

* * *

Reverend Eliphalet Nott swung his legs slowly out of the covers and eased himself from the bed so as not to wake up Skyo. They had spent the afternoon reading poetry to each other, then made love and fell asleep. What time was it? What were they reading? He slipped out of the bedroom, closed the door, and flicked on the kitchen overhead. Eight-twelve. Just dark. He stood naked on the tile floor thinking about the poetry, and then he took a Budweiser out of the fridge, popped it, and sat at the kitchen table. Old poetry, he remembered, not contemporary rambling. Something with flower petals that were swaying in images that reminded him of those sexy O'Keeffe irises. Skyo had brought the book. What was it?

The door to the church apartment opened, and Mountain Man Red Fields stuck his head in.

"I knocked."

Eliphalet stood up with a start. "Mountain Man."

Mountain Man stared for a moment at the naked Episcopal soulist holding the King of Beers.

"I'm . . . I knocked . . . I . . ."

"Come on in. I guess I didn't hear you. Beer?"

"Sure."

Eliphalet got another can out of the fridge.

"I'm not disturbing you?"

"Uh-uh. I guess we took a nap. What's the name of that poet who has a lot of, like, wet flowers in his poetry?"

"Ginsberg?"

"Shit no. Older guy. They wave. They undulate. They make you think about sex."

Mountain Man shrugged.

Eliphalet walked over to the window above the sink and looked outside. "You know what's weird? Falling asleep when it's really sunny out and waking up when it's dark."

They both seemed to consider this. Reverend Eliphalet Nott rolled a grin onto his face.

"Hey, man. Yale Strong is you."

"What?"

"Yale Strong. He's the foreman at the Norgan Ranch. He's doing you in the word-mural. The play. I'm a Conquistador."

"Yale Strong?"

"He's the real thing, man. He looks like Gary Cooper, only with black hair."

Mountain Man thought, Gary Cooper. "Really?"

"Brian Trujillo, who's also doing the downstream fishing, is playing Ticky."

Mountain Man popped his beer and put a dejected slump in his posture. "I guess I'm the joke, huh?"

The naked ecclesiastic walked over to Mountain Man and put his hand on his shoulder.

"Hey, man. Nobody is doing the joke thing on you. It's just out there. Kit Carson gets fucked, though. The two drunk Conquistadors—that's me and Jude McCormick—get fucked. But pretty much the rest is just facts."

Eliphalet went back to his chair and sat.

"What happens? What happens to me and Ticky?"

"Well . . . the playwright has Yale Strong making your case for going down the river, and he has Brian making Ticky's case. Although Yale and Brian both are on Ticky's side. That's all. Roarke—she's helping Kearney direct, but she does all the actual directing, and she is just inspiring—Roarke has them kind of face each other across the stage, and they just yell their ideas. You, Yale, make a great argument. He's sure and bold and all that, but Brian is so effective because he's flat and kind of nervous."

Mountain Man nodded and sat down. The moon was big in the window over the sink.

"I shared with Sheriff Myers."

"In an anonymous letter?"

"Nope. I just shared. He's looking into it. It came down to doing the right thing."

"Yeah, man."

They both sipped and thought how it was not always easy to do the right thing, things being what they were.

"I've been doing some soul-searching about my whole operation. The whole Mountain Man thing."

"Heavy-duty soul stuff?"

"Yeah."

Eliphalet put his head back and stared up at the beamed ceiling and the stucco in between. He rested his tall beer on his pubic hair.

"I been searching, too. The whole Episcopal thing."

"You don't think it's right for you?"

"I *know* it's not right for me. I've come to the conclusion that to be truly effective in the everyday sense of things, it appears that faith in God is essential for an Episcopal priest. I think my soulist shit is a fucking cop-out. But what would I do, man? I don't know anything, really, except this gut aesthetic feel for the spirit."

After a few quiet moments, Mountain Man stood up. "I just wanted to say thanks. Just thanks for listening and for recommending the book."

"My job, man."

Mountain Man nodded.

Eliphalet snapped his fingers.

"Wordsworth."

Thou hast seen nothing yet.

—Miguel de Cervantes, 1547–1616

50

rian Trujillo picked Roarke up at 5:00 A.M. in front of the rock house. She climbed into the high, twenty-year-old, immaculate orange-and-white Blazer.

"Hey," Brian said.

"Hi, Brian."

"Coffee in the thermos."

Roarke poured half a cup into one of several old porcelain cups lying on the console next to her.

They drove out of town on the dirt side road rather than Main Street and saw the banners and skeleton crews of protesters still there for what was being called "land warfare" in all the papers and TV stations. They were crossing behind the Creedemore Hotel when Jimmy the Kid walked out to his truck. Brian stopped and honked once to get his early-morning attention.

Brian turned his big mug toward Kid.

"Hey, Mr. Trujillo. Hey, Roarke. What're you guys doing up so early?"

"Well, boy, we're going fishing. What the hell *you* doing up so early?"

Jimmy the Kid did not miss a beat. "Running my lines with Miss Nellie Ordoñez."

"Well, now, boy, that's what Roarke says to do. Right, Roarke? Morning's the best time?"

"Right."

"Right."

Brian turned over the Bachelor Creek with a chuckle and headed along the Lake City road.

"I haven't been fishing in years," he said. "I'd go on into the water with Mags, my wife, and Chicky Martinez from Alamosa, who I grew up with, and Yale Strong's daddy, Sterling. Mags went with the cancer, and Bill, too, and of course Sterling struggled with the emphysema until it got him."

Roarke poured a little more coffee and listened.

"See now, it's a combination of solitude and companionship. It's good to be on the river. It's good. And don't get me wrong, it's good to be alone on the river, but there needs to be a summation at the end. How's that for a big word? What fly you used. Where it took it. How it went on a long run and maybe darted toward some brush caught in the rocks, but how you coaxed it back into the pools and played it and won. The story completes it. My dad used to say it's two phases of fishing for trout. One's the catching and the other's telling everybody about it at the dealership."

He smiled, and Roarke did, too.

She sipped the good coffee and put her feet up. "I never fished for trout."

"I got the stuff in the back."

"You're going to have to teach me."

"My pleasure—if I can remember." He laughed good at that.

"I grew up in Kansas, and we'd go for bass, bluegill, perch. We'd use worms. Night crawlers," she said.

"We could hook a worm if you like."

"I want to try fly-fishing."

They drove by Ticky's gate, and Brian pointed at it. "Ticky's gate," he said.

A little over five miles past the gate, Brian turned onto the dirt road that led to the public fishing area.

"I'm not going to say this is as good as any spot. Ticky's got some beautiful river, and of course there's the Norgan Ranch down below, but my Mags loved this stretch."

They got out of the Blazer and went around back, where Brian began to assemble the long glass rods.

"Green one was Mags's. That's what you're using. Bring sneaks?"

Roarke raised her feet up one at a time and showed him.

"We'll go without boots. This time of year, even the riffles aren't all that cold."

Brian Trujillo concentrated on bringing up the leader, one rod eye at a time.

Roarke watched his big fingers work it up and thought how much like an Indian chief he would look if he were wearing a headdress. His skin glowed as red dirt. Roarke imitated him and began to thread her line up the green pole. He watched her.

"Now, Jesus, Roarke, my God!"

"What?"

"How the hell did you get hands like that?" He looked at his own. "I did a lot with these. I coulda been king with those."

Roarke wiggled her amazing fingers at him, and he wiggled his septuagenarian stubs at her. He handed her a little leather pouch that opened flat, showing lambskin with rows of tiny flies attached. He put on his drugstore reading glasses and concentrated on the artificials.

"Okay. We don't use the hoppers because they're just not active till noontime. It's warming quickly, so we won't see many 'grammites drifting up from the bottom, so forget about those. If we see a hatch, it'll most likely be mosquitoes, but I'm not gonna bet the house on it at five-thirty in the morning. So see, we've eliminated the dries, most nymphs, and whatnot. So it's looking like old Mr. Red and Orange Woolly Worm."

He held up a long shanked hook with hair wrapping of orange, gold, black, and red. He bounced it in the palm of his hand.

"Weighted," Brian said.

Roarke took it and smiled. Brian took up his own woolly worm and leaned close to his leader. He threaded it through easily and held the line and fly up to Roarke's face.

"Now I'm going to show you the fisherman knot."

Roarke imitated him, her wondrous fingers tying it off with hardly a trailing. Then they walked down to the river.

"Okay, now. Watch." Brian moved slowly into the shallow, stony bottom of the river. "What we're aiming at is to coax them out of that far bank. It's good and deep, and they are there."

He wagged his rod high and fed out the heavy fly line with the leader attached, in a gradual flow. Soon perhaps thirty feet were out.

"You got them that have to throw a hundred feet, but they won't catch more. It's easy like this."

"It's beautiful."

"Thank you, Roarke. Let's see."

Roarke started slowly, got ahead of herself, and then found a center space so that the line eased out and didn't whip.

"Good girl. Now comes the presentation."

"I ought to be good at this. I'm a director."

Brian didn't get it. "Well, hell yes you'll be good at this. Watch."

Now Brian, with barely a sway from his forearm, brought the leader straight out from the fly line and drifted it down like a leaf.

"Wow."

"You can do it. Think how we want the fish to believe it's all nature's plan and not some New York director on the other end."

Roarke plopped it hard several times, then neatly drifted her woolly worm down.

"Now flick—watch me—it's a flick of hand and wrist, and when the current straightens it a little, throw again. That's good. That's a good girl."

297

Brian hooked one and led it in. He wet his hand, slipped the hook out of its lip, and they watched it swim away.

"Barbless hook." He shrugged. "Mags didn't like to kill them."

"Good for Mags. Is mine barbless?"

"Yes, ma'am. Okay, now I'm walking up to that rock, and we'll move upstream on the cast. Get going."

Brian Trujillo stood back and watched. Mags would do a kind of sidearm swipe, getting close to the overhanging grass on the bank. But Roarke did good with her high delivery. She was a caster for sure. He watched a little longer before walking up to the rock where he would throw.

*　*　*

They made love, made coffee, and got back into bed before the Canadian jays started their morning songs. They sipped in silence and listened to Bachelor Creek dribble over the small, smooth stones.

Molly Dowie put her coffee on the side table. "Roarke's gone fishing. I heard her leave."

"I hope she went fishing."

"Was I loud?"

"Pretty loud. Nice loud."

She snuggled against him.

"The run-through was terrific. Oh, it was wonderful. Even Cowboy Bob moved it along."

Steven thought how judicious were Roarke's cuts and how the piece was still resembling his own conception.

"Two hours and forty minutes," he said.

"Seemed quicker. I can't wait until you get it outside under the mural."

Steven finished his coffee thinking how miraculous her work was. How complete. How able to stand alone on many levels.

Molly kissed him and sat on the edge of the bed. She pulled on her big red flannel nightgown and walked toward the bathroom.

"Can you help me with those paintings?"

"I told you. Where?"

"Alamosa. Women's Club's having a showing. Last year I made fourteen hundred dollars."

"Yeah?"

"Three paintings. All trout. We can set up in twenty minutes. Want to take a shower with an old woman?"

She was undressed when he came in, and she turned and faced him. "Stop."

He stopped. "What?"

"From across the room. From right where you are. Does it bother you?" Steven marveled how taut and strong she seemed in nakedness and how very much her body contrasted with the sense of a frail waif she presented in her baggy overalls. The shoulders square and the sinew of biceps and thigh bursting with energy. She seemed taller, too. He had felt perfectly comfortable when they became lovers, but now his hands crept over his stomach until they covered as much of his soft flesh as they could. The feelings of his diminished art washed over him as surely as if he were already in the little tin shower stall. Could she see right through him? Did she judge him as a fraud, and a fat, played-out one at that?

"I'm . . . I think I'm losing some weight."

Again she went back to a flatness on her face.

"My tits," she said. "Tit, I mean."

"I thought you were talking about something else."

"Talking about what?"

He still tried to hide his belly as he stood naked on the cold bathroom floor.

"Talking about what a phony I was. My writing, I mean."

Now she squeezed her small hands into fists, and her knuckles went red and white. The little voice could have been swearing an oath.

"It's not phony. It's beautiful." She waited, and her face showed and her eyes fired.

Steven let his hands drop to his sides. "That is, too."

"What is?"

Looking across the space of tile, seeing her reflected in the bathroom cabinet mirror, front and now back, the wild new hairs, wilder still, morning-pink skin, eyes going brown to green in the light from the window's sun, chin set out in a dare, he smiled and perceived everything to have been worth it. His very lifetime of general human unease to have been acceptable, if that is what it had taken to set him down here, across from her, at this moment.

"What is?" she demanded again.

Molly Dowie, Molly Dowie, Molly Dowie, he thought.

"Your tit."

*　*　*

Ticky Lettgo arrived at the courthouse at eight-fifteen on the nose, driving himself in the big GMC pickup. Some boos and some applause, Petey noted, but mostly a welcome flatness of emotion. At last, except for a couple of diehards, this thing was wearing itself out.

Ticky surrendered his Colt .45 to Petey, handing over the holster belt, too, and walked into the building. Inside again, a smattering of boos and applause that rapidly abated. Mountain Man Red Fields gave a little wave, and Ticky returned it. On that one, Petey and Bobby exchanged glances.

Marge Klinger walked in from her office wearing her robes, and Dan Cryer announced her. She'd had her hair frosted recently, and Petey thought she looked pretty cute, considering how much scowling was required in her position.

"Good morning, ladies and gentlemen."

Some people answered her back. She arranged some papers on her desk.

Roger Hockney stood up. "Approach, Your Honor?"

She waved him up, and Les Vallejos followed.

"Your hair looks nice, Your Honor," Les said sotto voce.

"What, Roger?"

"Uh . . . yes, your hair looks nice," he whispered.

"Roger, what did you approach about?"

Roger had a grin from ear to ear. "Guess."

Marge looked up at that. "We are pals, Roger, but remember you can't be an asshole in my court."

"Sorry."

"Can he be an asshole out of court?"

"Les!"

"Sorry."

She looked over her half glasses at Roger, still trying to contain his grin. "What?"

"We want . . . he wants to drop the charges."

The three were quiet for a solemn moment.

"One more time," Marge said.

"Mountain Man doesn't want to go on with the trial. He wants to drop all the charges against Ticky. And he wants to read a kind of statement."

Les turned around and stared at Mountain Man, who sat straight-backed and tall in his chair. He'd even dressed a bit differently. Instead of a yuppie adventure uniform, he had opted today for a black suit, white shirt, and bolo tie. Les looked to share the moment with Ticky, but Ticky was in the middle of a dream at the defense chair, a slight smile fluttering across his veiny cheeks from his daddy's wedding toast. The old man had stood up in his church clothes, buttoned all four of the heavy suit-jacket buttons, and raised his glass of the champagne that Minnie's mama had shipped up from Dallas.

"Long life," Daddy said, keeping it brief and to the point. What more from a hard road salesman? Small talk was not his game.

The wedding was in Archer City, where Minnie's mama taught school in a

300

one-room house that turned into a Quaker meeting hall on the weekends. Her daddy had got himself shot dead the year before in Mineral Wells over certain political and social views that Minnie's mother had never been clear about, and they had never asked, although Minnie had the upsets pretty good over old Carl Longlook not being at the wedding.

The Lettgo-Longlook vows were quite the event. The entire Lettgo contingent and the Leedses on Mother's side drove down caravan-style and stayed at the Dixie Lady Hotel in Feeney, only a stone's throw from Archer City and St. Luke's Episcopal Church. That evening the rehearsal dinner was held at the ballroom of the Archer City Oddfellows Home, and Ticky was gratified at how the oak floor glistened and how the chicken was fried up wonderfully crispy brown. After the dinner Hollis Simmons and Lukey Appletoe and Ticky's dago pal Tony Finelli took him out to the Goodhaven Bar, and they all got smashed. Next morning, of course, the stomach upset got a hold of Ticky pretty good, a combination of shots of Ten High, Lone Star beer, and a grating uncertainty that maybe his marriage to the fetching Minnie Longlook was a mistake and doomed to be short-lived.

At St. Luke's, Hollis did the standing up for him, and Minnie's big brother, John Longlook, a five-year veteran of the Texas Rangers, took her down the aisle in his full-dress uniform. Minnie had a veil and seemed to float toward him. She was wearing a long, lacy wedding gown that her mother and mother's mother and mother's mother's mother had worn. That first one had made it herself from a tissue-paper pattern sold by the first national seamstress, Mme. Ellen Demorest, through the mail. But Lord our God, she was a pretty bride. Ticky watched her with a measure of pride. He could feel her brother John watching him, too. Yessir. John never said much, and he'd known Ticky's dad awhile, so he knew that the Lettgos were pretty damn solid folks, but still, before Ticky and Hollis assumed their places, Ranger John had taken Ticky aside.

"You look elegant, Ticky."

"Thank you, John."

"I just want to wish you a happy start."

"Thank you, John."

"You two are young, but you know that. Minnie's a real good worker. A real good girl. Hell, she's my only sister."

They both laughed a little. John put his hand out, and Ticky shook it. John held the shake.

"I can't give advice. You'll find all the hard spots on your own. But the main thing to avoid is ever, ever hitting or slapping. Avoid that, Ticky. Because this much I do know: If she is ever hit or slapped, I will shoot you dead without asking your side of it, and my friends on the Rangers will make sure nothing happens to me. You'll be dead with bullets in the heart and between the eyes, and I will be still chasing the bad men. But God bless you both. And your mama is so happy she's crying. I'm not supposed to tell you that. Best wishes, pardner."

Ticky never raised a hand to Minnie. Never would. But he appreciated the straightforward method of the Rangers and particularly of John. So important to get those kinds of statements out there. Marge's gavel brought him back.

Roger Hockney and Les Vallejos took their seats, and Ticky tried to catch the goings-on. Was today the day he'd have his say? His feet worked on the floor like little Fred Astaire's. Marge still had that unflappable tone going, but her eyes gave something away. Now Ticky shifted for a better look.

"Ladies and gentlemen, Mr. Hockney has a point of procedure," Marge announced.

Roger stood. "Yes, Your Honor, the people wish to drop all charges against Mr. Lettgo."

Ticky looked baffled. After a stunned moment, cowboys roared approval. Liberty associates roared back.

"Order!"

Petey, Bobby, and Dan went into the aisle dividing the two factions.

Marge looked at both Ticky and Mountain Man, banging her gavel again. "Mr. Fields? Is this your desire, to drop the charges pending?"

Mountain Man Red Fields stood. "Yes, Your Honor."

"And Mr. Hockney informs me that you also wish to make a statement?"

"Yes, Your Honor."

Marge Klinger spread her hands apart. "Be my guest."

Mountain Man came around the corner of the prosecution table. He paused to gather his thoughts and a green-and-brown-uniformed Liberty Society woman stood up and filled the silence.

"Goddamn sellout! Sellout!"

Marge clanged it again. "Sheriff Myers, please escort this woman to the pokey."

Petey sent Bobby down, and she went with him with one fist pumping. Her side applauded. Cowboys booed. Marge waited, and then it was quiet. She nodded at Mountain Man.

"Thank you. A little while ago, I had the opportunity to spend some time with Mr. Lettgo here, and after having a chance to talk with him, I decided that I like what he had to say and that maybe I had gotten everything wrong."

Mountain Man glanced over at Ticky, whose eyes were closed again, back in Archer City, Texas, watching Minnie float down St. Luke's aisle.

"I'd like to also add that I'm not giving up on the idea of the rafting experience, but that from now on I'll be asking permission to use passage, and I'll portage around anyone who refuses."

Marge and everyone else watched him.

"I think . . . I really, sincerely . . . I think it's time for the individual to assert some . . . some moral imperative over . . . over the group. Because, as Reinhold Niebuhr said, the individual is everything, and the group is . . . flawed. Of course I'm paraphrasing. That's it."

Now the relief Margie felt manifested itself in a loosening of her shoulders. The Lake City Ladies were going to get the real Marge "The Glove" Klinger back at shortstop.

"Well said, Mr. Fields. Case dismissed."

This time the factions stood raging. Bobby and Petey guided the cowboys out first, while Dan planted himself center aisle like a crossing guard. The Ticky group shouted the news to the world, staying in the parking lot to lord it over the Liberty Society and their allies.

Bobby shouted to Petey, "I don't think the cockhounds are gonna move, Sheriff!"

"I thought I was the only one who said 'cockhounds'!" he yelled.

"I been saying 'cockhound,' too!" Bobby yelled.

"Just let's get them over by Yale Strong's truck."

Petey felt the cameras, felt them hard, and for a moment felt Reedy there.

"What about it, Reedy? Is it a Boston Baked Ballbuster?"

"What?" Bobby asked.

"Where the hell are those staties? Jesus God."

Dan Cryer came out like a shepherd with an unruly flock. He stood on the top of the stairs, and Petey Myers signaled him to keep the Boulder crowd on their own side. Dan came down, red-faced, moving hard. The troopers stepped up now, in a Maginot Line of sorts, and Petey looked with satisfaction at the smart deterrent.

"There it is, Reedy. There you go."

"What?" asked Bobby.

The open top porch of the Creedemore Hotel had been requisitioned as a sort of news pool photography center. Videos whirred. Cameras clicked. But the state troopers held their line. Now Mountain Man Red Fields came onto the steps with Roger Hockney. A deafening roar of boos and applause. A switching of sides with some degree of fanfare. Onto his ensemble of black suit and bolo tie, he plopped on his final argument, a ten-gallon black Bronco felt deluxe cowboy hat. That's when Petey saw the gun.

It was just a glimpse really, concealed under the open Eddie Bauer utility vest worn by a thirty-or-so-year-old blond man, average size, in the outfit of the Liberty Society. Petey moved in an arc toward him, watching closely how he kept touching the area of the weapon. As Petey moved, so did the Liberty man, arcing himself closer and closer to Mountain Man.

"Jesus God," Petey mumbled to himself.

Yale Strong stood on his cattle freighter and let it go. "Three cheers for Mountain Man!"

The cheers rang out against a brilliant, cloudless morning. Mountain Man raised the hat over his head.

Petey had gotten to within three feet of the armed man. He played it in his mind.

"Here it is, Reedy. You want a gun in the West, you wear it outside. You announce it. If you're driving, you lay it *on* your seat, never *under* it. You never hide it."

Reedy would have reminded him about the Perini mob at the Falmouth Yacht Club swearing to God they were clean and then bringing those little guns up out of their socks and squeezing them off like squirt guns. Only they weren't squirt guns. Just ask Reedy's old sidekick Rick McGance. He didn't even know they'd killed him until Rick looked down and saw the blood coming out of that hole in his belly.

At the bottom of the steps, the blond man made a sharp gesture up to his side, the side where Petey had seen the black handle. Petey hunched and drew himself in, then struck hard at the man's kidneys. The man fell onto both knees. Petey reached over him and quickly pulled out the gun, then yanked him to his feet by his hair, keeping the confiscated weapon cold against the side of his head.

"If I shoot it once, I shoot it five times," Petey said flatly.

The young man's eyes were wide.

"He's got Alex!" someone shouted.

"Where?"

"Over there! The killer! The sheriff!"

Bobby made his way over, and Petey began pushing the man up the stairs.

"I can explain," the man said.

"Sure," Petey said, and led him into the courtroom and through the double doors to the corridor and sheriff's office.

The leading flank of Liberty Society members made a move at the stairs, sliding down their side of the state troopers' file. This drew both the state troopers and the cowboys.

Mel Prophit, who had stood off to the side on crutches, voiced his frustration. "Now, goddamn you people!"

Mel swung one of his crutches over his head and brought it down hard, through the gap of state troopers. It cracked the back of a head belonging to a tall, gray-haired academic and bounced madly off the teeth of an elderly Liberty Societarian, knocking her backward from her aluminum walker.

"Ha!" hollered Mel.

Now the state troopers and Liberty Society surged toward the conflagration. Mel Prophit fell back, lost a crutch, and hit the ground hard.

"Man down! Man down!" Yale Strong yelled from the top of his cattle freighter.

"Who's down?"

"Guy on crutches."

"Crutches?"

Yale directed the cowboys, who rolled toward the broken defensive line of state troopers. Someone on the Liberty Society side lobbed a cherry bomb onto the cowboys, some of whom responded by heading to their pickups for their rifles. Dan and Bobby stood firm, holding hands flat out as if preparing to push back a tidal wave.

Mel Prophit struggled to his feet, grabbed his missing crutch, and charged again. Two more cherry bombs were thrown. It was the one that exploded directly on top of Mel's Dallas Cowboys cap that set it off full.

*　*　*

Bill Clinings laid his tiny digital video camera on a dresser ledge and aimed it at the door of the motel room. Cia watched him. He looked through the viewfinder.

"Okay, you go outside and knock, and I'll start recording. I'll answer the door, and you enter. I'll say something like, 'Yes? Can I help you?' and you'll open up your raincoat and have nothing on."

"You're going to say, 'Can I help you?' "

"Something like that."

"Okay."

Bill Clinings let Cia out and punched the "record" button on the camera. There was a knock. He opened the door.

"Yes? Can I help you?"

Cia stepped into the room.

"Yes, you can," she said, and opened her raincoat.

Bill put both hands onto her perfect breasts and smiled. First at Cia and then at the digital camera. Then the phone rang.

"Goddamn it," he said, crossing to the camera, shutting it off, and picking up the phone.

"What?"

"When you weren't at home, I figured the motel."

The voice was whispery and hoarse.

305

"Sandy? Sandy? Jesus Christ, tell me it's you."

"Who the fuck did you think it was?"

"I'm— Are you all right?"

"Why wouldn't I be all right?"

"So where the hell are you?"

"I'm fine, thank you."

Bill sat on the bed of his Holiday Inn room and tried to calm himself. Her breathing sounded like a mountain storm.

"Sandy, the police have been in contact with me. They've gotten a hold of some rumor that you may be . . . planning something."

"Not me."

Bill Clinings felt his stomach muscles loosen. "No?"

"Absolutely, positively not."

"Thank God. For a while I thought that the cops were maybe right, and we have so much we have to ac—"

"Not *planning*, Bill. *Doing*. It's been planned. Now it's being done."

Bill felt his stomach knot again. Cia walked over and stood next to him.

"What?" he said quietly. "What is being done?"

Sandy laughed at that one. A guttural yuk like Bill imagined a bandito would make when he had you trussed up and hanging upside down over a cliff.

"You made the rules, Bill. You set down the society's bylaws."

"That's right. There's nothing in the bylaws that prohibits you from sharing with me the specifics of the plan."

"You sound like Todd."

"Put Todd on."

There was another long pause, but he knew she was still on because the heavy wind blew hard over the wires. Cia opened her raincoat again. Bill waved her off.

"Todd's a little tied up at the moment. Look, Bill, there's a codicil to the Liberty Society manifesto that you yourself added early last year, after you firebombed that earthmover outside of Boulder."

Bill stood and yelled into the receiver.

"That . . . that was a small device—a device, for Christ's sake! It was not— Are you listening to me, Sandy? It was not a firebomb."

"It blew up, it covered the mover with flames. What the fuck difference what you call it? Anyway, you added the Articles of Class Action."

Bill paced. He couldn't remember. He had added things concerning the society's whole gamut. He had added hundreds of things.

"Read it to me," he said now.

"I don't have a copy."

"Paraphrase the goddamn thing, then."

He imagined this fucking cow in all her smug glory. Jesus. Cia sat heavily in a tacky motel chair, pouting.

"You don't have to try to intimidate me, Bill."

Another pause.

"I don't even have to speak to you, Bill. You should be wondering who shared, not that I am making a stand for our beliefs. Or maybe they aren't your beliefs. Maybe you and that heap of academic blowhards have been playing at the whole thing all along. In any case it doesn't matter."

"Sandy . . ."

"Who shared?"

"What?"

"Who shared?"

Bill sat back down. His energy had flagged. It was as if the big woman had sucked it out of him over the phone wires. "I'm not sure, but I suppose it was Mountain Man."

Sandy guffawed, and Cia straightened.

"That sheriff who murdered those kids from Lake City and who arrested me out at the Lettgo place showed up in Boulder. Threatened to bring in the FBI."

He said it, and she was quiet. Her breathing only a breeze now.

"Sandy . . . listen to me, just listen. I know how frustrated you are over the trial and the property issues, otherwise you would never have left your business to come up here and . . . and . . . what is it, exactly? Is it a bomb?"

He could hear her, her silence dangerous.

"Okay, Sandy, a bomb. I figured it's a bomb. But—are you listening? We are the good guys, Sandy. We are the people who want to preserve and not destroy. We bend . . . we bend like the willows in our gentle protest. Our quiet, soft dignity . . . our . . . ARE YOU FUCKING HEARING ME!"

"Yes, Bill—'quiet . . . soft . . . dignity'—I'm listening."

"Just tell me if it's a bomb."

"Okay. It's a bomb."

"A big bomb?"

"Bigger than a bread box."

"Where?"

"Now we're getting into the area of the Articles of Class Action. I find them confusing. Todd finds them confusing. They are just confusing articles."

"Listen—"

"Hold on, putz. *You* listen. I'm so sick of you pindicks jerking off on my time. I should have done this long ago, asshole."

Bill Clinings squeezed the receiver. "Fat-ass," he replied.

"Cocksucker," she answered.

"Fucking lardo!" he shouted.

"Academic suck-ass," she yelled.

"Corpulent ignoramus!" he screamed.

"Second-rate lecturer!" she wheezed with a final whoosh and click. Bill Clinings looked at Cia.

"She hung up. She hung the fuck up. Bomb. She's got some kind of bomb."

His mad thoughts rolled into one, then separated into disconnected strands. One thing was preposterously clear, though: that everything has an ecology, even a movement, and its frailty is linked with people.

"People suck," he said pathetically.

Cia walked over and hugged him. The great man. The good man. Tears welled in her eyes. His, too. He took a deep and calming breath.

"Okay."

He dried his eyes with the palm of his hand and showed Cia a brave smile.

"Okay . . . you go outside and knock, and when I say, 'Can I help you?' or something, you open up your raincoat."

He led her to the door, then hit "record" on the camera.

51

etey Myers had Vi relay the news to Miss Wilma Kirk that for one twenty-four-hour period he and the staties were closing down town activities, including rehearsals for *The Creedemore Retrospective*. He was chatting with Sergeant Rosie Carnevale, the state police representative, when Wilma puffed into the office. Petey stood.

"Good morning, Miss Kirk. Have you met Rosie Carnevale?"

"I have indeed. Sheriff Myers, your lovely wife, and our excellent set designer, has informed me that the rehearsal for our *Retrospective* is not going to be allowed today."

"Well, yes, Miss Kirk. I asked Vi to talk to you."

"Why?"

Petey regarded the khaki-clad, pith-helmeted Miss Kirk and for a second thought about saying how much she reminded him of a western Winston Churchill, but he didn't.

"I figured—actually, *we* figured—a little time might quiet things down."

"Ahh. The conflagration."

"Yes, ma'am."

Miss Wilma Kirk wrinkled her eyes and nose and leaned against Petey's table.

"Now, Sheriff Myers, I would be remiss if I did not point out to you, at this juncture, this critical moment in the life of Creedemore, Colorado, that the entire essence, the actual precipitator of Mr. Steven Kearney's epic, was the potential explosion of emotions over property. And now that this has indeed come about, it is up to the arts community to put to the test the healing, indeed *cleansing*, power of the theater."

Miss Kirk reached out and squeezed Rosie's arm. "I've seen your interpretation of Williams's one-acts, remember. I *know* I don't have to convince you."

Petey shifted his feet. "People have been hurt."

"Exactly my point, Sheriff."

"We got two hospitalized. Weapons were fired."

"Over heads, wasn't it?"

Petey looked at Wilma Kirk with a nose wrinkle of his own. Man, those staties had a self-control he absolutely could not believe. After those Liberty cockhounds started throwing cherry bombs, after that cockhound Prophit had teed off on some elderly protesters, those goddamn cowboys pulled out their rifles. The line of staties calmly looked at them. Even when a couple of the cockhounds let off a round or two over Liberty heads. When was it the Black and White gang were shaking down shopkeepers on the Roxbury border—'79? '80? Him and Reedy got assigned to Benny O'Brien's task force. Nobody could believe that the blacks and Irish had formed up into a gang. So O'Brien has this Indian jewelry store that had been hit for protection money staked out. Petey and Reedy and Ducks St. Jean and two or three other guys. Everybody plainclothes. They weren't there twenty minutes when four black Fords pull up, and out step two young guys, one black, one white from each car, all in black or brown suits.

"Just like the FBI," Reedy says.

"Jesus."

"One of the great mysteries of law enforcement."

"Irish and blacks," Petey says, shaking his head.

Miss Kirk kept talking. "Our director, Roarke, would like to 'take it outside' for our first amphitheater run-through. Every rehearsal, Sheriff Myers, is most precious."

Rosie Carnevale poured some coffee. "I heard she's wonderful," she said.

"Extraordinary."

"If this darn trial security hadn't come up, I'd have been at your auditions for sure."

Miss Wilma Kirk smiled. "And I'm positive you would have secured a leading role, Sergeant. Now, what say, Sheriff?"

Miss Kirk fixed on him, and Rosie did, too, being clear she was not going to jump in here, at least on his side.

"Sheriff?"

Petey put on his hat and walked outside, saying over his shoulder, "Whatever you want Miss Kirk. Whatever you want."

Petey paused for a moment, trying to recall his easy decision to leave Boston for small-town policing and the restful, comfortable life among the stalwart, traditionally law-abiding, respectful citizens of the West. He chuckled to himself, although he did not feel like chuckling, and walked to his county Jeep. He slid into the driver's seat. Out of the alley between the rock shop and the Creedemore Hotel, the blond, gun-carrying Liberty Society member whom Petey had disarmed and arrested earlier jogged across the street and jumped into the Jeep, too.

Even though rehearsal would be in the Lumberjack Amphitheater with some lights, partial costuming, and most of the essential scenery, Roarke had her eighty-seven thespians assemble inside the Municipal Building. Two burned-out vehicles were being loaded onto an Alfonso's Tow Service flatbed truck, and Harry Cornell from the Creedemore Volunteer Fire Department stood alone with a garden hose watering down the smoldering paint on the parking lot side of the Historical Society Building.

Roarke greeted each cast member with a big hug as they entered, even Cowboy Bob, who arrived in his dress buckskins and white duster. He held the hug and then held Roarke at his short arms' length.

"I'm into my best cowboy suit
And my best artistic mode,
'Cause we're gonna hit the floor with boots
And get this show upon the road."

"Oh . . . oh, Cowboy Bob, you are something."

Cowboy Bob nodded agreement and rolled into the room on his towering heels. Miss Wilma Kirk stood on a chair, impossibly counting the company. She turned to Steven Kearney and shrugged. She clapped her hands together rapidly.

"Actors! Actors! Attention, please."

The cast settled and faced her.

"Ladies and gentlemen, thank you so much for responding to tonight's re-hearsal despite the recent calamity. Sheriff Myers has reported only three in-juries that required hospitalization. The two elderly people from Boulder who were attacked in the confrontation were treated at Monte Vista Community Hospital and released. Mr. Mel Prophit has been kept for observation of a pos-sible ruptured eardrum. I do not mean to appear callous, but fortunately none of the above are cast members of the *Retrospective.*"

Miss Kirk took a long, eccentric pause, sighed, and straightened.

"Before I turn the proceedings over to our director, allow me to add a fer-vent hope. As we begin our first run-through in the amphitheater, which in five short days will lead to our first performance, let us put aside, as artists, our differences in the world at large so that we may grow as a truly relevant and healing creative community."

Miss Kirk could think of nothing to add. A sweet contemplation filled the room.

"That's just like a prayer, Miss Kirk," Roarke said.

Miss Wilma Kirk clapped her hands again. "It's all yours, Roarke."

Roarke stood on her own chair. Shorts, pigtails, backward Yankee cap, little trout earrings Molly had made for her. She raised her arms out, and everybody stared at her electrifying hands.

"Usually when it's time to leave the rehearsal hall and begin in the theater, I have my cast just meet there. The reason I wanted us to meet here first is the sense of real discovery I want us all to have at the same moment. I want us all to stand under Molly Dowie's beautiful, amazing wall and have it flow all over you wonderful actors at the same time. Let's spread out and do our warm-up and then get to our theater."

They spread apart in the big hall, with an energy and commitment many, especially the older ones, felt they would never capture again. They stretched and vocalized, and then Roarke, Steven, Molly, and Miss Kirk led them on out. Rocks and Trees and Hills, Dinosaurs and Mica, Gold, Silver, Conquistadors, and Kit Carson, too. They walked down Main Street and cut behind the Western Market like a parade of liberators. They whooped in front of the mural, really seeing it for the first time. Molly wept a little. Roarke, too, draping her arms around Wilma Kirk and Steven. Even Cowboy Bob was getting sentimental until he spotted Roy Martinez in the crowd of actors and remembered how he had to cut his ears off in act 2, scene 3.

*　*　*

Bob Lobato had his Pep Boys cap in both hands when he stepped into the clearing beneath the leviathan earthen-and-cement Rio Grande Dam. Lois came a few steps behind, carrying a large porcelain casserole dish. Sandy Fiddler was on her back under the old trailer, packing a last, unseen fifty-pound bag of fertilizer. When she saw their legs, she slid quickly out and trotted to meet them. The twenty or so yards left her gasping.

"How you doin' there, little gal?" Bob said, giving her a tender hug.

"We are just worried. We are worried sick," Lois said worriedly.

"Sick," Bob agreed.

Sandy gulped for air.

"How's our patient?" asked Lois.

"Resting," Sandy gasped.

"Well, God bless him," Bob said. "Nothing as good as rest."

"It's as good as gold," Lois said.

"Hell yes. It's how you get your strength back. Now, little gal, is there anything we can do?"

"Just name it."

"Shout it out."

"It's what we're here for. It's why we're camp hosts."

312

Sandy Fiddler watched them with a kind of sadness. Sorrow, really. She simply could not believe she had five more days to wait before these old farts were under 200 billion gallons of water. Five days. It didn't seem fair.

"I really appreciate it, Bob, Lois, but Todd and I are independent people."

"Maybe we could just say hi?"

"He wouldn't recognize you."

Lois handed Bob the casserole and covered her mouth. "Oh, no," she sobbed.

Sandy nodded sadly. "Yeah. There," she touched her head. "Mesencephalon, pons, medulla oblongata. The works."

"But . . ."

"No buts, Bob. The last thing he said that made any sense was, 'Please tell Bob and Lois thank you for letting us stay here for five more days.' "

Bob and Lois Lobato could not speak. Bob handed Sandy the casserole and led the weeping Lois back to their camp. Sandy watched them disappear into the narrow pine- and aspen-lined path. She thought of heaving the casserole dish over her shoulder in a cool, casual gesture, but she noticed a layer of crispy noodles under the clear top. Was that cheese and tuna?

She carried it back to the tent site next to her nitrogen-packed trailer and laid it gently on the Styrofoam cooler. Glorious clouds drifted above, and a piney breeze blew light bursts of scent over her. She peeked into Todd's tent.

"How's my little dickhead doing?"

Todd's hair was messed, and a light reddish beard threatened on his face. His third day on the tranquilizer that Sandy had slipped into his trail pack of Del Monte fruit salad and continued every twelve hours was enough to turn a Bengal tiger into a house pet or a music theorist into a tent boy. He smiled strangely, and some drool slipped out of the side of his mouth.

"Ugh," grunted Sandy. "Gross. C'mon."

Sandy levered herself and pulled Todd out of the tent and to his feet.

"Jesus, asshole, you've got to fucking help, too."

She walked him over to a cluster of chokeberry bushes and faced him into them.

"Take it out first. C'mon. Dickhead has to go pee-pee."

Todd unzipped, and Sandy turned up toward the dam. The inconvenience of it all. Just when she thought he'd make it to at least within a day or two of the climax of "Operation Bernadette," as she had taken to calling it, Dickhead Todd Lehman had confronted her three days ago on the trail to the campground pay phone.

"Todd? Where are you going?"

"Where I'm going is my business."

"Why are you so . . . agitated?"

313

"Agitated? AGITATED? Why do you think I'm AGITATED? I have gone along with you and this scheme of yours for too long. We are not going to blow up anything."

"Sure we are."

"We are not."

"Yes we are."

"No we're not."

"Todd . . ."

"Let me ask you this, Sandy." Todd put his hands on his hips. "What exactly do you think will happen if you ever blew up our trailer?"

"*My* trailer, remember, dickhead? I paid for it."

"I would have helped you pay for it. You never asked. AND STOP CALLING ME DICKHEAD!"

"So you want out."

"I want no bomb. I want no part of no bomb. I'm calling Bill, and if you don't get that thing out from under the dam, I'm calling . . . I'm . . . the police, Sandy. There. It's said."

Todd pushed past her and headed down the trail.

"Okay," she called after him.

Todd stopped and turned. "Okay what?"

"Okay. You're right. I must have been crazy."

"Exactly."

"Out of my mind."

"You went loony bins, Sandy. Just loony bins."

She walked down the trail to him sadly. "Look. After lunch I'll hook up the trailer, drive it down to—what was that big feed store in Alamosa?"

"Charity Seed," Todd said, liking the plan so far.

"Charity Seed." She nodded. "I'll drive it down and see if we can make a fair sale. Not lose too much money. Think they'll go for it?"

Todd smiled gently and squeezed a handful of her triceps. "I'm sure they'll go for it. Let's call Bill."

"You know what, Todd? Let's eat some lunch, hook up the trailer, and call from Charity Seed. I want to get the hell out of here."

Todd smiled broadly, warmly. He would not lord it over her. He would allow her to think this was her own good idea.

"Whatever you want, Sandy. We'll call Bill from the Charity Seed. What's for lunch?"

"How does SpaghettiOs sound?"

"Yum, yum."

"And some nice fruit salad."

"My favorite."

Now that his hearing was coming back in starts, Mel Prophit's eardrum—his tympanic membrane, as the wetback doctor they assigned him at Monte Vista Community Hospital called it—was giving a brass-band concert inside his brain at the slightest sound. Last night was the clincher. Middle of the night, some big coon-ass male nurse comes sauntering through the door and drops a bedpan. Jesus. Atomic bombs could not sound like that. Mel just about flew up to the goddamn ceiling. Then the black son of a bitch wouldn't stop apologizing.

"Sorry, man. Man, Jesus. I am so sorry."

And that voice like the bottom of a well damn near popped the cotton plugs out of his ears. It all hurt. Even eating. Even drinking water. Jesus. Owww. And if he forgot for a second and crunched into some ice . . . well, it just clinched it some more.

Then that Bobby from the sheriff's office. Where the good horseshit was Myers? Sitting on his big old Boston baked ass, he bet. How the hell do you answer a question or even fill out a report if the goddamn pen running over paper is like a little Jap inside your head wearing gold shoes?

"What's your story, Mr. Prophit?" that snot-nosed kid asked, all official like. That notebook. Sunglasses on. Mel held his hand out and grimaced. Bobby watched him and grimaced, too.

"Need a doctor, Mr. Prophit?"

"No," Mel whispered, and signaled Bobby with one hand to come close and with the other hand to talk softer. Bobby got the first part. He bent down near Mel's face.

"What?" he said, loud and slow, as if to an old, hard-of-hearing man.

A volcano erupted inside him. This time not limited to his impoverished head. He was sure the discharge was shooting out his testicles.

"Ohhh," he moaned, and held his hands over his ears.

Now Bobby whispered. "Look, let's try this, Mr. Prophit. Let's try me talking real soft like this. Better?"

Mel nodded and dropped his hands.

"Okay, then? Okay. Sheriff wants to know your side of it."

Mel looked quizzically at him.

"The attack on the professor and old Mrs."—Bobby checked his notes— "Mrs. JoAnn Pombrel of Walsenburg."

"Walsenburg?" Mel whispered.

"Says that you got her with your crutches."

"Crutches? Me? Hit an old woman? C'mon now, Deputy."

"Says it careened off the professor's head and popped her in the teeth."

"Well, look, she's lying."

"What about the professor? Says you banged the back of his head. Saw stars."

"He's lying, too. They're all liars."

"That's your statement?"

"No . . . no . . . uh . . . look, here's my statement. I was on crutches due to recently being bushwhacked by some cockhound and—"

"Cockhound?"

"That's what I said—'cockhound.' "

"I thought me and Sheriff Myers were the only ones said 'cockhound.' "

"Jesus, boy, we been saying 'cockhound' since the fifties. Anyway, these people—one of them Liberty people—reaches through the line of state troopers and grabs my crutch and brings it back, you see, over his head like he's going to whack me but instead hits the . . . the . . ."

"Professor?" Bobby asked helpfully.

"Professor . . . right here . . . head. Wham. Then he turns around quick like and gets the . . . the old woman by accident."

"You want that as your statement, then?"

Mel pushed himself higher in his hospital bed, his voice a charged whisper. "Hell yes, that's my statement. Why the hell would I give it to you if it wasn't my statement? I swear on a Bible and to Almighty God that is what happened."

Bobby shook his head.

Hair's too goddamn long, Mel thought. No wonder these cockhounds can't get the respect of the bad men.

"You don't believe me?"

"Look, sir . . ."

Bobby had returned to a normal-size voice, and Mel instantly slapped his hands over his ears.

"Sorry, Mr. Prophit," Bobby whispered. "Sheriff Myers has got seventeen videotapes from different angles, including the one our surveillance unit in the second-floor window of the Municipal Building took, and you're on seven of them."

"Seven?"

"We got the cherry-bomb thrower, too. Animal-rights guy from Denver. Got four clear videos of him throwing. He swore to God, too. Said he saw the sheriff throw the cherry bombs."

"Lying bastard."

"Yes, sir, Mr. Prophit. Be seeing you."

* * *

Mountain Man Red Fields sat on the low front porch of his rental store sipping Coors Light from a can. The moon was bright yellowy orange, and the stars lit up the back street. He could hear coyotes above the old Corso Mine. He could hear the stir of voices in the Lumberjack Amphitheater. He drained the beer can, popped another, and walked up to the rehearsal.

Several work lights were on, but these were obviously not the lights that would glow the production. Mountain Man stood in the shadow of one of the bleacher rows and watched. On the periphery of the acting area, there seemed to be a kind of tableau, with about thirty people standing perfectly still. Only that cowboy, Jimmy the Kid, and that punk girl who used to have green hair moved and talked. The tall woman squatted in front of them, occasionally rising and whispering something, then returning to her squat.

As far as Mountain Man could tell, Jimmy the Kid and the punk were living a kind of surrealistic romantic dream. They were always inches away from each other but never touched, even when he seemed to look right at her and said poetry and blew it like a kiss, it was as if he were a million miles away. Mountain Man felt sorry for them. Sorrowful, actually. Across the parking lot, up toward the Municipal Building, a squad of state troopers stood apart from the Liberty Society encampment, whose ranks seemed to have grown since the battle of a few days earlier. Now he turned back to the actors when he heard a growly-sounding speech.

It came from Green Hair. The woman waved her hands and began whispering again. Vi Myers, the sheriff's wife, directed several people off to the side in the placing of a weathered gray outhouse.

Mountain Man sensed purpose. Resolve. Hopefulness. His eyes fell onto the market wall. The work lights did not completely illuminate the mural, but in its soft grayishness from the spill of light it actually appeared to move, undulating like history itself. Eliphalet Nott saw him in the shadows and walked over. He had on a Spanish conquistador breastplate over his T-shirt and a sword tucked into a chain-mail-and-leather belt that occasionally dragged on the ground. He held a heavy helmet in his hands.

"Hey, man."

"Hello, Reverend."

"Eli, call me Eli. Look at this. This is the real shit. Evan Santi brought it. Jude McCormick's got the same stuff. We're just trying it out."

"It's going good, huh?"

"I think so, but I'm in it, so it's hard to say. Hey, man, congratulations."

Mountain Man looked confused.

"Dropping the court case."

"Oh . . . yeah . . . well, it felt right."

"Yeah. Listen, a lot of us are going for beers up at Molly Dowie's house. Want to come?"

"Aren't some of the actors mad at me?"

"Yeah."

"Maybe I shouldn't."

"Hey, man. Fuck 'em if they can't take a joke."

* * *

Petey drove to the big log house he and Vi had bought in Ugly Acres. Neither of them understood why the small development of twenty-five homes had acquired such a moniker, except perhaps because of the proximity of one home to another. Stay the hell out of Boston, Petey had muttered to Vi the first time they heard it. Their beauty of a log cabin stood smack in the middle of a five-and-a-half-acre plot that sloped in the direction of the big river. They could hear it like rain in the middle of the night.

The two men walked into the house. The younger man followed Petey into the kitchen.

"Drink?" Petey asked.

"Soft drink."

Petey snapped two Sprites, and they sat at the table.

"Your superior in Denver was kind of pissed off at me for arresting you."

"Yes, sir."

"I saw the gun."

"Understandable."

"So you've been undercover how long?"

"Almost four months."

"You like undercover?"

"It certainly hones one's acting skills."

Petey stopped talking a bit on that one. Acting skills? Jesus God. Try acting *without* a nine-millimeter, cockhound.

The young man shrugged. "I guess that sounded kind of tight-ass. See, I *am* a kind of tight-ass."

Petey sipped his Sprite. "What made the FBI put somebody inside the Liberty Society?"

"Can I smoke in here?"

"Uh-uh. Vi's orders. Want to take it out on the porch?"

"I'll wait. About a year ago, they threw a kind of low-grade Molotov cocktail at an earthmover outside of Boulder. It was on a Sunday, so nobody was around. Nobody got hurt. But Agent Diver in Denver, who's mainly assigned to terrorist activities, saw a pattern of escalation. I went in under the alias of Alex Jordan, a graduate student in psychology."

"Clinings is a psychologist."

"Exactly. So I started going to their general meetings and got to know most of the group."

"And?"

"Couple of nuts, mostly well-meaning."

"I'd be forced to put Clinings in a third category. I'd say he was a cock-hound plain and simple."

The agent nodded. "Bill Clinings's priority is getting his hands on coeds. I'd say he started the whole thing just for that. Before he came up with the Liberty Society, he used to walk around campus in a beret with a backpack full of bad poetry."

"Jesus," uttered Petey.

"Now this demigod thing seems to be working for him. I doubt he'd jeopardize getting a piece of these girls by engaging in some stupid act of real violence."

"What about the big one? Sandy what's-her-name."

"Fiddler. Sandy Fiddler. Sheriff Myers, this is one angry woman. This is a capable one, at least under the profile Agent Diver compiled. We know she broke ranks, her and Todd Lehman."

"There's two now?"

"Can't figure Lehman. His biggest contribution to the Liberty Society has been organizing a 'crafts fair' fund-raiser and composing their theme song."

"They got a theme song?"

" 'The Preternatural March.' "

"Cockhounds."

They both sipped silently.

Then the agent said, "I think we coordinate our efforts. Me inside, you out. If you need to get in touch with me, call this number in Denver. It's Agent Diver."

Petey took the card and slipped it into his breast pocket. "Okay, and if you need me . . . well, I'm around."

They drove back to town. The work lights at the Lumberjack Amphitheater were visible as they cornered the tiny airport, and the Jeep rolled toward it and Creedemore proper.

Petey thought out loud. "When the micks partied from Dorchester, we used to bust our ass not to arouse those cockhounds. Calling them 'mister' and 'sir' even though the drunk little buggers were barely taking human form after gallons of that Narragansett beer. But we'd say, 'Now, sir, you'll have to please stay inside the club,' and 'Sir, no peeing on the sidewalk.' It used to piss hell out of me, but old Reedy, he never minded cutting them slack. But one time we take two fat micks—twenty years old, maybe, huge loads—out of one club because they keep taking out their schlongs and flashing the little things at the colleens, and all their buddies were laughing and so they just kept doing it, and this time Reedy did not let go with a mister or a sir. He took them outside and put their fat asses into our squad car. One of them is screaming how sorry he is, but the other fuck is spitting and threatening and calling Reedy a nigger and calling me a nigger lover. So we're on the road with the micks, maybe a mile from the precinct, and Reedy just pulls over, takes them out onto the Commons, takes off the cuffs, and we knock about twenty pounds of shit out of them."

Petey sensed the agent watching him talk and tried to explain it all another way.

"What I mean is, lawing used to be pretty damn pure."

The agent lit a cigarette, and they turned onto Main.

52

The day of the performance promised to be a dry one, although the night before, the final dress rehearsal had to be inside the Municipal Building to escape a torrential downpour. All things considered, back to taped areas and such, it went about as smoothly as could be expected, except for Cowboy Bob's last-minute attempt to soften Kit Carson's notorious bloodlust with an addendum of poetry pasted onto the events at Ear Grove. After the necklace of ears had been put on, Carson's stage direction called for him to walk by the narrator, Jimmy the Kid, playing Juan Carlos de Moreno. As Kit exits the scene, Teresa Herrera, played by the Marxist Nellie Ordoñez, steps into it and listens to one of Juan Carlos's love poems. He sends it out tenderly across time and space, and Teresa answers in her own dreamlike pentameter. So Cowboy Bob delivered his line perfectly, slipping the ears over his little head.

"I'm a man of my word. Now Ear Grove stands a hot testament to it."

He crossed Juan Carlos de Moreno, but before he exited the light and allowed Teresa Herrera to step into it, Cowboy Bob turned and removed the ears. Then, in his patented earth-warm drawl, he put it out there.

"I just want to add as a man of the plains
And a boy with his heart in the hills,
That Kit was a lad with a one and the same
Broken heart for those he was forced to kill.

We can go back as far as the year 1860,
When he took on the rustler McKay.
The gang blocked the tracks, acted mighty frisky,
But Kit shot 'em down anyway.

Some say he was mean, but I do not agree,
For I know in my heart he was kind.

But if one was unclean, even if it was me,
And Kit killed me, I still wouldn't mind."

Cowboy Bob paused and let it sink in. It sank in.

"Roarke? What think?"

"That sucks."

"Sucks? Who said that?"

Nellie Ordoñez stepped into the taped area representing the light. "I said that. C'mon, Bobby. Jesus Christ."

"Roarke?" he called out pathetically.

"I loved it, Cowboy Bob," Roarke said, coming around her director's table. "It's great, but, honey, you can't stick stuff in at the last minute."

"But—"

"Okay. It's a great lesson for us. One of the things I want my actors"—she squeezed Cowboy Bob's pouting shoulders—"my kids, to take from our whole experience is what we strive for in the theater. There really is no other way, at least no other honorable and moral and ethical way. We have to stick together. Stanislavski, the great Russian director who sort of guided people all over the world into the twentieth century of acting, had an emphasis on ensemble. He thought, and I agree with him, that you can be a great individual, like you, Cowboy Bob, but still be loyal to the play's life by subordinating yourself as an actor to the whole group of actors. He called it 'super-objective.' I call it 'sticking together.' "

"So I can't do the poem?"

Roarke smiled at him and returned to the director's table, speaking over her shoulder. "Kit Carson leaves. Here comes Teresa."

Now the sun was bright, and things were drying nicely. The evening's weather prediction was for mild temperatures with a slight breeze. Vi Myers and her crew of five began early with the finishing touches on the set and wiping rainwater off the bleacher seats. Tom Zaleski had secured major space in the market's storeroom for the ladies' dressing room. Yale Strong had steam-cleaned one of the Norgan Freighters, covered it with canvas, set up lights, chairs, and mirrors, and parked it adjacent to the Historical Society for the men's dressing room. Roarke, Steven, and Molly had walked up to the Corso Mine to release some nerves, but all were subdued and intensely quiet.

"Carol Connolly says the reserved seating is all gone," Molly said after a long interval. "That's one hundred twenty guaranteed. But she figures the rest will fill up easy. At least three hundred of them."

Roarke and Steven both seemed to be staring at the same mountaintop.

Molly thought how odd people drawn to the theater were. Even Roarke, who seemed so essentially healthy, appeared tottering on some imaginary ledge over a bottomless abyss as the curtain approached. Sure, there were enough weirdos in her own discipline to fill the Rio Grande Reservoir, but they did not seem nearly as self-punishing.

"Jesus," she said out loud.

Now she looked up at the mountaintops, too.

"You are both officially too old to beat yourselves up. I think you're both geniuses. You have to accept that. The word-mural . . . this . . . Steven, this is really wonderful. What a story you tell with people, Roarke."

They looked at her now.

"People as old as we are shouldn't waste any time on negatives. You guys have given them so much. I know you're thinking about it. I know it. I can see how you guys are just staring at the mountains and saying, 'What if it's not any good?' Well, it's great. You're great. That's it."

Roarke hugged her. "You know what, Molly Dowie? I wasn't thinking about the play at all. I was thinking how much I missed Niki. I called the last two nights and left messages, but . . . I guess she was out."

Molly looked at Steven.

He shrugged. "I wasn't thinking about the play either."

"No? What were you thinking?"

Steven regarded the women of his life on this precipice overlooking tiny, post-silver-boom Creedemore, and for the first time he could remember, he was not thinking about what he had written or what he was planning on writing. It was as if his mind had just at that moment divided into two compartments, with one big enough to encompass his poor dramatic words and one that would allow a life apart. He had felt it coming. It felt awful good.

"What?" she said again. That chin out. That silly bowler hat.

"I was thinking. . . . I was wondering if you would marry me?"

Molly Dowie opened her mouth, but nothing came out. Roarke opened hers, too. Creedemore heard it, and South Fork, too, and if the wind was with her joyous howl, they heard it in Monte Vista.

*　*　*

"Sheriff?"

Petey Myers looked up from the paper he was reading at the Seattle House of Joe. The morning sun caught him clear in the eye, and he reached for his aviators.

"I'm Bob Lobato. I'm camp host at the Ten Mile Campground."

"Sit down, Mr. Lobato."

"Call me Bob. Everybody calls me Bob."

"Coffee, Bob?"

"I'd take a cup."

Petey waved his cup at the little hippie girl behind the counter. "Can I get a refill and one more here for Bob?"

"Thanks, Sheriff. I'm not much on this fancy coffee, though. I'm for the basic A&P or Maxwell House. We perk it. These folks tend to burn it."

"I say that, too, but Vi, my wife, she says these new coffeehouses search around for exotic kinds of beans and then just roast the hell out of them. Reedy and me had a place in Boston where they'd do it in the big stainless dealies. Thirty-year-old dealies."

"Same deal by my Pep Boys. Jean's Diner. Every now and then, they'd fill up some scalding water and drip it over the grounds."

"Drip."

"It was hearty but not burned."

Petey sipped his black coffee. Bob added eight sugar packets and two dollops of half-and-half. Petey leaned back.

"What I find particularly weird about these new places is that it's like they just *discovered* coffee. Never mind all the silly things the cockhounds do to the coffee, all the 'au lait' and things, but plain old coffee has been around for a long time."

"Hippies had those coffee places."

"Beatniks."

"That's right. Those berets. Coffee like they just invented it, but I'll tell you, Sheriff, nothing warms you up to it like a good cup."

"Reedy would call it 'the revelation Styrofoam.' He put the mark on it."

"I like that."

They both sipped.

Bob chuckled to himself. "Oh, boy. My God. Had this Polish kid working in tires at the shop, and he got it into his head that what we needed was a coffee machine. I said, 'Now, boy, we got Jean's Diner right next door, for Chrissake,' but he talked about it and talked about it, and finally I just threw my damn hands up and said, 'Well, hell, if it'll shut you up.' So he gets this system—"

"Mr. Coffee?"

"I believe it was the Magic System out of Kansas City."

"Joe DiMaggio did some adds for Mr. Coffee."

"Joltin' Joe," Bob said with satisfaction.

"Now, we preferred Teddy Ballgame in Boston, of course, but good for Joe DiMaggio."

"Anyway, this Magic System ends up always being lukewarm and costing about a buck a cup. Got rid of it. About a year later, Polish kid joins up with American Tire across the street."

Bob shook his big old head, and Petey nodded.

"So what can I do you for?" he asked.

Bob Lobato reached into his Pep Boys manager shirt pocket, took out a folded piece of paper, and unfolded it, looking around as he did as if it were a secret. He laid it on the table facing Petey. Sandy Fiddler's face scowled up at him.

"That's one of my flyers, Bob."

"Saw it in the post office. I was mailing bills and such for Lois—that's my wife and my assistant camp host. Now, I believe that is a picture of a woman who is at our campground. Her and her cancer-stricken husband, Todd."

"Todd?"

"At least that's what they call him. What the hell's going on, Sheriff?"

Petey stood up and put some change on the table. "What number is their camp area?"

"That's the thing. They're not really in a camp area. She wanted to be under the dam. See, there's a clearing—"

But old Petey Myers was out the door, Reedy in his brain shouting instructions.

*　*　*

That same afternoon, Bill Clinings held the secret meeting in his room at the Monte Vista Holiday Inn. Jan from the humanities department paced by the window as Drew Lipton, the Liberty Society's recording secretary and owner of Drew's Natural Bistro in Boulder, read the minutes from the last meeting.

" '. . . and then Peter said let's wrap it up and then Jan seconded and then Bill led the Spiritual Preternatural Chant and then we left.' "

They watched Bill and sipped the wine coolers Cia had made.

"Didn't Sandy Fiddler say anything at the last meeting?"

"Sandy wasn't at the last meeting," Suzy Waldrop said, adjusting herself girlishly on the floor. She was seventy-three and professor emeritus of existential sciences.

"Todd Lehman?" Bill asked hopefully.

"Him either," Suzy said. She looked around the room with a quizzical expression. "Is Todd banging Sandy?"

"No!" Jan shrieked.

Everyone turned to her.

"No," she said quietly.

Cia squeezed Bill's hand. "Sandy hung up on Bill yesterday."

"What?" Andy Martin, a Liberty local out of Alamosa, uttered disbelievingly.

"I swear to God. Bill was right in the middle of a thought, and she just hung the phone up."

Bill took a deep breath. "Sandy is going to carry out some kind of quasi-environmental terrorism without the appropriate authority from the secret council. I tried to reason with her, explain that the correct procedure is group-oriented—"

"Except for that codicil you added . . . when? Last March?" Suzy interrupted.

"Suzy, that was added—"

"Articles of Class Action? That one?"

"March, was it?" Drew said, leafing through his pile of minutes.

Bill Clinings threw his hands up. "Okay, people, stop. Stop! Pay attention, now. Whatever Sandy and Todd are doing, they are doing under the auspices of the Liberty Society. We can say they didn't get permission or didn't go through proper channels, but who will listen? We, everyone in this room, will bear a share of responsibility."

"All for one, one for all," Suzy said, banging the floor with an open palm.

"You're missing the point, Suzy. What if she hurts someone? What if she blows something up?"

"Things get blown up all the time."

"No, Suzy, they do not."

"You blew up that earthmover."

"I . . . listen, I *flamed* the earthmover. It still worked. It was a semiviolent gesture."

"It made a whoosh."

"Scared me to death," Drew concurred.

"But no one was hurt. It was, by the way, an act which followed procedure from top to bottom."

Suzy shrugged. Everyone was quiet for a moment.

"Mountain Man stabbed us in the back," Cia said. "Just shared and quit."

Suzy reclined lower. "I thought you were banging Mountain Man."

"I'm not."

"I just assumed because you were always with him that you were banging the hell out of each other."

"People, listen," Bill said with authority. "It is time to fold our tents on this one. We have an opportunity for an honorable retreat. The sheriff has threatened to bring in the FBI."

"No way." Suzy snorted, pushing herself into a Buddha position.

"I'm only relaying his threats."

"Well, he wouldn't. He wouldn't want the FBI looking into his murdering those two children. I heard the girl was twelve. Can you imagine?"

"At any rate, we should steer clear of—"

"This is not like you, Bill. Not like you at all." Suzy struggled to her feet.

Cia inched closer to Bill as if to protect him. "Bill's trying to do what's best for everybody."

Bill Clinings smiled wanly.

"Are you two banging each other?"

"Suzy . . ." Bill said, trying to sound outraged.

"It distorts judgment. You yourself put in that codicil about Coveys of Five and Group Protest Dispersement, and it was very specific that the people inside each covey should not be banging each other. Or banging in general if the banging could unbalance esprit de corps within the boundaries of covey integrity."

"When was that?" Drew asked, leafing again through his notes.

Bill Clinings felt that hollow, achy feeling in his stomach, his will inching away. How did other leaders keep it going on? Where in the world did the tenacity come from?

Suzy was feeling strong. "I, for one, am going to keep the presence up. Mountain Man may think that he can simply walk away from the fray, but he'll soon see he can't."

His energy drained, Bill Clinings led the secret council in the Spiritual Preternatural Chant.

"We—we are here.
Liberty for all,
Land for all,
We—we are here."

Three times to the slow, methodical beat of Drew's tom-tom.

*   *   *

After the rope rigging for the winch and pulley that would fly the miners to the roof of the Historical Society was set tight and wheeled past the outhouse to where Vi stood guiding them into position, Mountain Man, Miss Wilma Kirk's newest assistant stage manager, received permanent working credentials in Puerite County when Yale Strong, foreman at the Norgan Ranch as his dad had been before him, slapped him on the back and said loud enough for everyone to hear, "Thatta boy, Mountain Man."

Mountain Man straightened up and smiled in that easy, unstudied way he'd forgotten. "Why, thank you, Yale."

It was a truly epic moment in his life. The complete turnaround. An upset victory. Mountain Man placed his hands on his hips and set his weight back toward his left leg and gazed at the sky. He needed to speak. To keep it going. This huge occasion.

"Looks like a perfect day for a play."

"Hell yes," Yale Strong agreed.

Mountain Man watched the hills and bathed in the glow of western acceptance as if he had just taken a Masonic pledge and knew something.

"Mountain Man," Miss Kirk boomed, walking over from Vi. "That thing we discussed last night? Operating the winch and pulley that transports the miners up and onto the market roof?"

"Yes, ma'am."

"Want to give it a go?"

"Whatever you want, Miss Kirk."

Mountain Man followed Miss Kirk off to where the running crew had set up the manual system of ropes and pulleys between the bleachers.

Cowboy Bob Panousus sauntered over to Vi. "Got a second, Vi?"

"If I can keep working."

"No problem. I'm still wishing we could adjust the position of that darn old outhouse. It's directly in my light."

Vi looked concerned and stopped moving. "It's in your light, Cowboy Bob?"

"Yes, Vi, it is. Smack dab in the middle of my light. Right when I make the deal with the mayor. 'I've come a distance, Mr. Mayor, and my word is gold. I don't have to remind you of Kansas. You read it true and straight. Kit Carson puts it down, you write it in stone.' "

"I love that moment, Cowboy Bob."

"Thank you, Vi."

"But I don't see how I can shift the outhouse without taking some of the space that Jude, Skyo, and Janice use in Mr. Kearney's configuration of Quartz Crystal, Gold, and Silver."

"I am so damn sick of having to adjust for a bunch of rocks."

Vi looked sympathetic. "Maybe if you mentioned it to Roarke."

"Maybe."

Cowboy Bob saw Tom Zaleski come from the alley adjacent to his hardware store with an armful of costumes, heading for the ladies' dressing area.

"Excuse me, Vi," Cowboy Bob said, and jogged off to intercept Tom. "Tom, we have got to talk about act three, scene two."

"What about it, Cowboy Bob?"

"Well, you've got me in the duster three times. Three times. The man had clothes, Tom. I'm saying Kit was no piker."

"Want to wear the waistcoat?"

"You know I do."

Tom pretended to debate himself. "I guess that'll work. Don't tell anybody or they'll all want to change things. That Nellie Ordoñez thought she should be bare-breasted in that— What's that scene where she's in Spain and he's up by Cathedral Rock? The Spanish lovers?"

"Bare?"

"Not *bare* bare. From here up."

Cowboy Bob never dreamed he would love the theater so. He thanked Tom and walked on up to the Municipal Building, where the cast was going to assemble again for the walk down to the set together. He stopped at the parking lot and waved to two of the troopers, who returned nods. The Liberty banners were unfurled, but the protesters looked lost. The cowboys had packed it up and left. Roarke and the playwright came from across the street, from the coffeehouse. They held hands. Cowboy Bob noted how Molly Dowie wasn't around and how they were supposed to be an item. Her and Kearney. Now here's Roarke and Kearney. Cowboy Bob furrowed his little brow and hooked his thumbs under his buckle. He had always preferred his solitary art of rhyme to this communal play thing where everybody had a say in something, but now, watching them walk in step, her swinging his arm, her astonishing fingers wrapped around that guy's hand and Molly Dowie somewhere, too—well hell, if you can't beat 'em . . .

* * *

JoJo would not exactly say he was glad his father had been hospitalized, but he was relieved, if that was the word, that for the time being, Mel was out of harm's way, even if the "way" was of his own devising. JoJo said hellos to the nursing staff and walked down the blue corridor to his dad's room in Monte Vista General. He gently pushed the door open so as not to wake him or Mr. Diaz, his elderly roommate, if they were sleeping. He stopped short.

"JoJo. Look who's here," Mel said.

JoJo slid into the room and closed the door behind him. Ronnie and Brian Coolette grinned from the other side of Mel's raised bed.

"Hey," JoJo said quietly, trying to smile.

"Hey, cuz."

"Hey, cuz."

"Ronnie and Brian came up to give you a hand."

"Doing what?"

Ronnie chuckled. "TCB."

JoJo was stumped.

"Taking care of business, JoJo. TCB. Elvis wore it on a gold chain," explained Brian.

"TCB," Ronnie said.

"Our place isn't too big. I can handle it. Couple of horses. Garden."

Mel pushed the "lift" button on his hospital bed, and the back rose up straight.

"I got some cotton in my ears. Got some baby oil on it to soften the sounds. Damn eardrum's about to break apart. What did you say?"

"I said our place isn't so big that I can't take care of it."

"It's not a big place."

"That's what I said, Daddy."

"Good thing, too. If it was any fancier, any bigger, your mama's sleazy lawyer would've taken it for her and that homo she went and married. Anyway, what about it?"

"What about what?"

"The place. Any problems?"

"No, sir."

"Horses?"

"They're good."

"Well, Ronnie and Brian are back now, so things'll be okay." Mel turned to his elaborately dull nephews.

They nodded and grinned. "Yes, sir. Everything's okay now."

JoJo shifted his feet and passed his cap from one hand to the other. "I thought . . . Didn't Sheriff Myers . . ."

"Goddamn son of a bitch," Mel muttered.

"Yes, sir, but didn't he tell Ronnie and Brian to get out of Creedemore?"

"Son of a bitch sees me attacked—bombed, for Chrissake—by those homo Liberty people, and does he help me? No, sir. Does he throw my sister's boys out? Yes, sir."

"They bombed you, Uncle Mel."

"I wasn't doing a goddamn thing. I'm exercising my personal freedoms, which the Constitution guaran-goddamn-tees, and they try to kill me."

Ronnie looked over to JoJo. Brian did, too.

"Anyway, we did get out. Went home and came back," Ronnie explained reasonably.

"Yeah. And that guy didn't say to *stay* out. He just said *get* out."

Mel gave his mattress a little punch. "There I am exercising my personal freedoms. Now, boys, I am telling you that God Himself gave us those rights, and here comes some cockhound—"

"Some what, Uncle Mel?"

"Cockhound. Cockhound."

"Oh."

"And he goes and throws some dynamite at me. BOOM! Eardrums gone, whatnot."

Ronnie and Brian each patted one of Mel Prophit's feet.

The generally addled expression on the Coolette boys momentarily focused on resolve, as if they'd both sipped curdled milk.

Ronnie sniffled. "Now, don't you worry, Uncle Mel."

"We're here, Uncle Mel. We'll get them. TCB."

"TCB, Uncle Mel."

JoJo watched his daddy's lips curl up into a smile. He watched him wiggle his toes.

*　*　*

She attached the folding aluminum chair to the back bumper of the Airstream with heavy clothesline rope and a full roll of silver plumber's tape. Todd watched her. He swayed and smiled and tried to say something, but only a burble of vowels oozed out. She straightened at the sound and glared.

"I'm not telling you again. Let me know when you have to pee or poop. Do you have to?"

He swayed. She watched him.

"Ah, what the hell. Go to town."

Sandy walked over, took his arm, and led him to the chair. She sat him down and taped his waist and chest and legs, leaving his arms free so he could feed himself the fruit-cocktail tranquilizer. He smiled and laughed.

Sandy Fiddler walked to the front of the trailer and examined the ten large mayonnaise jars of jet fuel chosen as accelerant and balanced on a makeshift plywood platform under the trailer's kitchen window. A twelve-volt battery, the negative line already hooked, awaited only the snap of positive, sending the sparks down onto a thirteen-pound can of gunpowder. The combined "passion of heat," as the terrorist manual put it, would be enough to act upon the nitrogen-rich fumes from the thirty thousand pounds of fertilizer. She was tempted to just do it then and there. What the hell. Touch it off and see you on the other side. She paused and looked up at the earthen-and-concrete wall holding back years of collected runoff from streams and rivers and snowmelt. Above her and to the side, she could see the yellow and green of El Grande Peak, its looming sandstone crest catching the afternoon sun. She could not make up her mind about it. Was it beautiful? Are mountains beautiful? And people? Are people beautiful, with their own great gorges and slides and glacial imperfections? No one had to inform her there. People were the interlopers of paradise. They were the mistake of the grand cosmic plan. But she would wait. Wait until the correct time. She unfolded her wrinkled flyer for *The Creedemore Retrospective: A Word-Mural*. "Six-thirty" was circled in red. She checked her watch and looked back up at El Grande. Two hours, twenty-six minutes, and counting.

53

omething was up. Dan Cryer hadn't been in law enforcement for forty-six years—forty-seven if you counted his voluntary capacity for old Petey Myers these past three months—not to know when something was up when all the signs pointed to something being up. The leftover crew of reporters and cameramen seemed on high alert on the balcony of the Creedemore Hotel. The troopers appeared antsy corralling those goddamn Liberties, who seemed to be swelling in numbers. Dan shook his gray head, plopped on an old sheriff's baseball cap, and wrinkled up his forehead.

Wasn't this godforsaken thing supposed to be over? Somebody stands up in court and says, "That's it, Judge. I'm throwing in the towel." Well, mister, that is it. That's how it always works. What part of it don't these Liberty Society birds get? He checked his Timex and got 5:25, although he might be fast. He tapped the face a couple of times and headed down to the Lumberjack Amphitheater.

Bill Clinings and Cia crossed over from their vehicle, parked way up by the fire station, and moved toward where Suzy had the Liberty contingency in a four-abreast marching line. Drew Lipton stood front right with his tom-tom, and two attractive coeds whom Bill had previously "mentored" held each side of the LIBERTY SOCIETY: A PRETERNATURAL ORGANIZATION banner. Several hundred yards down the street, he heard the happy din of the audience, now in a standing-room-only assemblage at the amphitheater. Suzy embraced him, and the hundred or so members and irregulars applauded. Bill waved weakly.

"We are truly on the march, Bill," Suzy said.

Bill looked around. "Will the . . . what about the state troopers?"

"There's no restraining order, and they know it," she said haughtily. "When we march, we march."

Cia gave his hand a squeeze. "I'm going for a walk."

Bill shrugged and looked far away. A moment later the door to the Municipal Building opened and Roarke stepped into the lovely late afternoon. Steven Kearney was with her, and an army of actors lined behind them. She took a deep breath, put her arm around Steven, and led them all out, in a fantastic costume parade, down Main Street to the Lumberjack Amphitheater. The reporters and camera people applauded, tourists on the walk snapped pictures. Rocks walked, and Dinosaurs, too. Cowboy Bob Panousus came from behind Yale Strong's horse trailer on an enormous white horse, his silver accessories throwing light. People at the amphitheater rushed out to see the parade. Even the troopers smiled and cheered. Mountain Man and the running crew came over to the side of the market and pumped fists as Roarke turned the corner at the alley between the market and the Historical Society Building and opened up to allow her actors access. She high-fived and hugged and kissed all eighty-seven of them. Steven, shy and hysterical, smiled with difficulty. He looked around for Molly, but she was not there. Only Miss Wilma Kirk held position. The actors did a once-around costume parade, and the audience went wild. Tom Zaleski looked on as his Quartz glistened and Conquistadors menaced. Brian Trujillo, dressed in his fishing waders for the downstream-fishing bit in act 3, scene 3, waved his nine-and-a-half-foot bamboo fly rod. Cowboy Bob sat tall, and his horse strutted in Panousus fashion. Finally, Miss Kirk pointed to the dressing rooms and entrance area, and the raw, spontaneous circling of actors formed itself into the highly drilled and efficient acting troupe of Roarke's making. Ticky Lettgo came out of the cheering crowd and spindled over to Mountain Man.

"Need help?"

"Got it pretty much under control, Mr. Lettgo. But hey, I got a great place to watch. Over where I'm operating the mining winch."

Ticky looked up at the rope pulleys coming out from between the bleachers and crossing high onto the roof of the Historical Society Building. "This winch?"

"C'mon, I'll show you."

Mountain Man walked Ticky over to his station. Cia watched from the crowd and followed.

Steven Kearney and Roarke crossed to Miss Kirk's running booth, a small plywood table with her light and sound board. The design and cues were taped above each machine. Miss Kirk wore complete black, and the effect was a kind of ninja eggplant. Action was her game. She examined her script, constantly checking and rechecking the pivotal staging areas.

"There is no confinement in the theater. You see it clearly for what it is. An infinite plain where honest play is conceivable," she pronounced.

Steven and Roarke watched her.

"Hey, Miss Kirk," Roarke said.

"Yes, Roarke?"

"I just love you to death."

Miss Kirk looked at them both. "And you are the genuine article. The absolute ideal. Tonight I'm happy to have put my trust in art. Now, if you'll excuse me, I have to call fifteen. Break legs."

They watched her walk off, arms swinging, toward the men's cattle-truck dressing room. Over Roarke's shoulder, Steven saw Molly coming quietly toward them. Tubby and Sarah Vinitti followed her. Niki Vinitti, too.

"Where's Molly?" Roarke asked.

"Uh . . . she had to get something."

"I hope she won't miss the light montage."

"She won't. What about Niki? You get in touch?"

Roarke looked at her feet. "Not answering her phone. Busy, I guess. I like Molly, Steven. She's so good for you. She's stalwart, you know? She'll be there."

"You think?"

"I know."

"There's two things, Roarke. Here."

Steven handed Roarke an envelope. "Don't open it now. It's half the pay from the Historical Society, and if you make a face or tell me I'm an asshole for giving it to you, you will just make me more nuts than I already am. There's a poem in there, too. The usual stuff. 'You're my best friend, I love you'—stuff like that."

Roarke laughed. "Okay. I'm keeping the money and reading the poem. What's the second thing?"

"I just remembered. I know where Niki is."

"Where?"

"Right behind you."

Roarke whirled.

Ronnie Coolette, milling near the alley between the market and the Historical Society, watched the sweet reunion and nudged his brother, Brian. "Did you see that?"

"Did I see what?"

"Over there. That tall woman kissed that other woman right on the mouth."

"You get the fuck out."

"So help me."

Brian watched now, but Roarke had grabbed Sarah and the impossibly huge Tubby in her beautiful hands. "She's kissing everybody."

"But—"

"She's kissing that fat guy. Look, Ronnie, got him on the lips."

Brian nudged JoJo. "Hey, cuz. She's a kissing nut. Ronnie's trying to say she's kissing that other girl on the lips, but see, she's kissing everybody. Ronnie's got the lesbians on his mind."

"Talk about your lesbians. JoJo. Brian took a lesbian to his prom."

"You lying fuck."

"She was."

"She was not. Not when I took her."

"She was when you brought her home."

Ronnie moved next to JoJo. "Stella Kreeger. Out to here with the boobies. Now she's bartending at a girls-only place in Dallas. And she was okay until old Brian took her to that prom."

"Asshole."

"Yes, sir. One date with Brian and she's done with men."

Brian smirked. "Well . . . when she's had the best . . ."

"You never did."

"I sure as hell did."

"You did not. JoJo, he did not."

"Wait," Brian said. "Look."

Ronnie and JoJo looked where Brian Coolette pointed. Jude McCormick had eased himself down from the back of the cattle-truck dressing room in his Styrofoam-and-aluminum-foil Puerite Rock costume and walked over to Tom Zaleski. He pointed to his back. Tom turned him around and adjusted a wild piece of Styrofoam obscuring a swirling vein of silvery aluminum.

"What's the plan, Ronnie?" Brian said.

"That little bastard."

"What's the plan?"

JoJo didn't want to whine, but it came out like one. "Listen, Ronnie. Brian. Why don't we just leave it alone? I don't want no trouble."

"What?" Brian asked him, as though he couldn't have heard what he heard.

"It's just—"

"He tried to kill you."

"Well, see—"

"Twice," Ronnie said. They were on either side of him, the way they always were at family picnics outside of Dallas. Them and their extended relations, the brooding and dangerous Coolettes, would pull up in Uncle Connie's crummy station wagon. Same deal. First chance Ronnie and Brian had, they'd get real close and start picking.

"Your daddy got shot account of him," Ronnie said.

Brian's awful breath burned on JoJo's neck. "Now he went and got him with dynamite."

"That wasn't McCormick," JoJo protested, sliding out of their circle. It closed again.

"Same difference," Brian said. "Maybe you're scared."

"I'm not scared. I just don't think—"

"Yeah, he's scared," Ronnie said with a little shove. "C'mon, Brian. Looks like we'll have to get him ourselves."

They simultaneously hitched up their tight jeans, pointed and centered their silver Marlboro belt buckles, and circled the arena toward Jude.

*   *   *

Halfway up to Lake City, just before the overlook near Brown's Lake where he took after Shari Tobias's murderers, Sheriff Petey Myers turned off onto the dusty dirt road toward the Rio Grande Reservoir. He checked and rechecked his watch and drove recklessly. At the first small campsite, below Llama Ranch, he sprayed a cloud of reddish dirt in every direction and saw angry campers shaking fists at him and worse, in his rearview.

"Sorry, cockhounds," he muttered. "You can't stop and explain your motives and your actions. You just can't stop at every goddamn corner and lay it out. Remember those three guys in Maine? Remember, Reedy? Figure they can come down to Mass Avenue, hit the Brookline Savings Bank, and go back up for lobster? Pursuit. When you are in pursuit, you got to pursue. That asshole from Internal Affairs? God Almighty, Reedy."

Petey thought about it and laughed.

" 'What were you two officers thinking?' Jesus Christ, Reedy. What *were* we thinking? They were shooting at us, and we were chasing them. You put the word on it, Reedy. You did."

Petey smiled contentedly.

"Well, sir, what we were thinking was we got us a carload of unidentified flying fuckers that are playing pop goes the weasel."

Petey's laugh carried him up over the high sloping ridge and dropped him toward the parking lot of Bob and Lois's Ten Mile Camp. He slowed and parked off to the side where his Jeep would be obscured by baby aspens and gooseberry bushes. He stepped out and waited for the engine to settle and the cooling fan to click, then set his ears in the direction of the big dam. A smooth rustle, like the wind almost, marked the flow into the Rio Grande from a release vent beneath tons of earth and cement. Petey checked his watch again and crossed the wooden bridge.

"Five minutes until the show, Reedy. Vi did the set."

He walked to the pump directly below Bob and Lois Lobato's mobile home and veered right onto a small, partially obscured Jeep road marked with a yellow warning sign spelling out that this was for state water bureau personnel only. The overhanging river willows covered parts of it so that when he stepped into the edge of the clearing, the looming earthen wall of the dam jolted him. Looking down, he saw the old trailer pushed hard against the structure. Again he checked the time. Sandy Fiddler lumbered around from the side and stopped when she saw him. Petey started on in.

"Something about six-thirty that has always driven me nutty," he said with a wave.

Sandy picked up a chair and moved it against the entrance of the trailer. She took a black box off a stepladder and deliberately set it onto the chair. Petey kept coming. Kept talking.

"Reedy used to love six-thirty. We'd be . . . well, most of the time we'd be on to home by then unless we had a dark shift, but I always had this uneasy feeling about six-thirty. I told Vi, 'Start the damn thing at six or seven.' You know."

She straightened and stood by the box. She wore a purple sweatsuit that had somebody's face on it. Petey couldn't tell whose.

"Clinings send you?" she huffed casually.

"No, ma'am. He surely did not."

"Well, that cocksucker would if he could."

"He's a cockhound, all right."

Sandy nodded and smirked.

"You Fiddler?"

"I am Sandy Fiddler. Soldier of retribution."

Petey regarded this big wild-haired girl and thought, Oh, boy. "Where's the other soldier?"

"He is not a soldier. He is a pussy."

"Okay. Where's the pussy?"

She pointed to the back of the trailer. Petey walked to the edge and peered around. Todd Lehman, his pants pee-soaked, strapped to the hanging lawn chair, smiled at him and drooled. Petey turned back to Sandy.

"Him?" he said, pointing.

"Him," she said, taking up a red wire. "I hate to say this, Sheriff. I hate it because of the cheesy colloquialism, but don't take another step."

Petey stopped. Damn, this was a big, challenging girl. "Don't take another step or what?"

Sandy moved the thin red wire. "Or I touch this positive fucker to that part of the battery there, and that accelerates my jet fuel, and that pisses off this nitrogen-packed trailer."

"Jesus, Reedy, the whole damn thing's a bomb."

"Who's Reedy?" she screamed looking behind her.

"He's my partner. Don't worry. Relax. He's dead."

They watched each other. Petey was scared, and she saw it.

"Not so tough now."

"No, ma'am."

"Easy when you're killing unarmed children."

Petey said nothing but thought, Oh, boy, for the second time.

"Now you know how they felt. You standing there, shooting point-blank. Not so fucking brave now. None of you are brave. Those bitches at the sorority house. So cool. So perfect. So fucking skinny, like a bunch of sticks. Now who's scared and who's not?"

Petey watched her hand trembling in a spooky blend of socio-revolutionary rage and considered drawing on her. Reedy was in his ear.

She got the wire for the fire. Looks like a Combat Zone hypothesis.

Petey thought, I don't know that one, Reedy.

Talk it out, baby. She's too close to the terminal.

"Talk it out," Petey repeated out loud.

"What?"

"I was . . . just talking to my partner, Reedy. In my head. Reedy's gone, except for here," he said, tapping his New England noggin. "And where old Sindy put him, of course. Cemetery in Roxbury. But old Reedy's here talking."

"So you're a fucking nut on top of everything else."

"Well, that *is* possible."

"Look, fucking nut, as far as I'm concerned, I'll touch this fucker off and be laughing the whole while."

"You'll be dead."

"You, too."

"And your friend."

"Dickhead? Fuck him."

Petey looked past her and crunched his old policeman brain.

"So they were mean to you at the sorority, huh?"

Sandy flared and shook her fist. "That's none of your fucking business, you old fuck."

"Well, I know that, but you brought it up, and I supposed it was on your mind."

They were both quiet for a moment, but Petey could hear her breathing over the windy *whoosh* of millions of gallons of water.

"Those sororities got foreign names, huh?"

"Greek."

"What was yours?"

"I never got in. They didn't want me. Theta House. I wasn't fabulous enough. I wasn't flawless. I wasn't perfect."

"Had to be perfect to get in, huh?"

"Had to think you were perfect. Had to let everyone else know you thought you were perfect. The whole fucking thing was such phony shit. They were nothing. Nothing. But they went on picnics and played tennis and . . . these perfect little bitches had these picnics on the front lawn of their house. Can you begin to imagine the arrogance of . . . glass wineglasses? No shit. So they could hold the stems in their perfectly delicate little fingers and sip their wine while the boys from Psi Epsilon walked by. And those dickhead fraternity boys would get quiet and respectful, even, and not be all gross, which was their norm, but they would poke each other to be quiet and, I guess, show the Theta girls they had the class to understand the function of the picnic. Because, really, it was all about a kind of graciousness you don't normally see . . . on a . . . on a campus."

Sandy's nose ran, and she sniffled. Her globoid cheeks glistened with some tears. Petey put his hands casually into his pockets and strolled a little toward her.

"Be nice to be at a picnic," he said.

Sandy shrugged.

"Be nice to just sit on some grass and sip some wine."

"I only went to . . . one. During rush. One of the girls' fathers had brought in some Chianti Classico. We sat out on Indian blankets and had . . . we had . . . I was being careful with what I ate. . . . I had salad, but the trays of little sandwiches were so lovely, and my girlfriends were all there because they were so interested in Theta."

"And were you?"

"Oh, I was. I was," she said girlishly.

"Then what?"

Now Petey was close, and she saw it. She dropped her heavy arms by her sides, and the red wire dangled.

"Then they didn't want me. And then my girlfriends didn't want me either."

Sandy stood weeping, making no attempt to dry her eyes or nose. She quaked in her sorrow. Petey listened for Reedy but didn't hear him. Didn't need him now. Reedy had shown the way so long ago with that hooker with the razor in the Combat Zone. Petey took two steps in, leaned, and kissed Sandy Fiddler smack in the center of her forehead. She looked up at him. Then she touched the bare tip of the red wire to the positive terminal of the battery.

*　*　*

Out of the canyon and across the grassy piedmont, Roarke had Miss Wilma Kirk hold the curtain for almost ten minutes. Then, with a nod, the general lighting dimmed to gray and a recording of thunderstorms boomed forth from ten speakers surrounding the Lumberjack Amphitheater. An array of lights, from lekos to streetlamps, flickered on and off under a pre-star western sky. It was way too early for the Creation effects to zing, but the audience got the idea and went with it. Cal Murray, the regional state police dispatcher, had been drafted by Miss Kirk to give voice to the disembodied First Narrator before Jimmy the Kid, as Juan Carlos de Moreno, took over midplay. Cal wheeled to the microphone and timed his initial vocal magic perfectly to coincide with a fading refrain of thunder. In Cal's confident, earthy baritone, a blend of Anglo-Hispanic cadence so richly groomed on the Alamosa Plateau, Steven Kearney's play began.

FIRST NARRATOR
    After the storm of storms,
    After the rain of rains,
    A small world racked by
    Glacial dreams, ten million years
    Of Pleistocene ice, changed again
    And again like clay in a
    Child's hands, bent and flattened
    And scooped by rivers,
    Heaving the broken stones up,
    Up from the earth.

        (ROCK ENSEMBLE begin to enter as lights rise:
        Quartz
        Feldspar
        Gold
        Silver
        Uranium
        Copper)

ROCK ENSEMBLE
    We are the sediment of ancient seas,
    Risen and fallen and risen again.

GOLD
    Precious to some.

QUARTZ
    Common to most.

FELDSPAR

Tricky like feldspar.

ROCK ENSEMBLE

Granite, gneiss, basalt, porphyry,
Serpentine, and coal.
Hardened volcanic crusts and snowy
Limestone. All wait. Wait. Wait.
Wait. Wait. Wait. For
The endless seas to end,
And come again.

(The ROCK ENSEMBLE rearrange themselves into a more formal
chorus.)

FIRST NARRATOR

Wait for life from ocean to land.

(Enter WALKING FISH.)

Cal Murray stopped, surprised at the long, spontaneous applause for
Mayor Ruby Onerati in Tom Zaleski's quite beautiful fish costume. Mrs. Mayor
stood ladylike across from the Rock Ensemble. When the applause fell off, Cal
Murray took the narration back up again.

FIRST NARRATOR

But what of the life in worlds
Old and new. . . .

Mountain Man Red Fields listened intently, considering the encap-
sulated physiographic history artful and informative and, more, a part of his
own story, accepted now into the actual flow of general western existence. Wasn't he after all just a present configuration sculpted by the same
mighty river that spread the valley so magnificently on either side of it? Wasn't
the same terrestrial topography that determined the curve of Creedemore
life patterns determining his own? Even Reinhold Niebuhr would agree that
he and the West had arrived at a sort of modus vivendi. He was part of it now.
He reached over and gave Ticky's shoulder a pat, but Ticky was sleeping
heavily in the assistant stage manager's chair, resting against Mountain Man's
winch and pulley.

"Red?"

Mountain Man turned to the soft voice. Cia was standing next to him. She looked different in her jeans and Liberty Society T-shirt. Older, maybe—he couldn't be sure. Her short hair was even shorter. She wore eye shadow and shiny orange lipstick.

"Cia . . . I was . . . how are you?" Mountain Man reached out and patted her arm. "You look . . . well, you just look great."

She watched him. He tried to force himself to keep looking at her and not at the *Retrospective,* but a burst of applause pulled him back to the play.

"It's great," he said apologetically.

Mayor Onerati had finished her monologue and crawled up from the rapidly evaporating Colorado sea. Behind her, entering in a swaying mass, were Yale Strong, Bob Lobato, John Torrey (from Rocks and Things), and Evan and Carla Santi, covered in a heavy, crisp canvas, with holes for eyes and mouth. This was the fabulous Cordilleran Ice Field and the cause of the initial applause, which amplified considerably when Jack Hill, Bob Marsden, and several Norgan Ranch wranglers slid onstage from the alley portraying the North and South Confluent Flows, which shimmered under sky blue vinyl.

"This is just so great," Mountain Man said again.

The applause subsided.

FIRST NARRATOR

    As if the sea and sky had dreamed
    The hills,
    So came the end of rain and snow,
    Replaced
    By salving winds.

CORDILLERAN ICE FIELD

    Slow, slow, slow,
    The valleys form and the mountains
    Cut away from
    Fertile plain.

NORTH CONFLUENT

    We are flow, the melt of ice.

SOUTH CONFLUENT

    And we, too, melt . . .

NORTH AND SOUTH CONFLUENT
. . . into the great river,
The Grand River,

ALL
The Rio Grande.

More applause for this starting point of a river of rivers. Mountain Man applauded joyfully and turned to Cia, who stood watching him.

"I'm . . . I'm an assistant stage manager, Cia. I'll have to be doing things . . . you know . . . pretty soon. So is everything okay? You look . . . happy. What a night."

"I have to talk to you, Red."

"Okay."

"Not here."

"I can't leave, Cia. I'm an assistant stage manager. See this winch and pulley? Later on, beginning of act two during the whole Carson thing, I have to—"

Cia raised an angry little handgun and pointed it a few inches from his stomach.

"Not here," she said serenely.

Mountain Man looked at the gun, turned, and began to stagger behind the bleachers toward Bachelor Creek across the road.

On the other side of the amphitheater, out of the throw of light, Ronnie and Brian Coolette watched the transposing poetical montage of Earth, Wind, Rain, and Fire, keeping an especially critical eye on the Styrofoam-and-aluminum Puerite that was Jude McCormick.

"He sucks," Brian whispered to Ronnie.

Ronnie nodded with a sneer but could not concentrate specifically on the rocks. He found the surrounding turbulence of theater, especially the colliding and undulating Cordilleran Ice Field, riveting. When the surging glacier split and joined each confluence of the Rio Grande, Ronnie joined the enthusiastic applause. He turned to Brian with a smile.

Brian snarled. "He sucks," he said again, and pointed at Jude's Puerite.

"Yeah, he sucks, but look at the river."

"What river?"

"Shhh . . ."

The narrator now lushly recited Steven Kearney's economical verse as Forests entered and exited and as Vi Myers augmented her design duties with a cameo as the Alamosa Plateau.

FIRST NARRATOR

But so the water burns to sky,
So, too, the melt flows back to
Mother sea,
Raising new life from old.

(WALKING FISH exits, South Fork preschoolers enter as SMALL LIZARDS.)

The wild, obviously child-made, colorful, papier-mâché-costumed reptiles received a laughing, prolonged standing ovation. Brian tried to look hurt that Ronnie was jumping up and down in applause, but he joined in, too.

(Lights flash, music of thunder.)

The audience let out a collective "oooh." Darker now, the lighting design had its effect.

(SMALL LIZARDS march and exit.)

FIRST NARRATOR

Life we know and
Life we know not.

(Enter FIRST TYRANNOSAURUS from alley.
Enter SECOND TYRANNOSAURUS from between bleachers.
Enter STEGOSAURUS, to the symphonic accompaniment of *Thus Sprach Zarathustra*.)

Miss Wilma Kirk brought in the recording perfectly from her stage-manager table. The deadly reptiles were created with chicken wire for heads and capped with glowing, scaly, blue-green foil. Each Rex rose twelve feet. Dave Page and Larry Holstedt from South Fork held poles inside the suits. The Stegosaurus was also chicken wire and cloth but looked like it weighed tons. Nellie Ordoñez, doubling as both lover and beast, moved easily inside at a lumbering pace. In the lightning storm, both big lizards, looking suitably vicious, charged the poor, grazing, oblivious Stegosaurus and devoured it to the swelling of timpani and violins and brass. Ronnie tensed up.

"Jesus," he said, pointing to the red liquid Nellie was squirting out from inside the poor old half-eaten Stegosaurus. Dave and Larry's growls ripped through the high air. As the character actors trudged offstage at the end of the battle, the audience again wildly applauded. Cal Murray waited patiently to vocally shuffle out the Antediluvian Flood and the Rain, Wind, and Sun Ensemble.

Brian moved in and shook Ronnie's shoulder.

"He's getting ready to leave," he said, pointing at the Rock mélange scraping slowly to an exit.

Ronnie snapped back from dinosaur reverie. "Okay. Remember we don't want that cockhound to get out of his costume."

"What?"

"His costume. He can hardly move in it, and we'll be—"

"Did you say 'cockhound'?"

"Did I?"

"I never heard you say it before."

"Well, I do. I say it all the time. It's mine."

"I think Uncle Mel says it."

"No he don't."

"I think so."

They carefully advanced in the shadow of the lighted arena toward the spot where Rocks were moving. By the corner of the alley in a narrow strip of dark, Tubby Vinitti stood snapping pictures. Sarah had worried that Tubby would start yelling back at the actors, like his outrageous performance at *Rent*, and so had sweetly suggested an activity as semiofficial production photographer. He was trying to feature each individual performer as well as ensemble scenes and was becoming concerned that the thirty rolls of film for his point-and-shoot might not be enough.

"Move it, fat-ass," Ronnie said.

Tubby looked at the big boys. "I'm sorry?"

"You sure as shit are, you tub of shit."

"Ronnie said move your fat ass. You're blocking us."

Tubby wondered what place people come from that go up to strangers and call them names. He thought of Bigs Mianelli, the Sicilian queen, who enforced for Sarci in Newark. He wore tight suits and lavender ruffled shirts and same-colored sandals with everything, and he curled his hair and had a huge red opal ring dazzling his pinkie on his hanging wrist. Who was it called him a fag? Bertonelli? Yeah. Bertonelli the fighter. Called Bigs Mianelli a fag. He didn't even want to think about Bertonelli. Point is, you never know who you're talking to. Tubby sighed and looked up at the boys. He looked like three hundred pounds of burlap lumps stuffed into huge flowery Bermudas. The men on his construction crew would say pretty much the same thing, only substituting nails for burlap.

"You gonna move your fat ass?" Ronnie said.

"Or we gonna have to move it for you?" Brian finished.

Brian did not stand up well to the short, controlled little thump to his diaphragm and sat sucking air on the ground, holding his belly, unable to make a sound. The tall one, Ronnie, surprised Tubby with the delicacy of his facial tissue, as it was only a light backhand that coldcocked him and pretty clearly broke his nose.

Tubby looked around. He couldn't be sure, but it appeared as if the tall one had fallen where either the Antediluvian Flood would exit or the Mastodon would enter. Either way he didn't want these morons blocking the offstage area. He liked this show pretty much so far. Steven had a language going he appreciated. He liked that Roarke had arranged fun pageantry around his words. He liked that no actor was wagging a weenie at him. Tubby wrapped Ronnie over his shoulder and picked up Brian by the back of his neck, carried and pulled them to a patch of grass behind the Historical Society, and waddled back to photograph the exit of the ensemble and the entrance of Skyo Overstreet and the Reverend Eliphalet Nott inside each end of a hairy, brown, ten-foot Mastodon.

Cal Murray watched for Miss Kirk's cue. She pointed emphatically at him without taking her eyes off her running script.

FIRST NARRATOR

They came following. Following other flows
Of life.
They came from lands of snow over
Bridges of earth,
Following the game of prehistory.

(Enter MASTODON down right into circle of light. Cue drums.)

Tom Zaleski worked the high-school kettledrum in sync with Skyo and Eliphalet's choreographed steps.

FIRST NARRATOR

For ages upon ages upon ages,
From deepest Northwest across
Icy straits, they followed, followed, followed.
Until from the walls of cliffs and floors
    Of deserts, they followed into this
Fertile field of life.

(Enter PREHISTORIC INDIANS.)

Tom had chosen leather and fur, which he fitted over ankles and wrists and into a kind of quasi–caveman–cum–Anasazi look. They entered in a ritual dance. These were the Sons of the Anasazi Dance Lodge out of Del Norte, consisting mostly of Hispanics passionately aware of their Indian lineage and two Japanese graduate students from Adams State College in Alamosa. Slowly they bounced and slid their way around the Mastodon until a circle was closed.

Steven Kearney suddenly stood and walked down the space between the bleachers. Molly Dowie watched him abruptly turn up toward Bachelor Creek and started to follow. Roarke, holding hands with Niki, grabbed Molly's sleeve with the other.

"Don't," she whispered.

Molly watched until he was out of sight and sat back down. "He's missing it."

"I'm amazed he stayed this long."

"But it's wonderful."

Roarke nodded and smiled and the prehistoric hunting party, which had inadvertently followed their prey into the beautiful valley, raised their spears.

* * *

Up by the airport, the only headlights on for miles between Creedemore and Lake City pendulated side to side as the road curved and dropped in blackness. An elk darted fifty yards in front, and a smaller one followed.

"Elk," Petey Myers said, pointing up ahead as he slowed to around thirty. Todd Lehman, inching out of crazy fruit-cocktail dementia, looked confused and frightened. He was sitting shotgun, and Sandy Fiddler sat in the back, her hands cuffed in front of her. Petey looked at her through the rearview and pointed at the elk again.

"I'm up here from Boston maybe a month when this call comes in that some skiers up at Wolf Creek Pass had hit an elk. Bobby was off. Vi was on the console. Dan's only voluntary, and I think he had to get down to his daughter's in Colorado Springs, but the main thing is, I figured, 'What the heck can be a big deal about that? Kill an elk? Wreck a part of your car.' So I drive on up through South Fork in the Jeep. Climb up toward the pass, and off on the side of the road, swear to God, now, was this late-model Pathfinder squeezed like an accordion. One guy dead on the spot. One girl dies a couple of days later. Other two had the shit shook out of them. So I say to one of the folks who saw it, I say, 'Where's the elk?' And guess what? Elk squeezed the Pathfinder and pranced away."

Petey looked back at the road. Even the stars couldn't shed any light on this stretch. Todd tried to say something.

"Wha . . . we . . . if coo . . . if coo . . ."

"Jesus," muttered Sandy.

Petey gave Todd a pat on the leg. "Let it rest up, kid. You'll be okay. In fact, I guess, all things considered, you're kind of a hero. I'm assuming it was this guy here who put water into your jars of—what did you say?"

Sandy let out a what-the-hell sigh. "Jet fuel."

"We'da been long gone."

"That's right."

Petey grinned at the rearview. "Wouldn't have come down yet."

Sandy smiled, too. First to herself, then at Petey Myers, and they turned finally up toward Cathedral Rock.

* * *

As the Sons of the Anasazi led the Mastodon carcass away and the parade of Wildflowers, Sage, Indian Paintbrushes, and Aspen entered along with the Buffalo-Mountain Lion Ensemble, Steven Kearney walked past Mountain Man and Cia, up toward the Corso Mine. Mountain Man smiled wanly, opening and closing his eyes in a vain attempt to communicate.

"Hi, Steven."

"Hi, Mountain Man," he said. He looked over at Cia, her hands inside a light jacket. "Hi."

"Hi," she said quietly.

"Taking a walk, huh?" Mountain Man asked.

"I guess."

"That's great. Maybe I can walk with you?"

"No," Cia said.

"Hey, have a nice one."

Steven continued along the dirt road, climbing up to the overhang next to Cathedral Rock that marked the mine.

"That's . . . that's our author."

Across the street and over the creek, more laughter and applause rose and fell like waves.

"I'm one of Miss Kirk's assistant stage managers, and pretty soon, when the miners . . . when . . . after, you know, Kit Carson clears out the red men, then I have to get the— Yale Strong and a couple of guys play the miners, and we've built this . . . well, it's symbolic, but it's like an ore car, and instead of tracks we have this pulley, and my main job—although I also give the cue to the Carson gang—I . . . my . . . I kind of fly the miners up to the roof of the—"

"You shared," Cia said matter-of-factly, taking the revolver back out of her pocket. Once more Mountain Man found himself temporarily muted.

"You shared, even though you knew the penalty."

Over Cia's shoulder Mountain Man saw the glitter of metal from the amphitheater a football field away. He heard the steady roll of drums and knew that Jimmy the Kid, Reverend Nott, and the other Conquistadors were making their entrance. It was his second-favorite part, after Carson and the ear scalpings. He looked back at her and felt words working.

"This is one of my favorite parts."

"I don't care."

"Yeah? Well, I do. Look, I shared because after I talked to Reverend Nott, I got ashamed I even had to run it by him at all. I mean, c'mon, Cia, I saw you with Clinings and everything, but you have to admit the guy's an asshole. Pure asshole. I wasn't supposed to share that he wanted to ruin everything?"

Now there was shouting over her shoulder. He knew that the battle was joined. Anasazi, Ute, Conquistadors.

"He didn't want to ruin everything."

"That's what he said at that meeting."

"He just wanted to ruin some things."

Another shout across the road. Swords clanged. War whoops.

"I can't miss this. I don't want to get shot, but this is really great so . . . I guess . . ."

Mountain Man walked around her toward the conflagration. Cia raised the pistol, two hands, police-style, and aimed between the big man's shoulder blades.

*   *   *

Above them Steven walked heavily alongside Bachelor Creek, often stopping for a deep breath. He walked up past the Foxledge Mine and the Mary Day and the Rhode Islander, all posted with yellow warnings, most of the shafts having fallen back on themselves. The amazing Corso Mine above was maintained as a tourist spot, and now Steven moved under one of the still-standing pine towers that at intervals served the Corso Mine's sky-high tram system and on up to the Visitors' Center. He ducked under a wooden barricade and walked around the center to a stone overview where Creedemore spread out like an arrowhead. He lit a cigarette and watched the glowing amphitheater below.

*   *   *

Cal Murray eyed Miss Kirk closely as the last dying Ute staggered offstage. She flicked her finger at him, and the Conquistadors' moment had arrived.

FIRST NARRATOR
 They set then young and hard,
 Victories in the moment, these

Men from another world having
Vowed to king and country
To return, return with
Ransoms of gold and precious stones.

CONQUISTADOR #1
Gold is law.

CONQUISTADORS #2 & #3
Silver is law.

(JUAN CARLOS DE MORENO steps apart from the others.)

JUAN CARLOS DE MORENO
I came toward this distant world
Without the dream of wealth
To see the flag of wondrous love unfurl.

FIRST NARRATOR
Juan Carlos de Moreno. Poet, scribe,
And warrior.
Lost, lost in his dream of love,
Of Teresa Herrera still in España.

(Lights rise on TERESA HERRERA.)

TERESA HERRERA
Is this the beginning or the end of joy?

JUAN CARLOS
Beginning a dream, perhaps a hope.

TERESA
Perhaps a phantom cord or rope.

JUAN CARLOS
Or savage nature being coy.

(Lights fade out.)

The audience applauded, and Cal came back on.
"Ladies and gentlemen, there will be one ten-minute intermission."

More applause. Mountain Man looked over again at Ticky deep in sleep and gave his pulleys and winch a tug. Yale Strong had been standing beside him to get a good look at the first romantic interlude.

"Nellie growls, huh?"

"What?" Mountain Man said, noticing him there.

"She kind of growls her words when she's talking to Jimmy the Kid."

"You think?"

Near the winch, Tubby rolled over to where Roarke, Niki, and Sarah sat. They all gave him a kiss.

"Hey, c'mon. Jesus."

"They're just kisses," Sarah said. "Take them like a man."

"Tubby lost over forty pounds," Niki said.

"Big deal," Tubby said.

"Forty pounds. Wow! How?" Roarke asked.

"No sugar, no milk, no bread, no desserts. No bread is tough. Plus, I been working out."

"Jogging," said Sarah with pride.

"Big deal," he said again. "Where's Steven? I love this shit."

"Went for a walk," Molly said.

"You did that," Tubby stated with a point at the mural. "I mean, who can *do* that?"

"It is wonderful," Niki said.

They all looked up at it, sprayed with light, floating against the whitewash of grocery wall.

Miss Kirk stopwatched the intermission and started the preset music nine minutes to the second after the break began. At ten minutes she cued Jimmy the Kid, who as Juan Carlos de Moreno—Conquistador and narrator—took it out into the arena.

Molly stood and whispered, "I've got to change."

Juan Carlos de Moreno narrated the disastrous effect of gold fever on Captain Miguel Sánchez and his soldiers, took everyone through the smelting of gold at the Lost Diablo Mine and the death by burning of Friar Joaquín Santaló. Rapidly the conquistador moment at the headwaters of the Rio Grande was down to the poet and lover. Alone. Living in a cave and making oaths from one world to another. Jimmy the Kid brought it soft but clear.

JUAN CARLOS
    (On his knees.)
My withered soul has set only thee as prize,
A remembrance of this bitter, bitter end.

(TERESA HERRERA steps into the light as if she feels and sees his agony.)

TERESA

And, beloved, if I my heart could lend
Or see you only once with aging eyes . . .

(JUAN CARLOS DE MORENO falls dead.)

After a split-second pause, the big crowd yelped and hollered. There it was, then. Love and life are fleeting yet appreciated events. Lights slowly dimmed to black. Nellie Ordoñez left to change into a Brown Trout and Jimmy the Kid slid into the narrator's seat next to Miss Kirk, who had arranged his script and marked the starting point. He watched her closely now, and she gave the cue as she took up the lights. Juan Carlos de Moreno, as narrator, led the valley to its tranquil return, bringing back a pastoral dance by the Sons of the Anasazi. The space of tender history between Spaniard and Carson.

When the dance was done and Juan Carlos had interpreted the "cycles of earth law," Tom Zaleski worked his drums again. A new and darker story was coming. One that resonated through the valley still. One kept alive by the Committee to Keep Kit a Hero, with chapters in Colorado Springs and Hays, Kansas. Roarke had foreseen the interest and let as much quiet descend on the stage as possible. Tom quit his drums. The dancers seemed tense in anticipation. The audience felt it and stood and looked high and low.

Cowboy Bob kept his big white horse, Lulu, as quiet as conceivably possible, but when neither of them could stand one more second concealed behind Yale Strong's dressing trailer, Cowboy Bob gave the reins a tug, and horse and rider galloped into the arena. Cowboy Bob rode twice around the semicircular amphitheater, waving his big cavalry hat at Indians and audience alike. He stopped center stage, his head bowed humbly, his hat hanging by his side. The crowd went nuts for Carson. A prolonged standing ovation followed, during which Cowboy Bob rode several more passes around, even dismounting once to walk into the bleachers and sign autographs.

"Is that in the script?" whispered Niki.

Roarke was smiling broadly and cheered, too.

"I love this shit," Tubby said. "I got to get some pictures."

At her key position, Miss Kirk did not appreciate the deviation from the text. The order that gave a kind of mathematical signature to her previous stage-managing duties had obviously broken down. But certainly she understood the nature of such an artist as Cowboy Bob and waited patiently, if not irritably, for him to resume the work. After yet another pass, he paused at center as the applause faded and the audience sat.

(A roll of drums again. Enter MAYOR OF DEL NORTE.)

MAYOR

That's our tale, then, Mr. Carson. Seems as though the Utes won't listen to reason. Why, just the day before yesterday a farmhouse was burned at Aspen Grove, this side of Wagon Wheel Gap.

There was a small round of applause from the campers and ranchers who hailed from that craggy, willowy bend in the river below Creedemore now known as Ear Grove. Cowboy Bob waited for silence before speaking. He had chosen to vocalize Carson with a delicate crossing of Clint Eastwood and Charles Bronson. When he spoke, his lips hardly moved.

KIT CARSON
(On horse.)
The Utes haven't done anything to me, Mayor.
And I don't know nothin' about no burning
farmhouse. Give me a better reason to help.

MAYOR

A better reason? You mean money?

KIT

I mean a better reason. Here it is, then, and your town can think it over. Ten dollars a head.

MAYOR

But, Kit, how will we know if you really got 'em or not? For ten dollars each.

KIT

When I'm through, I'll meet you and some others in Aspen Grove. I'll bring two ears off of each one.

(The MAYOR reaches up and shakes KIT's hand. The deal is confirmed.)

Steven watched from above. He could imagine the dialogue, and when he saw the Mayor exit and leave Kit Carson alone, he could almost hear Cowboy Bob spinning his plan in a canny soliloquy.

Cia had composed herself enough to rejoin Bill Clinings, still standing, with the neat marching ranks of the Liberty Society. She wanted to confess her cowardice, say she had at least tried, but Bill was in a desperate power struggle with Suzy. Several of the Liberty members had stood with Bill, but a surprising number of them seemed to be in agreement with Suzy and her existential rant of action, inaction, and "a priori." Cia stepped beside Bill at the very moment Psychology and Philosophy collided.

" 'A priori,' my ass. You have to stretch it out as tight as your slacks to get any determination of 'a priori' into a justification of this stupid idea."

Suzy watched him with the self-assuredness of one who had long ago discarded God for the *cogito*.

"So you think an orderly show of rank, a demonstration of resolve is a 'stupid idea,' " Suzy said with an understanding nod. She turned to her cohorts. "I was correct in my initial assessment. He *is* banging her."

Now they all looked at Bill and also at Cia. Some of his most loyal enthusiasts who had broken the military-like ranks looked, too.

Suzy shook her head sadly. "The very man who coined the Articles of Action, whose codicils stimulated our certitude over land redistribution, has been surreptitiously banging away. Just banging away. Bang. Bang. Bang."

Now the state troopers were looking, too. After another withering eyeballing, Suzy faced in the direction of the glowing arena and its roaring crowd.

"Atten . . . hut," she commanded.

The large flank of Liberty Society soldiers came to a kind of stiffer alertness.

"Suz . . ." Bill said pathetically.

"Bang away," she said. "Tonight we do the duty of the people. Mark time . . . mark."

Suzy marched in place, and the other preternaturals followed her lead.

A tall, lanky redheaded state trooper stepped up to Suzy. "Ma'am . . ."

"Don't even think about it. Without a restraining order, you cannot stop us."

The redhead looked over to another trooper. "Del? Where's Sergeant Carnevale?"

"I think she's watching the show."

"Better go get her."

"Forward . . . march."

Suzy set out in a left-right quasi stomp, and the rank moved, too. The two coeds carrying the banner high-stepped a bit, like drum majorettes.

"What do we do, Bill?" Cia asked.

Bill Clinings watched his handiwork shuffle down toward the amphitheater. Of course Suzy would choose this clinical kind of obstructionism against her enemies. Hadn't he, after all, framed the Liberty Society's constitution complete with the occasional codicil such as his now-regrettable Socio-Interruptus? How did he put it? "Any event that precasts or even postdates events not advantageous to the society is ripe for sustained physical protest." Something close to that anyway. Jesus God Almighty, Bill thought. Cia tugged at his arm. He looked down at her and wondered why the fuck he couldn't get that goddamn professorship. Then he'd transfer his ass to a college back East and stick to poetry to nail the coeds. God, he hated the fucking West.

"What do we do, Bill?" Cia asked.

The army advanced slowly and uniformly. Some of the audience saw them and wondered if they were part of the show. Carson's men, maybe.

Cowboy Bob Panousus had the last ear laced tight and dropped the gruesome necklace around his neck. He began his soliloquy under a starry, red-streaked sky.

KIT CARSON

This is the way, then, a man of his times conjures up the dark hour, the black clouds of his western moment. The bounty of ears, then, and dollars for my brave men.

Suzy and her force had now reached the grass bordering the parking lot, and Sergeant Rosie Carnevale was waiting.

"And . . . halt," Suzy said.

She stepped out of rank and confronted Rosie.

"Step aside, instrument of the state. We will not be deterred."

"May I see your parade permit?"

Suzy scoffed. "Don't try it. We have a right to protest the results of the trial."

Rosie smiled unchallengingly. "Sure, but you can't ruin the show."

"We've talked enough," Suzy said. "Stop us if you can. Atten . . . hut."

Still standing in front of the Municipal Building, Bill Clinings saw the sheriff's Jeep pull up to Rosie.

"Hi, Rosie," Petey said from the cab.

"Mark time, mark," commanded Suzy.

Petey was not surprised to see them clomping in place. Maybe he'd never be surprised again. Rosie tensed, facing down the parade. Petey eased himself out.

"What's up?"

"They're gonna march through the show," Rosie said through her teeth.

Petey knew that Reedy would like this, wherever he was. Watch *this* now, partner.

"Well, I guess we can't stop them. Let me get my prisoner out of your way. Rosie, I got a woman named Sandy Fiddler in the backseat was fixing to blow the Rio Grande Reservoir. Kill probably four, five hundred in the string of campgrounds alone. How about that?"

Many in the ranks broke out to peer inside the Jeep. Sandy stared back. Petey kept talking to Rosie.

"Yes sir, Sergeant. Looks like we'll have to be rounding up members of the Liberty Society for conspiring to commit murder. And let's start with any hard-core member who marches one step further."

What think, Reedy? Pretty good, huh? Talk it out, huh?

"He's bluffing!" yelled old Suzy. "Don't forget he's a convicted murderer!"

"Folks, you know that's not true. It's one thing to follow these nuts around and want free land and things, but sometimes you got to think for yourself."

And Suzy found herself alone. A marching officer without company. Petey nodded at the others as they stepped away. Suzy snatched the sacred preter-natural tom-tom from Drew Lipton. She stared for a moment at Sandy through the glass. Sandy stared back. Turning away, standing alone, she straightened herself and thought how authoritative Sartre had been. How utterly correct in the existential tracts. Existence does indeed precede essence. Man is an iso-lated being capable of creating destiny by choice of will. She looked back at Sandy, who still watched her. Suzy smiled a small, recognizable smile. A smile she believed all true existentialists all the way back to Pascal and Kierkegaard would smile. A smile shared by scholars of unique inner vision and courage. Sandy smiled, too, and muttered, "What an asshole," to herself.

Now Suzy began marking time on her own. Little clouds of dust encircled each weighty foot. She beat her tom-tom, too, with hard, semirhythmic whacks. Petey looked over to Rosie and shrugged. The army was down to one but still attacking. Suzy stepped around the county Jeep and, swinging her heavy arms, marched on.

(Enter MAYOR OF DEL NORTE.)

MAYOR

Good job, Kit. You did it true. You did what you said you would. Your word is gold.

(Holds bag of money.)

Here's your reward. Five silver dollars per set of ears.

(KIT and his men circle MAYOR.)

Steven saw the encircling of the Mayor by Kit and his boys from his high perch at the Corso Mine. He knew that in a moment Kit would break the silence with a reiteration of the correct terms. Ten dollars a pair of ears. Soon the Mayor would be shot dead and Aspen Grove would become Ear Grove in a kind of quasi-geographic linking of man and mountain pass. He could see the line of Miners, Ministers, Whores, Card Sharks, and assorted Gunmen waiting in the alley between the market and the rock shop for the discovery of that Corso vein of gold.

Steven thought Kit to be in midspeech when he saw a squat figure enter the stage area in an exaggerated, arm-pumping walk. He stood and searched his mind. He did not remember this triumphantly marching gnome. Did he write it? Carson, the Mayor, and all their supporting actors seemed to be stopping and looking.

Cowboy Bob could not believe he was being interrupted at perhaps the most significant moment in the depiction of the *Retrospective*. On top of it all, the old gal was chanting in a considerable bass-baritone.

Suzy marched back and forth in the arena, making crisp about-faces at each corner.

"We—we are here.
Liberty for all,
Land for all.
We—we are here."

Tubby came up behind Roarke. "Where's her costume?"
"She's not in the play."
"Honest to God?"
"Honest to God."

Twice Kit Carson attempted the speech ordering his men to murder the Mayor and his council members before riding down to Del Norte and burning it to the ground. Twice the one-woman parade seemed to raise the already booming level of her voice until poor Cowboy Bob Panousus had to give it up in frustration. He turned toward the mural as if some history might pop off the wall to silence this interloper. His eyes set on Molly Dowie's Carson. A coldness Cowboy Bob had not agreed with played over his acrylic eyebrows. No doubt what Kit would have done, a mission being what it was. That ancient warrior code. The specific calling of the Western Man. Conflict and resolution.

Kit Carson reared up on his enormous stallion and turned back to his men.

KIT

(To his men.)

Lay them out in a line, put the mayor at the front. I ain't a-wearing ears for my health.

The men began to form the Mayor and his three Councilmen into a line and worked their way into a firing squad despite the disruptive chant. Kit kept his dangerous eye on Suzy Waldrop. When she turned a right-face in order to march through the tableau, the actor-poet and outlaw-lawman merged. He cut off her advance with his horse and drew his mahogany-handled sidearm, the barrel still warm from the Ute Indian attack. Roarke turned to Niki with a blank expression. Her beautiful hands made little circles in the air. The audience let out an overlong "oooh" and waited. Confronted by the horse and rider and not wanting to break cadence, Suzy marched in place. Cowboy Bob glanced over at Roarke with steely resolve, then settled back on Suzy.

"I'm a man of peaceful means,
But I have to tell you true
That my daddy taught me never
To be dumb—
And it ought to tell you reams
That I've got the draw on you,
So you'd better turn around and
Start to run."

There was a scattering of applause.

"I love this shit," Tubby whispered.

"Don't be coarse," Sarah whispered.

Roarke had never seen anyone improvise quite like Cowboy Bob. She made more circles in the air for Niki.

Suzy's in-place marching pumped the scholar's blood into her already stuffed brain. She smirked at the rhyme and breathing heavily to the rhythm of her steps shouted:

" 'I am responsible for myself and for everyone else. I am creating an image of man of my own choosing. In choosing myself, I choose man.' Jean Paul Sartre!"

Cowboy Bob would have had to think about that one for a while, but when he heard another round of applause for her retort, he simply lost it. He reared up and fired two quarter-load blanks a foot or so over her head.

Now Ticky Lettgo had been inside the dream good. Minnie had that tummy going with Jefferson. Six months then. That little tummy and they had gone down to the bend in the big river. Those days, when they came up to Creedemore from the Feed 'n' Seed in Wichita Falls, they stayed at that hotel in South Fork. So they packed the picnic, and him and Minnie and Jefferson in her tummy drove through Creedemore and out past the mines to that pretty bend in the big river. Minnie spread out her mama's Indian blanket and got out tomatoes and those big cukes and dove breast cut up thin and cool thick coffee.

"Over there," she said in her little-girl voice.

"Over there what?" he said, his mouth mashing at cukes and bird.

"Over there on that flat rise, that meadowy rise, that's where we should build it."

"Build it? Build what?"

"Build a place."

"Build a place there?"

"I said it, didn't I?"

Minnie patted her round little belly, and her smooth red cheeks went high into a smile. "This boy will need a place up here."

"Boy?"

She didn't have to say any more. Ticky knew right then he was up against it. Had to find out who owned this piece by the river and how dear it was going to be to get it. He was smiling deep until the first quarter charge brought him out of it in time to see Kit Carson getting another one off on a civilian. A woman at that.

"You son of a bitch!" Ticky yelled weakly, coming to his feet and drawing the long Colt .45 at the same time. He braced himself against the pulley-rigged mine-shaft car and fired with both hands. The shot went low, skipped off the ground, and thudded hard into Vi's outhouse.

"Jesus!" Cowboy Bob screamed.

Mountain Man, standing by his winch and pulleys, waiting for his mine-shaft car to get filled up with the three miners so he could start act 4, scene 1, by flying them to the roof of the market during Juan Carlos de Moreno's narration of the gold and silver decades, watched with mouth agape as Ticky got off another one, this time a direct hit on the outhouse, whose door flew open.

Cowboy Bob did not have the presence of mind to drop the stage gun, his hands gone white on the handle and trigger. Steven on his perch watched the scattering of audience and actors alike amid echoing screams. Ticky brought his gun back up, and Mountain Man, ten yards behind him, went for the pulley. The wooden-framed mine-shaft car bumped low, and Ticky fell back. Both arms flopped over, and the big Colt dangled, not falling to the ground until the pulley jammed with Ticky fifteen feet over the middle of the arena, his legs straight up and working a wild little dance.

Roarke made her way to Miss Kirk's control table. Miss Kirk sat behind it with her stage manager's book open and a look of catatonia on her round face. Mountain Man picked up Ticky's gun and ran it over to Roarke.

Petey arrived on the run with Bobby. "Jesus," he gasped.

"Mountain Man got the gun," Roarke said. "Everything's okay."

Roarke took up the narrator's microphone. "Ladies and gentlemen, I'm afraid this has to count as our number-two intermission, so let's resume our seats."

The crowd's jovial mood seemed to return instantly, as if this had all been part of the show. Many were convinced it was.

Petey took the microphone from Roarke. "Ticky?"

The mine-shaft car wiggled, and his feet disappeared. Soon his little noggin popped over the side. "What?"

"Are you okay?"

"Well, I guess so. Jesus. My behind hurts."

Petey turned to Mountain Man. "Get him the hell down."

"I've been trying to. It's stuck. Rope went under the whatchamacallit."

Petey thought about a ladder but didn't like it. "Hey, Ticky?"

"What?"

"Do you mind if we get you down after the show?"

"What show?"

"The—I don't know—the play!" Petey yelled up, spreading his arms.

"Carson and such? Indians? Rocks?"

"Yes."

"Okay."

Suzy Waldrop kept marching through it all, and her septuagenarian calves were feeling the altitude. Petey walked over to her. He could not decide if this was somebody Reedy, who normally liked everybody, might not like. She had glossy confrontation set into her eyes and all the way up to her forehead. He walked alongside her. Her chant was down to a breathy whisper.

"Now, ma'am, I'm thinking that you've made your point and it's time to let the play go on."

She snorted. "Oh, 'The show must go on.' Is that it?"

"Yes, ma'am."

"Oh, 'Please don't exercise your existential rights.' Is that it?"

People started stomping their feet. They wanted Kit Carson. They wanted the Mayor of Del Norte opened up like a ripe watermelon. Cowboy Bob and his men had retreated with the Del Norte council behind the market when the real gunplay began. Petey regarded the raucous audience and turned back to Suzy.

"Okay," he said.

"Okay what?"

"March your ass off."

Petey walked over to Roarke and Miss Kirk at the stage manager's table. He shrugged. So did Roarke, who turned to Miss Kirk.

"Cue Cowboy Bob."

"But . . ." Miss Kirk said, gesturing to the marcher.

Roarke looked up to where Steven would be. The lights popped in her eyes, and she saw stars.

"Cue him, Miss Kirk. It's okay."

Kit Carson charged on with new resolve, although he did stop once and gaze angrily up at Ticky, hanging above the stage. Ticky applauded happily, and Cowboy Bob and his boys blew the Mayor and his Councilmen away. Soon the Gold and Silver were replaced by bluish Titanium actors and Coal actors and a Phosphorous Chorus.

Presently the Trout Ensemble entered to the "Fanfare for the Common Man." Nellie Ordoñez as the German Brown Trout and Skyo as the Cutthroat Trout flanked Molly as the spectacular Rainbow Trout.

Steven watched them. They twirled in small circles, and he knew that his poem "Riverlife" was being recited. He saw the parade of miners, cowboys, and liars. He watched old Mr. Trujillo fly-fish downstream to the delight of the guffawing trout fishermen.

Just when Mr. Trujillo got to the point in the story where his granddad was telling his uncle in no uncertain terms that if he fished downstream he'd probably scare his nephew half to death, Suzy collapsed with a gigantic groan. Roarke jogged in with some bottled water, and Niki ran over, too. They got her into a sitting position. The audience stood and waited.

Ticky looked directly down on them. "What the hell?" he said.

"She's fainted," Roarke said.

Ticky turned to Brian Trujillo. "But what the hell happened? Don't tell me the son of a bitch actually fished downstream."

"He sure as hell did!" Mr. Trujillo yelled up.

Ticky just looked at him. Stunned into silence.

"I'll tell it in a second!" Mr. Trujillo yelled.

Rosie Carnevale in her uniform and another trooper joined Roarke. After a few minutes, they raised Suzy to her feet. The audience cheered madly, as if a running back with a bad knee was walking off the field under his own power.

She waved oddly and allowed Rosie to walk her to a seat. Roarke pointed to Mr. Trujillo as she cleared. He took it up to the point where the satellite television reception was being carried to the valley and then to the last scene before Juan Carlos de Moreno's poetic monologue on the everlasting valley. Jimmy the Kid had taken position for his entrance and watched with everyone else as Mr. Trujillo, back as Ticky Lettgo, and the legendary Yale Strong, portraying Mountain Man Red Fields, took their places. Emboldened by the big yuks of his downstream-fishing scene, Mr. Trujillo fell into an easy, earnest explanation of Ticky's position on private property. Yale Strong, looking like a muscular Gary Cooper and sounding a little like Willie Nelson, emphasized the textual belief of land use for everyone.

"What? Jesus, Yale! Of all people!" yelled Ticky, swaying above them.

"It's a play, goddamn it!" yelled Mr. Trujillo.

"What?"

"It's a play! A play! C'mon, Ticky! Listen, will ya?" Yale yelled.

And soon they were finished with a handshake, a Roarke touch that most liked.

"Well, Jesus!" yelled Ticky.

Now the lights lowered to black, except for a single spot in the center. Juan Carlos de Moreno stepped into it, in full Conquistador regalia. The audience hushed. A low growl floated out from somewhere. In a tangy accent tempered by Roarke's reminders of clarity, Jimmy the Kid offered up the forty-stanza finish to *The Creedemore Retrospective*. He moved speaking the words in a circle, even breaking choreography once to direct some language up at Ticky, who listened transfixed. Then he was at the alley and with a wave exited to:

Join the earth and mountain
And river.

Steven saw the audience rise as one, shouts and hats flying. Juan Carlos de Moreno entered as planned, to more applause. Teresa Herrera, still dressed as a German Brown Trout, joined him. Cowboy Bob brought Kit Carson in on his horse, followed by Mr. Trujillo, and then they were all out, waving and applauding back. Ticky waved at the audience, too. After perhaps three or four minutes, Jimmy the Kid brought up Roarke, who brought up Miss Kirk. Costumes, sets, lights, and running crew joined them. Mountain Man strode on importantly.

Steven watched the settling crowd. He couldn't hear what Roarke would say, but he didn't have to. It was the *event*, he knew. The *involvement* of both sides of the stage that she would evoke as the essence of her theater. He lit another smoke, puffed it, and looked at it. The smoke wiggled sideways. He'd have to stop this. Hard enough to breathe up here even without the smokes. He dangled it back on his lips and looked over to the ragged mountaintops and the moon beyond them. He wasn't thinking about writing. Not poetry or prose. No battling sentiment, no colliding plots going on inside his head. Maybe there never would be again. He heard another crescendoing laugh and drew on the cigarette.

54

By early October the aspens started gold and the whole tone of the valley altered. Wildflowers had closed it up, and deer and elk and enormous transplanted moose got bolder, coming down to the big river in afternoon light, all in their own way anticipating the usually harsh late fall and winter.

This Saturday morning came warmish, a sort of reprieve from high-altitude reality. They loaded the easel and paint box into her pickup and drove to the river where it intersected the Norgan Ranch and where a decrepit railroad trestle crossed it.

He pulled out the easel and started to set it up. She stood staring at the trestle.

"Not there."

He waited.

"There."

He took it over and set it up.

"Sure you're going to be all right? I should be about three hours." Usually Steven had Saturday and Sunday off from his job with South Fork Log Homes, but Buff Cryer, Dan's brother, who owned and operated the business, had asked him for the favor, and he was happy for the work. A fellow from Colorado Springs wanted to get in as soon as possible, but the plumber was only available today or two weeks from the coming Monday. So Steven was Buff's plumber's helper for the day. It took just under four hours to get it all up and flushing.

Heading back to the trestle, he stopped for sandwiches and sodas at Ear Grove and put them in a small cooler. Where the valley started narrowing into the craggy groves, he saw that she had moved her easel to another spot so that she looked down on the shattered old bridge. He pulled the truck off to the road's shoulder and watched her for a few minutes. She stood with her charcoal frozen on the paper looking hard for something. Finally she pulled her hand off and walked away from the trestle, glancing over her shoulder as she moved. She stopped, made a mark on the ground with her foot, and went for the easel.

He watched her move it, her strong arms, her sturdy steps. Then she was working the charcoal fast and sure across the slightly tilted paper. He felt as if he were hallucinating this new life. This new sense of things. She saw him and waved, and he started across the valley floor and the little gullies and rises that were part of it.

THE CREEDEMORE RETROSPECTIVE: A WORD-MURAL

291 pages
The life and history of an American town.
© 2004
Produced